STARS
MAGE

ALIEN ARCANA

BOOK FOUR
OF THE STARSHIP'S MAGE SERIES

This edition published in 2018 by:
Faolan's Pen Publishing Inc.
22 King St. S, Suite 300
Waterloo, Ontario
N2J 1N8 Canada

ISBN-13: 978-1-988035-61-1 (print)
A record of this book is available from Library and Archives Canada.
Printed in the United States of America
2 3 4 5 6 7 8 9 10

Second edition
First printing: September 2018

Illustration © 2016 Jack Giesen

Faolan's Pen Publishing logo is a trademark of Faolan's Pen Publishing Inc.

Read more books from Glynn Stewart at faolanspen.com

STARSHIP'S
MAGE

ALIEN
ARCANA

BOOK FOUR
OF THE STARSHIP'S MAGE SERIES

GLYNN STEWART

FAOLAN'S PEN
PUBLISHING
faolanspen.com

CHAPTER 1

PROFESSOR YOSHI KUROSAWA, Mage, Rune Scribe, and hold-
er of PhDs in xenoarchaeology from several of Mars's most prestigious
universities, would not have described himself as bored. He had an entire centuries-old alien facility to investigate.

But after a year in the Andala System, digging through the scraps
and the wreckage of what had once been *someone's* refueling station,
Yoshi was starting to wish they would find *something* interesting.

The Rune Scribe was on Andala IV because the ruin there was the
only evidence humanity had ever found of aliens with interstellar travel—and humanity only traveled the stars by the magic of the Jump
Mages and their runic jump matrices.

He'd hoped, when he'd agreed to the placement, to find alien runes
in the wreckage. The complex wasn't *small*, after all. Six domes, each
over six hundred meters across, on top of an underground structure that
stretched dozens of levels into the ground.

It had been a refueling station once. They hadn't found any evidence
of gas extraction facilities at the gas giant in the system, but the ruins
had once contained massive, billion-liter tanks of hydrogen. Their con-
tents were long evaporated now, but the tanks remained.

Checking his breather, Yoshi wandered deeper into the ruins.
While the humans had attached a prefabricated habitat to the
alien dome that had been the focus of their investigations so far, the
planet's atmosphere was toxic to humans. There was enough oxygen

in it to be breathed, though, so simply filtering out the high carbon monoxide and carbon dioxide content was enough for humans to survive.

The domes were mostly intact and had shielded their interior structures and the underground tunnels from the planet's weather. Over three years of investigation, the archaeologists had cleared and cataloged twelve floors and subbasements of three of the domes.

Water and collapsed tunnels had stopped them going deeper. The current plan was to clear and catalog *every* dome as deep as they could go, which frustrated Yoshi to no end.

He'd seen the drone video of the rest of the complex. There were no runes there, not even where there *should* be. No gravity runes. No defensive spells. No emergency atmospheric magic. None of the things that humanity would have included in this facility.

It was possible, of course, that the aliens *did* have a technological method of faster-than-light travel, in which case they wouldn't have the magic that Yoshi wanted to find. Except that the technology they *had* found was no more advanced than humanity's—cruder, in many cases, than modern human tech.

Yoshi wasn't *supposed* to come down and stare at the collapsed tunnels leading deeper into the alien base. As he was one of the most senior scientists and the only Mage in the research team, though, there wasn't really anyone to tell him *not* to.

The walls around him were smooth rock, either cut or smoothed by lasers long enough before that humanity hadn't even *had* the technology. Some failure of design or intervention of nature in the centuries since had first bowed and then shattered the roof of the curving stairwell leading deeper into the underground complex.

Magic twitched in his hands, the Gift of his Martian bloodline *itching* to serve his curiosity, and Yoshi laughed softly to himself. Opening up the lower levels would take time and energy for the rest of the Expedition. They would bring in heavy equipment and carefully remove the rubble, shoring up the roof with supports and bracing.

He could just...open it.

There were a hundred reasons why he shouldn't, but at that moment, deep in the bowels of an alien base that utterly *refused* to reveal its secrets to him, none of them came to mind.

Softly humming to himself through the breather, Yoshi gave in to temptation. Power flowed through his body as he carefully considered the debris, continuing to hum as he reached out his hands and unleashed the energies he commanded.

Yoshi Kurosawa was a Martian-born Mage by Blood, born to one of the oldest families of Mages and descended directly from the survivors of the Eugenicists' Project Olympus. For all that he was an old man now and had been an academic his entire life, he was a *powerful* Mage.

The fallen stones bent to his will. They lifted, adjusting and merging together to form a new supporting archway through the debris. It wasn't large, just enough for Yoshi himself to walk through, and he wasn't a tall man.

A few minutes of magic, an exertion of will no one else in the research team could match, and a tired-but-pleased Yoshi walked through his new tunnel to see what secrets the debris had hidden.

At first, his light fell on the same smoothed stone and ancient light fixtures that had been present on the other side of the cave-in, but he hadn't expected anything different.

Carefully and gently, he walked deeper into spaces where no human had ever set foot. His breather warned him the air here was different from outside. Staler. It still had enough oxygen for the machine to function, though, so he carried on.

Turning a corner, however, he stepped into an open gallery, and his breather calmly informed him it was now redundant. Surprised, he checked the readings on the device through his wrist computer. The air still wasn't perfect for human consumption, but it was far closer than it had been even a few steps back. The carbon dioxide and carbon monoxide had been reduced to levels that wouldn't harm him.

Yoshi looked around him. Someone, long before, had gone to a lot of effort to make the gallery look as welcoming as a two-hundred-meter-long cavern could. He stood on a balcony around a third floor, looking down at a floor ten meters below, centered around what had clearly been some kind of fountain. Murals of strange and alien trees, now flaking and faded, had been painted on the walls.

Part of the roof had collapsed at some point in the intervening centuries, leaving debris scattered across what had once been some kind of market concourse, but this had clearly been a place for rest and relaxation for visiting ships' crews—and had been set up to preserve atmosphere somehow.

Yoshi knelt next to the murals, brushing aside debris and dirt as he searched for what he *knew* had to be there. No technological solution could have lasted this long.

It wasn't in the murals, he realized after a moment. It was in the *safety railing*. The safety barrier around the balcony had been laser-carved from the original stone, and the top layer then bleached white—and inlaid with familiar silver runes.

"Yes!" Yoshi shouted aloud, pulling his camera around to take pictures and record *everything*. It wasn't much—just a simple spell to maintain atmosphere in this massive space—but they were *runes. Still-functioning* runes of an alien race.

He was starting to salivate over the potential lessons humanity could learn from studying a completely different species's approach to magic when his computer happily started popping up recognition notes for the matrix.

He stared in shock as his computer happily translated the matrix into normal human diagram summaries. It recognized the symbols. That was *impossible*.

Dropping to his knees once more, Yoshi Kurosawa studied the silver inlay with a critical eye. Looking for it now, he saw what his computer, following its basic programming, had seen instantly. The runes weren't alien. They weren't even just similar to the Martian Runic script humanity used.

It *was* Martian Runic.

But no being of any kind had set foot in these buried lower levels since before humanity had relearned magic. They'd *dated* the debris—the tunnel he'd opened had collapsed before Martian Runic had been invented...which meant...

"Damn," a voice murmured softly behind him. "I'm sorry, Professor. I'd really hoped you wouldn't find anything."

Yoshi jerked back to his feet, turning to find Samara Hollins behind him. His tall, athletic student wore the same breather as he did—but instead of carrying a light, she was wearing light-gathering optics. Military gear that would have enabled her to sneak through the abandoned base without being seen.

"What are you doing here, Samara?" he asked, then shook it aside in the excitement of his discovery. "Come take a look at this," he told her. "These runes! They're Martian Runic—*exactly*. That means..."

"I know," she cut him off coldly. "I know what they are, I know what that means. I don't suppose I could convince you to stay quiet about this?"

Yoshi stared at her in shock.

"This is the find of a lifetime!" he snapped. "What can you possibly mean, *stay quiet about it?!*"

In answer, his student conjured blue witch fire around her hands—burning off both the gloves she wore and another layer of skin-toned covering he'd never realized she wore. A chill ran down Yoshi's spine as he realized Samara had a projector rune carved into her hand—a rune only given to *Combat Mages*.

"You're a Mage?" he demanded. "I don't understand."

"I was sent here to make sure no one discovered what you just found, Professor," she said sadly. "If you will not keep silent, then my orders are to silence you."

Witch fire flashed from her hand, but she'd talked for too long and Yoshi was no fool. A shield of frozen air flashed into existence between them, Yoshi backing away as he drew on half-forgotten training to try to defend himself.

More fire hammered against his shield, and a tug of force tore his feet out from underneath him. The old professor fell, feeling his bones *snap* as he slammed into ancient stone.

"I'm sorry, Professor," Samara said gently. "But there are secrets I am sworn to keep."

Yoshi Kurosawa would *not* die on his knees. Power flashed through him, lines of force supporting old and broken limbs as he rose to his feet once more and *attacked*. Waves of pure force flashed across the space between them, throwing Samara back as he struggled to remain standing.

She used magic to control her movement, twisting in the air to land on her feet like a cat and then sending more fire hammering back at him.

Focused on standing, he'd dropped the shield. Witch fire hammered into his flesh, setting muscles and nerves alike on fire. Somehow, he remained up and flung lightning and force back at her.

She dodged, sidestepping his wild attack with the ease of practice. Whatever Samara Hollins was, she was *not* a xenoarchaeology grad student!

Her counterstrike hammered into a hastily raised shield, force and flame flinging him backward. Yoshi barely had time to realize the only thing behind him was the railing when he slammed into the old carved stone with an echoing *snap*.

It was only when his legs and hands refused to respond to him that he realized he'd snapped his back in multiple places against the safety railing. He tried to summon his magic, bring himself back to his knees, but only sputters of power answered him.

Then he *was* rising, but not under *his* power. He looked down at Samara, who held him suspended in the air.

"Dammit, Yoshi," she whispered, "you could have been one of us."

Then she threw him over the balcony.

CHAPTER 2

DAMIEN MONTGOMERY, Hand of the Mage-King of Mars, found detention center interview rooms spectacularly creepy. He didn't have particularly fond memories of them, though today was the first time he'd been on the *interviewing* side of one quite so reminiscent of his stay in a Corinthian cell so many years ago.

The young woman sitting across from him would probably have looked small and harmless to most, but Damien was easily ten centimeters shorter than she and even skinnier. He didn't underestimate his *own* threat level, so he doubted that Roslyn Chambers was as harmless as she looked.

She sat silently, judging him in turn while probably wondering why she'd been summoned there. The closed golden fist of his symbol of office hung openly outside his suit, a stark contrast to the shapeless jumpsuit the Tau Ceti Landing City Juvenile Detention Center had stuck Chambers in.

"Care to tell me why I'm here?" the girl demanded. According to the records Damien had been shown, she had turned eighteen in detention and was being released shortly, her youth sentence finally up.

"You have an interesting record, Miss Chambers," Damien told her in half-answer, projecting the details he'd been given onto the plain metal table from his wrist personal computer. "Let's see."

He tapped a command, zooming through the list he'd read when Chambers's counselor had sent it up to Damien's ship with her request for a favor.

"Brilliant student, pride of the Chambers family, one of Tau Ceti's first and most famous Mage families," he noted. "Until, at age fifteen, everything seemed to go to pieces. Four allegations of assault, one dropped, two settled out of court, and one where the individual tried to press charges. The note here suggests that after interviewing the witnesses, the young gentleman who tried to press charges ended up facing charges of his own.

"Suspected association with an illegal Mage duel," he continued. "Resulted in over fifty thousand in damages—paid by a third party, and the owners of the property declined afterwards to assist in the investigation.

"No less than *fourteen* incidents of vandalism you were either linked to or implicated in, but, *strangely*, none of the damaged parties chose to press charges," Damien noted dryly. "A curious Tau Ceti Bureau of Investigation officer turned up that the damaged parties were all compensated for damages in exchange for ironclad nondisclosure agreements.

"And not quite lastly, seven counts of minor to moderate petty theft that the TCBI is sure of, all settled without police involvement," he concluded.

"I have to wonder, Miss Chambers, how many incidents aren't in this file that your parents covered up before you stole—and *wrecked*— Royal Tester Karl Anders's personal car while he was visiting their estate."

"Nothing except Anders's car was ever proven," Chambers told him, her nose elevated slightly as she managed to look down on him despite the fact she was handcuffed to a chair.

"A pattern still emerges," he pointed out. "What pattern do you see, Miss Chambers?"

"That I'm handcuffed to a chair with a creepy dude reading my life story to me," she replied. "What's the damn point?"

"I can tell you the pattern the Navy recruiter saw," Damien said quietly. "Ninety-eighth percentile in Practical Thaumaturgy. Ninety-fourth percentile in Thaumaturgic Theory. Average ninety-fifth in all secondary

eventually, you found something even your parents couldn't
noney and influence.

me, Miss Chambers"—he leaned forward to hold her dark
y—"given what I'm guessing, why is Ronald Armstrong still
Even at fifteen, you could have broken his neck. Hell, even
n alive, you could have told the prosecutors what happened
ne else could see."

an't know about that," she snapped. "*No one* knows about that.

bers sank her face into her hands.

d Karen in confidence," she whispered. "I couldn't... I
"

Jakab is the cousin of the commander of my cruiser," Damien
She begged a favor of him and he begged a favor of me—and
e Jakab more than I can count. So, I'm here. Looking at a girl
idiot ruin her life. Sound about right?"

idn't lift her face.

t do you *want*?" she repeated, her voice very quiet. "My par-
..well, my parents"—a pair of senior judges in Tau Ceti's
Judicial system, the separate justice system for Mages—"but
g... his father was the *Governor*."

h had meant that Ronald Armstrong had dodged facing adult sex-
lt charges—something he wouldn't have dodged for an attempted
rge. It also meant that he'd been dumb enough to try to charge
rs for assault after she'd punched him out and fled the party.

ng arrested and dropped into Tau Ceti's Juvenile Detention sys-
its mandatory counselor visits was probably the best thing that
ve happened to Chambers after that, short of her actually talking
arents. Something that Damien could almost understand her be-
illing to do.

ce, not that long ago, I sat where you are, in a room very much
one," Damien told her. "I faced having my magic stripped be-
o one would believe what I said. While where you sit isn't quite
, you've lost a lot."

academic testing *except* Law and Eth
and Ethics. A pattern of dysfunctio
family.

"Mages by Blood sometimes belie
their actions. Your parents tried to shi
Martian Navy is not *blind*, Miss Chamb

She wilted in the chair.

"All I ever got was 'rejected'," she ad

"I should also note," he continued,
viction for grand theft auto, while a you
ents' influence, has still resulted in your
Mage Academy being revoked.

"You walk out of here in three days
nowhere to go but home."

"So, what's the fucking point of this,
by Right here to gloat over one of the lu
up? What do you *want*, Montgomery?"

Damien hadn't actually given her hi
surprised that she knew who he was. Tl
Mars were his roving warrior-judges who
what the Romans had once called *imperiu*
Protectorate military.

There were also only fourteen of them
sive as Damien was, people tended not to
images of Lord Hand Damien Montgomer
fice and could draw the connection.

She was a smart kid. Which was, of cou

"I'm wondering how someone with so
up so badly," he responded bluntly, throwi
face. "Though I'll note that I see a different
ers did when you took the intake exam."

"And what pattern does the mighty Hand

"Someone in pain," he told her. "Lashir
have the consequences smoothed away by th

you. Unti
bury with
"So t
gaze leve
breathin
leaving
where n
"You
Except...
Cha
"I t
wouldn'
"Ka
told he
I owe
who let
Sh
"W
ents a
Comp
Armst
W
ual as
rape
Cham
G
tem
could
to he
ing
like
caus
that

She nodded.

"But you've been a model prisoner and your counselor thinks you have a great deal of potential, so I'm here," Damien concluded. "You still want to be a Navy officer, Roslyn Chambers? Why?"

"Yeah," she admitted. "Because...because...someone has to stop the bullies of the world. No matter the scale," she finished fiercely, finally raising her head to look back at him.

"Good," he told her. "Here's the deal: you walk out of here in three days. The next intake exam for the Navy is in six months. You stay out of trouble and keep seeing your counselor for those six months and *pass* the ethics chunk of the exam, and I'll put a letter on file that has your record ignored.

"You'll enter the academy a year late, but having *seen* your test scores, I don't think that will slow you down," Damien finished. "Do you think you can do that, Roslyn? I can tell you the Protectorate needs every smart Mage it can get into uniform."

"Even battered ones who've fucked up everything?" she asked.

"That's why I'm offering you a chance to *un*-fuck everything," he replied.

"Well?"

Damien nodded silently to Warden Conner, gesturing for the older man to show him to his office. With a sigh, the Warden obeyed. The instant obedience of most public officials to Damien's office always bothered him. He shared dark hair and a slim build with the Warden, but Conner was easily thirty centimeters taller than him.

Entering the sparsely furnished office Conner ran the planet's largest juvenile detention center from, the lanky prison warden repeated his question.

"Well? What do you think?"

"There's a good kid in there," Damien told Conner, looking around the man's office. If you didn't know you were in a prison, you'd have thought you were in a high school teacher's office. The shelf of books on teaching and connecting with teenagers belonged in either, but the cheerful motivational posters had gone out of style everywhere *but* high schools.

"There's a good kid in almost all of them," the Warden replied. "There aren't many irredeemable sixteen-year-olds, my lord. Some—but most of those end up in adult prisons. You think she'll take you up on it?"

"I think so," the Hand told him, squinting in thought. "I hope so, anyway. The Navy could use her."

Even with Conner, he couldn't admit that the Navy was quietly starting to prepare for war. No one expected anything *soon*, but Damien and the other Hands kept finding Legatan supplies and agents buried inside the conflicts they were sent to resolve.

Every smart young Mage was needed. Damien wasn't certain what was coming—but he had his suspicions.

"I'll leave a letter of instructions for the Navy recruiters with Miss Jakab," Damien continued. "My understanding is that she'll continue to act as Chambers's counselor after her release."

"That is generally our preference, though I'll admit our counselors are *always* overloaded," Conner admitted with a sigh. "We have just over twelve hundred kids in this place, and we cycle through over three thousand every year. I'm...honestly shocked you made the time to come down here."

"You do good work here," the Hand told him. "Though, admittedly, I'm on vacation and I owe Karen Jakab's cousin a few dozen favors." He smiled sadly. "Not least, I'm 'on vacation' because I got his ship shot up, and for some reason, the Navy wanted to *fix* it."

Conner paused, clearly digesting that.

"Doesn't Karen's cousin command a battlecruiser?" he asked plaintively.

"Yes," Damien confirmed. "The Navy lends it to me as a transport, and we got in some trouble last month."

The prison warden shook his head at the concept of someone *shooting* at a cruiser of the Royal Martian Navy and checked his wrist-comp quickly.

"It's almost time for the assembly you agreed to," he noted. "I hope you don't mind, but I pulled in all of the detainees, Mage and mundane."

"If you hadn't, Warden Conner, you'd be spending the next few minutes scrambling to fix that," Damien replied. "If my time here leads even one of these kids to make better choices when they leave, it was a worthwhile side trip. Show me the way?"

CHAPTER 3

BEING ON VACATION, as much as a Hand *ever* actually went on vacation, meant that Damien had the *time* to do things like address an entire prison full of teenagers on how they could turn their lives around. He doubted any of the teenagers actually *believed* he'd been a wanted fugitive at one point, but if even a handful of them listened and ended up in a Protectorate uniform, it had been worth it.

Since *he* was on vacation, though, he'd sent his *staff* on vacation. That meant that instead of Julia Amiri watching his back, he had a very earnest squad of Royal Martian Marines—who were intimidated enough by the Hand and his history not to argue when he'd told them to go grab a bite to eat with the prison guards.

Despite that, three of them were waiting for him when he left the auditorium stage, their faces grim.

"Sir, we just received a transmission from Mage-Admiral Segal," said the squad leader, a Combat Mage-Lieutenant named Denis Romanov who was almost as earnest as Damien suspected himself of being. "He's requested a secured channel to you as soon as you're available."

The Hand glanced back at the door behind him. Conner was still speaking to his detainees on the other side.

"Did he say how urgent?" he asked the Mage.

The young Mage-Lieutenant clearly thought that *any* request from an Admiral was high priority and shrugged in response.

"Corporal Levant," Damien turned to one of the two junior Marines. "Could you please pass my regrets on to Warden Conner? It appears duty calls."

The soldier nodded his agreement, and the Hand turned back to the commander of his temporary bodyguard.

"Lead the way, Lieutenant Romanov."

Since he mostly made his home on a Navy warship, Damien also used a Marine assault shuttle as his personal transport. It made life easier for his bodyguards, in the worst-case scenario he could fly it by himself, and it was often helpful to impress on people that the barely one hundred and fifty centimeter–tall quiet man in a tailored suit was dangerous.

It had other advantages, though. Since it was designed to function as a mobile command post as well as a delivery system and weapons platform, the shuttle had a small officers' compartment tucked in behind the cockpit, with a full communications suite.

Activating the privacy shield, Damien brought up the encryption system and entered a sequence that would connect him to Mage-Admiral Segal's flagship. A burly young man with pitch-black skin and hair appeared on his screen.

"Lieutenant Salil Ali speaking, how can I assist...Hand Montgomery!" Without even rising from his chair, the youth managed to stiffen to attention and salute crisply. "What do you need, my lord?"

"Admiral Segal requested to speak with me," Damien replied. "Is he available?"

"He's on the flag bridge, but he left orders for you to be connected to him immediately," Ali replied. "Give me a minute, my lord."

The screen faded into the stylized rocket-and-red-planet logo of the Royal Martian Navy for less than a minute, then a new image appeared on his screen.

Mage-Admiral Aaron Segal was a short man, not much taller than Damien himself, with broad shoulders and salt and pepper hair. He was turned out as perfectly as always, his navy blue uniform perfectly crisp and gold stars polished to a shine.

Something about his eyes, though, told Damien all was not well.

"My lord Hand," he greeted Damien. "How was your visit to the detention center?"

"Hopefully productive," the young man replied. "It doesn't take many minds changed to make a trip like that worth it. I received your message. What did you need to talk to me about?"

"Are you familiar with the Andala System, Lord Montgomery?" Segal asked.

Damien ran the name through his mind, remembering what he'd heard about it.

"Uninhabited system with alien ruins," he dredged up. "We have some kind of research base there, right?"

"We do," Segal confirmed. "Jointly funded by the top, oh, thirty universities in the Protectorate. I haven't seen anything more exciting than a pottery party out of the expedition until the weekly courier dropped back into Tau Ceti two hours ago and transmitted an urgent priority message."

"What kind of urgent priority does a camp full of scientists have?" Damien asked.

"Murder," the Admiral said flatly. "Professor Yoshi Kurosawa apparently made an unauthorized breach into the previously sealed lower levels. He was a Mage and a Rune Scribe, and the lack of any evidence of magical capability in the Andalan facility's upper levels bored him.

"His students found his body," he concluded. "He was killed with magic, Damien—and he was supposed to be the only Mage in the system."

"So, a mystery," Damien murmured. Despite himself, he was intrigued—though he still didn't see just why the Admiral had reached out to him. "I believe the Martian Investigation Service has a Tau Ceti station. We can spare a Marine escort with a few Combat Mages to keep the MIS team safe, can't we?"

"We can, but I did contact you for a reason, my lord," Segal replied. "Damien...Kurosawa found what he was looking for. His students found at least one fully functioning rune matrix in the room where they found his body."

A fully functioning rune matrix.

A fully functioning *alien* rune matrix. That was the dream of any Rune Scribe like Kurosawa—and Damien finally understood why Segal had contacted him.

"I could send an MIS team and a dozen Rune Scribes," Segal told him. "Or...I could ask a Rune Wright, who'll sort out in an hour what would take the Scribes a year, to take a look.

"And since said Rune Wright is a *Hand*, with more investigative and police authority than any MIS team..."

Damien snorted and conceded the point.

There were, to his knowledge, exactly five Rune Wrights in the Protectorate. Two were the minor children of the Mage-King of Mars. Two others were the Mage-King of Mars and his sister. The last was Damien Montgomery himself.

Unlike other Mages, the Rune Wrights could *see* the flow of magic in runes, understand the use of a rune matrix in a glance instead of taking painstaking hours to read it. The additional understanding meant that Damien and the others could do many things ordinary Mages couldn't—among other things, design the Runes of Power that they carved into their flesh, dramatically augmenting their own power.

That same Sight would enable him to read alien runes, understanding them regardless of how much or little they shared with humanity's script.

"I'll still need the MIS team," he told Segal. "My Secret Service detachment is down to the bare minimum. I *am* on vacation," he pointed out. "I'll also need a ship. *Duke of Magnificence* is several weeks from being ready to deploy again."

"I have a Navy armed courier I was going to put at the Investigation Service's disposal," Segal replied with a grin. "I can place it at your command instead."

"I'll take it," Damien agreed. "I'll need to speak to His Majesty first, though. This does seem sufficiently low-key, I think he'll agree to let me cut my vacation short."

Unlike the Andala System with its tiny research base or even many of the poorer systems of the Protectorate, Tau Ceti had a Runic Transceiver Array. Unlike even wealthier systems, Tau Ceti had two—one for each of the two inhabited worlds, Tau Ceti *e* and Tau Ceti *f*.

The system had been one of the earliest settlements after the first Mage-King concluded the Compact that defined the relationship between man and Mage, and it had the wealth and industry to show it. Massive stations orbited ahead of each world, shielding them from the fields of meteors and comets that had regularly shattered the biospheres of both worlds before humanity had settled them.

Amidst the many signs of wealth and progress were the RTAs. Many systems didn't have any. Damien's own homeworld of Sherwood had been more able to afford an entire *fleet* of warships than a single Array. The Sherwood Array, partially funded by the Protectorate after the events of the last few months, would come online soon.

The nature of the Arrays prevented more than one being installed on a planet: they flung the voice of a Mage inside them across the galaxy to the target world and were only so accurate. Even an entire planet was a tiny target on that scale.

Tau Ceti was the only system with two of the massive black spherical facilities. Sol alone had more, with one each on Earth, Mars and Ganymede.

Damien's rank and authority cleared him a fifteen-minute slot at the Tau Ceti *f* Array. His Marines led the way through the rune-encrusted obsidian hallways, his pair of Secret Service agents trailing behind. He'd given the Array short enough notice that they clearly hadn't informed all of their staff, and he felt guilty as the various functionaries and administrative staff either pressed themselves against walls or cleared out of the way.

"Lieutenant Romanov," he said softly, gesturing for the Combat Mage currently acting as his chief bodyguard to drop back and join him. "Remind me next time to warn them I apparently bring multitudes."

That got a glimpse of a smile out of the perpetually serious soldier.

"I'm in contact with Array security," Romanov murmured back. "We should be clear to the transmission chamber now."

The number of staff the Marines had to gently move aside dropped off as they progressed, until the final layer of the immense onion-like structure of obsidian walls and silver runes was completely clear except for a single redheaded Mage in a uniform-like robe.

"I am Transceiver Elva Santiago," she told him. "We have cleared the secondary receiving chamber as requested, though we do have a recorder running in case any side transmissions come in. Per Guild rules, of course, we will remove your transmission from the recording, and you may verify this yourself afterwards."

Damien smiled at the older woman.

"Miss Santiago, I have studied the history of the Protectorate with a careful eye, and *never* have the Transceiver Mages broken their oaths of confidentiality," he reminded her. "I appreciate your efforts, however. A review of the recording will not be necessary this time."

She inclined her head.

"The chamber is prepared for you," she told him.

"So, both Segal and I agree that a Rune Wright would be ideal," Damien concluded after summarizing the incident at Andala. "Which means me, my liege. While I hesitate to call the murder unimportant, I'm not sure a Hand is needed for that investigation—but if a Rune Wright is needed anyway, I see no reason not to handle that as well."

"You *are* supposed to be on leave," Desmond Michael Alexander the Third, Mage-King of Mars and Protector of Humanity, answered calmly. "That whole mess in Sherwood and Mínglïàng was rather enough trouble. Are you sure you're up to this?"

Damien sighed. A *lot* of people had died when a mining rights conflict between those two systems had nearly been fanned into open war. While he was reasonably comfortable now that there hadn't been much else he could do, the dead had joined many others in his nightmares.

"It's one murder in a base with barely a thousand people," he pointed out. "It can only go so wrong—and we *do* need a Rune Wright. It's almost a continuation of my vacation."

He couldn't *see* Alexander. Despite almost two centuries now of research, the only thing an RTA could transmit or receive was the voice of a speaking Mage. Any kind of data transmission had proven impossible—including, in one more experimental thought, via replacement of a volunteer's voice box with an implant.

He could still *hear* his King's sigh.

"Only the men and women I pick as Hands would call a murder investigation a vacation," he pointed out. "Which perhaps says more about what I normally ask of you than anything else. Your support is also on vacation. I assume you have a plan?"

"I will be borrowing several investigators from the MIS and a squad of Marines from Mage-Captain Jakab," Damien confirmed. "Mage-Admiral Segal is placing an armed courier at my disposal. It has the space for twenty passengers, exosuits for the Marines, and a combat shuttle. I checked."

Alexander laughed.

"All you needed to tell me was that you had a plan, Damien," he pointed out. "You didn't get that golden chain because I don't trust your skills, and you've proven those skills again and again. Go to Andala, my young friend. See what our eyes can see of what the aliens left behind.

"You don't need my permission, but you have it. And my blessing. Keep me informed."

"There's a weekly courier run already. I'll send back reports via the Tau Ceti RTA."

"Then good luck," Alexander told him.

A moment of silence marked the end of the conversation, and Damien sighed. Even now, over a year later, the authority and independence that the Mage-King had bestowed on him was mind-boggling. Hands had to keep the King *informed*, but they didn't exactly ask for *permission* as a rule.

He still had time left on his slot and he checked his wrist-comp to make sure he had the right numbers and angles for his next transmission. Once he was sure, he channeled power into the runes and around him and spoke aloud.

"Ardennes RTA, are you receiving?" he asked.

A moment passed. Then two.

"This is the Ardennes RTA; we confirm receipt," the cheerful voice of the Transceiver Mage on Ardennes replied. Damien had become a Hand on that world. He'd been supposed to be an apprentice, but everything had gone *very* wrong, and the Hand he'd accompanied had been murdered.

More importantly right now, however, was that Julia Amiri's boyfriend was currently running for governor of the planet in an election that was shaping up to be functionally an acclamation, and she'd gone there to "provide moral support" to the ex-professor and ex-rebel turned politician.

"This is Hand Damien Montgomery. Please record a message for relay to Special Agent Julia Amiri," he said stiffly, following it up with a string of numbers that would reach her personal wrist comp.

Another pause.

"We are standing by to relay, my Lord Montgomery."

"Julia, this is Damien," he said calmly. "This transmission is for your information only; you are *not* to cut your visit to Ardennes and Riordan short. There has been an incident in the Andala System requiring my specific skills."

That was as close as he'd come to talking about being a Rune Wright via a relay. He'd trust the Transceiver Mages to wipe the recording of his time here on Tau Ceti, but anything relayed into the normal datanets was vulnerable.

The existence of Rune Wrights was classified at the highest level, mostly as Damien himself was the only one they knew of who wasn't a member of the Royal Family. Surprises were handy.

"I'll be traveling with both Marine and Secret Service escorts," he continued. "I'll be fine. I'll see you when you return to Tau Ceti, Julia. Tell Mikael good luck from me."

CHAPTER 4

MAGE-LIEUTENANT DENIS ROMANOV waited outside Major Kennedy's office patiently. He did *everything* patiently by nature, something many people found at odds with his lanky build, red hair and bright green eyes. Despite humanity's diaspora to the stars, certain stereotypes survived—and despite his last name, Denis was from Ireland on Earth and *looked* it.

"The Major will see you now," the burly sergeant who headed the staff section for *Duke of Magnificence*'s Marine detachment told him.

With a grateful nod to the noncommissioned officer, Denis stepped through the door into Major Sherry Kennedy's office—only to stop immediately as he saw Mage-Captain Kole Jakab sitting in a chair off to the side of the Major's desk, leaning back and watching him carefully.

"Sir," he said crisply, hiding any hesitancy behind protocol. He was familiar with Kennedy's office, a relatively standard military office aboard a Protectorate warship with a denser-than-normal "I love me" wall of citations and medals.

The comfortable chair Jakab was sprawled in hadn't been part of the décor in the past. Neither had the chair in front of the plain metal desk, a far more comfortable seat than the normal one.

"Get in and sit down, Romanov," Kennedy barked. The stocky, platinum-blond commander of *Duke*'s Marines had a command voice Denis could only hope to one day match.

"Yes, ma'am." He took the indicated seat, poising on the edge and consciously keeping his back ramrod straight.

"You've been running close protection for the Hand for the last two weeks," Kennedy told him. "Your thoughts?"

"Close protection for a man who lives on a battlecruiser is easier than a lot of VIP details I've been on," the young Combat Mage said slowly. "His Secret Service detail has been generous with their time and cooperation as well; I would have expected more pushback after needing to ask for our help. I...suspect Montgomery wouldn't allow it, though."

"Any problems?" she asked.

"None," he told her. "But things have been quiet, and I understand we'll be turning responsibilities back over to his Secret Service detail shortly."

"That's been preempted," Jakab said calmly. "How do you feel about a longer-term assignment, Lieutenant? A potentially more active one?"

Denis glanced to Kennedy, who gestured for him to answer.

"I go where the Corps sends me, sir," he finally replied. "If the Marines need me to guard Montgomery, I will guard him wherever he goes."

"The Hand is leaving Tau Ceti on what *should* be a low-key, low-intensity mission," Kennedy told him. "Hands are Hands, however, and I have the suspicion it won't *stay* as low-intensity as Montgomery may think. We're sending a squad with full heavy combat gear, including exosuits, to keep him safe."

"I would be honored to continue the duty, ma'am," Denis told her. "Though I will confess..." He considered how to phrase it, only to be cut off by Jakab.

"That it seems strange to guard a man who could wipe out your entire squad without thinking?" the Mage-Captain asked dryly. "Hands of the Mage-King are, after all, terrifyingly powerful Mages. Roughly what you were thinking, Lieutenant?"

"Yes, sir."

"Powerful as Montgomery is—and if you're being assigned to his personal guard on a more long-term basis, I'll see that you're cleared for the footage of the Ardennes Planetary Command Center assault—he is still human," Jakab said grimly. "He has defenses, but he *can* be surprised, and if somebody manages to shoot him, he *will* die.

"I don't need to tell you that the Mage-King will be *upset* if we allow one of his Hands to get broken," the Mage-Captain finished dryly. "You're also there to provide Montgomery with a strike force at his personal command," Kennedy pointed out. "Phenomenal cosmic power is all well and good, but he can't take prisoners or board ships without boots on the ground. The armed courier you'll be taking has enough space for a squad of Marines and their full gear, including exosuits, heavy weapons, and anything *else* you can think of in the next eighteen hours."

"Any particular squad I'm taking?" Denis asked. "For that matter, what about the rest of my platoon?"

"You should only be gone a few weeks at most, and *Duke* won't be out of the docks in that time," the Major replied, with a glance at Jakab, who grimaced his agreement. "Your sergeant can handle the rest of the platoon for that long. You know your platoon best, so pick the best squad for this.

"We will be reinforcing you either way," she noted. "The Tau Ceti Marine base is sending over a second Combat Mage to back you up, a Mage-Lieutenant Karina White. She's junior to you and this is your op either way."

"It's Montgomery's op, last I checked," Denis pointed out. "I'm in, ma'am. If we're leaving in eighteen hours, though, I have work to do."

The Royal Martian Navy armed courier TK-421 wasn't much of a ship in the grand scheme of things. Larger than many of the couriers that provided mail service across the Protectorate, the ship was still only seventy meters from bow to stern, an unadorned tube of metal thirty meters across.

It was also very clear to Damien Montgomery that Mage-Lieutenant-Commander Beata Pokorni loved every millimeter of her undersized, barely-armed command. Pokorni herself was as unprepossessing as her command, a notably overweight woman with Mars-born dark skin, slanted eyes and frizzy, graying hair—but she was the senior of the six Mages aboard, excluding Damien.

"We have four missile launchers and a single laser mounted along the keel of the ship," she concluded as she led him into TK-421's simulacrum chamber. The magically perfect liquid silver model of the starship floating in the center of the chamber—the exact center of the *ship*—was the key that made TK-421 a starship. With it, a trained Jump Mage like Pokorni or Damien himself could teleport the ship a full light-year in an instant.

Like most military ships, TK-421's bridge and simulacrum chamber were the same space, with computer consoles looking oddly out of place against the spherical, rune-encrusted screen that made up the simulacrum chamber's walls.

From here, Pokorni could jump the ship, engage with its weapons, and if someone was actually stupid enough to *attack* a Navy armed courier, demonstrate the distinct and terrifying difference between a ship like TK-421 and a regular courier.

A civilian courier had a jump matrix, a set of silver runes woven throughout the entire hull that amplified a small-scale teleport to the point where it could cross stars. A warship or an armed courier like Pokorni's ship had an *amplifier* matrix, capable of amplifying *any* spell. From the simulacrum chamber of her courier, the Mage-Lieutenant-Commander could utterly destroy any ship foolish enough to approach too closely.

"She's an impressive ship," Damien told her. "I'll admit I've never been aboard one of our armed couriers before. Destroyers and cruisers, mostly."

"My understanding is that HQ decided that if they wanted an armed ship, they'd send a destroyer," Pokorni replied. "They can only build three ships like TK for the price of a destroyer, and if they've got to come up with eighteen Mages *anyway*..."

Damien laughed.

"Budget isn't *irrelevant*," he noted, "but a courier crew's worth of Jump Mages is harder to come by."

A strong, practiced Jump Mage could jump after four hours' rest. Once. Maybe twice. Navy and Guild regulation called for limiting jumps to every *eight* hours outside of emergencies, so a ship with a single Mage only traveled three light-years a day.

A courier with *six* Mages aboard traveled *eighteen* light-years in the same day, putting, for example, the fourteen-light-year-distant Andala System within a day's journey of Tau Ceti.

"Is there anything you need to be ready to leave on schedule?" he asked. "I know Navy couriers tend to get most of what they need, but *nobody* tends to argue when a Hand shows up on their com screen."

"We are good to go," she replied. "The last of Mage-Lieutenant Romanov's people's equipment from *Duke* is arriving aboard your assault shuttle in fifteen minutes. Once that's here, we can leave whenever you want."

"Good." Damien smiled, actually impressed. That was two full hours ahead of when he'd expected to be able to leave. "If we're ready early, head out as soon as we are," he ordered. "While I don't have the impression the situation on Andala is likely to deteriorate, but I'd still like to be on site as soon as possible."

"We'll make it happen, my lord," Pokorni promised. "Would you like to join me in the simulacrum chamber for the first jump?"

"I would," he confirmed cheerfully. "I'll even promise not to try to make the jump myself!"

It ended up taking them over an hour to get everything aboard, which was a surprise to no one at all.

The Royal Martian Navy was a professional, well-funded, well-respected military force—but it was also a *peacetime* military. Things went wrong.

In this case, Damien found out about the addition of Mage-Lieutenant White to his bodyguards roughly two minutes before he'd been about to order TK-421 out. In the end, her shuttle had made rendezvous and delivered the young Mage—now the *ninth* aboard the courier, which made the little ship probably the highest concentration of Mages in the Protectorate—with an hour to spare before the original planned departure time.

"Lieutenant White reports that she is aboard and says, I quote, 'Thanks for waiting for me,'" Pokorni's executive officer, holding down what would be the tactical officer's console on a ship with a larger crew, reported. He was a white-haired Mage-Lieutenant, noticeably old for his rank even in a peacetime Navy, which led Damien to wonder at the older man's story.

"The shuttle has detached and we are clear of umbilicals from Tau Ceti Orbital," he continued. "My lord, ma'am, we are clear to depart."

Pokorni glanced over at Damien but he gestured for her to continue. TK-421 was *her* ship. He was simply a glorified passenger with a few gold trinkets.

"Take us out," she ordered. "On line for the Andala System, fifteen gravities."

With six Mages as part of the crew, courier ships could afford the time and energy to maintain *extremely* powerful gravity runes. Most civilian ships couldn't afford any and either used a constant one-gravity acceleration or rotating sections to provide a semblance of "down" to their passengers when not under way.

Navy ships maintained gravity runes capable of offsetting up to ten gravities of acceleration. Both Navy and civilian couriers, however, had the Mage on hand to maintain even stronger runes. Those allowed them to accelerate faster and carved hours and potentially even *days* off the time needed to reach a space they could jump from.

It would take a destroyer or cruiser three hours to be clear enough of Tau Ceti's suns and planets to jump. A courier made the same trip in two and a half hours.

They were quiet hours, and Damien spent them on the bridge with Pokorni's crew, getting a feel for the people responsible for keeping him alive through the depths of space. The trip was less than a day each way, but taking deep space for granted was an easy way to end up dead.

Pokorni's people were competent enough. They weren't the finely oiled machine of Mage-Captain Jakab's bridge crew aboard *Duke of Magnificence*, but few ships were. Jakab had led his people into battle repeatedly while acting as Damien's transportation and *Duke* was likely now the most battle-experienced crew in the Royal Martian Navy.

If Jakab's well-honed machine was a five, Pokorni's people were a two—but so was most of the Navy!

By the time they reached the point where the influence of the system's masses was low enough to be safe to jump, Damien was relatively content with the crew of the courier. All he needed them to do, after all, was not break the ship during fourteen jumps.

"Gravity scanners report we are clear of influences," the XO reported.

Damien watched quietly from the back of the room as Pokorni stepped up to the liquid silver model of the ship at the center of the room and placed her hands on it. It was still a novelty to him to watch someone *else* jump a starship.

With his Sight, he could see the exact moment that the runes inlaid into the Jump Mage's palms made contact with the blank spots on the simulacrum meant for them. It was like a circuit closed, and suddenly, power *thrummed* to the ship in a way that only he could hear.

He could See and feel the other Mage channel energy, focusing it in *just* this way, *just* this angle...and then release it.

There was a flash of both light and nothing, and then TK-421 was a light-year away, on its way to Andala.

CHAPTER 5

DAMIEN SPENT most of the trip studying the information that had been available in Tau Ceti on the Andala Expedition. Launched three years ago, two years after a corporate survey looking for mineral deposits had found something *very* different, the Expedition was led by one Dr. Johannes Kael and had *already* produced at least fifty papers of various degrees of importance.

The Hand had a university degree, a minor and three years of focused postgraduate training under the Mage-King himself. It took him less than an hour to skim the papers sufficiently to work out which fourteen actually contained useful information.

So far as the Expedition could tell, the facility had been calmly closed up between two hundred and fifty and three hundred years before, during the Eugenicist War between Earth and occupied Mars. There were no bodies or even—strangely—images of the occupants, so they had no idea what the aliens had looked like.

The absence of any seating arrangements recognizable to humans suggested that the creatures had been at least different from humans, but analysis of the interior of the facility also suggested that they'd breathed the same air, seen on roughly the same wavelengths of light, and needed spaces only slightly larger than humans.

And, in three years of study, that was basically every piece of conclusive data Kael and his people *had*. There were a lot of guesses and qualifiers in the documents Damien had but nothing solid. The aliens had removed a lot of tech and destroyed much of what they hadn't removed in place.

Until Kurosawa had broken into the sealed lower levels, there'd also been no evidence of magical use in the facility. Legatus had put up a good chunk of the funding for the Andala Expedition in the hopes of finding the UnArcana World's holy grail: an FTL drive that didn't require Mages.

It seemed they were going to be disappointed.

Another flicker of *nothing* passed through the ship and Damien checked his computer to confirm what he already knew: they'd arrived in the Andala System.

Lightspeed delay in communication was a fact of life. Since they were in no hurry—no one had left the facility since the murder, according to the report Damien had received—and multi-second gaps in conversation weren't conducive to mutual understanding, he waited until they were in orbit before reaching out to Dr. Kael.

The man who appeared on his wall when the channel finally connected couldn't have been a more stereotypical professor if he *tried*. He was a portly, balding older man with his remaining hair gone shockingly white and a distracted, grumpy look on his face.

"You must be the MIS team," Johannes Kael began immediately, cutting Damien off before the Hand could say a word. "You look too young, though. Whatever," he said, cutting off his own question.

"Get down here at once," he ordered. "You'll coordinate with my security chief, Volk. You will *not* interrupt my people's work or distract me until you have an explanation for Kurosawa's death. We are very busy here and I will not tolerate interference!"

Damien was silent for a moment in pure shock. Even if he *had* "merely" been a Martian Investigation Service Inspector, Kael's peremptory orders would have been unacceptable.

"Did they send the rune person with you?" he continued abruptly. "How *nice* of the Navy to send a ship—make sure they know they won't be permitted on the planet. I shudder to *think* of the chaos those uniformed thugs would cause!"

"Dr. Kael," Damien finally snapped. "Shut. Up."

The academic administrator stumbled to a halt, tripping over his own tongue—then started to inhale, clearly about to launch onto a tirade.

In response, Damien leaned forward, making sure both the gold medallion at his throat—the one that marked him as a Mage, with symbols carved into it denoting his training as a Jump Mage, Combat Mage, and Rune Scribe—and the chain and amulet of his rank were fully visible in the camera.

"I am Hand Damien Montgomery," he told Kael softly. "Your conditions are unacceptable, Doctor. This investigation is under the jurisdiction of Mars and will be carried out as *I* choose. Do you understand me?"

"We didn't call for a Hand!" Kael barked.

"But a Hand is what you got. I speak for Mars, Doctor, and my assistance is not under discussion," Damien told him calmly. "I am both your investigator and your rune expert. My shuttle will be departing TK-421 shortly, I expect to arrive within the hour, and I will be meeting with *you* as soon as I land.

"I will be accompanied by my shuttle's four-person crew, three Secret Service Agents, three Martian Investigation Service Inspectors and a squad of Royal Martian Marines. Please make sure you have quarters ready for them," Damien instructed. He paused, eyeing the now-silent academic.

"Will there be any problems, Dr. Kael?" he asked, his voice softer now. "Believe me when I say I have no intention of interrupting your people's work more than I must, but Dr. Kurosawa's discovery is of critical importance to the Protectorate—which makes his murder my concern as well."

Dr. Johannes Kael visibly swallowed and slowly nodded.

"I had not considered it in that light," he admitted. "I am concerned about both our research and my people's morale, Lord Montgomery," he continued, "but I will try not to impede your investigation."

"Thank you, Dr. Kael," Damien told him. "We will speak once I have landed."

He cut the channel with a sigh. He'd give Kael the credit of his words, but somehow he doubted the man was going to manage to *not* be a problem.

The shuttle dropped away from TK-421 with all the grace of a brick dropped from a plane. The Royal Martian Marine Corps did not build their assault shuttles to be pretty or graceful. They built them to land in the face of hostile fire, take hits, and deliver their payload of Marines alive.

Damien's detachment was smaller than the platoon the shuttle was designed to deliver, which thankfully meant there were safety harnesses for everyone. Among other things, the RMMC didn't bother with gravity runes in their shuttles, so multi-gravity combat maneuvers were painful affairs.

In the absence of incoming fire, the MIS Inspectors had clearly thought the harnesses wouldn't be required. Luckily for them, Mage-Lieutenant Romanov had insisted—and the Navy pilot of the assault shuttle promptly dropped them toward the planet at four gees.

"Are we actually in this much of a hurry, my lord?" Inspector Mara Dragic, the senior member of the MIS team Damien had "borrowed" on his way out of Tau Ceti, asked. The dark-haired, hook-nosed police officer looked vaguely ill under the force of the acceleration.

"No," Damien allowed. "But the people responsible for our safety, Inspector Dragic, take it very seriously. They may take unnecessary precautions—but the day those precautions turn out to be necessary, you will be very glad they were taken."

She looked confused for a moment.

"When would this become necessary?" she finally asked.

"It was on Ardennes," Damien said shortly. "A squad of Marines and a Navy flight crew, much like these men and women, died to get me to the ground alive then. So, you are right, Inspector, that I do not expect this to be necessary today. But I didn't expect it to be necessary then, either."

The whole mess on Ardennes was public knowledge, though given the size of the Protectorate, Damien doubted few of the Mage-King's citizens knew more than the headline blurb of "A Hand falls, another rises, Governor removed for treason."

He was okay with that.

"Landing in ten minutes," the shuttle pilot reported. "We have a storm incoming, and despite my best efforts, we aren't going to miss it. It's going to get bumpy."

Dragic looked even more horrified for a moment.

"This *isn't* bumpy?"

The planet Andala IV wasn't habitable by humanity but that didn't mean it lacked life. A strange forest of blue-green trees with spindly branches and strange cylindrical leaves shifted and trembled in the hammering rain and vicious wind as the assault shuttle finally touched down.

Inspector Dragic had managed to make it all the way to the surface intact, but as soon as she attempted to rise, she crumpled to her knees and vomited. The ever-handy Romanov had a bag in her hand the moment before she lost it, and the mess was at least contained.

The new Mage-Lieutenant, a stockily androgynous blonde woman Damien had been introduced to as Karina White, moved up to the airlock with a quartet of Marines. All five wore small metal breathers over their mouths, and another fire team of Marines was passing out the devices to everyone else.

"We'll sweep the pad for threats," she said calmly. "Please remain aboard until we report it clear."

If White was surprised by her fire team suddenly acquiring a suited Secret Service agent after her announcement, she didn't show it. She led all five of her companions out into the airlock and cycled it behind her.

"Are you all right, Inspector?" Damien asked Dragic.

"Yes, my lord," she confirmed, taking a proffered cloth from one of the Marines to clean her face before putting on the breather.

"Pad is clear," White reported over a radio channel. "Dr. Kael is wait-ing inside the facility."

"Let's go," Damien instructed, only to get a raised hand from Dragic.

"Shouldn't you be wearing a breather, my lord?"

He smiled. Once, long before, he'd been a mere apprentice to an older and wiser Hand who had told him it wouldn't do for a Hand to appear like "a soaked rat." Appearances were important, and not needing the breather or being bothered by the storm they'd landed in were com-ponents of projecting power in a way Dr. Kael would understand.

"I am a Hand," he told the Inspector. "I'll be fine. Let's go."

From the shocked double take Doctor Johannes Kael made when Damien walked in from the rain and poisonous atmosphere outside his climate-controlled camp site without a breather and bone dry, the point was probably made.

"Welcome to the Andala Expedition Research Facility, my lord." The balding scientist offered his hand to Damien, who calmly shook it.

"Thank you, Doctor."

Damien glanced around the reception area for the facility, such as it was. Kael had only two companions with him, who he gestured to im-mediately.

"Allow me to introduce Miss Jessica Volk, our head of security and facilities," he waved toward a tall woman with soft features and a clean-shaven head. She bowed slightly at Kael's introduction. "She is see-ing to quarters for your companions, but it's taking some time."

"We were using the space as storage, to be honest," Volk told Damien in an unusually deep voice. "I don't have a lot of people, so it will take us most of the day to get the spare quarters freed up."

"Romanov?" Damien asked. He didn't need to specify what he wanted.

"Kitcher, Chan," the ever-serious Lieutenant barked crisply. "Take your fire teams and help Miss Volk out. If the extra hands would be of use?"

It sounded like a question, but Damien didn't think anyone in the room was fooled. In addition to helping clear out and set up the quarters, the two Marine teams would make sure they were safe.

"Of course," Volk agreed cheerfully. "If you'll excuse us, Dr. Kael?"

"Yes, yes, of course," Kael said shortly, and gestured the third person with him forward. "This is Jarek Zitnik. He was Professor Kurosawa's senior student and the one who found his body."

"Ah, good," Damien said, offering his hand to the youth. Dark-haired with tanned skin, tall and muscular, Zitnik looked more physically able than some of the Marines, hardly what he would have expected of a xenoarchaeology student.

"Professor Kurosawa was a mentor and a friend," Zitnik told him in noticeably-accented English. "If anything I can do will help catch his killer, I am more than willing."

"Let's take this conversation somewhere more private," Damien suggested. "Inspector Dragic's team will start interviewing the rest of the staff, starting with Kurosawa's students."

"I can arrange some..." Kael trailed off at the Hand's gesture.

"No," he ordered. "*They* will arrange things, with the support of the Marines. Surprise, I'm told, is helpful in these affairs."

Kael visibly swallowed again.

"I wish I could say it was just an accident," he whispered. "Just a damn fool old man who fell off a balcony."

"You saw the body, Doctor," Zitnik told him.

"I did," the Andala Expedition's senior scientist confirmed, drawing himself back up with a firm nod. "The compound is not particularly large, Lord Montgomery. My office is nearby. Shall we?"

Mage-Lieutenant Denis Romanov watched the Hand disappear deeper into the prefabricated modules making up the research camp, trailed by his three Secret Service Agents for now, then turned to the two Martian Investigation Service Inspectors and his remaining Marines.

"Carmichael, your team is with White," he ordered, gesturing the other Mage to him. "Mage-Lieutenant, I want you to sweep the exterior of the research camp *and* the alien base. Set up the scanners we brought with us—I don't trust a bunch of scientists to have set up systems able to see anyone sneaking up on us."

"Of course," she said crisply. "Should I pre-cache supplies and weapons as well?"

"Munitions, breather filters, SAMs," he confirmed after a moment's thought. "We should be able to deploy in armor and with weapons, but extra ammunition and air supplies won't go amiss."

It was paranoid, but it was his *job* to be paranoid.

"Make sure the Service Agents know the location of the caches as well as our people," he ordered. "And include ammo for their systems, too."

The Martian Secret Service was charged with defending the Mage-King, his family, his Hands, and the members of the Council of the Protectorate. Their preferred weapons systems were lighter and more transportable than his Marines' gear—and traded having higher maintenance requirements and lower ammunition capacity for comparable performance.

The only real flaw Denis saw in the Secret Service's heavier gear was that it *couldn't* trade ammunition with the RMMC rifles. Thankfully, the Service, the Marines, and the MIS all used the same *sidearm*, so ammunition for that wasn't a concern.

"Isn't that a little paranoid?" one of the two MIS agents asked as White led Carmichael's fire team back into the airlock. "This is a murder investigation. Why would we end up outside, living on emergency caches?"

"I don't know," Denis told the cop. "But my job until Special Agent Amiri gets back is to make sure that Damien Montgomery survives. Since almost nobody is stupid enough to go straight at a Hand, that means we prepare for what we *don't* expect to happen."

He glanced around the prefabricated reception area and concealed a shiver. They had a single armed courier in orbit and the research camp had no defenses. No communication, no support, no backup. He wondered if the Hand had even registered how vulnerable this place was if someone decided to come after him.

"But our job today is to find a murderer," he told the Inspector with a smile. "My people will stick to yours like glue, but this part is your show. How do you want this to work?"

CHAPTER 6

THE SPARTAN NATURE of the plain entrance and sterile white hallways that made up the prefabricated habitats of the Andala Expedition's "campsite" didn't prepare Damien for the crowded reality of Dr. Kael's office.

It seemed that the Professor had understood exactly how long-term his position as head of the Expedition was going to be, and had brought all of the comforts of home. A massive wooden desk with an old-fashioned leather-and-chrome swivel chair held pride of place in the office—and represented the only clear surface in the room!

Wooden bookshelves had been lined up along every wall, all of them full to bursting with books, printed reports, and miscellaneous artifacts and bric-à-brac collected across a lifetime. There were three comfortable-looking chairs in the room, but all three had books and data disks piled on them.

A side table had been stuffed in beside the desk to add extra workspace and had apparently been sacrificed to the gods of clutter that ruled this place. Unlike the desk, it was covered in the same papers as the rest of the room, only with dirty plates and cups added to the mess.

"You can move the papers on the chairs," Kael instructed. "Just make sure they stay together—there is a system, though I know it isn't obvious."

Damien twitched his fingers and the piles on all three chairs lifted up, neatly organized themselves, and dropped onto the corner of Kael's desk. Interesting, despite the mess of the *rest* of the office, the professor clearly twitched at there being something on his desk.

The blatant display of power, much as Damien *hated* making it, seemed to settle the point though. The theatrics required for his job grated on him sometimes, but he had no intention of letting the Expedition's leader mistake their relative positions.

Taking one of the comfortable chairs himself, he waited for Dragic and Zitnik to sit, then gestured for the MIS woman to begin.

"I'll have questions for you both with regards to Kurosawa's time here," she noted, "but for the moment, let's start with the most obvious. I understand that Mister Zitnik here found the body. Can you tell me exactly what happened?"

The athletic xenoarchaeology student nodded, taking a moment to compose himself.

"About half of the people researching here are postgrad students," he began. "We're all assigned to a specific professor, usually on a one-to-one basis. Since Runic Studies is a relatively small specialization, especially for non-Mages, Kurosawa agreed to mentor the three of us in that specialty who ended up here."

"How did three Runic Studies–specialized students end up here?" Damien asked.

Zitnik coughed and looked uncomfortable.

"Well..." He sighed. "There were no runes here to study, so it was the posting that was left over for the non-Mage students."

Damien winced but nodded. Non-Mage students in a field like Runic Studies would be at a disadvantage to begin with, since a non-Mage couldn't be a Rune Scribe and Runic Studies was mostly a precursor to that title. Since non-Mages were rare among those who could *teach* it, mundane students would be the last choice for any work placement.

It made sense, though it also resulted in an immense barrier to creating the non-Mage rune specialists whose unique points of view had been key to many advances in magic over the last quarter-millennium.

"Who are the other students of Doctor Kurosawa?" Dragic asked.

"Myself, Samara Hollins, and Talin Davidyan," Zitnik told them. "We're each from different universities—different *worlds*, even. I'm from Tau Ceti, Hollins is from Mars, and Davidyan is from a Fringe World I'd never heard of."

"All right," Dragic said after a moment. She was taking notes on her wrist computer via a holographic keyboard only she could see. "So, you were looking for Professor Kurosawa? Why?"

"With the regular courier in system, I'd just received feedback from my university on my draft thesis," Zitnik told them. "It was positive, but they had some key points I wanted to run by the professor. He wasn't in his office, but I knew he'd been wandering the facility to try and get a feel for how the Strangers thought.

"He's also been *really* frustrated over the decision not to open up the lower levels," the student continued, glancing over at Kael.

That *had* to have been Kael's decision, Damien realized. It was supportable, certainly, but he doubted the Legatans who'd been underwriting the lion's share of the Andala Expedition were happy with the pottery and circuitry scraps that had been sent back. *Those* worthies wanted proof of technological FTL.

"He and I hadn't *talked* about it, but I knew that we had one access to the lower levels that's close to the base site, and he'd been going and, well, staring at it in frustration," Zitnik admitted. "I went there to see if I could find him, and found that he'd opened a path.

"It was...impressive, to be honest," he noted. "The professor had just...moved all the rocks and locked them into place. I've seen magic before, but wow."

"And the professor's body was past the new entrance he'd created?" Dragic asked.

"Yes," the young man confirmed with a nod. "I'll admit I was curious, too. *I* couldn't just open a tunnel into the lower levels, but I wasn't going to turn around and leave when it was there!

"I saw his light pretty quickly and went to find him. He'd found some kind of gallery, probably an old market area, at a first guess—and the air was *clean*. The runes were still functioning. It was incredible..."

Zitnik sighed, shaking his head.

"And then I realized he wasn't with his light," he said softly. "There was a balcony. He'd gone over, fallen about ten meters. He was..." The student swallowed hard. "He was still warm by the time I made it down there, but he was dead."

"The fall killed him?" Dragic asked. "Could it have been an accident?"

"Miss Volk has his body in cold storage; you can see it for yourself," Zitnik told them. "He'd been *burned*, Inspector. Like someone had hit him with hot coals. And he was too far away to have fallen—he was thrown. Looked like magic to me, though I'll admit I don't know *anything*."

"He was a good man." The student looked at Dragic and Damien desperately. "I...don't know why anyone would kill him. *Everyone* liked him."

"It does sound like magic," Damien agreed. "Dr. Kael, just to confirm what I've been told, there are no Mages in your Expedition?"

"Without any runic artifacts or evidence of magic on the Strangers' part, there was no need," the Expedition leader replied. "Doctor Kurosawa was here for his general expertise in xenoarchaeology, not his knowledge as a Rune Scribe. Nobody here could have killed him with magic!"

"We'll need to inspect the body to be sure," Dragic said calmly, with a somewhat repressing glance at Damien that he probably deserved. He *had*, after all, agreed to let her run the investigation without interference.

"But first, I think I'd like to go over Doctor Kurosawa's things, and then I want to interview each of you separately," she continued. "We have a lot of work to do."

"Of course," Kael allowed. "I do ask that you interfere with our research as little as possible. Our work is important."

Damien managed not to audibly snort, barely. The Andala IV *site* was important, but his study of the literature produced by Kael's people suggested that their work wasn't going to find anything of value anytime soon.

"The only interference that is unavoidable is one you probably won't notice for a bit," he told Kael. "As of our arrival, no one is permitted to leave or land here without my direct permission. We wouldn't want our murderer to escape, after all."

Kael swallowed.

"Of course," he said faintly. "May I show you to Doctor Kurosawa's room?"

Damien had brought along the Martian Investigation Service Inspectors for two reasons: firstly, while he was qualified to carry out witness interviews, he didn't have the time to interview even the dozens of people in the research base who had worked directly with Professor Kurosawa, and secondly, because he was *not* able to do forensic investigation himself.

Entering Yoshi Kurosawa's quarters, his main responsibility was not to interfere as Mara Dragic did her work. Barring Dr. Kael from the room was the work of a moment and a few quiet words, leaving him and the MIS Inspector alone.

Keeping his hands in the pockets of his tailored suit jacket, the Hand surveyed the room. He wasn't sure how long the professor had been on Andala IV, but he'd tried to make his space homelike. A series of cloth scrolls with calligraphied Japanese poetry hung on the walls, helping cover up the plain metal walls of the prefabricated structure.

Everything else in the room was neatly organized. It wasn't a large space, basically a bachelor suite with an office instead of a kitchen, but everything was neatly organized and appeared to have a place. The office screens had been shut down and rolled away, and the paper that was there had been neatly organized.

No clothes scattered on the floor, no dirty dishes, nothing. Kurosawa had hardly been an ascetic—there was a tidy little set of glasses around a half-empty carafe of what looked like whiskey to Damien—but he had been organized.

Dragic was making a methodical sweep, a set of tweezers in one hand and a case of bags and tags in the other, but she didn't seem to be finding much.

The room was...too neat. Wondering, Damien reached for his Sight and swept the room again. He'd never met a Rune Scribe in his life who didn't have *some* unique little trinket he'd charged with magic, and what it was and where he'd hidden could give the Hand insight into Kurosawa's character.

He Saw nothing.

With a sigh, he focused more, looking for the glow of energy and channeled magic. If nothing else, a Mage had *lived* here. That left some signs behind.

They were there, but they were...muddled. Mixed up. The whiskey carafe was in the wrong place—Kurosawa had apparently amused himself by using magic to pour his drinks, but he'd done it in the *office,* and the carafe was next to the bed.

There were hints that something quite strongly magical *had* been kept in the desk, but it wasn't there anymore.

"Are you finding anything, Inspector?" he asked softly.

"Nothing," she replied. "The room hasn't been touched since he died. The murderer didn't come here."

"Hmm," Damien hummed stepping further into the room. "No, Inspector," he said softly, "someone was here. The glasses have residual magic attached to them: Kurosawa was...playing with them, for lack of better description, before he died. There."

He tapped the edge of the desk.

"A runic artifact was removed from the desk," he continued. "I would guess...about a day ago. After the professor's death. Check his file archive," he ordered. "Full forensic sweep. I suspect you'll find a number of his files were deleted *very* cleanly about twenty-four hours ago."

Dragic stared at him, then looked to the glasses and back to him. He'd briefed her on just what his Rune Wright Gift entailed on the way there, but he suspected she hadn't believed him. Now...she wasn't so sure.

"Let me check something," she snapped. Suddenly being *much* less careful, she stepped back to the door and yanked open its control panel, pulling a pair of leads from her wrist computer and plugging them in.

A moment later, she swore.

"Someone entered the room twenty-five hours and sixteen minutes ago," she stated calmly. "They wiped any record of it from the main systems, but the door has a local log of when it operates to assist with maintenance.

"There were no physical signs in the room," she continued. "My lord, somebody swept this room and did it so cleanly, *I couldn't find a sign.* We're not dealing with a crime of passion. This was a *professional.*"

Damien sighed.

"That's what I was afraid of," he admitted. "Check Doctor Kurosawa's files. See if you can identify what was deleted. We'll touch base this evening and compare notes."

"What are you doing?" she asked.

"I'm going to go examine the only thing it makes sense for him to be killed for," the Hand told her. "It's time I took a look at these alien runes."

Kael was still waiting outside the room, his arms crossed and tapping his foot, when Damien emerged. The three Secret Service Agents not so subtly blocking the path away suggested why he remained despite his clear irritation.

"Find anything, my lord?" he asked.

"Not yet," Damien told him. "Inspector Dragic will continue her investigation here. I need to take a look at the runes Kurosawa found. Can you show me to the alien base?"

"I can have..."

"Doctor, please," the Hand said quietly, "you know the Strangers' base better than anyone here." If he didn't, Kael wasn't doing his job, and that wasn't *quite* Damien's impression of the man. "I can read the papers everyone has written, but that doesn't tell me much. I need your take on this."

The Andala Expedition's leader sighed. That was apparently the right tack to take, though, as the man nodded his agreement.

"All right, my lord Hand. Follow me."

As he led the way through the plain metal corridors of the research site, Kael waved a hand around genteelly, taking in his entire facility.

"Our quarters and research labs were built in modules on Terra herself," he told Damien. "The best equipment from across the Protectorate was loaded into them, and they were delivered here by a chartered ex-military transport.

"There's only one site worth investigating on the planet," he continued as they reached a different airlock from the one they'd entered through, "so we set up right next to it. We have a covered tunnel that connects our site to the stranger base, but we concluded that pumping breathable air into the old base could cause irreparable damage to some of the artifacts."

"Could you?" Damien asked, curious. "It's still airtight?"

"Not entirely anymore," Kael admitted, "but it definitely was initially. Whoever the Strangers were, they were no more able to breathe Andala Four's air than we are. We've found several air intakes with filters that, well, look blocky and obsolete to us *now*, but they were *abandoned* over two hundred years ago." He gestured to a locker by the door out.

"Grab a breather, my lord...if you want, I suppose?" he considered aloud, clearly remembering Damien's arrival.

Damien chuckled at the administrator's discomfiture but grabbed a breather. He checked over its telltales and made sure it linked to his wrist comp, then put it on.

A few adjusted straps later, and he was breathing carefully filtered air. Glancing back, he confirmed that his three trailers had *also* put on the breathers. They were here to protect him, but he figured that responsibility was reciprocal.

"After you, Dr. Kael," he instructed the other man.

The older scientist led the way into the airlock and cycled it with the push of a button. Since the only real concern with the planet's air was the toxin concentrations, the outer door opened immediately and Kael led the way into a tunnel of flexible plastic.

"The Strangers built their facility with local materials," he told Damien. "The domes are local rock, pulverized and cast in a chemical matrix. High-tech concrete, basically. There are six of them," he said, pointing through the translucent plastic. "Each is roughly six hundred meters across and a hundred high—this was not a small facility."

"But according to your papers, it wasn't a colony?" the Hand asked, studying the shapes as they approached the closest dome. The tunnel had several forks, other covered paths heading out to the three further domes.

"It was a colony in the sense that they clearly aren't *from* here," Kael replied, more energized now that he was talking about what was clearly his favorite topic. "The degree to which the facility is sealed from the local atmosphere tells us that, as does the lack of any *other* ruins on the planet.

"There are also utterly massive fuel tanks underground here," he continued. "There's no evidence of cloud-scoop infrastructure on the gas giant, but it had to be there. This was some kind of refueling station with some groundside recreation and shopping opportunities. There are a dozen facilities like it in human space."

"That's why we're sure they had interstellar travel?" Damien asked.

"There would be no other reason to have a facility like this," Kael told him. "This is the only place we've ever seen which was clearly settled by aliens from a different system—we've never found ruins that weren't clearly from aliens evolved around that star."

And ruins were most of what humanity had found of other alien races, Damien knew. A tiny handful of races had been discovered with tech ranging from Stone Age up to one mid–Steam Revolution species, but anyone beyond that had died out. The intact races were carefully watched by quiet Navy pickets to make sure nothing avoidable happened to them.

The evidence humanity had was that a single system species was *terrifyingly* vulnerable to natural disasters on an astronomical scale—but the Andala IV base was the only place they'd ever found evidence of a multi-system species.

Reaching the end of the tunnel, they reached what clearly had once been an airlock. Without power, it had simply been forced open and wedged in place. The presence of the flexible plastic tunnel meant no more of the planet's air made it inside than had already been there, but from Kael's comments, the interior had been the same as the outside, anyway.

"The upper layers in the domes are built much as you would expect," the scientist told him, leading the way into the alien structure. Tiny but powerful lights had been strung down the main corridors, providing the light the ancient facility's systems no longer could.

"There's a few open spaces, but mostly they're buildings. Built of concrete made of local rock, same as the domes themselves. Dimensions suggest a species not much taller than us but noticeably *wider*." He gestured at a door as they passed, and Damien saw what he meant.

While the gap in the concrete was only a bit over two meters high, not even out of the range for human doors, it was almost as wide as it was high, a very different set of dimensions than for a "normal" door.

"What do we know about the Strangers?" he asked as he followed the other man deeper into the dome.

"Mostly? They didn't like to paint pictures of themselves," Kael said, his tone irritated. "We've gone through the entirety of four domes and were working our way down toward the points in the tunnels where we were blocked off. There's a surprising amount of art—probably more than we would have—but most of it is abstract. What isn't abstract is landscapes. Not Andala Four's landscapes, but no creatures, and certainly no aliens."

"Inconsiderate of them," Damien agreed. They were underground now, and the lights were getting sparser. He appreciated the scale on which the Strangers had built their base quite a bit!

Kael pulled out a pair of flashlights and passed Damien one. He seemed to have forgotten the Secret Service Agents, but they all produced small but powerful lights from inside their suit jackets. It was rare, in the Hand's experience, for his bodyguards *not* to produce whatever minor tool was needed from inside their jackets.

Since his own jacket was of a very similar style and design, he wasn't entirely sure how they did it.

"We're passing the area where we've completed our sweep and set up lights," he said. "This section is...safe, but it's also where the collapses occurred. Keep your eyes and ears open."

"This doesn't look quite the same as above," Damien noted, pointing his light at the walls. The stone was smoother now, without even the minor casting-mold lines the dome corridors had.

"Laser-cut," Kael replied. "Or, at least, laser-smoothed. We could build something similar, of course—not sure we could have when this place was built, though."

"The Olympus Mons Complex was built around then," Damien pointed out. "Much the same way: blasted out with explosives and then smoothed with lasers."

"I didn't know that," the older man admitted. "Not many people go inside the Mountain, though, my lord Hand."

"All relative, I suppose," Damien said quietly. The Complex itself had a population of over a hundred thousand, and the city that sprawled across the slopes of the immense mountain was home to over twelve *million* souls.

"But we're also not sure when this place was built," Kael continued. "Easier to date when it was abandoned. We have a range of over a hundred and fifty years for when it was built—and at the high end...well, let's just say it *probably* wasn't built before nineteen fifty."

The Hand whistled silently. That was *five hundred years* earlier. Before humanity had even launched rockets to orbit.

"What happened to them?" he asked. Andala IV was only twenty-two light-years from Sol. An alien facility had been occupied for between a hundred and *two hundred and fifty* years, basically in humanity's backyard, but humanity hadn't seen any other sign of the Strangers.

"We don't know. They just...packed up and left. We have some evidence that it happened in stages," Kael noted. "When they finally left, only one dome was in operation."

He shook his head and gestured forward to where a bright light marked a collapsed tunnel and two guards carrying stun-guns.

"We've reached the collapse," he told Damien. "Once we're through here, we're walking in spaces only a handful of beings have seen in centuries."

CHAPTER 7

WAITING FOR HIS Secret Service Agents to check the other side of the admittedly intimidating and dark tunnel that Kurosawa had made through the cave-in, Damien spent the time studying the tunnel itself. It was impressive: the Mage had lifted everything into place, moving hundreds of kilos of stone, then flash-transmuted it to solidify it there.

Damien would freely admit that transmutation was one of his weakest points, something he generally overcame by the sheer brute force that the Runes inlaid into his flesh allowed him. Kurosawa's arched tunnel was anything *but* a brute-force approach—but had still required an immense amount of power.

"I'm impressed," he told Dr. Kael. "Kurosawa was powerful."

"Martian and Mage by Blood," the chief scientist replied, as if that answered the question. "My understanding is that he was very powerful, as these things are measured. Not sure how he could have been killed by magic!"

"He wasn't combat-trained," Damien said softly, considering the archway. "But his power would have allowed him a decent chance against any Mage that *wasn't*."

"What does that even *mean?*" Kael demanded.

"That you have a combat-trained Mage hiding among your staff," the Hand told him. "Which suggests that this was hardly personal. Kurosawa's killer was a professional."

The Expedition head didn't get a chance to reply before one of the two Secret Service agents who'd gone forward returned.

"The gallery we were told about is clear," he told Damien. "We haven't checked further, but we've got sensors on the entrances. Should be safe."

"Come on, Johannes," Damien told the doctor. "Let's go take a look at the Strangers' magic, shall we?"

The gallery was impressive from what Damien could see, which wasn't much with the limited light of the flashlights. They picked out the railing of the galleries glittering off the silver band he presumed to be the runes Kurosawa had found.

"Give me a moment," he ordered the other men. Even Kael paused, unsure whether or not to argue, long enough for Damien to channel energy through his Runes and conjure a cool-but-bright ball of light and pitch it into the air.

A moment's concentration put the small artificial sun in the middle of the room, hanging a dozen meters above the dry ancient fountain. Murals in odd purplish colors covered the outer walls, and the half-rusted poles of long-ago vendors' stalls and tents still stuck up from the ground.

With the room lit up, it was easy for Damien, at least, to pick out the signs of a Mage fight. Scorch marks covered the wall behind him and parts of the railing. It was also sadly easy to pick up where Professor Yoshi Kurosawa's life had ended: a chunk of the edge of the old fountain was the reddish-brown stain of recently dried blood.

"His body, of course, is in storage at the base," Kael said quietly. "We...well, we didn't have the gear for forensics, so I ordered the lower levels guarded and kept for your people."

"Inspector Dragic will go over both the body and the crime scene," Damien told him. "Is anyone in the Expedition qualified to do an autopsy?"

"We have a couple of medical doctors, but...I don't think so."

"Then the Inspector will walk them through it," the Hand replied with a confidence he wasn't sure he felt. *He* certainly couldn't run an autopsy.

Leaving the others behind, Damien walked up to the edge of the railing. The sensors on his breather, linked to his PC, told him the main function of the runes as he glanced at their results. The toxic levels of carbon monoxide and carbon dioxide had been scrubbed from the air. The oxygen content was increased above levels humans would find comfortable.

While it had been made decorative and part of the life of the base, this gallery had been a magically secured emergency shelter, its air purified by a heavily secured and charged spell that had survived *centuries* without maintenance.

Damien was impressed.

Kneeling next to the stone railing with its strip of silver inlay, he looked at the runes and Saw. Where anyone else would only see the silver itself, he saw the flow of power itself through the silver. He also saw that while it *had* worked unmaintained for centuries, it wouldn't do so much longer.

There hadn't been much power left in the runes, and they'd taken damage in the fight where Kurosawa had died. What power was left was sputtering out, supercharging an effect that wouldn't have been powerful enough to fully purify the air, but also reducing its lifespan to a matter of days.

He blinked, shaking his head. The pattern looked *very* familiar. Too familiar. He'd been a Jump Mage before he'd been a Hand—the two runes required for that job were still inlaid into his palm—and he *knew* what an emergency air-purification spell looked like.

It was strange. It looked the same but different, and he couldn't put his finger on it. Like he was reading a sentence he knew in a foreign language but was still able to puzzle it out because they were both Latin languages using the same alphabet...

"That's impossible," he whispered, but he brought his PC up to take a photo and run it through his software regardless.

The piece of code he used had been custom-written by the current Mage-King before he'd taken his throne. Both Desmond the Third and

Damien had worked on it since then, and it was able to recognize any arrangement of the seventy-six characters and fourteen connectors in the Martian Runic script and reduce them to a circuit diagram.

Normally, the Rune Wrights didn't need it. The program had been made for Hands *other* than Damien, none of whom were Rune Wrights. But right now...he needed the confirmation.

A confirmation by the software happily popped up, unaware of how deeply its simple conclusion shook the foundations of human knowledge of the universe.

"Dr. Kael," Damien said levelly. "You are certain no human was in here before Kurosawa?"

"Absolutely," the Expedition leader replied. "We dated the rubble back when we were mapping the facility. The cave-in was just over two hundred years ago. The Protectorate barely existed then. No one had been to this star system." He paused. "Why?"

"Because if we hadn't found this behind a cave-in, sealed away for hundreds of years, I would say someone was playing a prank on you, Doctor," the Hand told him. "But since we did, I'm afraid I know what Kurosawa died for.

"These aren't alien runes, Dr. Kael. These are ours. Martian Runic."

"That's *impossible*," the xenoarchaeologist replied. "I'm no student of runes, my lord, but even I know Martian Runic was only developed in the twenty-third century by the Eugenicists!"

"Earlier than that," Damien said quietly. The Olympus Mons amplifier had, after all, enabled the Olympus Project to identify children with scraps of the Gift for their forced breeding program that had started in the twenty-one-fifties. "But much of the details of the origin of human magic was lost when the Mages overthrew the Eugenicists," he admitted.

"But that is details," Damien continued, staring at the runes. "Because you're right. This facility uses the same runes we do and *predates human magic.*"

The stunned expression on the scientist's face—and his bodyguards' faces, for that matter—told him everyone else had caught up.

Unlike anyone else here, Damien *knew* that Martian Runic was not an entirely efficient way of organizing magic. He'd discussed revamping the language with the Mage-King, but the current conclusion was that it was just too huge a project.

Aliens would have—*must* have—developed their own not-entirely-efficient language.

There was only one way these runes could be the same as humanity's: if humanity had learned rune magic *from* the Strangers.

CHAPTER 8

DESPITE DR. KAEL'S clear impatience, Damien took another half-hour to carefully review the rest of the runes in the ancient gallery, the cold light of his false sun lighting up the silver even more clearly than daylight would have.

The matrix that covered the railings didn't change anywhere along the way. A regular Rune Scribe would have recognized the runes, but the layout and structure were sufficiently different that they'd have problems being certain what they did without taking time to review it in detail.

The runes were sufficiently the *same* that even the most recently graduated Rune Scribe *would* be able to break down the purpose and function of the runes. It wasn't just the script that was the same. Reading the alien runes was like what he imagined reading Spanish as a Portuguese speaker would be. The script was the same and the syntax and grammar were similar enough to help, but the words, while similar, were different.

"We'll need to sweep the entirety of the lower levels for any other samples of runes," he told Kael. "Not today, but before I leave. This is...huge."

"This is *unimaginably* huge," Kael replied. "My lord, this could make the career of every scientist here! We'll need to bring in real experts, not Kurosawa's mundane students, as soon as possible!"

"We'll see about that," Damien said sharply. If nothing else, the three who'd worked with Kurosawa were who was *available*, and he wasn't sure just how far he really wanted to spread the knowledge of these runes just yet.

Someone had *died* for it already, after all.

"I need to go over *everything* you have on this base," he concluded aloud. "Not just what's been published, but every scrap of data, every artifact analysis, *everything*. There are patterns I may see that you haven't."

"Of course, Lord Montgomery." The administrator paused. "Does this...mean the Protectorate will be taking over?"

"Probably," Damien admitted. "We're unlikely to change up too much. At least initially, we'll just bring in more security and some specialized Mages."

Most likely, Kael would be left in place heading the civilian side until or unless he pissed someone off. Based off the Hand's experiences with him so far, Damien figured that could take as little as six hours or as much as six months, depending on the temperament of whoever ended up in charge there.

"Let's get back to the base," he ordered. "Malcolm, Connor, lead the way."

The two Secret Service Agents had been guarding the passage back to the human base since arrival, while their third companion had been trailing Damien around the gallery. At Damien's order, they swept the tunnel with their lights, making sure at least the first few meters were clear before everyone entered.

Once Damien and Kael had reached them, they led the way back, their lights illuminating the hallway and side corridors as they advanced. They'd already come this way, but the Martian Secret Service didn't train their people to make assumptions.

The lead pair made sure there was at least two meters' distance between them and their charges—two meters that saved everyone *else's* lives.

Damien didn't see the tripwire *or* the mines. He could see magic where others saw only silver, but that didn't allow him to see technology no one had ever touched with a spell.

Neither of the two Agents saw them either. Malcolm stopped in the middle of the hallway as he hit the tripwire—and had just enough time to look back at Damien and yell "Shield!" before the mines went off.

The Hand's sense of danger was as sharply tuned as anyone's, so he had a shield of solid force in front of him before the Service agent had finished yelling.

It took *time* to stretch it forward and shield the two people out in front. Time Malcolm and Connor didn't have. Half a dozen directional mines had been mounted on each side of the wall since they'd come in, and they all detonated simultaneously, filling the ancient corridor with fire and deadly projectiles.

Both lead Agents went down, dead—*shredded*—before they hit the ground, but Damien's shield was in place in time to save the rest of them. The projectiles hammered against his barrier, testing his strength, and then it was over.

And then the shooting started.

"Down!" Damien was hit in the middle of the back by the remaining Secret Service Agent, flung to the ground as an automatic weapon sprayed the corridor with bullets. The man rolled off Damien and came up firing his own weapon—only for a blast of flame to rip the weapon from his hand.

Gunfire and Mage-fire resumed a moment later—and slammed headlong into Damien's shield, now covering them from the front as he rose to his feet.

"Get back, both of you," he ordered the scientist and bodyguard. "This one's mine."

The next salvo was a string of grenades, and Damien winced as the energy transfer rippled back into him. It was roughly equivalent to the recoil of a large pistol, far less dangerous than the grenades but uncomfortable. Stopping more of the energy would take more of *his* energy—and he had other uses for that.

"I am Hand Damien Montgomery," he snapped down the corridor, using his Sight to track where the firebolts had come from. *There.* He started walking toward the attacker. "You know how this has to end. You have thirty seconds to surrender."

The response was...disturbing. Another mine had been concealed at the height of his arm on the side corridor he was following the attacker down, and went off as he passed it.

His main shield was along the corridor path, but he'd still wrapped a lesser shield around himself. The explosive sprayed its deadly projectiles into his right arm, smashing against the shield and smearing metal across his jacket arm for a moment.

The suit jacket was wrecked. His defense had stopped the mine from killing him, but enough heat and melted metal had burned through to shred the suit. Its expensive-looking fabric concealed an expensive flexible composite, though, that had sacrificed itself to save him.

Under the wrecked suit, the Rune of Power inlaid into his forearm was now fully visible, and with a chill, Damien realized that the mine hadn't been meant to kill him. It had been meant to break or damage the Rune, one of the five that made him, born a Mage of average strength, the second most powerful Mage alive.

No matter *who* his attacker was, they shouldn't have known about those Runes. One was inlaid on the right forearm of every Hand—more than one was only possible when a Rune Wright was designing the Runes on themselves, unfortunately—but the source of the Hand's extraordinary power was kept secret.

"Right," he muttered aloud, forcing his shield forward as a second salvo of grenades launched out of the darkness. "Time's up."

He caught the grenades with his power and flung them aside as he charged forward. A tighter shield wrapped around him now, protecting him as a series of mines at the right height and angle to hit a Hand's Rune fired off as he passed them.

Another sweep of power caught up the projectiles and explosive force of those weapons and brought them with him. His Sight picking out the Mage in the tunnels with him, he *threw* all of that force directly at them.

The speed and power of the shield they conjured answered his question. His attacker was a trained Combat Mage—and almost certainly Kurosawa's killer.

"Why'd you kill the doctor?" he demanded, following a trail he was sure the assassin didn't know they were leaving.

"Orders," a feminine voice replied, though his Sight showed she was somewhere different from the source. Probably a speaker. "Same as you. Some secrets must be kept, no matter the price."

"You know you can't kill me," he said quietly. "Turn in your employers and I can arrange clemency."

"You have no idea what you're talking about," she snapped. The voice was still coming from in front of him, but she'd taken another tunnel and was sneaking around behind him, using the speaker as a distraction. "I am a Keeper and my oaths *will be kept!*"

She lunged from the corridor, a long rune-encrusted knife, presumably designed to cut though a Mage's shield, in her hand.

Damien's power *flared* in the underground tunnel, the Runes of Power across his body flashing with heat as he caught her arm, overcoming the knife's runes with sheer overwhelming power and stopping her in mid-strike.

Frozen in the moment, he got a good look at his attacker for the first time. She was dressed in the same plain lab utilities as everyone else on the base and wearing light-gathering optics above her breather. He couldn't see her eyes, but the cast of her face made her anger clear.

She *twisted* to escape his hold—and then her arm *snapped* like a twig, the knife falling from nerveless fingers as Damien tried to maintain his hold. Her *other* had lifted the deadly-looking carbine she'd been firing earlier.

He lashed out with a bolt of pure force. He was trying to just stop the weapon, but he lost a degree of fine control when he was doing multiple things at once. Her arm snapped back, the second limb snapping in a handful of moments.

"Others will come," she told him, her voice thick with pain. "The secret will be kept."

Then she spasmed, the distinct convulsions of poison. Damien dropped her, pulling clean air around them as he desperately tried to pull off her breather to force out whatever pill she'd taken.

Despite his power, he was only human. By the time he got the face mask off, her mouth was full of foam and her convulsions were weakening. He stared at her in horror as she gave one final full-body con-vulsion...and stopped.

CHAPTER 9

THE TUNNEL BEHIND DAMIEN had collapsed as the explosions rippled through it. They'd been closer to the surface than he'd initially thought, though, as he could see the sky through the holes. If he hadn't already been wearing a breather, the atmosphere could have been a problem.

The assassin was a slight woman, not much taller than Damien but easily beyond his ability to carry. With a sad sigh, he wrapped gentle bands of power around the body and lifted it up after him as he climbed up the debris into the ruins of the surface portion of the Strangers' base.

"Corei, do you read me?" he said, opening a channel to his surviving Secret Service Agent. "Are you and Dr. Kael all right?"

"We're okay, but the tunnel you went through collapsed. Where are you?!"

Damien glanced around him. Despite the base being abandoned for centuries; the local plant life was only now beginning to break through the sealed concrete. There weren't many exterior structures there, but there had been garages and even what looked like had been the site for a set of surface-to-space missiles. The immense domes rose all around him and blocked his view of the prefabricated models of the base camp.

"I'm on the surface," he told his bodyguard. "Take Dr. Kael back to the base. I'll coordinate with Lieutenant Romanov's people to get back inside myself."

"Sir, we're responsible for your safety!"

"Corei..." Damien sighed. "I need you to make sure Malcolm and Connor's bodies are retrieved and prepared for return to Mars. Romanov is capable of seeing to my security, and you can't do it on your own. Besides, the assassin is dead. While I suspect our problems are far from over, I don't think there are any other immediate threats here."

"Understood, sir. I'll see you at the base camp."

Shaking his head, Damien flipped channels to bring up the Marine commander.

"Lieutenant Romanov, this is Montgomery."

"Sir, we registered explosions and gunfire," the Combat Mage replied. "I have a fire team strapping on exosuits. What do you need?"

"I've been separated from the Secret Service Agents and I'm on the surface," Damien told him, pausing for a moment to consider before continuing. "I need you and those exosuited Marines to rendezvous with me on the surface. Kurosawa's killer attacked me. She's dead now, but I'm not willing to *assume* we're all safe just yet. Put your people on high alert."

"White is outside with a team right now," Romanov replied. "I can have her meet you immediately."

"I'm not *that* worried," Damien said dryly. "Leave her and her team to their work. I'll see you when you're out, Lieutenant."

"Yes, sir."

Denis Romanov had *not* expected to find out that someone had attempted to kill the principal while the Hand was in an abandoned alien base accessible only through a single tunnel linked to a prefabricated base camp full of *scientists*.

Given that one of those scientists had murdered another one, he supposed it should have been a possibility, but when the principal *was* a Hand, you tended to assume that most attacks were going to be...grander than an assassin in the dark.

"Keep loading up," he ordered the team with him. They were halfway into their exosuit armor, but their commander wasn't joining them in the heavy gear. Working magic through the heavy powered armor was *possible* but annoyingly difficult. He'd be going out in a breather and light body armor, which had been much easier to put on.

"I'm going out to rendezvous with the Hand," he told the Corporal leading the team. "Follow as soon as you're ready."

"Yes, sir."

Leaving the squad behind him, Romanov entered the airlock. The inner door slid shut behind him...and then the lights cut out and the air exchangers stopped.

"What the hell?" he asked aloud, tapping at the controls. "Team Charlie, check in—the airlock just shut down. Is the facility secure?"

There was a pause.

"Yes, sir," the Corporal replied calmly. "I've got red flashing on the airlock, but that's it. Lights and air are on in here."

Denis considered for several seconds. The only reason to block the airlock, in his mind, was to *stop* the Marines getting out to join Montgomery. He knew the Hand hadn't wanted to interrupt White, but...

"Delta Team, break off your perimeter and move to secure the principal," he ordered. Silence answered him and a chill ran up his spine. "Fire Team Delta, Corporal Carmichael, report. Mage-Lieutenant White, report."

Only silence answered him.

"Corporal Chan," he said very calmly. "Set up an emergency airlock in that room and follow me as soon as you're able. I am breaking my way out...now."

Blades of force flashed into existence around his hands as he slung his battle rifle, channeled magic and *struck*. The airlock was a civilian structure, though designed for vacuum rather than its current purifier duties. It resisted him for less than a moment before the steel door fell outward, cut to ribbons in his hurry.

"Lord Montgomery, please confirm your location," he asked over the radio.

His only answer was a sharp buzzing that hadn't been there a moment before. He was being jammed.

"I need to find that jammer," he said aloud, fully aware no one could hear him.

"I'm afraid I can't let you do that, Denis," another voice replied. "I have new orders, and I can't let you interfere."

He was somehow unsurprised to find Mage-Lieutenant White standing on the concrete, framed by the blue-green trees behind her as she raised her hands. The projector rune at the top of her hand *flashed* with power, and only years of training got Denis out of the way before fire hammered through where he'd been standing.

"Whose orders?" he demanded. "You don't *fuck* with a Hand, White—that's *treason*."

"Orders from high enough, Romanov," she said flatly. "Surrender and you can leave with me. Push it and I'll leave you dead in the dirt with everyone else."

"I won't betray the Hand and I *won't* leave my men," Mage-Lieutenant Denis Romanov told her. "Go to hell, White."

He was suddenly *very* sure why Fire Team Delta hadn't answered his call—and it wasn't because they were being jammed. A shield of energy snapped into place as White attacked him again, and Denis was forced a step away from the airlock door.

He conjured lightning, his own projector rune warming in his flesh as it helped him channel his power over greater distances. White dodged, but it bought him time to start moving.

A Royal Martian Marine Corps Combat Mage was one of the deadliest beings alive short of a Hand. They weren't necessarily *trained* to fight each other, but the thought had certainly crossed his drill sergeant's mind.

Shields helped, but either of them could burn through the other's shield in a matter of moments, given the chance. Mobility was everything, and Denis wrapped power around himself as he *leapt*, crashing to the ground a dozen meters from where White's next attack landed.

A dozen sparks flashed from his fingers, each carrying a charge that would short out a tank or stop a human heart. White dodged most of them, flicking the last few aside with a shield, and replied with a sheet of fire that dropped on Denis, trying to envelop him so he couldn't jump aside again.

This time, he ripped her attack with spikes of force and sent those spikes, accompanied by her own conjured flame, hurtling back at her. She dodged away, and he leapt again, landing on the ancient alien dome and looking down at the traitor.

"We'll find the jammer, White," he taunted her. "You'll pay for my men. I don't know what you think you're getting out of this, but all you *will* get is a traitor's death."

She answered with force and he wasn't moving fast enough. Blow after blow slammed into his shield, forcing him to pour all of his energy into trying to stay alive.

"I get to live," White told him. "And fulfill my oaths. Look to the sky, Romanov. Your death is coming."

She was a stronger Mage than he. He tried to slide down the dome, but her force strikes picked him up and *flung* him back up the ancient concrete. His shield prevented injury, but she had him pinned. He couldn't move.

She *wasn't* moving, standing in the uniform she'd dishonored and looking coldly up at him as she gestured above their heads.

"The secret will be kept," she promised him. "Not that you'll know. Sorry, Romanov."

White had looked back up at the stars when he opened fire. Both of them had ignored their rifles for the entire fight—at this range, magic was far more dangerous than any battle rifle. Her magic was enough to pin Romanov in place, and she was slowly crushing down his shields— but not strong enough to do that *and* shield herself.

Heavy bullets slammed into her torso, ripping apart the other Mage in a spray of bullets. Her eyes still to the heavens above them, Karina White fell.

The pressure released and Romanov rose to his feet. Considering White's words, he looked up—and swallowed hard.

There was a new star. A big star, one screaming across the sky toward them at an impossible speed.

A ship. One that wasn't supposed to be there.

Damien had picked up his pace back toward the base camp as soon as he realized he was being jammed. The sounds of fire and lightning magic led him to break into an all-out run, but the domes were *huge*.

He finally made it to a point where he could see what was going on, to find Karina White collapsed on the ground, very obviously dead, and Denis Romanov staring at the sky in horror.

Following the Marine's gaze, Damien spotted the same rapidly approaching light.

"Please tell me that's TK-421," he shouted toward Romanov as he approached over the curve of the alien ruin.

"TK is in orbit," Romanov replied. "They're *approaching* orbit and decelerating hard; that's why they're so visible."

The Marines, Damien reflected, had a *lot* more reason to train in identifying what ships were doing from the ground than he did.

"I can't raise TK-421 to confirm what *they* see, either," Romanov continued. "I'm pretty sure the men who went out with White are dead and she's set a jammer up somewhere."

"Can you localize it?" Damien asked.

Romanov pulled up his computer, studying it. "I don't have enough data," he admitted after a moment.

"Link to my PC; we should be close enough at this point."

Another moment passed, and the Marine shook his head, gesturing toward the nearby forest.

"It's that way," he said, his gesture encompassing an arc of several hundred meters of forest, "somewhere between five and six hundred meters. Not really helpful."

"You'd be surprised," Damien told him dryly. "Does your combat gear suggest there's anything alive over there?"

"What?"

"Your helmet has thermal and motion sensors," Damien reminded the Marine. "Is anything except the trees in that area you just described?"

Romanov turned his head, scanning the forest. "No, but...what are you going to do?"

Normally, Damien tried to keep his open use of magic inside what one of the Marine Combat Mages could achieve. Even when he wasn't doing *that*, he tried to stay inside what the other Hands, with only *one* Rune of Power to his *five*, could do.

Something about today's events, though, left him very, *very* nervous.

All five of his Runes flared with a gentle warmth as he channeled magic, drawing energy from the alien earth beneath him and from the web of the universe. With a broad gesture, he unleashed it, conjuring a vast wave of flame that swept over the arc Romanov's scanner had indicated.

Trees *popped*, the local cellulose equivalent no more resistant to that heat than Earth's trees would have been. Blue-green bushes and leaves vanished in an inferno that filled the area the jammer had to be in...and then *vanished* when Damien loosed his will once more.

The jamming stopped.

"TK-421," he snapped into his radio. "Pokorni, what the hell is going on up there?"

"Oh, thank goddess you're alive," the armed courier's captain replied. "We couldn't reach anyone down there! A ship jumped in a couple of minutes ago and opened fire! We're outgunned—we've been forced to abandon orbit, and she's incoming fast."

"Dammit, Pokorni," Damien snapped. The armed courier had an *amplifier*. There wasn't much that could destroy her before reaching the range of her captain's enhanced magic. *That* was going to be a problem for another time. "What am I looking at?" he demanded.

"She's not a freighter, too small, too fast," the Mage-Lieutenant-Commander replied. "Some kind of warship, but not like anything I've ever seen. *Szar!* My lord, they've dropped a rock toward the planet."

"A rock?" Damien demanded. "Not a bombardment weapon?"

"Looks like just a chunk of asteroid, my lord."

Damien glanced up. A rock wouldn't accelerate much until it hit the core of Andala IV's gravity well, but if the ship was at an approach velocity, it would still only take a minute or so to hit the ground. It was slower than an actively accelerating smart kinetic bombardment project-ile but would be perfectly effective at wiping the research base and the alien ruins from the planet.

And it would look natural. Unless, of course, there were witnesses.

"Listen to me, Pokorni," he said quickly. "Run for safe space and *jump* as soon as you can. *Keep* jumping. Cycle your entire crew in the next ten minutes and make random jumps. Return once you can do so safely, with at least one Mage ready to jump you *out* if they're still here!"

"What about you, sir?"

If she'd *really* cared, she might have tried *fighting*, but Damien sighed. TK-421 couldn't face any real warship, not one with an amplifier, anyway.

"That's up to me now," he said grimly. "*You* need to get away so that no matter what happens, Mars knows this wasn't an accident. Do you understand me?"

Pokorni swallowed hard enough that he heard it on the voice link.

"Yes, my lord."

"Then *go*."

Cutting the channel, he turned to Romanov. "Please tell me we have some kind of sensor network set up."

"I'm linked into the research base's traffic control radar," the Marine replied. "My people were supposed to set up more, but none of them are turned on and...well, I think White killed them."

"Link me in," Damien ordered. "Then track the vector for the rock. I'll need your help."

"What are we doing?"

"You're calling directions," the Hand said grimly. "*I'm* stopping an orbital bombardment."

Romanov paused, looking at him very carefully.

"Can you *do* that?"

"I'll tell you in about ninety seconds," Damien replied.

CHAPTER 10

SECONDS PASSED with excruciating slowness. The bright light that had detached from the ship grew lower and larger as the chunk of whatever rock they'd acquired continued on its deadly route, and Damien studied its path on the pathetic excuse for radar the research base had assembled.

He inhaled deeply as it drew nearer. This would be something beyond even *his* experience. Without an amplifier and its attendant simulacrum and sensors, he couldn't deflect or destroy the projectile with a carefully timed strike as he would an incoming missile.

He was going to have to *stop* a rock that had been dropped from orbit. At least Andala IV was a relatively low-gravity world. Even that one-tenth gravity difference compared to Earth would make a huge difference to the final velocity of a dropped rock with no acceleration.

"Aimed well," Romanov noted. "It's headed right for the center of the ruin. Won't leave much of this place but a crater." He paused. "Fifteen seconds."

Damien nodded and exhaled the breath he'd drawn in. With that exhalation he drew power into his Runes, feeling them heat up. A simple shield of force sprang into existence above the ruin and the research base.

Simple. But immense. Even with the vector they had, Damien needed to cover several square kilometers of sky—with enough strength to stop a probably kiloton-range weapon.

He could *feel* the Runes. Despite what most non-Mages thought when they saw them, they weren't tattoos. Each of his Runes of Power was made of a flexible silver-polymer inlaid a full millimeter and a half into his skin, and he could feel the heat from every bit of that surface as he channeled more power than he ever had before.

Then the rock hit.

It was a twenty-five-ton projectile carved out of a nickel-iron asteroid. The attempt to make it look natural meant it came in slowly for a kinetic bombardment weapon, and the attackers had made up for the lack of speed with sheer size. Traveling at over a hundred kilometers a second, it hit Damien's shield with the force of a thirty-kiloton bomb.

The sky above them lit up with white fire fading to sparks as drops of molten metal flung themselves dozens of kilometers in every direction. Damien physically lurched away from the blow, the force of the impact cracking the concrete under his feet as he passed the force he couldn't control through himself.

"My god," Romanov whispered, staring at Damien. "How... That's *impossible.*"

"I am the Hand of the Mage-King of Mars," Damien whispered, wavering on his feet as a wave of exhaustion swept through him. His breath came in short, heavy bursts, but he was alive—and so was everyone else. "And even I wasn't sure that was possible," he admitted with a grin, suddenly feeling *very* young.

"Damn. Why do you have bodyguards again?" Romanov asked, returning the grin around the breathers they both wore.

"Because I only have one set of eyes," Damien pointed out, then paused as Romanov was suddenly refocused on the computer again.

"New launch," he said grimly. "I'm tracking an active projectile, moving *fast*," The Marine swallowed. "Sir, that's a Talon VII. That's *ours.*"

Somehow, Damien wasn't surprised in the slightest. The downside was that the Talon VII was a multi-impactor weapon capable of over a thousand gravities of acceleration. Each of the Talon Seven Orbital Impactor's submunitions would arrive with almost twenty times the kinetic energy of the rock they'd dropped before—and as the name implied, it would deploy seven of them prior to impact.

"ETA and vector?" he asked, his voice far calmer than he felt. Stopping the rock had been hard enough. He really didn't think he *could* stop a Talon VII. Certainly, even if he could, *no one else* could.

"Sixty-five seconds. There." Romanov pointed. "It's separating," he said grimly. "Sub-impactors activating their own engines."

"Only one target; they'll go for different angles," Damien said aloud, thinking through what he had to do. Shielding *everything* was the only option.

"I'm sorry, Mage-Lieutenant," he told Romanov. "I don't know if I can do this. But I'll do what I can. If you're religious, I'd suggest praying."

"God helps those who help themselves, sir," the Mage-Lieutenant replied seriously. "They're splitting up, as you predicted."

Damien swallowed, nodded to the Marine, and raised his hands to channel power once more.

A shimmering barrier of pure kinetic force, the energy field that science fiction had predicted and science had failed to deliver, snapped into existence, an invisible dome over people who were barely aware they were under attack.

The Runes inlaid in his flesh *burned*. He wondered if he'd have been able to smell his own flesh without the breather—his suit certainly didn't appear to be surviving the process, as curls of smoke rose around him.

The first impactor drove him *through* the shattered concrete under his feet. The ancient artificial rock crumbled into dust as kinetic energy ran through him into the ground. Suddenly, he was several centimeters into the soil under the concrete.

The second and third impactors arrived simultaneously, driving him to his knees in agony, but he still held the shield.

The next *three* arrived in the same instant from different angles, lighting the sky up with fire as they hammered against Damien's shield. His power, *somehow*, held as the infinitesimal fraction of surviving force ground his knees into the pulverized concrete and alien soil. He could feel blood dripping down his face, and he didn't have the time or energy to wipe it away.

The last missile came directly down the middle, trailing the rest by a tenth of a second due to an overestimation of how long the rest would take to adjust their courses. It hammered into his shield from above, lighting up the sky like an impossibly close sun, and Damien *felt* his shield crumple. Bend.

He crumpled and bent with it, his shield failing as his eyes wavered, unwilling to see as his entire *body* screamed against the strain of what he'd called on his power to do.

He let the shield go as he found himself face-first on the cracked alien concrete. Part of his mind wondered, almost idly, where all the blood had come from.

While Denis Romanov had never seen thaumic burnout in person, it had been covered in his training. Like the Navy it worked with, the Royal Martian Marine Corps was fundamentally a peacetime military—but it tried to be a well-trained, well-equipped one.

There was enough blood leaking from Montgomery's face that the Marine really wasn't quite sure what to do. The normal rule in this situation was to relieve the overwhelmed Mage and replace them with someone else, even if that person couldn't do the job quite as well.

Denis himself was the only Mage available, and he couldn't do what the Hand had done at *all*. He knelt by the collapsed, bleeding Hand and tried to check for a pulse.

"I'm alive," Lord Montgomery told him, coughing behind his breather. "Where are our friends?"

Denis checked. His helmet was only showing a ghost icon now; the attacker had gone over the horizon.

"We're out of line of sight—and probably fire," he told the Hand. "The base's sensors suck, but my comp is calling it thirty to seventy minutes before they complete their orbit."

Montgomery slumped onto the shattered ground around him for a moment, then raised his bloodied eyes to look at Denis.

"Your people were laying out SAMs," he noted. "Where did they end up?"

"I don't know," Denis admitted. "White was with them and I haven't heard from them."

"*Find them*," the Hand ordered, his voice harsh. "Most likely, they'll assume I can do that again, in which case the next step will be to send in ground troops."

"I...only have sixteen Marines left, sir."

"That's why you need the SAMs." A small click in Denis's com system announced that Montgomery had opened a wider channel.

"Dragic. I need you to coordinate with whoever the hell you can find in charge in there," the Hand told the MIS Inspector. His voice was even harsher now, and Denis wondered just how much damage the other Mage had done to himself.

"We've got Dr. Kael out," the Inspector replied. "What do you need?"

"You have twenty-five minutes to get every single person in that compound into the lower levels of the alien base," the Hand ordered. "We're under orbital attack and I expect to see ground landings shortly. The civilians will be safest at the bottom of a hole, and conveniently, the aliens left us a deep reinforced one."

Silence.

"I'll make it happen," she said steadily. "Be in touch."

Ignoring the brusqueness of the Inspector, Denis brought up his own links.

"Marines, come in," he snapped. "We are under attack. Anyone in an exosuit needs to get out here and find Carmichael's fire team and the surface-to-air missiles they were supposed to be caching.

"The rest of you, get *in* exosuits and come join me outside. We have work to do."

Cutting the channel, he turned back to Montgomery.

"What happens if they *do* bombard us again?" he asked, eyeing the bloodied state of his boss.

"We die, Lieutenant," the Hand told him. "So, we'll plan for the alternative."

Dragic was more efficient than he had any right to expect, Damien reflected. The time frame he'd given her was impossible, but she'd managed to get over a thousand people organized and streaming into the lower levels of the ancient base before it ran out.

He'd spent the same time trying to wipe blood off of his face with only moderate success. He couldn't spare the energy to purify air for himself, so he'd had to leave the breather—and the dried nosebleed under it—in place.

"We found the rest of the SAMs," Corporal Kitcher, leader of the exosuited Marine fire team sweeping for Corporal Carmichael and his people. They'd found three of the caches placed exactly as per plan, each containing two Hyper-Interceptor two-stage surface-to-air missiles.

"We've found Carmichael's people," Kitcher concluded. "White took them out with magic from behind. They would never have seen her coming." The Marine paused. "She disabled the last six SAMs. Initiator stages are bled dry; they're just antimatter bombs now."

"Bring them back anyway," Romanov ordered. "They may still come in handy."

What was disturbing to *Damien* was that three caches had been placed as planned before White had turned on the Marines. It was like she'd been doing her job, perfectly efficiently, until someone *else* had told her to stop—and she'd immediately, without hesitation, turned on and murdered the Marines working with her.

Something *stank* to Damien and he didn't like the implications.

The Marine Mage-Lieutenant was looking at Damien, his expression hidden behind his helmet. Romanov had been the last of his people to get into exosuit armor, but the palms of his suit had small runes inlaid into them, allowing him to still use his magic.

"Is there anything you can do, my lord?" he asked quietly.

"If I *do*, I definitely won't be able to stop another bombardment," Damien admitted. He didn't think he could stop a bombardment either way—but he needed to conserve *all* of his energy for that possibility.

"We'll do what we can," Romanov replied. "We're going to fall back underground pretty quickly in that case."

"I have radar signatures," Corporal Chan, leading one of the three fire teams that had joined Lieutenant Romanov out with Damien, interrupted. "Not the ship, not yet, but I'm reading ten shuttles."

"Any kind of detail?" Damien demanded.

"Not with *these* sensors," the Corporal said bitterly. "We got five minutes until they're on top of us."

"Lieutenant," Damien said quietly, "you are authorized to shoot them down. No warning. No second chances."

"They tried to *nuke* us, sir," Chan demanded—and Damien could feel the Marine's questioning glance through the man's faceless armor.

"And that is why we are going to kill them all," Damien told him. "But the responsibility remains mine."

"Kitcher, you've got the birds," Romanov ordered, ignoring the byplay between his superior and his noncom. "Fire at will."

The Marines must have been setting up the remote-controlled weapons as they found them, as a Hyper-Interceptor took two minutes to set up and needed a thirty-meter safety zone to launch...and all six missiles lifted off inside five seconds of the order.

The first stages burned for twenty seconds, old-fashioned chemical rockets that lifted the missiles past five kilometers' altitude, clearing a safety distance for the *second* stage.

The sky lit with brilliant fire as six *antimatter* engines lit off, the missiles seeking targets at hundreds of gravities of acceleration. There were countermeasures—and the flash of a dying missile told Damien that the attacking shuttles *had* them—but inside an atmosphere, there was almost no time to deploy them. Anti-missile lasers nailed *one* SAM.

The other five slammed head-on into their targets, wiping four shuttles and their cargo of ground troops from the air in flashes of antimatter annihilation.

CHAPTER 11

AS THE MARINES headed for the hole the assassin's explosives had opened in the ground, Damien found Romanov standing next to him. It wasn't possible to read the emotions of someone locked in a two-meter-tall suit of exosuit armor, but somehow the Lieutenant still managed to appear impatient.

"We need to get *you* underground, too," he noted. "If we let *you* get killed, there'll be hell to pay, no matter what."

The Marine gestured toward where the shuttles were sweeping in. "Once they have those boots on the ground, they're not going to nuke their own people. If we're going to make a tunnel fight of this, I'd rather not leave the most important objective on the planet *outside* those tunnels."

"Touché, Lieutenant," Damien allowed. The runes they'd found in the lower levels were probably more important than he, but he doubted he'd be able to convince the man charged with keeping the Hand alive of that.

"Let's go."

Damien couldn't see the rapidly approaching shuttles, but he could *hear* them by the time they'd reached the open wound the assassin had ripped open trying to kill him. It was a larger opening into the underground tunnels than any of the handful of ancient airlocks that had been forced open.

"Are we leaving this for them?" he asked the Marine as he dropped into the hole.

"For now," Romanov replied. "If nothing else, we don't want them going through the labs. Plus, I have a *plan* for this hole in the ground."

They passed by a fire team of exosuited Marines just inside, clearly setting up whatever plan Romanov had. Deeper in, another set of Marines was ushering the last stragglers of the research team toward the hole Kurosawa had opened to start this whole mess.

"This is my stop," Romanov told Damien. "I don't expect you to go hide behind the civilians, my lord, but this kind of tunnel knife fight is our job. Leave us to it."

Damien didn't *like* it, but the Marine was right. With a nod and a sigh, the Hand left the Marines behind.

Denis waited for the Hand to pass through Kurosawa's tunnel behind the rest of the civilians and then nodded to the Marines waiting there. They unfolded a portable blast shield covered with runes on the "safe" side to reinforce its flimsy frame, over the tunnel.

It wouldn't stop anyone who actually *made* it to the tunnel, but it would stand off gunfire or even major explosions. Since Denis had sixteen Marines, including himself, to stand off six shuttles' worth of attackers, explosions were a major part of his plan.

"Here they come," Chan reported, feeding everyone the datastream from the camera drones they'd left all over the domes and alien ruins outside. "Those...yeah, those are our shuttles, boss."

Denis flipped to the visual feed from the tactical map he'd set to update, and nodded his silent agreement. The paint job was different, pitch-black instead of the Marines' dark gray, but it was recognizably the standard assault shuttle the RMMC had built for their own *exclusive* use.

The visual suddenly fizzled and grayed out.

"EMP sweep," Chan reported.

"It's always nice to deal with professionals," Denis said calmly. "Bring up the second wave of drones."

The visual feed and the tactical map returned, showing him the assault shuttles sweeping back around, their scanners poking for any sign of defenders. Denis had enough time to recognize the flight pattern—the pilots, whoever they were, had been trained by *Marines*—before a *second* electromagnetic pulse swept the area, killing his second wave of eyes.

"*Paranoid* professionals," Chan told him. "We've only got one more set of eyes, boss. What do we do?"

"Hold for sixty seconds," he ordered. Once the enemy troops were on the ground, the shuttles couldn't keep pulsing their EMP weapons, but his spy eyes were only truly hardened when turned off. When to bring up the last set was always a question of...timing.

The seconds of blindness ticked away with agonizing slowness, time Denis spent checking his links to the network of secondary nodes they'd carefully set up before going underground.

"Now," he ordered. "Bring them back up."

Everything flared back into existence on his helmet screens in the darkness. Four of the shuttles were grounded now, with two more orbiting about a hundred meters above them.

"Not quite where I hoped," he observed, studying the shuttles as their landing ramps extended and soldiers in black exosuits started to pour out. "It'll have to do."

He glanced around at his men. All of his people were in exosuits now, which would shield them from just about anything that wasn't right on top of them. The blast shield and the ancient alien concrete *should* shield the civilians...and that was really all he could give them.

"Fire in the hole," he told his squad, then hit the prepared command.

The antimatter fuel cell in a Hyper-Interceptor missile was a marvel of engineering, built of permanently magnetized materials that held their payload of antiprotons suspended in a contained vacuum. Rated to withstand being dropped, crushed and even *shot* at, the fuel cells were extraordinarily hard to rupture.

With enough explosives, of course, *anything* was possible.

Six separate charges, crudely made from the missiles' own warheads, went off where they'd been hastily concealed in the dirt. Six fuel cells ruptured, each containing a fraction of a gram of pure antimatter.

All told, twenty kilotons of fire swept the valley between the domes, incinerating the ancient ruins of the surface structures, two of the shuttles and dozens of the exosuited soldiers.

If Denis hadn't already been certain his enemy had RMMC gear, the fact that two shuttles and easily a quarter of the exosuited troops *survived* the explosion would have confirmed it for him. Even buried underground, waiting for their enemy, his people were buffeted by the shockwave and covered in dust and loose rocks.

He'd lost over half of his eyes on the surface—less than he'd expected—but what was left was enough for him to confirm that one of the shuttles would never lift again.

The other *did*, sweeping for other threats as the last two hovered low enough to drop their own payloads of soldiers.

Of a hundred and twenty exosuited ground troops, his enemy was now down to sixty. It wasn't *enough*, not when he had less than *one* squad against their three, but it was a start.

"Get ready," he ordered. "Now when they get down here, they're going to be *pissed*."

The massive explosion had collapsed the portion of the tunnels that the earlier assassination attempt had opened up. It had also, Denis hoped, melted or collapsed shut any of the ancient airlocks the attackers may have wanted to use.

Sheltered by one of the ancient domes, the research camp had survived unscathed, but he was unsurprised when the strangers didn't head that way. The prefabricated modules didn't have great security, but with all of the airlocks double-locked, they'd slow the attackers down.

Instead, four of the exosuited soldiers dropped into the hole and placed charges before leaping back out with their augmented muscles. A moment after they were clear, the shaped explosives detonated, opening a new hole into the underground tunnels.

"Fire Team Alpha," Denis said calmly. No further orders were needed. Corporal Kitcher knew what to do.

The first black-armored soldiers charged through the hole they'd opened, two full fire teams sweeping into the dark tunnels with heavy exosuit battle rifles in their gauntleted hands. Whoever these strangers were, they had access to the absolute latest in RMMC gear. Low-flying combat drones went ahead of them, sweeping for the traps and waiting soldiers their masters knew had to be there.

"Now!" Kitcher snapped to his fire team as Denis listened in. A preset EMP charge went off in the middle of the corridor, blinding their enemies' extended eyes. A moment later, a salvo of grenades flew down the corridor, landing amidst the attacking soldiers in a flurry of smoke and explosions.

Denis's squad hadn't come prepared to fight exosuits. The armor-piercing grenades that would have had any effect on their enemy were still aboard TK-421—but the black-armored attackers didn't know that. They paused as the grenades landed in their midst—taking the best position to survive the high powered, exosuit-threatening grenades they thought they were facing.

Corporal Kitcher's men, however, knew the grenades were no threat to *their* exosuits and followed them far more closely than the enemy expected. The black-armored soldiers were *good*—but by the time they realized the grenades weren't a threat, the Marines had opened fire.

Exosuit armor was tough, tough stuff, but both sides had heavy battle rifles designed to penetrate it at ranges of hundreds of meters. In a point-blank tunnel fight, three of the attackers went down in the first seconds.

Denis watched the fight through the helmet cameras relaying into the encrypted network of his squad, and for a moment, he thought Kitcher was going to take down the entire first wave without any losses.

The attackers reacted too fast for that. They were returning fire before the first bodies hit the ground, and helmet links died as the ancient tunnels turned into an abattoir of fire and death.

"Corporal Kitcher, respond," he ordered. All four helmet links from Fire Team Alpha were gone. Silence answered him and a chill ran down his spine. "Chan, I need eyes on Alpha," he snapped.

"On it."

They'd expended most of their drone eyes outside, but they'd held a small reserve of flying drones for just this purpose. Chan sent it hovering back up the tunnel, sweeping for any evidence of their enemies or their own people.

Abattoir turned out to be a good word. Against the kind of pirates or other half-trained-at-best opponents the Marines normally faced, Kitcher's trick would have likely taken them all out with no casualties.

Against twice his numbers of equally-equipped, equally-trained soldiers, it had turned into a point-blank firefight where even exosuit armor had failed in the face of the high-powered weapons both sides carried. None of the attackers had lived through the ambush—but neither had any of Kitcher's people.

"Damn," Denis murmured. "Pull the drone back," he ordered. "Pull back from behind the mines and secure the entrance. These people are way too damned good."

The Marines watched through their aboveground robotic eyes as the second wave of black-armored soldiers moved into the hole the explosives had opened up. Two fire teams of scouts had been shot to hell, so whoever was in charge was now sending in two full squads, leaving the twelve remainders of the initial squad behind to cover their rear.

Forty exosuits moved into the tunnels, and they didn't do it quietly or subtly. Explosives blasted open accesses to other tunnels, and in a matter of minutes, Denis Romanov and his people were looking at six fire teams advancing down six different corridors, with four more hanging back, still in the tunnels, and three left on the surface.

He only had three fire teams left.

"Blow the charges," he ordered Chan. "Then get ready."

With the enemy drones sweeping ahead of them, there was only a small chance of actually catching the attackers in the mines and charges they'd placed in the tunnels, but they might still knock out a few of the soldiers—and in any case, it would reduce the approaches to where they'd dug in to a single tunnel.

The ground trembled again, the explosives much closer though far less powerful than the antimatter bombs they'd set off on the surface.

Tunnels collapsed, taking the handful of scattered eyes Denis still had underground with them and leaving only one clean approach to his position and the civilians behind him.

The area outside the initial cave collapse had been a larger crossroads area of some kind, an open space large enough to let half a dozen of the Marines easily fire down the single remaining corridor leading in—and to allow all of the remaining Marines to fire on anyone who actually made it in.

It was as good a defensive position as Denis had found. If they were going to hold these strange soldiers anywhere, it was going to be there.

"Here they come," Chan announced over the network, hefting his own battle rifle as the seconds continued to tick by with agonizing slowness.

And then the enemy was there. The Marines saw scouting drones first, but Denis saw no reason to give the attackers a good look at their position.

"Take them down," he ordered, firing as he spoke.

A sharp salvo of fire rang through the underground complex, knocking the half-dozen low-flying robots to the ground. The enemy now knew where they'd find the Marines, but without the drones, they knew nothing of Denis's positions.

Now it was a question of what they'd do. There were arguments, Denis knew, for both a sacrificial scout force and an all-out rush in this situation.

He had his answer thirty seconds later as a volley of grenades came bouncing down the corridor. Unlike his people, he assumed their attackers *did* have armor-piercing grenades—and so his people had taken cover behind several more of the portable blast shields they'd covered the entrance to the lower levels with.

The shields on their own might not have been enough, but combined with the collapsed stone the exosuits had more than enough strength to move, they short-stopped the grenade attack entirely, allowing Denis and his people to watch for the people who'd thrown them.

It started with a single fire team. Four exosuited soldiers swept forward, taking the most covered positions they could find and spraying suppressive fire in the direction of the Marines.

A second fire team leapfrogged them, adding their own fire to the suppression as a third team of four moved forward. The attackers were clearly using IFF linked targeting systems, allowing them to spray fire down the corridor while being *mostly* sure they wouldn't shoot their own people in the back.

"Sir..." Chan said, quietly questioning as the *fourth* fire team started moving down the corridor. If they leapfrogged the first few teams by the same amount each previous team had, they'd be the first actually into the gallery.

"Hold fire," Denis ordered, waiting and watching until that fourth fire team *did* enter the gallery, and for a moment of hesitation, the suppressing fire slacked. The possibility that his people had moved on was clearly sinking into the attackers' minds and that made the moment..."Now!"

Rising over his cover, he opened fire himself. He'd taken one of the positions that could fire down the whole corridor, and he did just that, starting his fire at the farthest fire team and working his way forward.

Exosuited soldiers went down, penetrators punching through the heavy armor in sprays of sparks and blood. Over half of the attackers were down in the first moments, but the black-armored troopers were *very* professional. They opened fire immediately, and the Combat Mage could only shield *some* of his men and still fight.

In the middle of the firefight, the loss of his men barely registered. He knew he'd mourn them later, but for now, they had to *survive*.

And somehow, they did.

The smoke and fire cleared, and Denis realized he was still alive. So were over half of his people, seven Marines still standing and two, including Corporal Chan, wounded but alive.

Half of the rear two attacking fire teams had managed to retreat, but of the twenty men they'd sent at him, sixteen were now dead in the hallway. Little by little, the odds were shifting in his favor.

"Sir...look at the surface footage," Chan told him. The Marine had lost his left arm at the elbow, but his suit appeared to have that under control—enough for him to still be watching the cameras, anyway.

Denis pulled the video footage up on his helmet and inhaled in sharp surprise. The shuttles had landed again, and the fire teams that had stayed on the surface were now pulling back aboard. As he watched, the reserve teams from the tunnels followed.

His last round of explosives had done more than he thought. He'd only confirmed twenty-four kills, but only twenty-nine of the strange black-armored soldiers retreated back onto their shuttles.

"They're giving up?" Chan asked.

Denis shook his head.

"No," he said quietly. "They're pulling back so their ship can bombard us again. Move that blast shield," he ordered. "We're going to need the Hand."

CHAPTER 12

THE RUNES in the ancient alien gallery might have been broken in the fight that killed Kurosawa, but their dying gasp of overcharged purifying was serving more purpose than their centuries of low-level function. It was bad enough that they'd crammed hundreds of people into the underground cavern, but the ability for everyone to take their breathers off stopped it from becoming completely unbearable.

Damien had even managed to clean most of the blood off his face, staying mostly separate from the crowd of scientists and researchers. They mostly seemed upset that their work had been interrupted, cursing out the utterly implacable Dragic and her two companions.

Santiago Corei, his last surviving Secret Service Agent, had been waiting for him when he'd joined the civilians. The agent, a dark-haired and -eyed young man from Argentina on Earth, was holding his carbine close to his chest while guarding the tiny tunnel leading back up to the surface.

Damien was probably the only person still in the gallery that realized that Corei's "little gun" fired high-powered penetrators capable of punching through exosuit armor. If the strange soldiers broke in, Corei and Damien would be the last line of defense for these people.

His face finally clean, Damien linked back into the Marine tactical network. Codes hidden in the golden hand of his office allowed him to override much of the security the Marines were using. If he'd been able to link into the frequency of the attackers, he'd probably be able to override *their* security, too—but the landing team was using frequency hoppers with an algorithm his system didn't have.

As it was, he linked into the tactical network, with its helmet and spy drone cameras, in time to watch Romanov's people throw back the assault on the corridors outside Kurosawa's tunnel. He was familiar enough with the network protocols to establish how many people the Marines had lost, and he felt sick to his stomach.

Looking at the images from the surface, however, that sickness intensified. He hadn't known what Denis was planning, though he'd have approved it if he had, but to see the surface ruins wiped from existence hurt. Only the sheer scale of the main domes had protected them, and he wondered how many little things they would never learn about the aliens now.

He spotted the shuttles sweeping in for a landing and the troops retreating in good order. They were pulling back, which, unfortunately, probably meant a second round of bombardment.

With a sigh, he mentally poked at his internal reserves. It wasn't something he'd had to worry about in years; the five Runes of Power amplified his strength enough that he hadn't come this near to thaumic burnout in years.

He wasn't sure if he could stop another attack. He just knew he had no choice.

"Corei, with me," he ordered, replacing the breather on his face as he headed back to the hole leading up. "Romanov?"

"You saw," the Mage-Lieutenant replied. "We're moving the blast shield; we'll need to hustle you to the surface."

Damien paused, then sighed again.

"It's honestly probably better if one of your people carries me," he admitted. "I am still, well...shattered."

The trip through the tunnels while being carried by Corporal Chan was not the most dignified experience of Damien's life by any stretch of the imagination, but it got him to the surface in time to watch the final shuttles taking off.

"Do we have a link into the research station's transmitters?" Damien asked. They'd gone from "incoming strange ship" to "we're being bombarded" so fast, he hadn't even *tried* to talk to these people. It was almost certainly a waste of time, but anything that distracted the enemy might be worth it.

"Yeah," Chan replied. "What, think they'll piss off if you ask nicely?"

"Asking nicely isn't exactly what I have in mind," Damien told him. "Put me down and link me in."

A few commands later, he was linked in to the big traffic control transmitters, his voice going out omnidirectionally on every regular channel.

"Unidentified ship, this is Hand Damien Montgomery," he told them. "You have launched an unprovoked attack on a research facility under the protection of Mars *and* an open attack on a Hand of the Mage-King.

"These are not actions that Mars will allow to go unpunished. You have already failed to overwhelm me and my Marines. Surrender now and Mars may show mercy. Continue on this course and the galaxy knows the fate of those who attack Hands."

He cut the channel, waiting for a response he didn't actually expect to come.

"They won't surrender," he noted aloud to Chan and Romanov. "But *knowing* they're firing on a Hand may make them hesitate."

Unmentioned was the *other* item he'd sent along with his voice. The codes and programs included in the files concealed in the golden hand symbolizing his office had many, many purposes and utilities. Some could be called "backdoor viruses" if you were being *rude.*

"Not so much," Romanov agreed. "I've got another Talon Seven... wait, no, make that *three.*"

Damien swallowed. His bug was in the *ship* software now—and, as they spoke, should be preventing further weapons from being launched—but it might not have made it into the missiles themselves.

"One last chance, gentlemen," he said quietly.

"What's that?"

"I dropped a Hand override virus into their system," he told them. "If it made it into the missiles, this will work." He tapped a command on his screen.

Seconds passed. He'd thought some of the waiting before had lasted forever, but this was worse.

"Damn...two missiles down," Romanov reported. He paused, swallowed. "Third has remained on course and deployed submunitions."

Damien nodded sadly. It was time to see whether even a fully-trained and upgraded Rune Wright could stop multiple mass bombardments in an afternoon.

"I'll do what I can," he told Romanov and Chan. "I...may fall. Please try not to let me hurt myself; I may well not be conscious when this is over."

The exosuits containing his Marine companions were expressionless, but he didn't need to *see* their faces. No Marine wanted to stand by while a Hand died, but no one else could do this.

With a gesture and a renewed surge of burning heat into his Runes, Damien once more wove a barrier of solidified air and power around the ancient base and its modern symbiont. A glance at the screen showed that this last weapon had been better programmed than the first one. All seven of its projectiles were going to hit, from seven different angles, at roughly the same time.

There was no way he could brace himself for this, but he steadied himself as best as he could, counted down the final seconds, and then threw every *erg* of power at his command into informing the universe that, no, the people under his protection were *not* going to die today.

CHAPTER 13

FIRE AND THUNDER lit up the sky above Denis as the bombardment projectiles slammed into the Hand's shield. The Mage-Lieutenant was trained in the theory of the type of shield the Hand had raised, and was even practiced at using it at a smaller level to protect himself and the troops around him from incoming small arms or even artillery fire.

To his knowledge, no Mage in the Royal Martian Marines could have stopped even the first round of bombardment, let alone all three. His surprise at being alive distracted him for several moments before he realized that Montgomery had collapsed.

"Check the skies," he ordered Chan as he knelt next to the collapsed Hand. Still clad in his armor, he couldn't directly check for a pulse, but the suit thankfully had its own sensors—which informed him that Montgomery was *alive* but unconscious, with an elevated body temperature and accelerated pulse.

The Marine didn't even need to see the blood oozing out around the other man's eyelids and breather to recognize a classic case of extreme thaumic burnout.

"Sir, our friend is running," Chan told him. "Whatever Montgomery did to their systems spooked them—they're burning away from the planet at what looks like twelve gravities, though with these sensors, that means anything from eight to sixteen."

"Good," Denis snapped. Another round of bombardment would have finished them, and it looked like the *last* round might have killed the Hand—*not* something he needed on his watch.

"Dragic." He pinged the leader of the MIS team. "It looks like our mystery visitor is leaving. We still want to hold off on letting the civilians back in—but I need you to bring whatever doctor they've got to their clinic right now. Montgomery is hurt bad."

"Shit. I'll have Corei drag them if needed," Dragic replied. "What about you?"

"My people will keep an eye on the sky, but I'm bringing Montgomery to the clinic. See you there."

The mysterious ship kept running the entire time it took Denis to carry the Hand to the clinic and the entire time he spent stripping out of his armor while keeping an eye on Montgomery. He was trained in battlefield first aid, but with a doctor on site, there was no point in the battlefield expedient for thaumic burnout of "pack his head in ice."

He was considering it anyway by the time Corei arrived, dragging the Expedition's senior doctor with him by the arm.

"This is entirely unacceptable," the woman snapped. "What the hell is going on?"

"What's going on, Dr. Mandela," Denis told the black woman softly, "is that Hand Montgomery nearly *died* saving every one of your lives. We need *you* to make sure it stays 'nearly.' Do you understand me?"

Dr. Hope Mandela paused for a moment, then produced an elastic hair-band and pulled her long black hair into a practical ponytail in a practiced motion. "Show me," she ordered. "What happened?"

Surprised by her sudden about-face, Denis led her to where he'd put the Hand.

"Thaumic burnout," he told her. "He stopped three rounds of orbital bombardment. It was like nothing I'd ever seen."

"I have no experience with burnout," Mandela warned. "I've been trained on it, but that's it."

"His life is in your hands," Denis snapped. "Do what you can."

"Of course," she snapped back. "Let's start by cooling down his head— You, in the suit!" she barked at Corei. "You dragged me up here without my nurses, so scrub down." She pointed at a sink. "I need extra hands and you're volunteered."

Corei leapt to obey and Denis followed him without even asking.

"The main risk is brain damage from overheating," he told the doctor, even as she was removing ice packs from a freezer he'd missed amidst the clinic's many, *many* cabinets and pieces of equipment. "I don't know how long it'll take for his temperature to drop; I've never seen *anyone* use that much magic."

Passing the cold-packs to Corei, Mandela hooked up the scanners on the hospital bed, positioning one directly above Montgomery's head and another above his chest. Looking at a series of numbers that meant nothing to Denis, she shook her head slowly.

"I'm going to give him a hibernation agent," she told them. "It'll put him in an induced coma and slow his metabolism; it *should* get his body temperature down and protect his brain."

She pulled out a hypodermic and filled it with a disturbingly purple fluid.

"Keep those cold-packs on him," she ordered. "Everything we're doing is just buying time, gentlemen. I have *no* idea how to handle this beyond keeping him alive until his body recovers."

"We need to get him to Tau Ceti," Denis said grimly. "But he sent the courier away."

"Then we better hope they come back," Mandela replied. "Because this is bad, and I doubt I *can* do more than buy him time. This is out of my league."

"Chan, where are you?" Denis asked as he leaned against the door of the clinic. "I need an update on our mysterious friend."

"I'm in the Expedition's Space Traffic Control Center," the Corporal replied. "I've got people guarding the door; we're in complete control of coms and sensors, boss."

"Good." Denis was *reasonably* sure the only threat in the Expedition itself was dead, but the lanky Marine was utterly unwilling to take risks at this point. "And our trigger-happy friend?"

"A light-second away and accelerating fast," the noncom replied. "I expect to see them jump in another hour or so."

"Good," Denis repeated. In the attacker's place, *he'd* probably be running with his tail between his legs, too. They had no evidence Montgomery couldn't just swat aside every single attack they threw his way. Denis wasn't sure exactly *how* the Hand had been able to do that, but he suspected it had something to do with the runes that had literally burned their way through the other Mage's clothing.

"Keep an eye on them," he ordered. "I'm coming to join you."

If Chan already had the STC secured, that gave them at least one place they could plan in private.

"Afolayan," he pinged his other surviving Corporal. "Once your team is out of the suits, I need you to proceed to the infirmary. Place yourself under Agent Corei's command; he is in charge of Hand Montgomery's security.

"*No one* except Dr. Mandela and her staff goes in that room unless they're unconscious or *dying*; understand me, Corporal?"

"Yes. On our way," the Corporal replied in his thick accent—his colony had actively preserved the tribal languages of western Africa, and English was Kweku Afolayan's *seventh* language, if Denis understood the man's history correctly.

The Mage-Lieutenant was also sure that the Corporal often exaggerated his accent to make people underestimate him—a dangerous mistake, as Afolayan was probably the smartest man in his squad.

"Thank you, Corporal," he said quietly, then flipped to another channel. "Inspector Dragic."

"How are we doing, Mage-Lieutenant?" she asked. "Is Montgomery…"

"The Hand is critical but still with us," Denis told her honestly. "We need to talk next steps, Inspector. As I understand the Hand's chain of command, *you're* in charge now. Meet me at the Space Traffic Control Center? We have it secured."

"I'll be there in five," she promised.

It was a somber group that gathered amidst the screens and blinking lights of the prefabricated space traffic control room. Dragic had brought both of her subordinates with her, and Denis had Chan, whose Marines stood guard outside the door.

"I have *no* idea what the next step is," the senior Martian Investigation Service investigator admitted once the door closed, separating them from the rest of the compound. "I'm a cop, Mage-Lieutenant. I was brought here to investigate a murder, not... I don't know what this is. A war?"

"A conspiracy," Denis said bluntly. "An organization able to plant assassins both in the Expedition and in my Marine squad. An organization with access to a ship of a type I've never seen before, with tech and weapons that are restricted to the Martian Navy and Martian Marines."

He shook his head.

"My understanding is that the Navy doesn't even like *Hands* having access to specialized orbital impactors," he told the cop. "*Duke of Magnificence* surrendered hers when she was tapped to act as Hand Montgomery's personal transport. But someone fired *four* modern orbit-to-surface kinetic weapons at this base and then followed up with troops who may as well have *been* Marines."

"This is...way over all of our heads," Dragic replied. "What the hell do *we* do?"

Denis Romanov sighed and stepped over to look at the screen showing the mystery ship.

"How much data did these sensors actually *get* on that ship?" he asked Chan.

"Less than a proper planetary net would have grabbed," the dark-skinned man with the slanted eyes said quietly. Unlike many in the Martian Navy, he was actually from China instead of being the ambiguous mixed brown with epicanthic folds of a Martian native. "We've got enough we can identify her if we see her again, but for any real analysis, we'll want TK-421's sensors."

"Did Pokorni make it out?" Denis asked.

"She did. Our friends lobbed half a dozen missiles at the courier, and she ran like a flushed rabbit," Chan told him bitterly.

"Armed or not, TK-421 wasn't designed to get into fights with warships," Denis said. "She'll be back, and with that sensor data. Once she's here, we'll load Montgomery onto her and head straight for Tau Ceti. The big Navy Hospital there has the people and facilities to treat him; we certainly don't."

"Will he live?" Dragic asked.

"The doctor says he needs better care than she can give," he admitted. "The sooner TK-421 is back, the happier I'll be. Once we're in Tau Ceti, we can send a squadron to make sure this place is safe. What we need— what *Montgomery* is going to need when he wakes up—is more data."

He was looking at the MIS team, and Dragic met his gaze with calm confidence. She might not know how to handle someone trying to blow her apart from orbit, but she could do data gathering.

"There are a pile of dead guys in the tunnels," he reminded them. "A bunch of crashed shuttles with more dead guys and gear. We need to go through them all, see if we can find serial numbers, identification plates, *wallets*—anything we can use to identify these assholes or who supplied them.

"It's ugly work," he concluded, "searching the dead. But we need to know what is going on here."

"*That*, my dear Lieutenant," the MIS Inspector said brightly, "we can do. We'll learn what we can."

CHAPTER 14

"WHAT DID you *do?"* Inspector Mara Dragic demanded as the survey buggy they'd borrowed from the Expedition rounded the exterior of the dome shielding the base camp and she saw, for the first time, the hell zone their defense had turned the ground between the alien habitat domes into.

"Six two-hundred-milligram antimatter fuel tanks," Denis told her simply. He pointed out the locations. "We set them under the most likely landing spots and cracked the casings with the warheads from the missiles we ripped the tanks out of. Nailed two of their shuttles and crippled a third."

"That's what we'll start with, then," she decided aloud. "Take us to the intact shuttle."

"On our way already," he confirmed. They were short enough on troops and people they trusted that he was the only Marine with the MIS trio, and he was driving the buggy himself. He'd left the rest of his battered squad guarding the traffic control center and Montgomery.

Pulling up to the shuttle, he studied the lines and sighed. The spacecraft had been picked up by an antimatter blast, flipped at least once in the air, and slammed back down onto molten ground. Its hull was warped, its landing struts and engines were bent and broken, and several of its struts were embedded in melted and resolidified sand—and it was still recognizably an RMMC assault shuttle, coated in radar-absorbing paint.

"The entrance will be over here," he told Dragic. "This is...definitely one of ours."

Nodding, the three Martian Investigation Service Inspectors followed him around the forty-meter-long craft. As they reached the door, his communicator chirped.

"What is it, Chan?" he asked.

"Our friend finally jumped," the noncom manning the sensors informed him. "We have clear skies, Mage-Lieutenant. What do you want me to do with them?"

Their one assault shuttle and its Navy crew weren't going to do any good even if they put it into space.

"Wait," he ordered. "Let me know the moment TK-421 returns to the system. We'll need to haul ass spaceward with Montgomery as soon as Pokorni's back, but there's no point even moving him until she is."

"Understood, sir," Chan replied. "I'll keep an eye out for our lost Navy puppy."

Shaking his head, Denis turned his attention back to the wrecked shuttle in front of him. They'd reached the end of the ship, where the landing ramp had been blown clear by the emergency explosive bolts.

It clearly hadn't saved anyone. A dozen exosuited figures were scattered through the back half of the shuttle, eternally frozen in positions as joints had overloaded and the occupants had died.

"Roshan, check those suits," Dragic ordered. "Tane, check the shuttle systems. Lieutenant, anything in particular we should check for?"

"Serial numbers on the gear," he told her. "Mostly scanned by radio tag these days, but we also inscribe them into the upper portion of each piece of the armor. The shuttle should have an ID number of its own—at the base of the ramp and in the cockpit, same number."

"What about the computers?"

"We'll probably just want to physically pull them," he admitted. "The Hand might be able to override their security, or the Navy computers back in Tau Ceti might be able to crack it, but I'd bet both my fathers *we* won't be able to open whatever encryption they have."

"We have some tools that might surprise you," Dragic told him.

"Umm...Mage-Lieutenant," Roshan interrupted, the MIS investigator having started to dismantle the armor. "I need you to take a look at this."

The troop compartment of the shuttle wasn't particularly large, and Denis joined the investigator in moments, looking down into the armor suit Roshan had started dismantling. The investigator clearly had at least some passing familiarity with the exosuit, as he'd opened up the back first, the chunk of slightly thicker armor that *should* have contained the central CPU and its links to the helmet and armor.

Instead, it contained ashes and burnt-out circuits. Ignoring the corpse—and *very* glad his breather blocked his sense of smell—Denis reached in and grabbed several specific locations. Exerting a practiced force, he yanked the entire back plate of the armor off, exposing the mess of circuits and wires that was the core computing component of an exosuit.

All of it was gone, burned out by a dozen tiny explosives and electrical surges.

"That wasn't your bomb, was it?" Roshan asked.

"No. That's a deadman-activated computer suicide switch," Denis said grimly.

"Is..." Roshan considered how to ask his question. "Is all Marine armor set up to burn itself out like this?"

"No. Check his wrist, see if he has a PC," the Marine ordered. The investigator obeyed promptly, opening up both vambraces and exposing a shade of mixed-brown skin that could have originated on *any* of the Protectorate's ninety-plus worlds.

No computer. No dog-tags either, Denis confirmed quickly.

"The computer is heavily protected," he noted. "The primary memory is *supposed* to survive the death of the wearer, to allow their data to be retrieved for later analysis." He tapped the largest of the scorch marks. "It was directly under one of the kill charges. This was specifically designed as part of the armor."

"So...if not *all* Marine exosuits do this..."

"It's an option that can be installed," the Mage-Lieutenant admitted with a sigh. "Force Recon Commandos use it, and I *suspect* that something similar ends up in black ops units nobody would tell me about.

"But these guys...they weren't Force Recon," he concluded. "Two platoons of Force Recon against my squad? We'd all be dead. Some kind of black, unlisted unit...obviously, I guess."

"But it's weird," Dragic said calmly.

"Yeah."

"Let's check the shuttle systems."

Denis was unsurprised to find similar charges had been set throughout the shuttle. The three-woman crew had died when the shuttle had flipped—they'd all been out of their restraints, coordinating with the landing force, presumably. The crew members and the officer in the communications / tactical center had all been clad in insignia-less black fatigues.

No personal computers. No dog tags. Every computer on the ship destroyed by explosives, whether triggered on the death of the three crewwomen or by remote control, the investigators couldn't say. The panel on the ship that *should* have contained the manufacturer's identification number had clearly had an extended encounter with an arc welder and a file.

The armor pieces had been similarly rendered anonymous. Dragic took DNA samples from everyone, but Denis had little hope. The attack force had been *completely* sanitized prior to landing. He doubted their DNA would show up in any databases that he or Dragic could access.

"We're also taking material samples," she told him, rejoining him at the exit from the ship as he looked out over the desolate waste he'd created. "There are a few points in the ship deep enough to be protected from the antimatter blasts."

"Will it help?" he asked.

"We'll probably be able to identify *where* the ships and armor were made," she said.

"Sol or Tau Ceti," Denis told her bitterly. "Only two places the RMMC manufactures these shuttles and this armor. It's all *our* gear, Inspector. The pilots flew like Marines. The soldiers fought like Marines."

"They weren't Marines, Mage-Lieutenant," Dragic reminded him. "They might have fought like them, but they *weren't* Marines. Protectorate Marines don't hide who they are."

"That we know of," he replied. "But we wouldn't know, would we? These people were just as well trained as mine. Just as well equipped. We beat them off by luck and massive application of explosives, and I have *no idea* who they were. They could well have been Marines. Hell—*White* was a Marine."

"Romanov, they *attacked a Hand.* They dropped kinetic weapons on civilians. I think it's pretty safe to say they weren't Marines," the MIS Inspector told him harshly. "You just saved a thousand lives. We'll find who attacked this planet. We'll find who White was working for."

She smiled grimly. "That's *our* part of the job, Lieutenant. Your part was to make sure everybody lived this far, and you did that with style."

Andala was setting over the shattered plain, the star just starting to dip behind the "western" dome, when TK-421 finally returned.

Denis had left the wrecked shuttle to the forensics experts, pacing the half-melted concrete and sand his desperate improvisation had created. The devastation was oddly contained, the ancient alien domes standing up to being functionally nuked at point-blank range with surprising aplomb. Each bomb had been *relatively* small, after all, and the concrete mountains had channeled the force back into the plain in the midst of them.

For all that, the damage seemed entirely out of scale with the actual *deaths* inflicted. All told, the antimatter bombs had killed fewer than eighty people but turned a kilometer-wide, roughly square plain of concrete to glass and dust.

To the Marine, that sounded like...well, whatever the opposite of over-kill was. If he'd done this much damage *and* killed all of his opponents, he might have accepted the possibility of overkill. Since his enemies had still had sixty exosuited soldiers to send into the tunnels after him, he clearly hadn't tried hard enough.

His PC chirping interrupted his thoughts, and he linked his helmet communicator back into the network.

"Romanov here."

"It's Chan," his subordinate told him. "We just picked up a jump flare. TK-421 is back. She's about five light-seconds out."

"Link me in anyway," Denis ordered.

"You're live."

"Mage-Lieutenant-Commander Pokorni, this is Lieutenant Romanov," he announced. "We need you to get into orbit ASAP and prepare for a medical evacuation. Hand Montgomery has been injured and we need to relay him back to Tau Ceti as soon as possible."

Seconds ticked by as his message crossed space at the occasionally seemingly slow speed of light and Pokorni's response returned at the same speed.

"What happened, *Lieutenant?*" her voice snapped on the channel, emphasizing his junior rank. "Where is Montgomery?"

"Hand Montgomery is in the Andala Expedition's infirmary in medically induced hibernation," he explained patiently. "He is suffering from a severe case of thaumic burnout, and nobody here or on your ship is qualified to treat him. We need to evacuate him immediately."

More waiting.

"We're talking about a Hand," Pokorni finally said. "What did he *do?*"

"He stopped an orbital bombardment. Three times." Denis shook his head. "An orbital bombardment from the ship *you* allowed to enter orbit without being challenged."

"You're on dangerous ground, *Lieutenant,*" the courier Captain responded. "I'll need my staff to review the Hand's condition, but we can pick him up as soon as we reach orbit."

"*Hurry,* Pokorni," the Marine replied with a sigh. "Believe me, Lieutenant-Commander, there is *nothing* you can threaten me with that's worse than the day I've had."

He owed Damien Montgomery his life and the lives of the men and women under his command. If saving the Hand's life in turn required him to board and seize a Navy ship by force, well, he'd already nuked an irreplaceable ruin today.

Denis Romanov smirked under his breather. He really *was* having a bad day. Pokorni was an annoying coward, but she wasn't *stupid*. They'd get Montgomery to Tau Ceti safely.

CHAPTER 15

DAMIEN WOKE UP with a splitting headache to a darkened room. Unsure of where he was, he reached for his magic to light up the space.

It refused to answer. He could *feel* its presence, but the usual easily summoned warmth stayed stubbornly buried inside him, weakly flickering in complaint at his demands.

Never in the over two decades since his Gift had been discovered and he'd been trained in its use had it ever simply...*refused* like that, and he panicked.

He lurched from the bed, displacing sensors and tubes he hadn't realized were dug into his flesh. He swore in pain as an IV ripped itself out of his wrist and a shunt half-tore from his chest.

Despite everything in his way, Damien made it *off* the bed before his limbs simply refused to cooperate anymore and he crashed to the floor— and at that point, the *catheter* came out to an even louder round of cursing.

The sensors around him added a series of braying alarms to the cacophony, and then the door to the room slid open and the lights came up.

Finally able to see, Damien recognized his surroundings as a Navy hospital's private room, an intensive care space for officers and dignitaries.

A pair of male orderlies stood in the door, neither apparently quite sure *what* to do, before a doctor cut between them.

"You weren't supposed to wake up for several more hours," the tall black man in the white coat and military insignia. "Are you all right, my lord?"

"I can't access my Gift and I just ripped out a catheter," Damien replied between sharp inhalations. "I've had better days."

"Reynolds, Hart, get him back on the bed and hooked up," the doctor snapped. "I am Surgeon Mage-Commander Aziz Mohammed. You may be awake, my lord, but you are still extraordinarily weak. If you had arrived at my hospital even a dozen hours later, I'm not sure even the frankly *brilliant* idea to put you in forced hibernation would have been enough to save you."

"Last I remember," Damien said slowly, wincing as the nurses *tried* to gently reinsert the tubes he'd yanked out, "I was on Andala IV." Hoping he was able to stop even one more set of military impactors. He was more than a little surprised he was alive.

"Where I have *no* idea what you did," Mohammed said cheerfully, "but you managed to give yourself the single worst case of thaumic burnout I have seen in forty-six years as one of the Navy's medical Mages."

The doctor wore the same gold medallion at the base of the throat as every other Mage in the Protectorate, but *his* bore the caduceus of the medical profession. To Damien's knowledge, less than five hundred Mages in the entire *Protectorate* had the right to wear that symbol on their medallion.

"I was in good hands," he acknowledged aloud as the orderlies finished their work. He hadn't struggled against them—he physically *couldn't*. "How bad was it, Doctor?"

"Out," Dr. Mohammed ordered his staff. Both obeyed with a cheerful alacrity, saluting both the doctor and the Hand as they left. Once the door slid shut behind them, the white-coated Navy Mage pulled a chair up next to Damien's bed and sat.

"I've only seen runes like yours once before," he said quietly. "On another Hand, who had one of them, not five. I don't even need to be *told* never to tell anyone else what I've seen, Lord Montgomery. I can guess what they do."

The doctor shook his head.

"Two days ago, I would have said that the human body could only handle a certain level of thaumic burnout before a fatal aneurysm," he said clinically.

Damien winced at the mental image regardless. That had *almost* been him.

"Your runes, in addition to clearly allowing you to channel more power than a regular Mage, *also* appear to enable you to absorb more burnout," Mohammed concluded. "Not only can you conjure more power, but you can also take more backlash. I'd call it unfair, but I *saw* the amount of scar tissue you've picked up regardless."

"How long was I out?" Damien asked slowly.

"Four days," the doctor replied. "And you're not leaving this room for at least two more. You are magically and physically exhausted. Your body has no reserves left in either sense."

"My magic will come back, though, right?"

"Relatively quickly at this point, yes." The doctor shook his head. "I had to go into your head with magic to lower temperature and relieve pressure, my lord. It's a delicate, slow, dangerous process. If you had gone anywhere else, you would have died. Only Sol would be certain to have doctors trained in the same process, and you would have died before you reached Sol."

"I need to be briefed on what happened in Andala, Doctor Mohammed," Damien told him. He paused. "For that matter, where are Mage-Lieutenant Romanov and Agent Corei?"

"Agent Corei and Mage-Lieutenant Romanov are running security on this ward," the doctor replied. "Using, as I understand, only Marines who were with you in Sherwood. Brigadier General Ihejirika, whose Ninth Marine Brigade normally has responsibility for our security, has thrown up a *second* cordon around us in addition to the *normal* security of the Tau Ceti Navy Hospital." The tall black man shook his head. "I wouldn't be surprised to discover Admiral Segal has moved his battleship over here to watch over the station. Everyone is being *very* paranoid about you."

"Reassuring," the Hand said slowly. "I'll cooperate with being locked up in here, Doctor, if you can arrange a briefing for me."

Mohammed chuckled.

"Son, I'm under direct orders to inform the Admiral the moment you're awake. I believe he intends to take care of that personally."

Damien had managed to get about three hours' sleep and was feeling slightly more human by the time Mage-Admiral Segal arrived. The stocky, perfectly turned-out Navy officer brought Mage-Lieutenant Romanov with him and was escorted in by Doctor Mohammed.

"We need to discuss with Lord Montgomery in private, Doctor," Segal told him.

"I understand," the doctor accepted. "You have thirty minutes, and I'm watching his vitals from the other room. If I don't think you're up for more, Hand Montgomery, I'm kicking everyone out and you will *all* listen to me, understand, sirs?"

"Yes, Doctor," Damien allowed, gesturing Segal and Romanov to the seats in the room. With one last admonishing glare, Mohammed let himself out of the recovery room and shut the door behind him.

"Apparently, I'm locked in here and hooked up to these machines for at least twelve more hours," he told Segal and Romanov. "After that, my understanding is that I'm to remain under observation for at least one more day."

"That seems reasonable," Segal said calmly. "The Mage-Captain here said that it was a near-run thing, and that everyone *else* would have died without you."

The Hand blinked and realized he'd missed the change in Romanov's insignia. Where the young Mage had previously had a single silver bar on his epaulets, he now boasted two: the insignia of a Royal Martian Marine Corps Captain.

"Congratulations," Damien told the Marine. Despite his occasionally paternal feelings toward the soldiers set to protect him, Romanov was only a year younger than he was. He'd probably been due for a company anyway, but his actions on Andala IV must have sealed the deal.

"He also tried to downplay his *own* accomplishments," the Mage-Admiral continued, "in the finest tradition of His Majesty's Marines. His subordinates' reports and the files Inspector Dragic sent along with him made his actions very clear, however, and Brigadier Ihejirika pinned his Captain's bars on him last night."

He coughed somewhat delicately. "To be fair, that rapid a promotion requires an extra level of authorization. The Brigadier and I can make it stick, but if you would be prepared to sign off..."

"Admiral, Captain," Damien said, smiling and shaking his head, "I watched Mage-Captain Romanov hold the line against six times his numbers with ingenuity, courage, and the finest traditions of the RMMC. If you hadn't pushed through a promotion already, I'd be asking you to. I would be *honored* to sign off on the promotion of the man who saved my life."

"You saved mine first," Romanov pointed out, his voice quiet and serious. "And after."

"What happened after I went down?" the Hand asked. "I don't remember anything after raising the shield."

"I'm not surprised," the newly minted Captain told him. "You went down hard once the last salvo of impactors hit. You stopped them, obviously, or neither of us would be here. After that..." He shrugged. "After that, they left. In their place, I'd have assumed you could *keep* stopping their bombardment."

"I also shut down their weapons," Damien said with a harsh cough. Once the coughing fit let up, he half-grinned at Segal's horrified expression. "We didn't put backdoors into our ships' *defenses* or engines, but yeah, the Hands can shut down your bombardment launchers."

"If it's only the bombardment launchers, I'm okay with that, I think," Segal said beatifically. "Still a nerve-wracking thought, no offense, my lord."

Damien let the Admiral keep his illusions. *His* understanding was that he could, if he had the chance to upload the codes, shut down every single offensive system on a Navy ship. Managing to actually upload those codes was extremely unlikely, but he'd assumed that his message would at least be *listened* to by the strange ship.

He'd guessed right. If he'd guessed wrong, he and a lot of other people would have been dead.

"Inspector Dragic and I went through the wreckage and learned what we could," Romanov continued after a moment. "Which...wasn't much. Whoever they were, they thoroughly sanitized every shuttle, every soldier, and every piece of equipment they sent to the surface.

"Dragic is still on Andala IV, pulling together whatever she can, but she sent her initial analysis and samples back with me. They're currently at the Tau Ceti MIS HQ, undergoing forensics testing with a guard of Marines I absolutely trust."

"Thank you, Captain," Damien said quietly. "Well done. What about Andala IV itself?"

"I had a destroyer squadron moving ten minutes after TK-421 made it back here with you," Segal told him. "Their first return courier arrived after you woke up. There's been no trouble since—but I'm not moving that squadron, either. This whole mess has me looking for targets painted on my back."

"I suspect the target is painted on Andala IV and anyone who knows what they found there," Damien admitted. "Has anyone been briefed on that?"

"On what?" the Admiral asked, with a sharp glance at Romanov.

"It...was my impression that what the Hand found should be regarded as classified," the Marine Captain said levelly. "I...*may* have informed Dr. Kael that it *was*." He met Damien's gaze. "No one in Tau Ceti has been briefed, sir."

Damien sighed and nodded. That was a relief. He needed to talk to the Mage-King before he made a decision on who to tell about the alien runes in the ruins and their nature as the source of Martian Runic.

"Well done, Captain," he told Romanov.

"Can you tell *me* what's going on?" Segal demanded. "I'm a soldier, my lord; I can *take* 'you don't have need to know,' but someone just tried to blow a planet under my protection to pieces and I'd like to know why!"

"This is classified at the highest level," Damien told him. "As in don't tell your staff, don't tell your wife, don't even tell *another Hand*. Understand?"

Segal exhaled, nodding. "How bad is it?" he asked.

"There are alien runes in the lowest levels of the Andala IV base," the Hand replied. "The higher levels I'm now guessing were *intentionally* scrubbed of them, but the people doing that work didn't have access to the lower levels.

"Those runes predate human magic. Hell, I think they may predate human spaceflight—and I'm talking *Sputnik* here," Damien warned. "They predate everything...and those runes are written in Martian Runic."

The Mage-Admiral paused, clearly shocked in mid-thought.

"That's..."

"Only possible if we got Martian Runic *from* them, Admiral. If the *Eugenicists* got the runes they used to identify Mages—the key component of the Olympus Project—from aliens," Damien said harshly.

"One of the worst and longest forced-breeding experiments in human history, gentlemen. My family didn't come from that, but both of yours did. We know who to *blame* for it, but we always wondered where they got the runes. Why they didn't understand that Olympus Mons was an amplifier.

"But if they were *given* the runes, and it wasn't fully explained what they had...a lot makes more sense. On the other hand, if aliens gave the Eugenicists the ability to breed magic into humanity...why did they? What did they want?"

Damien was lost for a moment, remembering the strange ruins with their impossibly familiar magic.

"And if they were in contact with the Eugenicists over three hundred years ago, where did they *go*?"

"There's another question, too, my lord," Romanov pointed out. Both of his seniors looked at him and the redheaded Marine shrugged. "These are all key questions—so why is someone willing to kill to stop them being asked?"

CHAPTER 16

THE FIRST PLACE Damien went once Doctor Mohammed finally released him from the hospital was back to the surface of Tau Ceti *f* and once again to the reassuringly solid mass of the Runic Transceiver Array.

This time, Mage-Captain Romanov had spoken to the facility in advance *and* sent a platoon of Marines ahead. In the absence of his proper Secret Service detachment—still on their way back from their leave—the Marines had assigned Romanov permanently to Damien, along with an entire company of troops "borrowed" from *Duke of Magnificence* with Captain Jakab's blessings.

When Transceiver Elva Santiago met him this time, it was in an empty hallway whose exits were blocked by Royal Martian Marines. Nonetheless, the formally robed Mage seemed utterly unperturbed as she led the Hand to the transmission chamber.

"As last time, we have cleared the secondary receiving chamber, and we have a recorder running in case any side transmissions come in. The recording will be reviewed by Agent Corei and any record of your conversation removed from it before it is passed to us."

"I apologize for the extra inconvenience," Damien said quietly. "We have...reason to be paranoid."

"The Guild exists to serve the Protectorate, Lord Montgomery," she told him. "If we are told it is a matter of Protectorate Security, we believe you. The primary chamber is waiting for you."

With a grateful nod to the woman, Damien walked into the shadowed sphere that would allow him to talk to his boss.

"Damien," Desmond Michael Alexander's voice rumbled into the chamber. "It's good to hear from you. When the first reports came in after you got back, we were worried."

"I'm fine and you can tell Kiera and Des that," Damien replied. He got along well with the Mage-King's two children, at least when Kiera Michelle Alexander wasn't teenage-crushing on him and Desmond Michael Alexander the Fourth wasn't teenage-hero-worshipping him.

Or, well, teenage-crushing on him as well. Eighteen-year-old Des was officially into breaking hearts of *all* genders. Life in Olympus Mons was always fascinating for Damien.

"I hope I'm not interrupting anything," Damien continued. "I...presumed you'd want to talk to me as soon as I was able. We found something of a mess."

"You only interrupted me reviewing the latest set of 'suggestions' and 'advice' from the Council of the Protectorate," Alexander said dryly. "I may need to arrange for the Councilors to receive remedial training in 'not giving orders to their sovereign.' Some days, I have a lot of sympathy for Charles II attempting to compromise with a Parliament determined to strip him of his power.

"Of course, both Charles and his Parliament were assholes, a problem we are thankfully in shorter supply of on both sides, I think," the Mage-King finished. "And speaking of orders. What happened on Andala, Damien? That trip was supposed to be a glorified working vacation! Tell me *everything*."

Damien obeyed, detailing everything he remembered and everything Dragic and Romanov had reported. Electronic copies of everyone's reports were aboard couriers headed for Sol that would arrive within a day or so, but even that day could make a huge difference sometimes.

"Damn," his King said when Damien finished. "And you're okay?" he demanded. "I'll admit I've never tested whether a Rune Wright could stop an orbital bombardment before."

"I'm still weak," Damien admitted. "Even this is taking more energy than I'd like, but I'm recovering. I'm going to get to the bottom of this, sir."

He paused, considering. If there was *anyone* in this galaxy he trusted, it was his King, but someone had, so far as he could tell, dropped *Martian Marines* on his head.

"Sir...did you know?" he asked. "That our runes were alien in origin? That our *magic* was alien in origin?"

The transceiver chamber was silent for a long moment.

"I can understand why you have to ask," Alexander replied. "No, Damien. I didn't know. And no, I'm *not* aware of a covert special ops team using our tech and our training to murder people who might find out."

"I wasn't going to ask," Damien told his boss. He *had* wondered, but he hadn't been that far gone into his paranoia. Yet.

"The first Mage-King, my grandfather, *might* have known," the third Mage-King admitted. "But...he was dead before I was born. My father was a child of his second century, and both of them ruled for a hundred years. Remember that my grandfather was...a strong man, a *good* man—but also a man who was used as a stud stallion for seven years.

"He was broken in many ways, and my father was only born because the Protectorate *needed* an heir. I would not have put it past my namesake to have decided certain secrets should die with him."

"And now someone seems determined to make sure that those secrets die with whoever else learns them," Damien said with a sigh. "I'm meeting with the MIS forensics team that's been going over Dragic's samples shortly."

"Damien...we both know your answers are likely here," Alexander told him. "A third of the shipyards in the Protectorate that could have built that ship are in Sol. If *any* information about dealings with aliens by the Eugenicists was written down anywhere, it's in the libraries of Olympus Mons.

"You're wounded and you've been betrayed, my Hand. Come home."

Damien smiled softly, touched by the concern.

"I will," he promised. "But there are still questions to ask here. I'm not leaving this mess to someone else. Who would I trust?"

"I do have other Hands," his liege reminded him.

"This is my...quest now," the Hand replied. "People under my command died for this. I'll find my answers. I promise not to get killed along the way."

"I'll make discreet inquiries here. Frankly, I agree that this should be kept close to our chests for now."

"Not forever," Damien insisted.

"No," Alexander agreed immediately. "This secret has already killed too many. I wonder how many have died we don't even know about. For now, though, I will keep this under wraps. Indeed, as much as possible, I believe we should keep this within the Hands for now."

"I'll be using other resources here," Damien warned, "but that makes sense to me. *Duke* should be repaired within the week, and Amiri is already on her way here. Once I have my bodyguards and my ship back, I'll return to Mars.

"Until then, I will poke around Tau Ceti and see what I can find."

"Be careful, Damien Montgomery," Desmond Alexander ordered his Hand. "We had enough problems before this. With Legatus running spies across half the galaxy and the Council pushing for more control, I *need* you. Don't make me avenge you."

"I have no intention of requiring vengeance, only delivering it."

CHAPTER 17

TAU CETI *f* was a wet, chilly world on the outer edge of the system's Goldilocks zone. Debris and meteor strikes had prevented it from developing life much more complex than fungus before humanity arrived. Now a massive defensive constellation protected the planet from that bombardment, one large enough to be visible for about half the day and night from anywhere on the globe.

Early afternoon was station-rise in the capital of Asimov, and Damien took a moment standing outside the Martian Investigation Service's Tau Ceti Headquarters to watch it.

Asimov was an impressive city. The designers and architects had apparently decided early on to try and offset *f*'s dreary skies and drizzle with a cacophony of strange designs and bright colors. If there was a gray skyscraper in the city, Damien couldn't see it from the hill the MIS HQ stood on. He *could* see red, blue, green, orange and purple, plus a small handful of glittering glass edifices—common still on Earth but standing out like lost gems here.

While he'd spent more time on Tau Ceti than anywhere other than Mars or his home of Sherwood, Damien could still count the number of times he'd been able to stop and watch station-rise on one hand.

The MIS had built their headquarters, a steeply sloped jewel-toned pyramid of green glass and steel, on the top of one of Asimov's highest hills, allowing him a clear view of the horizon as the first of the visible stations rose. At first, all you could see was lights, stars barely visible in the horizon during daylight.

Then the core station, the Tau Ceti f Impact Defense Platform, rose over the horizon. The two IDPs were among the largest humanmade structures in existence, exceeded only by the Centurion Accelerator Ring the Legatans had built to produce antimatter without Mages. It was still a tiny shape in the sky, but unlike its newer and smaller supporting platforms, it was a visible *shape*, reflecting back Tau Ceti's rays to the planet below.

"Sir?" Romanov asked questioningly. They'd dispensed with most of the *overt* security there, though the three armored cars that had delivered the Hand still had a full squad of Marines between them.

"We have a few minutes before we're supposed to meet people, and I wanted to see station-rise," Damien told him, gesturing toward the platform. "If we can build *those*, surely we can manage to get through a few hundred years of civilization without killing each other?"

"We mostly do," the Marine said quietly. "It's just you and I have jobs where we see every place our civilization *breaks*."

"Depressing, that," Damien murmured. "All right, Captain. Let's go talk to the forensics people."

The front lobby of the building was lit with a pale green wash, an inevitable result of the green tint to the glass outside. While there were dozens of ways the MIS could have reduced or eliminated the effect, they had instead chosen to *augment* it by choosing dark green couches for the waiting area and pale green marble for the reception desk.

"Lord Montgomery," the cheerfully green-washed young woman behind the desk greeted him as he walked in. "Welcome to the Emerald City! Director M'Bogo is waiting for you; if you'll take a seat, he'll be down to meet you in a few moments."

"Thank you," Damien told her. He'd barely started toward the couches with his close-in detail in tow, however, before an elevator door swung open and a tall, white-haired man with pitch-black skin emerged and made a beeline for him.

"Hand Montgomery," he greeted Damien, offering his hand. "I am Director Alex M'Bogo, head of the Martian Investigation Service in Tau Ceti."

Damien shook M'Bogo's hand.

"It's a pleasure to meet you, Director," he told the other man. "We Hands tend to swing through everywhere at the highest levels, but we do know who helps keep order behind us. I do apologize for the level of disruption this whole mess has created, though."

"It's been...difficult, I will confess," M'Bogo said carefully. "It's not often I lose an entire floor of my building and two of my top forensics teams behind a wall of Marines. We *do* serve the same master in the end, my lord Hand."

"We do," Damien agreed. "I apologize for the necessity, but this is being kept under wraps at some of the highest levels. Even the Marines being used are only those who've served with us before."

M'Bogo sighed but nodded.

"Indeed. And we are willing to cooperate," he replied. "But it is...difficult. Speaking of that, however, if Captain Romanov and Agent Corei wish to have one of their people join our surveillance supervisors, Miss Penny here"—he gestured at the young woman behind the desk—"can show them to the center."

Damien gestured for his bodyguards to sort it out, but apparently, it had been discussed previously. One of the two Marines backing the Captain immediately joined the young woman at the desk.

As they disappeared into one elevator, M'Bogo led Damien and his remaining crowd into another elevator, one thankfully large enough for all five of them.

"We have two levels of forensics here at the Emerald City," the Director told them, using the inevitable nickname without even blinking. "When we were asked to provide a secure area that would need to be completely locked down, we offered Sublevel Ten. It's the lowest level of the building—actually below our high-security cells—and was most easily secured."

Ten levels below ground or not, the elevator smoothly delivered them to the lowest level in barely more time than it took M'Bogo to explain the location. The doors opened onto a secondary lobby, clearly primarily a security checkpoint with badge scanners and sealed doors.

Two fire teams of Marines occupied the space. Two of the eight were in full exosuits, looming over everyone present, while the other six wore fatigues and slung submachine guns.

All promptly saluted as Damien and Romanov entered.

"This is where we leave you, Director," Damien gently told M'Bogo.

"What? But this is..."

"Still not your need to know," the Hand told him, keeping his voice calm. "We'll give you your people back shortly, but they'll be under a Royal Seal. This is a matter of Protectorate security for now, Director."

The tall man sighed and nodded slowly.

"I apologize," he said gruffly. "I'm not used to being mistrusted enough to be cut out of the loop in my own building."

"It's not a question of trust," Damien told him. He wasn't even entirely lying, though right now, he wasn't sure he trusted *anyone* who hadn't at least been shot at with him. "It's a question of those highest levels of security. We all serve the people of the Protectorate, Director. Today, we serve them best by keeping this quiet."

"I don't know what can of worms you've dug up, my lord," M'Bogo told him. "But I hope you get it under control. Good luck."

Past the secure doors, Damien found the sublevel to be institutionally bland. He expected a forensics lab to be full of blinking lights and fascinating machines, but instead he found white corridors with numbered doors. Presumably, each door hid a laboratory of some kind with those fascinating machines, but without a guide, he felt more than a little lost.

Fortunately, they were met almost immediately by a stocky older woman with a bun of graying hair and a white coat.

"I am Dr. Millicent," she said calmly. "You must be Hand Montgomery—which makes you the reason I've been living with guards for the last few days. It's certainly...odd, though from the briefing Captain Romanov here gave me, I understand the necessity."

"I don't recall being told that the good Doctor's people were being locked in here," Damien said to Romanov, his voice carefully low.

"They are not," the Mage-Captain replied. "We *have* had them assigned bodyguards until the conclusion of the project, however."

"Ah."

"It is not an impediment," Millicent told him. "Just...odd. If you'll come this way, please, we've prepared a briefing on what we've discovered."

Damien followed the older woman as she led them to one of the many numbered doors. This one turned out to contain a relatively standard-looking conference room with a white-coated older man with the faded brown skin and slanted eyes of a Martian native.

"This is Dr. Rose, the other senior investigator here," Millicent told them. "My team is pathology and biologicals; his is tech and materials. He has more useful things to say today than I do. Please, be seated."

Damien grabbed one of the seats, as did Romanov. Agent Corei and the remaining Marine, however, took up flanking positions at the door. Just in case someone attacked the building, made it past the squad of Marines outside the building, all of MIS's own defenses, and the *other* squad of Marines guarding this specific floor to attack them in this specific room, the Hand supposed.

"Since my report is the easiest, I'll start," Millicent told them. With a wave of a hand across a sensor, she turned on the screen at the front of the room and then tapped a command on the screen itself. A series of numbers and symbols promptly filled it.

"Inspector Dragic retrieved just over two hundred biological samples," she noted, tapping one of the columns that Damien realized was a number sequence from one to two hundred and nine. "Some were unusable and others turned out to be from the same individuals.

"All told, we have biological samples from one hundred and two individuals. Genetic markers do not suggest any particular commonality of origin, ethnicity, age or sex. The largest grouping, sixteen individuals, were from Mars. All were physically healthy, consistent with being ground troopers of some kind."

Millicent shrugged. "I ran every comparison I could think of," she told Damien. "There are no commonalities to lead us anywhere or give us a better starting point for analysis. I ran all hundred and two sequences against the identification databases for the MIS Offender Registry, the Tau Ceti and Sol medical databases, and the Royal Military databases.

"There were no matches," she concluded. "Various markers suggest at least six individuals were born in Tau Ceti, but none of their genetics are on file as having been born here. Most likely, the records were scrubbed.

"I apologize, my lord, but whoever these people were, their tracks were carefully covered. We can't identify them."

"I didn't expect you to be able to," Damien admitted. "According to the briefing I received, their gear was completely sanitized. I'd be surprised if they hadn't made sure their people couldn't be tracked."

"As for their gear, I'll speak to that," Doctor Rose interjected. He tapped several commands on the screen, bringing up an image of a crashed assault shuttle.

"The samples we were brought were from the interior of this shuttle," he noted. "Inspector Dragic also sent us some wreckage samples from one of the shuttles your people shot down when the Nineteenth Squadron sent their first courier home. We've analyzed both, plus the video footage and scan data provided, in detail.

"I'm sure no one is surprised that this is a Royal military craft," he continued, tapping the image. "It's a Model Twenty-Four-Forty-Five Assault Shuttle. They're manufactured in three plants: one in orbit of Tau Ceti *e*, run by Tau Ceti Nova Industries, and two in Sol—on Mars and in Jupiter orbit, respectively.

"Without serial numbers or intact computer systems, we can't verify the exact origin or manufacturing timeline of the spacecraft ourselves, but what we *could* confirm was the exact isotopic makeup of the materials used."

Dr. Rose paused, as if expecting applause or some more positive reaction. When Damien simply waited for him to explain, he sighed.

"The isotopic makeup is unique to a given source of, say, titanium," he explained. "While the processing removes many of the impurities, it is still often possible to trace even a manufactured metal to its origin.

"We reviewed the shuttle fragments and armor samples provided by Inspector Dragic. They had four different points of origin—but all four were extraction facilities here in Tau Ceti."

"So, the shuttles were built here?" Damien asked.

"Almost certainly," Rose confirmed. "The exosuit armor as well. The weapons retrieved were Martian Armaments gear, manufactured on Mars, but MA gear is scattered across the entire Protectorate in the hands of Royal and system government troops."

"We have a lot more detail in our reports and analysis," Millicent told Damien. "You can review it at your leisure, but those are the high points." She paused. "Don't let Rose fool you," she noted. "What *his* team did was almost impossible."

"Somehow, that doesn't surprise me," Damien replied with a chuckle. "And thanks to you, Dr. Rose, I now know where to go next."

"My lord?" Romanov asked.

"I'm starting to miss my staff," the Hand said. "Now I'm going to need to make an appointment with Tau Ceti Nova Industries' Board of Directors."

CHAPTER 18

RETURNING TO the main floor, Damien reacquired his various body-guards and informed the squad guarding Sublevel Ten that they could pack up and return to *Duke of Magnificence*. Everything the two teams had found was now sealed under his Hand, and he was relatively sure he could trust it to stay that way.

Probably. He was having a bad week.

"My lord," a new receptionist greeted him. This one was a dark-haired young woman to Miss Penny's blonde, but otherwise appeared to have been pressed from the same attractive, overly-cheery mold. Somehow, he suspected they were both armed and deadly.

"We have an incoming aircraft," she reported. "I have a verbal request to ask you to hold on until they arrive, so I've taken the liberty of setting the HQ to condition two. Your Marines have been notified and are standing by."

"I see," Damien allowed. "Thank you, miss..."

"Amber, sir," she replied. "Tiffany Amber. The helicopter will be arriving in less than two minutes, sir. I'd suggest you stay inside—the front 'glass' is transmuted titanium."

Smiling at the woman, if shaking his head at the paranoia of the whole situation, Damien took a seat on the edge of one of the couches, watching through the tinted glass as his Marines began quietly drifting out of the armored cars and settling into using them as cover.

Less than thirty seconds after Amber's warning, he spotted the incoming aircraft. It was a particularly unintimidating thing, and he relaxed—slightly—as he recognized the plain gray-green aircraft that the Royal Martian Navy used to run people around on the surface in a hurry.

It dropped to the ground on the clear pad in front of the building intended for just that purpose, and immediately disgorged six dangerous-looking young men and women in black suits. For a moment, Damien started to tense again—and then the last person left the helicopter.

She was a tall, broad-shouldered woman with short-cropped black hair, wearing a perfectly-cut suit and carrying a slung Secret Service carbine. She also wasn't supposed to be back on Tau Ceti for another two days, but Damien was nonetheless glad to see her.

"You can stand down the building, Miss Amber," he told the receptionist. "They're Secret Service. They're with me."

Leaving the MIS receptionist behind, the Hand strode out of the building to greet his significantly taller bodyguard.

"Julia Amiri!" he shouted over the rotors. "I thought you were supposed to be on Ardennes, backing Riordan's election campaign."

"You haven't heard?" she replied, gesturing for the Secret Service agents with her to take up position around Damien. "I guess you wouldn't have. I hitched a ride *on* the news courier. Election was three days ago. Mikael won. My boyfriend now runs a planet." She shook her head. "Which takes some adjusting to, *unlike* the fact that you tried to get yourself *killed* while I was gone."

"I wasn't *trying*," Damien noted. "It was supposed to be a quiet murder investigation."

"Who's been watching your back?" she demanded.

He gestured at the pair behind him.

"Agent Corei and Marine Mage-Captain Romanov."

Amiri stepped up, sizing both of them up with an appraising eye.

"Well, the little guy's still breathing, so you did okay," she said critically. "Where to, Damien?"

"Back to *Duke of Magnificence*," he told her. "I need to brief you and I need to borrow some poor junior officer to chase a CEO's staff." He glanced around. "Where did you find *our* Agents?" he asked, gesturing at the suited men and women.

"They arrived in system just before I did," Amiri said with a posses-sive smile. "They just aren't *quite* as capable as I am of getting Captain Jakab to tell them where you were. Just...*why* is the dear Captain acting like a professional paranoid?"

"Because I told him to," Damien said shortly. "Like I said, I need to brief you."

"So, that's the summary version," Damien Montgomery told his body-guard two hours later. The repairs on *Duke of Magnificence* were now most-ly complete—sufficiently so, at least, that he'd been able to reclaim the ob-servation deck he'd turned into his office when he'd moved aboard the ship.

His senior bodyguard leaned back in her chair, sipping her cup of excellent coffee—the Hand's only major vice—as she took in everything he'd said.

"I see Romanov is more directly responsible for you still being breathing than I thought," Amiri finally said. "That was a near-run thing, Damien. There's a *reason* you're not supposed to go places with just a three-man detail, for crying out loud!"

"I brought Marines," he pointed out. "And it was *supposed* to be a work-ing vacation, not kicking open the biggest can of worms that's crossed even *my* desk in recent memory. Hell, Julia, I'm not sure who to trust any-more. A *Marine* stabbed Romanov's people in the back."

"*Duke*'s crew seems safe enough," Amiri said thoughtfully. "They've walked into hell with you; I doubt any conspiracy can offer most of them enough to betray you. But...seriously, boss? Mystery ships? Navy bom-bardment weapons? What *have* we stumbled into?"

"A secret the first Mage-King may have meant to die with him," Damien said grimly. "What worries *me*, Julia, is that the first Mage-King may have set up something to make *sure* the secret stayed dead. It seems... possible that we are facing an organization operating at the highest level of the Protectorate, under black orders from Mage-King Desmond Alexander the First himself."

He hadn't said it aloud yet to anyone—he hadn't even briefed Romanov on everything the Mage-King had said—but that was the worry in the back of his mind. The King might back *him*, but if the King's *grandfather* had created these secret-keepers, they might have access to all of the resources that he did.

"But His Majesty has our back, right?" she asked.

"I've never known Desmond to lie to me," Damien said quietly. "That doesn't mean he didn't or wouldn't, but... Yeah, he's with us. This whole mess is dangerous, Julia. I won't drag you into it if you want out."

She laughed at him.

"Dangerous, huh?" she asked. "And stepping into the middle of an incipient civil war wasn't? Launching a *revolution* wasn't? I'm here to keep you alive, Montgomery. That means I go where you go, *especially* when it's dangerous."

He shook his head at her and raised his coffee cup in salute.

"Ever thought of a different career?" he asked.

"Used to be a bounty hunter," she reminded him. "I like this better."

Something in her eyes and the way she quickly started drinking her coffee suggested that he'd hit a nerve. If it was important, though, Damien knew she'd tell him.

"I've reached out to Captain Jakab," he told her. "With my staff still scattered across at least three systems—the Professor is still a *week* away—I'm leaning on his people. His poor communications officer is trying to pin down TCNI's CEO and Board for a meeting. We'll probably end up having to give them the data in advance to make the meeting worthwhile."

"That officer has one hell of a name to conjure with," Amiri pointed out. "I'm pretty sure you'll get your meeting."

"The Mage-King's name opens many doors," Damien agreed, only to pause as his bodyguard laughed and shook her head at him again.

"I doubt he'll even need to *mention* the King," she told him. "*Your* name is a pretty potent conjuration all on its own."

Damien shivered. Hand of the Mage-King or not, that was never a comfortable thought.

CHAPTER 19

IT TOOK JUST over two days for the bureaucracy of a major inter-stellar megacorporation to grind through the gears sufficiently to acquire Hand Damien Montgomery a meeting with Tau Ceti Nova Industries' CEO and Board of Directors.

In Damien's admittedly uneducated opinion, that was basically a miracle.

Despite the horrendously overbooked schedules of corporate exec-utives at that level, however, the Hand found himself flying into their headquarters in orbit of Tau Ceti *e* barely three days after being released from intensive medical care.

His plan to fly the shuttle himself, his normal habit, was prompt-ly vetoed by, in order, Amiri, Jakab and Doctor Mohammed. Instead, a young Lieutenant from *Duke of Magnificence*'s contingent of pilots named Vanessa MacDonald and her crew of Petty Officers took on the task.

MacDonald delivered them to the station perfectly on schedule, and Amiri led the way onto the station.

While Mage-Captain Romanov and his company had effectively been permanently assigned to Damien, this task called for a gentler touch. If Damien's Secret Service detail had still been scattered to the winds on vacation, he'd have used the Marines anyway, but since his people were starting to re-coalesce now, he'd use the right tool for the job.

Two suited Agents followed Amiri, sweeping the station corridors like hunting hawks. Two more followed Damien as he boarded the station. It all felt a little ridiculous to him still, but after someone had tried to use *orbital bombardment* to kill him, he was no longer prepared to call it overkill.

The group waiting for him seemed completely unbothered. The set of three executives, two women and a man, all cut from the same hard-eyed-but-graying cloth, had their own set of guards, a quartet of burly young men in security uniforms.

"Welcome to Nova Central Station, Hand Montgomery," the taller of the women greeted him. "I am Andrea Volk, CEO of Nova Industries. These are Lucía Fierro, my Senior Vice President in charge of Internal Audit, and Quanah Comanche, our Chairman of the Board."

"Miss Volk, Miss Fierro, Mister Comanche," Damien greeted them. "I understand we are meeting with the entire Board?"

"We are," Volk confirmed. "Miss Fierro has been responsible for the research into your data and will be carrying the core of the presentation. If you'll come with us, please?"

Damien had, in his nearly a year as Hand of the Mage-King and three years training under the Mage-King, seen conference rooms on half a dozen worlds, put together for heads of governments, rulers of space stations, and the Protector of Humanity.

The conference room that Volk led him to put most, though not *all*, to shame. It was a two-tiered, horseshoe-shaped affair, floored in Sherwood oak imported from Damien's homeworld. The gravity runes had been inlaid into the expensive hardwood with care, and then lacquered over. It made them more difficult to charge but protected them and the imported floor from traveling feet.

Each tier had its own table, each space marked with a carefully stuffed leather chair and an interface setup for personal computers and communicators. The table was soft-pink marble, *probably* from the marble quarries on Tau Ceti *f*, though there were other quarries in the galaxy it could have been imported from.

Damien was led to the middle of the lower tier and given the central chair, where he could see everything. Amiri took a seat near the door without asking, and her agents flanked the door like silent black-clad statues.

Volk took her own seat to one side of Damien, and Comanche took the seat on the other. No one introduced the fourteen members of the Board who had been waiting in the room, though Damien could have named each of them from his briefing on the way over.

"The room is sealed," Lucía Fierro announced, stepping up to the lectern at the center of the horseshoe. "No electronic communication in or out is now possible. Hand Montgomery, you are of course welcome to step outside at any time, but you impressed upon us the importance of secrecy and confidentiality of the data you provided and asked us to review."

"Your caution is appreciated," Damien said mildly. "Carry on."

"My lord, you provided us with material scans, sensor data, and a wealth of other information on several assault shuttles involved in the attack on you," Fierro began. "My Internal Audit analysts have reviewed this data and we agree with the MIS's conclusion: we can confirm that the spacecraft that was intact enough for thorough examination and sampling was manufactured here in Tau Ceti by us.

"You will understand I hope, my lord, that the full internal audit to attempt to identify any missing spacecraft will take time," she warned him. "Months at least.

"We have done, however, a full preliminary analysis from materials acquisition to spacecraft delivery. While it is possible our data systems have been compromised at some point, I can assure you that would not be *easy*. Our purchased materials for this program are fully accounted for, as is every shuttle manufactured for the program."

Fierro looked uncomfortable.

"Every Model Twenty-Four-Forty-Five assault shuttle we manufactured was delivered to either the Royal Martian Marines or the Royal Martian Navy. Much as I dislike the thought myself, I suspect the craft were diverted *after* they entered His Majesty's service, not while they were in our possession."

Damien nodded slowly.

"I will need to have my people review the analysis," he noted.

"We should be able to provide that," Fierro told him. "It will take us a few days to turn my people's internal analysis into something useful to those unfamiliar with the data, but we can have that to you quickly."

"Very well. What about the ship?" he asked.

Fierro tapped a command on the lectern, and an image appeared on the wall behind her. It was an odd-looking ship to Damien, far from the sharp lines of the pyramids the Martian Navy preferred. A sharply curving bullet-like shape half a kilometer long according to the scale on the screen, it was very different from anything he'd ever seen.

"Between the surface scan data and TK-421's sensor scans, we have a relatively detailed image of the ship that attacked you," Fierro told Damien. "Roughly six million tons, five hundred and two meters long, one hundred and fifty meters wide. Antimatter engines, current Navy-issue weapons; she's a *very* unusual ship."

"Unique, so far as I can tell," Damien replied. "A custom build is my guess."

"That is my own assumption as well," the auditor confirmed. "We unquestionably have enough data to identify the vessel if she were in our records." She paused. "We've scoured everything, my lord. Including records that are technically supposed to be sealed without a court order. We did not build this ship."

Damien sighed. He *wanted* to believe them. Wanted to trust them. But this was the same system where someone had managed to attach an *assassin* to his bodyguards—and Mage-Admiral Segal's MPs had so far failed to even find a *trace* of the orders reassigning White to that task.

"I will need to see that data as well," he said finally.

Fierro shifted uncomfortably, and gestured toward Comanche.

The Chairman of the Board of Directors cleared his throat.

"My lord, Miss Fierro was not exaggerating when she said there were records reviewed that would not have been opened for a request from a lesser authority," he said calmly. "We have signed confidentiality and nondisclosure agreements, and have a moral and ethical obligation besides to protect our clients' interests.

"Providing you the data would not allow you to prove a negative," Comanche said flatly. "I spent four hours sitting with Miss Fierro's analysts this morning, Hand Montgomery. Once they got over the shock of having the Chairman of the Board in their offices, they walked me through their analysis from beginning to end.

"I swear to you, Lord Montgomery, that Fierro speaks the truth. I can provide no greater assurance, but we *cannot* simply hand you this data. We would be in violation of a dozen or more contracts."

"All of which are subject to override by court order," Damien said flatly. "I remind you, Mister Comanche, that my orders *are* a court order."

"And under the Charter, we have sixty days to comply," the Chairman replied. "It would take almost that long for us to find a reasonable compromise between your needs and our own moral and legal obligations. We *will* take that step, if you insist, but my lord...we have worked with His Majesty's government for decades. Over a century, in fact.

"We provide you with detailed files on every ship we build for the system governments," he pointed out. "We work with you on every file. We are *being* cooperative. I am...not certain what more you want from us."

"Certainty," Damien said flatly. Anything they manipulated, anything they *touched* before they gave it to him, was suspect. The Board wouldn't even need to know the data had been manipulated—the people he was looking for wouldn't hesitate to lie to TCNI's Board as well.

"Ladies, gentlemen, I am dealing with a conspiracy that threatens the very safety of the Protectorate. Even a filtered dataset would be insufficient. I fear I will require unfettered access to your files."

"*That* we also have sixty days to comply with," Comanche said quietly. "And while I can begin to see your need, understand that we would be remiss in our obligations to our shareholders, our employees and our clients were we to permit you that access without challenging it all the way to the Council of the Protectorate and the Mage-King himself.

"We will put together as complete a supporting package of our analysis as we can," he finished, nodding to Fierro, who looked determined.

"We *want* to help. But we *cannot* simply hand you access to all of our confidential files, my lord."

"I understand," Damien said stonily. "I would appreciate that package being provided as soon as possible."

"I will have all hands on deck, my lord," Fierro promised. "I cannot guarantee anything, only that you will have it as quickly as you can."

The Hand nodded. They might be honestly trying, but it wasn't enough.

He was going to have to find an alternative.

CHAPTER 20

"THAT'S IT," Romanov told Damien, gesturing out the tinted window of the black government car.

Asimov was the capital city of a star system with two inhabited planets and just over seven billion human beings. Traffic control and design continued to advance every year, but there was only so much that could be done. Stuck in traffic in the downtown core, the black vehicle was moving slowly enough to allow inspection of the building without being obvious.

It didn't stand out much. Amidst the glittering multicolored jewels of Asimov's downtown, the black ten-story building almost disappeared, beneath anyone's notice. Anyone who paid attention, though, would note that the building had even more cooling vanes than most, with narrower windows and heavier shutters.

Two uniformed guards stood just inside the door, but a lot of corporate buildings there had at least a small uniformed presence to secure their assets.

This *particular* corporate building was a server farm for a computer services company that was, on paper, utterly independent of Tau Ceti Nova Industries—but had long ago had its entire capacity subsumed by the bigger corporation. The servers here didn't support TCNI's operations—but it was their secure backup facility.

"What do we know about it?" the Hand asked as the car slowly moved on. The Marine Mage-Captain, Amiri, and the Secret Service agent driving the car were the only people he'd mentioned anything to about this arguably questionable course of action.

"We only know it's here since our contracts say they have to tell us where the records of Navy production are stored," Romanov pointed out. "I had a couple of my Sergeants pull all the records they could find as a 'training exercise', though, so I have a few details."

"And?"

The Mage-Captain glanced at the tinted windows, as if making sure no one could see what he was doing, then tapped a command on his wrist computer that opened up a holographic image of the building in front of him.

"It's not a military facility," he pointed out, "so security is relatively light. Doors are all secured by codes in the staff's wrist computers, everyone who doesn't work in the building has to check in at the front desk, and there is a surveillance system in place which monitors *everyone's* arrivals and departures.

"There are three ground-level accesses: the front door, the staff entrance, and the delivery dock. All are guarded twenty-eight/seven." Tiny red holographic figures appeared at each of the doors. "During the day, there are two guards at each entrance. At night, the delivery door is physically locked down and unguarded; there is a guard at each entrance, and four patrolling guards."

"How would you gain access, Captain?" Damien asked softly, eyeing the hologram.

"Assuming full sanction...we go in with stunguns and jammers," the Marine replied. "Jam the emergency callcode, SmartDart any guards that get in our way. Glorified smash-and-grab; even with the jammer, we'd only have a few minutes.

"Since it *does* hold military records, any significant attack will result in the security company escalating to Marine Rapid Response Teams. We could override those, but that will raise a lot of questions."

"And make it obvious it was us," Damien said quietly. "Let's...presume we don't want anyone to get in trouble for this. Amiri? Thoughts on sneaky options?"

"Marines," she sighed aloud with a gentle smile at Romanov. "Any kind of assault is overkill: it's a *server farm*. It's full of people in suits, most of whom don't know each other, running around on half a dozen tasks.

"You want to sneak in, not shoot up the place."

"I can override the locks," Damien admitted, "but the *guards* are going to be looking for something a bit more solid."

"What you need, my lord, is a distraction," Romanov noted. "I have a company of Marines, sir. I can arrange a bar fight."

"No," the Hand said slowly, "that's not going to draw corp security guards to check it out. We need something more immediate."

"You sound like you have an idea," Amiri noted.

"I do. I just need to find someone."

Somehow, Damien was not at all surprised that Roslyn Chambers wasn't at home. He was mildly *pleased* to discover that her "home" wasn't her parents' sprawling estate twenty minutes' flight from Asimov but a small apartment in one of the city's calmer areas.

The Mage-King's officials on any planet paid a stipend to any Mage who asked for it, no questions, no applications. It wasn't much, but it was enough to live on or tide over a difficult stretch in your life. Its purpose was to try to keep Mages out of the criminal underworld, a purpose it succeeded at surprisingly well.

No one expected that they could keep *every* Mage from crime, but the stipend softened the kind of financial need that *forced* people into it. According to the records he had accessed, Chambers had walked out of the penitentiary and had her mother drive her to the nearest Guild office, where she'd formally requested the stipend.

She hadn't even *been* to her parents' estate from what he could tell. She'd had the apartment she was living in registered to her name by the end of the day she'd left juvie.

Fortunately, Damien's Secret Service agents had full access to the city's cameras, and it had taken them less than two minutes to track down his young Mage.

The Hand assessed the situation with a practiced eye as he rapidly grew more and more amused. Chambers had settled herself down in a corner café, with the cheapest drink on their menu going cold on the table in front of her as she paid more attention to the convenience store across the street.

With a sigh, he gestured Amiri and Romanov to a different table and dropped himself into the empty chair at Chambers' table.

"I seem to recall telling you to stay *out* of trouble," he told her genially.

"What? Who? *How?*" the dark-haired girl spluttered, staring at him in shock. After a moment and a deep inhalation, she glared at him. "Last I checked, drinking coffee might not be *good* for me, but it's hardly getting in trouble."

"Miss Chambers, please," Damien replied. "You are acting as lookout for at least one, perhaps more of your friends who are about to try and rob that convenience store. It's completely automated, so I'm assuming they have some kind of hack that will cause the machines to hand over either money or goods, and you are here to make sure no cops see what's going on."

She looked guilty and he smiled coldly.

"Call it off, Roslyn," he said gently. "I can help you get into Fleet, but not if you rob someone in *front of me.*"

The young woman sighed, and tapped an icon on her wrist computer.

"Roger Wilco, people."

"What? Roger Wilco? There's nobody…" a voice replied.

"Roger Wilco," she repeated. "We're done."

"If this is for nothing, O'Kane'll have your head."

Chambers flashed a brilliant smile at Damien across the table.

"I don't think so," she said calmly. "Tell him we're done. And he *knows* what I can do if he wants to push it."

Killing the channel, she met his eyes challengingly.

"Now that I've pissed off the boss of the gang who runs my apartment building—who is *also* an ex-boyfriend, so my tears are limited—why the fuck is a Hand of the Mage-King at my table?" she demanded.

"I need a favor," he admitted. "I need some people distracted, and I can't get anyone officially associated involved."

"Okay." She leaned back and eyed him. "I can make that happen. What do I get?"

"I can make sure you're not bothered by O'Kane?" He gestured at her wrist-comp.

She laughed.

"O'Kane won't bother me," she replied. "He's a small-time petty thief with delusions of grandeur, but he knows not to fuck with a Mage."

"You already have a letter that will get you into the Academy if you don't get charged with a crime between now and then," Damien pointed out. "Something that made your stunt today *damned* stupid, if you ask me."

"It was a favor," she admitted, flushing. "O'Kane got me the apartment so I didn't have to spend any time at the estate. It was help with a few jobs or fuck him, and I didn't feel like making my way on my back."

"Fair." Damien waved it away. "I can ignore it," he told her, "which leaves me, I suppose, with a simple question: what do you *want* for your help?"

Chambers paused for a long moment, then laughed.

"I have no clue," she replied. "Why do you *need* me?"

"Because I'm facing a conspiracy in my own government and don't know who I can trust," he told her quietly.

"Damn." She was silent for a second. "You're not shitting me, are you? This is the real deal?"

"Yes."

"Fuck it. I'm in."

CHAPTER 21

DAMIEN STOOD impatiently in the alley behind the server building, waiting to see just what Roslyn Chambers unleashed on the two unsuspecting men chatting next to the staff entrance. Signing in wasn't the best option, but he could easily override the secured entrance—if he had about a minute without interruption.

Despite Amiri and Romanov's protestation, he was going in himself. Only the codes in his Hand could override the security on TCNI's servers, and without knowing *exactly* what security they were using, he couldn't give them one-time codes as he'd occasionally given Amiri before.

His pair of minders lurked nearby, ready to swoop in if something went *very* wrong. He didn't expect to need them, but it was reassuring to know they were there. It was always possible, after all, that some part of Chambers's plan would raise more havoc than expected.

He was starting to worry that the young Mage had flaked out on him, when she finally appeared in the side street, heading deeper into the maze of alleyways that linked Asimov's downtown away from the main thoroughfares.

She'd managed to find a skirt and shirt ensemble that, combined with tying her hair back into pigtails, managed to make her look both even younger than she was *and* scandalously underdressed. The two guards, both old enough to be her father, were clearly uncomfortable as she approached them.

"Can you help me?" she asked as she reached them. "I'm trying to find an office around here, but the datanet map is confusing!"

"Certainly, young miss," the older of the two guards told her. Sensibly, the other remained steady, watching the door as the first stepped over to Chambers to help her with her manufactured directional difficulties.

She pulled her wrist computer around to show the guard the map she had projected on it, a movement that both showed the guards what Damien suspected was a dangerously distracting amount of skin and allowed her purse to slip down her other arm.

Exactly like that had been a prearranged signal, another teenager emerged from the shadow nearby, yanked her purse out of her loose grip, and bolted down the street at full speed.

"My purse!" Chambers squealed in a pitch that Damien doubted she had ever used without intent in her *life*. "Help!"

There was a moment of hesitation on the part of the guards, but the door *was* locked behind them and this was a young woman, likely the age of their own children, in dire need.

Both men took off after the runner, abandoning their post and allowing Damien to quickly approach the door without attracting attention.

"I need a full minute," he told Chambers, who was looking after the guards with a sad expression on her face. "Think your friend will get us that?"

"He's a champion sprinter," she said quietly. "He'll get us that and they won't get close enough to even *ID* him before he loses them. Those are good guys, Montgomery. They don't deserve to get into trouble for this."

"They won't," he said, activating a series of codes on his wrist computer. "I promise you that."

The light on the panel flashed green, the door accepting his Hand override at last.

"Thank you," he told her. "And I promise you—*no one* is getting in trouble for this. I swear it."

The inside of the building was sterile and corporate. Plain white walls, small plaques with numbers and names, offices and server rooms all around him.

According to the information TCNI had provided the Navy, the most secure backups were stored in the basement behind another set of security doors requiring a higher level of access. So, conveniently, were the recordings of the systems surveillance network, which Damien would need to plant a bug in before he left.

TCNI was still working to provide him their compromise data. He didn't really want them to know he'd snuck into their building and illegally accessed the data they hadn't been willing to give him.

His staff had been *far* too willing to assist in his blatantly illegal break-and-entry, too. That gave him more pause than he liked to admit. They were technically breaking the law at his request, confident that he was in the right and that he could shield them from the consequences.

It gave him an eerie insight into how the shadowy figures he was facing could draw Marines like Mage-Lieutenant White into their conspiracy—the beginnings of a slippery slope that could end in their turning on their fellow Marines.

No one in the building questioned him. He was better dressed than most of the people he saw running around, but there were enough people in suits that his went unquestioned. He knew where he was going, and he'd found that a suit and a determined expression got most people out of your way.

Reaching the bottom of the stairs into the basement, he took a quick glance through the tiny window in the door, a moment's paranoia that spared him potentially serious issues.

There was, indeed, another set of security doors blocking access into the secured archives in the basement. However, unlike what the data Romanov's people had acquired had said, there *were* guards down there.

Two men, both in TCNI Security uniforms and carrying stunguns, stood in front of the security doors, clearly watching for any potential intruders. If Damien had barged through the stairway exit, he'd have found himself doing some uncomfortable explaining.

As it was, he had to deal with two armed guards without raising an alarm or attracting attention. Neutralizing them, even non-lethally, would be easy enough—he could step through the door and electrocute them with a charge equivalent to what the auto-calibrating SmartDarts in their stunguns would deliver.

That would, unless the guards' employer was incompetent, almost certainly trigger an alarm. A subtler measure was required.

Breathing carefully, Damien reached out with his magic and manipulated the air around the men's heads. Not the air in the room—strange variations in that would likely trigger another alarm—just the air in a tight, invisible bubble around each man's head.

It was the exact *inverse* of the spell he'd used to breathe on Andala IV's surface without a breather, slowly lowering the oxygen level in the air around them. It had to be a careful, subtle thing, and it took time... but neither guard even noticed it as they slowly grew more tired, both settling into chairs...and then passing out.

Damien stepped into the room, sweeping his spell away as he checked on both men. Their pulses were strong, their breathing steady now that they had proper oxygen access again. They'd wake up with ugly headaches but otherwise be unharmed.

He felt painfully guilty nonetheless as he overrode the lock and stepped into the secured archives. None of the guards he'd tricked or gassed on his way in had deserved it. Hell, even if they *had* built the ship, *TCNI* probably didn't deserve this.

He just had to *know* they hadn't.

The inside of the basement archive was a chilly room with racks of floor-to-ceiling black cylinders. Each of them was a server containing an amount of information Damien could barely comprehend, usually accessed via specific links from the outside, but there had to be *some* local access.

It took him a minute to find the set of cubicles and link his Hand to the consoles there. Like almost all technology built in the Protectorate, the secured console chugged its objections for a moment but then turned on and gave him full access.

Transferring into the console the search program he and Amiri had put together before he'd arrived, he set it to run while he found the security office. One preprogrammed virus installation later, and all record of him would be wiped from the records.

No one would ever know he was there unless he got caught on the way out, and he already had a plan for that.

There was *nobody* in the basement, which was helpful for Damien if a bit creepy. All of these servers, though, were just that: servers—and backup servers at that. Everything on them was accessible remotely and also kept in more easily accessible, higher-grade servers.

The set of four cubicles and consoles he'd taken over were basically there to enable maintenance of the server towers. There were guards, because this was sensitive data, but no one would be down there unless something had gone wrong.

It was still creepy.

Returning to his suborned consoles, he saw that about half of the search programs were done. Looking through each individually, a sinking feeling settled into his stomach.

Nothing.

Nothing.

More nothing.

They'd put together twenty-two different searches and crawlers, looking through TCNI's files in every way smarter people than Damien could devise, and each one came back with the same result.

The Board had been telling him the truth, and he'd broken into their building and assaulted two of their security officers for nothing.

"Damn," he whispered.

The sound of movement caught his ears and he realized the guards outside were awake now. Muttered cursing echoed through the walls, and he sighed. His plan had been to simply walk out the front door to avoid potential complications, but since that wasn't an option...

He brought up a program on his PC, quickly checking vectors and distance against its internal map. Once he was sure, he channeled power through his runes, casting the spell that, aboard a starship, could teleport the entire ship a light-year away.

Seven hundred and eighty-six meters was child's play.

CHAPTER 22

IT WAS NOT Julia Amiri's job to tell Damien Montgomery when he was being foolish. It was her job to tell him when he was putting himself in danger—which she had done—and to make sure his foolishness didn't *kill* him.

That last duty was why she found herself sharing a blue covert armored car tucked into a side street with a Marine, waiting for Damien to finish his *latest* foolish escapade, waiting for an emergency signal that responding to would open not merely the can of worms but the entire barrel.

"You've been with Montgomery a while?" Romanov asked. Julia didn't know him *well*—she'd only peripherally interacted with the Marines aboard *Duke of Magnificence*—but she'd met him before.

"Since the beginning," she agreed. "Though I don't know if that counts as a while. He became Hand when Alaura Stealey died on Ardennes, and that was only a year ago."

"I was there for the end," Romanov replied. "Hell of a day. Did he really go into the Governor's bunker on his own?"

"He did," Julia confirmed. "Didn't kill the Governor, though. After all he'd done, Vaughn died stopping his pet madman from blowing up his cities. Guess he still had a conscience left."

Memories. It had been odd to go back to Ardennes and visit Riordan. The ex-rebel had been doing a spectacular job of helping the interim Governor bring peace to the warring factions there—too good a job. The interim Governor was now the "Peace Commissioner," and her poor boyfriend had managed to get *himself* elected Governor.

"You seem distracted, Special Agent," the Marine said quietly.

"It's none of your business, Captain," she replied harshly, but his flat gaze in response got a chuckle from her.

"Right now, Special Agent, I work for you," Romanov pointed out. "But I also work for the Hand, and if you're distracted such that you can't protect him..."

"Fine," she snapped. "Don't tell him, though. Understand?" The Marine nodded. She didn't need to specify the him. "My boyfriend was just elected Governor of Ardennes. He's putting together his cabinet, and he needs the best person he can find for Minister for Defense to help put the shattered wreck of the system militia back together."

"He offered you the job," Romanov guessed.

"And a fucking ring with it, if you'll believe it," she said. "Planetary First Lady and Minister for Defense. Me. An ex-bounty-hunter-turned-bodyguard."

"I'm guessing you didn't say yes," the Marine noted.

"I didn't say no, either," Julia admitted. "I may...have dropped the ring on the ground, fled the building and grabbed the first courier back here." She shrugged sheepishly. "I didn't even know Damien had been injured when I left Ardennes."

The Marine turned away and started making small convulsive motions. It took her a full ten seconds to realize he was laughing into his hands.

"Oh, fuck you, Romanov," she snapped.

"Please tell me you at least emailed him with 'I'll think about it' or *something*?" the Marine asked as he regained his composure.

"Well, yes...eventually," Julia admitted. In truth, *he'd* called *her* while she was heading out-system, and she'd calmed down enough to at least promise to *consider* the idea. She'd said it at least as much to make him realize she wasn't rejecting *Mikael Riordan*, just panicking at the thought of being a Minister and a First Lady.

"And you haven't told Montgomery?"

"What would I tell him? 'Your badass bodyguard can't handle a marriage proposal'?"

"Special Agent, I've watched you in action," Romanov replied. "No one is going to take you being flustered personally with any ability to not do your *job*. But you should probably tell Montgomery. Especially if you might take the job."

Shaking her head, Julia looked around for a change of subject and checked the time.

"Wait...shouldn't we have seen distraction girl by now?" she asked. "She was supposed to meet us here."

Romanov checked the time himself and nodded grimly, a short-barreled carbine materializing in his hands as he scanned the area around them.

"She had a com code and she knew to look for the blue car," he agreed. "We should have heard from her if nothing else."

A pause.

"I'll go look for her," they both said simultaneously.

Shaking her head again, Julia made a "go ahead" gesture to the Marine.

"You go," she ordered. "I'll watch for Damien."

Damien winced as he hit the ground, even in the soft soil. He had emerged just over two meters aboveground in the middle of a park, a position that, while awkward, would be clear of people—and then he'd messed up his landing.

His ankle twisted under him and he ended up face-first in the dirt, adding minor injury and dirty scrapes to the insult of realizing he'd gone to a lot of effort and risked major political consequences to...basically confirm that the TCNI auditors had told him the truth.

With a sigh, he levered himself off the dirt, waved shakily to a small boy who'd watched him appear and fall, and limped toward the alley where he was supposed to meet everyone. If anyone in the little oasis of pure greenery in the heart of Asimov thought a Mage appearing out of thin air and spraining their ankle like an idiot was strange, they kept it to themselves.

Entering the alley, he spotted the blue car and started limping toward it. To his surprise, Romanov emerged from around the corner and was heading to the car as well—and the Marine looked worried.

"What is it?" Damien asked, reaching the armored car and leaning on it as the Marine joined him.

"Chambers is missing," Romanov said flatly. "I checked all the way back to the door where she was distracting the guards. She's gone."

"She may have just skipped on us," the Hand replied. He tapped a series of commands on his PC, wincing as he put too much pressure on his twisted ankle. The small screen happily popped up a NO CONNECTION notice.

"I already tried calling her," Amiri said, stepping out of the car. "Her PC is either off or refusing calls."

Damien tapped another icon, a command code that would override a call refusal. The computer still informed him that Chambers's PC was unavailable.

"It's off," he said grimly. "That's...not right. Neither of you saw anything?"

"We were watching for your emergency signal and keeping an eye for her," Amiri replied. "She didn't come into the alley at all."

"Any sign of a fight?"

Romanov shook his head. "Nothing I recognized, but untrained or not, she's a Mage. Anyone doing a snatch-and-grab would know they needed her disabled *fast*."

Why would someone grab *Chambers*? Damien wasn't sure, but he suspected he wasn't going to like the answer.

"TCNI is clean," he told them bitterly. "Let's make sure the kid doesn't suffer to have proven that. Head to her apartment."

The car had barely started moving when *Damien's* computer buzzed with an incoming call. It flashed up as UNKNOWN CALLER—something that wasn't supposed to *happen* with a military-grade personal computer linked to the full databases.

"This is Montgomery," he said sharply. "Who is this?"

"Who I am is irrelevant," a calm, unrushed voice with an identifiably English accent replied. "What is relevant is that I am the one with Roslyn Chambers in custody. She is quite unharmed and will remain so barring further unpleasantness."

"I guarantee you," Damien said quietly, "that if you *don't* release her, there will definitely be 'unpleasantness'."

"Please, Lord Montgomery, let's not be hasty," the voice said. "Miss Chambers was picked up as...surety, let's call it. We knew you'd want to access TCNI's files, so we were in position to acquire an asset of yours when you moved.

"The plan was to pick up Miss Amiri, so you can imagine my operatives were pleased that you utilized a teenage girl. I am...less impressed."

Amiri threw Damien a hand signal to note that she was tracing the call. She would need him to keep talking.

"I do what I must," he told the stranger. "What do you want?"

"We need to meet, my lord Hand. The situation has already grown out of hand and we need to calm it down."

"You're with the people who bombed Andala."

"I am," the speaker admitted. "My brethren went too far. I believe an amicable solution remains possible; therefore, we must meet."

"And if I refuse to meet with you?"

"Then I am afraid Miss Chambers's parents will be mourning the child they should have spent more time with," the voice said grimly. "I have no desire for unpleasantness, but we do what we must."

"Harm her and I will crush you."

"I have dealt with Hands before, Lord Montgomery. I cannot threaten you. I can only make you responsible for the lives of others. I am not asking you to betray the Protectorate or dishonor your oaths. Just to meet with me.

"Isn't the safety of the girl worth at least that?"

Damien glanced at Amiri, who shook her head. They couldn't trace the call. Whoever the speaker was, he was *good*.

"Fine. Where and when?"

"Good. You can be reasonable."

CHAPTER 23

THE STRANGER'S instructions took Damien to the open-air patio of an old restaurant on the outskirts of Asimov's downtown. The sign proudly announced that the Golden Hare Public House had been opened in twenty-two-sixty, which would probably make it one of the first restaurants opened in the Tau Ceti system.

It looked the part, if nothing else. There'd clearly been renovations and expansions over the nearly two centuries since the restaurant had opened, but the core structure was recognizably one of the prefabricated residences shipped out in their millions in the first wave of colonization.

Mostly metal and plastic, many of those prefabs had survived surprisingly well. The Golden Hare had clearly been successful and expanded. Damien spotted two outside seating areas, a bar, and at least two separate indoor dining areas.

Given his name, the hostess saw him onto the rooftop patio, an outside seating area built on top of the expansion of the ground floor, and to a table tucked away in a secluded back corner, out of sight of the vast majority of the patrons.

"We have a clear line of sight to the table," Amiri reported over his earbud. "We're running facial recognition scans and Romanov's team has the suit in their sights. If he tries anything, we'll drop him."

Damien sighed and shook his head. It was the only response he could make, but with the cameras, shotgun microphones, and sniper rifles trained on this rooftop, it was one he was sure Amiri saw. His body-guards had reacted to the invitation with professional paranoia, and he had the sneaky suspicion they'd done more than they'd *told* him about—and he'd been *told* about the squad's worth of Marine snipers scattered around the area.

"The suit" was an older man with shockingly white hair and pale skin, exuding an air of frailty as he rose carefully and offered Damien his hand.

"Lord Montgomery," he said, his voice the same clipped British ac-cent as on the communicator before. "Welcome. Thank you for meeting with me."

Damien left the hand hanging in the air, looking up at the taller man with cold eyes. The other man might want to fake the niceties, but he was there because of an explicit threat to an innocent. Frail-looking or not, the man could rot.

The stranger waited a moment, his hand wavering slightly, then sighed and turned his outstretched arm into a gesture of invitation at the other chair.

"We can play that way, too," he said calmly. "Sit, my lord. I insist."

Damien obeyed, though he did so carefully to make sure he could still draw the pistol concealed under his suit jacket.

"While I presumed you wouldn't be willing to have a meal with me, I did order some appetizers and wine so the waitress would leave us alone," the white-haired man told him. "I should also note, my lord, that your bodyguards won't find me in their facial recognition database. Believe me, I would not be so foolish as to meet with you if I thought you'd be able to find me."

"Most people simply choose not to threaten His Majesty's Hands," Damien told the other man quietly. "I presume you have a name?"

"Which I am not going to give you," the stranger replied. "You may call me...Winton."

"All right, Mister Winton," Damien said slowly. "You threatened an innocent young woman to get me here. I suggest you get to the point before I decide tearing the planet apart to find her is more convenient."

"Please, my lord, patience," Winton told him. "Miss Chambers is fine and will be returned unharmed so long as *I* leave here unharmed. I simply wish...ah, here are our drinks."

A young man in plain slacks and a white shirt appeared out of nowhere with a tray of freshly baked pretzels, a salty smell that assailed Damien's determination not to touch anything Winton had arranged for, and two glasses of a pale pink wine.

With his delivery complete, the waiter vanished and left Damien and Winton alone in the secluded corner.

"Well?" Damien demanded.

"Please, my lord," Winton told him, "my goal here is to find a peaceful compromise. I'll confess my brethren may have been a little...hasty at Andala. The situation had accelerated well beyond any preparations, and the man on the scene attempted to, well, *erase* it."

"Your 'brethren' tried to kill an archaeological expedition," the Hand pointed out. "That's a level of mass murder I'm not particularly inclined to write off as 'being hasty'."

"Says the man who ordered an entire city destroyed as a backup plan?" Winton asked.

"That," the Hand said carefully, "proved unnecessary and was a *last* option. Your people seemed to go to mass murder as the first one."

"The first choice was to wipe the runes before anyone saw them," Winton explained. "The lower levels weren't scheduled to be opened for another six months. We'd already arranged to control the safety inspections that would be part of that so we could make certain that the runes were destroyed before anyone who wasn't a Keeper saw them."

"Like you did with the upper levels."

"Exactly," Winton confirmed calmly. "When Kurosawa decided to ignore everyone's schedules, he threw our plans off course. Our agent on the scene acted to minimize the risk, but then that foolish grad student found the Professor before she could reseal the lower levels. "Kurosawa's actions sealed his fate. Everything that followed was unfortunate necessity."

"Kurosawa did his job and made the discovery of a lifetime—and your people murdered him. I'm not seeing the necessity here at all, let alone the 'unfortunate necessity'."

"And that is because we have done *our* job for two hundred years," Winton replied. "We have bought humanity time, protecting them from themselves, no matter the price."

"And how many have you killed for this fantasy?" Damien demanded. "You tried to kill a thousand last week. Is that a rounding error for you? Unnoticed amidst the piles of bodies you've buried in 'accidents' and 'disappearances'?"

"Less, my lord Hand, than even a most conservative estimate of what would follow if the secrets were unveiled."

"What secrets? That aliens gave humanity magic? That aliens gave the *Eugenicists* the tools to unleash their reign of terror and to carry out the *scientific* murder of tens of thousands to perfect the human Mage?"

"You're guessing," Winton pointed out. "Even your...unique gifts provide no proof."

"It's pretty damn suggestive that our runes are *identical*," Damien replied. "You're saying that you *have* proof?"

"I'm saying that you have no idea of the scope or magnitude of the shadows you begin to fumble in—and no concept of the consequences of unveiling the secrets I am sworn to keep."

"Keepers, huh?" the Hand said. "Secret Keepers?"

"The Royal Order of the Keepers of Secrets and Oaths," Winton reeled off calmly. "We serve Mars, Lord Montgomery, the same as you. We are sworn to a sacred oath to guard a deadly secret until the right time. And like you, we are sometimes called on to make harsh choices and hard sacrifices to preserve the Protectorate."

"I guard the Protectorate from real and present dangers," Damien said. "You... I don't know what you guard us from, and I question its validity."

"I can explain everything, Lord Montgomery," Winton told him. "But there is a price that must be paid."

"What, that I join your little Order?"

"Exactly. You join the Keepers, and you order everything that happened at Andala IV sealed. You *have* that authority."

"Not anymore," Damien told the stranger. "The Mage-King has already been informed. Everything I know is in his hands or will be shortly. *He* will decide what happens now—unless you think your precious 'Order' will defy our *King*."

For the first time since he'd arrived, Winton looked taken aback. He took a long moment to take a slow sip from his wine glass.

"That is unfortunate," he said quietly. "While the Order has concerns about the rule of the current Desmond, we would prefer not to move against him."

"You somehow feel you have the right to judge the Mage-King?"

"When his weakness and compromises undermine the Charter and have led us to the brink of civil war, yes," Winton said flatly. "Compromise was not how our Protectorate was built. He weakens our cause and encourages his enemies. We will allow no man, not even the Mage-King of Mars, to weaken Mars in the face of the threats to come."

"The Protectorate is built on compromise. The alternative *is* civil war."

"The Protectorate was built on force," the old man replied. "Desmond the First *imposed* the Charter; it was not a compromise. Weakness on the part of the Mage-King threatens us all and has allowed Legatus to undermine the very fabric of our civilization."

"If you think not compromising would have *weakened* Legatus's hand, you're mad," Damien told him. "Every time we make peace, every time we show another world the Protectorate fights for *everyone*, we buy ourselves friends and loyalty that will stand in the face of any threat, internal or external."

"You are young, Lord Montgomery, and naïve. Time will season you, open your eyes. Strength is required to face what is coming, and Desmond the Third does not have it," Winton said. "But a Rune Wright must sit the throne at Olympus Mons. As you have no doubt surmised by now, that amplifier wasn't built to be usable by humans. Only a Rune Wright can command its full power."

The frail old man studied Damien, who was busy processing the fact that the man clearly knew a *lot* more about Rune Wrights than anyone *not* one themselves should know. For that matter, *Damien* hadn't known the unimaginably powerful amplifier in the throne room in Olympus Mons, with its simulacrum of the entire Solar System, required a Rune Wright to function.

It made...too much sense for him to disbelieve.

"Of course," Winton said softly, "if *you* were to join the Keepers, another option would be available to secure the safety of Mars."

Damien stared at the other man, trying to parse what he was suggesting. He couldn't *possibly* mean...

"We could use one of us upon the throne," the Keeper told him bluntly. "Likely as Lord Regent, not Mage-King, but—"

The Hand had heard *enough*. Power and anger *flared* through his body and he lunged to his feet, his magic tearing Winton from his chair and suspending the man in the air by his throat.

Damien's hand, clad in black gloves as always to conceal his Runes, crooked toward Winton as the man struggled to draw breath.

"If I die," the Keeper choked out, "so does the girl."

Damien jerked convulsively, throwing the man *through* a table and into the restaurant wall as he released the magic around Winton's throat.

"I will never betray my King," he told the older man as he advanced on the wreckage. "I will *never* murder innocents or cover up your atrocities for you. I don't know what secrets you guard, but I will learn them. I don't know what resources you command, but I will break them. I will hunt the perpetrators of your crimes at Andala to the ends of the galaxy or to the heart of Mars, wherever you have hidden them, and I will burn your Order *to the ground.*"

Winton had looked frail enough *before* he'd been thrown through furniture. Now, cringing in the shattered fragments of the Golden Hare's patio table, he just looked pathetic.

"Go," Damien ordered. "But if Chambers isn't safely returned within the hour, know that I *will* find you."

The white-haired old man rose carefully to his feet, wincing as he moved.

"She'll be in her apartment in five minutes," he said harshly. "We made a deal. You won't see me again."

"So certain?" Damien said coldly.

"Yes. Even if you survive to keep your word, Lord Montgomery, you won't find me. Unlike many you have faced, I *do* know what it means for a Hand to go to war."

CHAPTER 24

MAGE-CAPTAIN Denis Romanov scanned the apartment building hallways as he made his calm, implacable way toward Roslyn Chambers's thirteenth floor apartment. He didn't spot any sign of whatever agents had dropped the girl off—*assuming* the creepy old man Montgomery had sadly not been able to choke to death had actually kept his word and returned her.

The place the young Mage had found was on par with where Denis had grown up. Cheap but well maintained, with residents and owners who clearly cared. While the apartment building was only thirty stories to the three-hundred-story building in Ireland his mother had lived in, it had the same feel of "poor but decent".

The kind of place that smart people on Mage-stipends or other social assistance lived in. The pension of a Marine Mage-Lieutenant killed in the line of duty wasn't nothing, but health had stopped his mother working.

It was only when he'd been about to sign up himself that Denis had realized that the massive friendly man at the end of the hall who'd always had candy or advice for him, whichever he'd needed, was a vet—and a Marine who'd served under his father. *No one* had been willing to tangle with the Sarge to harass Mrs. Romanov.

He smiled at the thought as he exited the stairwell onto the thirteenth floor. The last letter he'd got from his mother was that their delicate, decades-old dance had finally resolved with ex-Sergeant Wil Harrison asking Jessica Romanov to marry him. Time and past time, in her son's opinion.

Harrison had *always* been his second father, their wedding just made it official.

The hallway outside Chambers's apartment brought back less-pleasant memories. There was a still in the air, an absence of traffic and a smell like a storm about to break. A human storm. The smell was nervous sweat.

Denis paused right outside the apartment door and listened.

"Come out," he finally ordered aloud. "I can *smell* you, I can *hear* you, I may as well be able to *see* you."

Three young men, two in torn old T-shirts and jeans and one in *much* nicer clothes, a local designer label from the looks of it, emerged from around the corner. All three were carrying, the two minions with cheap revolvers that might have arrived on Tau Ceti with the colonists, and the boss with a neat little concealable auto-pistol that was *completely* illegal on Tau Ceti, even *with* a license.

"I don't know what you twinkles *think* you're up on," the leader told Denis, "but this is my vixen's hole, and the comings and goings are making me *witchy*. What up?"

Twinkles, as Denis understood current Tau Ceti slang, covered anyone in a suit or uniform that looked out of place or done up. *Vixen* he could guess. Apparently O'Kane, if the boy was who Denis thought he was, wasn't actually *aware* he was Chambers's *ex*-boyfriend.

Keeping his hands where the *idiots* could see them, he turned so that his uniform—*including* the Mage medallion at his throat, though the likelihood they knew what the swords meant was low—was fully visible.

"You would be O'Kane," he said flatly. "*I* am Marine Mage-Captain Denis Romanov. I grew up in a building like this—it seems a peaceable place and I don't want to start trouble. I *will* finish it.

"Now, the last *I* heard," he continued, "was that Roslyn told you, specifically, to fuck off. Now, normally, I suspect the young miss could enforce her own orders, but you're rubbing me the wrong way. So. Fuck. Off."

"Marine" would normally be enough. "*Mage*" would normally be enough. Apparently, O'Kane was either angrier or stupider than he looked, however, as he lifted the gun to point it at Denis's head.

His grip was better than a lot of wannabe gangsters, a proper two-handed stance that gave him enough stability that he might have even managed to *hit*.

Of course, his two flunkies *evaporated* the moment he pointed a gun at Denis, and the Marine simply smiled and snapped his fingers.

A tiny blade of force sliced the gun in half immediately in front of O'Kane's fingers, leaving the kid holding only the grip of the auto-pistol as the barrel and extended magazine clattered on the floor.

"Do I need to repeat myself?" Denis said calmly. "Chambers is now a Navy candidate, if you hadn't heard. We watch our own. Walk."

Staring at the half of a gun in his hand, the youth backpedaled several steps, then turned and fled after his minions.

Knocking on the young woman's door garnered no response, but the lock turned out to be...lacking. Making a mental note to see someone install a better lock on her door—this one hadn't kept out the Keeper agents and probably wouldn't have even stopped O'Kane—Denis hotwired it and entered the apartment in under ten seconds.

The suite was small and plain, lacking almost anything in terms of personal decoration. It had a kitchen, a sitting/dining area with cheap furniture anyone who'd grown up poor in the entire Protectorate would recognize the ancestry of, and doors leading into the bathroom—open, showing a plain white space, with a counter covered in cosmetics the only sign the apartment was lived in—and the bedroom, which was closed.

Denis rapped on the bedroom door, then, unsurprised by the lack of response, pushed it open and entered the room. The furniture was of the same ilk as that in the living room, even Chambers's bedroom lacking in much of personal touch beyond clothing strewn across the floor.

The Marine breathed a sigh of relief to see the young woman on the bed. She'd been dropped there in the same clothes she'd been in when she'd been playing distraction and, thankfully, didn't look too much the worse for wear.

Just unconscious.

Part of the light combat gear he was wearing included a pouch of various medical patches, including a stimulant patch that he figured should counteract whatever sedative they'd given her. He peeled the test patch off the back, confirmed she wasn't allergic with it, then applied the main patch to her neck.

It took a few minutes to kick in, so he carefully draped the blanket over her so she was covered, and stepped back to a distance he hoped was nonthreatening to wait.

Chambers convulsed upward after a minute, clutching the blanket to her as she stared around in panic.

"What the *fuck?*"

"You were kidnapped," Denis told her gently. "Once they'd got what they wanted from Montgomery, they dumped you at home. He sent me to check on you."

"Fuck," she repeated, then blinked as nausea clearly swept over her.

A few moments later, she was in the bathroom and Denis was calmly waiting on the couch. The *stim* wouldn't be causing this reaction this quickly, so whatever they had given her had to be nasty.

Finally, she emerged once again from the bathroom, rubbing her mouth with a towel and a faint greenish tinge to her face.

"I've probably had worse wake-ups," she admitted. "But not that I can think of. You're...Montgomery's Marine watchdog, right?"

"Close enough." He chuckled. "You okay?"

"I'll live. Last thing I remembered is being grabbed and, well"—she touched her neck—"stinging."

"Hypospray from behind," Denis concluded. "Professionals."

"What did they *want?*"

"They used you as a bargaining chip to get Montgomery to meet with them," he told her. "He did. It didn't go the way they wanted, but they let you go regardless." He smiled grimly. "I think they realized they had zero chance of hiding you from us for more than a day, so it was give you back or kill you. And the Hand would have ripped the system apart if they'd killed you."

"Why? I'm nobody," she snapped.

"They grabbed *you,* an innocent, to get to *him*. That would have been enough," the Marine pointed out. "Plus, he thinks you have potential. Signed a letter to get you into the Navy if your nose is clean at intake. Not that that seems to be getting you to *keep* your nose clean."

She sighed.

"I guess I didn't really believe him, to be honest. I ended up in juvie for a reason. Pretty much fucked up everything."

"And the Hand, for his own reasons, has staked a portion of his own personal reputation with the Navy to open a new door for you," Denis pointed out. "Though, admittedly, right now he feels guilty for dragging you into this. You weren't supposed to get *this* caught up."

"Fucking bullies," she sighed. "At every level, I guess. From tenement gang lords to government conspiracies. How do you deal?"

"You really asking me?"

"Yeah," she said after a moment's thought. "You're a soldier, an officer, a Mage. Everything I wanted to be, that you all seem to think I *can* be."

"One day at a time, one asshole at a time," he told her. "You don't stand by when someone's being pushed down. You don't walk away from someone calling for help. You put on the uniform, you face the bad guys. You check in on the poor kid who got sedated because your enemies saw a weakness," he finished with a sigh.

"No one is going to *make* you sign up," Denis reminded her. "But the Navy needs every Mage who can meet their standards, and everything I've seen says you can—if you grow up a little."

She flushed and stiffened at that.

"I can do whatever it takes," she told him.

"Good. Then you can make it five months without getting arrested or kidnapped again, can't you?"

She flipped him a very old universal hand gesture, but she was laughing as she did it. Denis would make sure a medic swung by later, but it looked like Chambers was going to be okay.

CHAPTER 25

THE NEXT MORNING saw a weary Damien Montgomery looking out the massive window of his observation-deck office aboard the battle-cruiser *Duke of Magnificence*, studying the massive shipyard tucked in behind the defensive constellation shielding Tau Ceti *e*, a large world with barely tolerable gravity, from the system's debris fields.

Where Sol and Legatus, the other key shipbuilding centers of the Protectorate, had spread their construction capacity to multiple locations across their systems, the debris danger in Tau Ceti was such that the yards were concentrated in the lee of the *e* constellation. While the Tau Ceti *System* was only the third-largest producer of sublight and jump-capable spaceships in the Protectorate, these yards *were* the biggest single *shipyard* in the Protectorate.

In the center of his view was the nearly complete hull of the Royal Martian Navy's thirteenth battleship, soon to be christened *Thunder of Glorious Freedom*. While *Thunder* had been the only battleship under construction when she was started, shortly before Damien became a Hand, he could see the skeletons of two more beginning to take shape beyond her.

Three more were under construction in Sol, along with more...covert projects. *Someone*—Damien had his guess and a lot of circumstantial evidence to back it—had tried to trigger a civil war between the system militias of two systems only a few months before. Similar agitators had been attempting to provoke planetary rebellions and crises across the Protectorate.

The Navy was expanding to deal with the threat. While some members of the Council had argued that battleships were unnecessary, that cruisers and destroyers were the best tool to keep the peace, the Mage-King commanded the Navy.

So, the battleships were being built, and a peacetime Navy slowly began to gird itself for a war they hoped they would never have to fight.

And while they did so, it fell to the Hands to make sure no one stabbed them in the back.

"So, we failed to track Winton," he concluded aloud, not turning around to look at the other people in the room with him. "I'm not entirely surprised, but how exactly did he manage it?"

"He was picked up by a black car, went downtown, mixed it up with at least a dozen other identical black cars, and then eight of those cars randomized their VIN beacons," Amiri told him, the bodyguard's voice a mix between apologetic and impressed.

"It was prearranged," she continued. "We managed to track and localize all eight cars eventually, but by then, they'd all been abandoned. VIN beacons and physical labels were destroyed and the vehicles had been flash-sanitized of any genetic traces."

"That's not a particularly survivable process for a car interior," Romanov pointed out.

"No. The cars are write-offs. It was an expensive, though effective, way of thwarting pursuit."

"Whether or not these people actually *are* a Royal Order constituted by order of one of the Mage-Kings, they have enough resources that they may as well be," Damien pointed out. "Any one of the four Talon VIIs they fired at Andala cost as much as a dozen luxury cars.

"They have funds and resources to burn, and a disturbingly accurate threat profile for *our* capabilities. Winton knew I was a Rune Wright, for example," he told them. "Captain *Romanov* was only cleared for that after I woke up. The existence of the Wrights is one of our most closely guarded secrets.

"What about Chambers?" he asked the Marine. "She's all right? Any sign of whoever dropped her off?"

"She was unconscious for the whole affair," Romanov replied. "Local cops and a couple of friends at the Asimov Marine barracks are going to keep an eye on her just in case, but she seemed like she was going to be fine.

"As for the people who dropped her off...nothing," he said flatly. "The building's security systems *exist* but are so full of holes and pre-planted worms, they probably automatically delete more footage than they save. Her return to the building isn't recorded at all."

"So, what we have learned is that our opponents are very capable, extremely well resourced, intimately tied into our own government... and that their damn ship wasn't built in Tau Ceti," Damien summarized aloud.

"We also know that the Mage-King is not involved," Amiri said grimly. "Given how much access these people seem to have, that's...not an insignificant win."

Damien winced but nodded. She wasn't wrong.

"The ship remains our best and clearest starting point," he told them. "She's a warship and a big one—the size of Sherwood's new frigates or even a bit larger. There's only so many shipyards in the galaxy that can build a six- or more million-ton starship."

"Nine, now that Sherwood has bootstrapped themselves into the list," Romanov confirmed.

"And three are in Sol," Damien finished. "Two more are in Legatus, which...well, I'm unlikely to get access to the records for either, and I don't think a conspiracy based in the Mage-King's court would buy from them anyway.

"Sol is our best bet. No one there outside the conspiracy will even consider denying a Hand, and we have His Majesty for backup." Looking away from the shipyard at last, he turned back to his staff.

"We're going to wait for the Professor to get back and for *Duke of Magnificence* to be repaired, and then proceed to Sol."

He grimaced.

"I'd prefer *not* to find my enemies in my home," he said quietly, "but I'm afraid that's *exactly* where they're hiding."

Damien found Mage-Captain Kole Jakab in his office aboard *Duke of Magnificence*, carefully rearranging the wall of medals and still images that he'd had to put away while the ship was being repaired. The *Duke's* commanding officer was a tall man, with the pale skin of a lifelong spacer for all he was Terran-born.

"Good to be home, Captain?" the Hand asked from the doorway.

"Yes," Jakab said simply. "Our yard people are the best, but you're never *sure* you'll get your command back intact when you hand her over.

"Come in." He waved Damien to a chair, smiling as he placed his Martian Cross—the RMN's second-highest award for valor—carefully in the center of the display, directly above the model of the ship.

He'd earned the Cross charging *through* hostile fire to make orbit of Ardennes to support Damien and the rebellion there. *Duke of Magnificence* had been one of the ships in position when Damien had ordered the Navy to bombard the command center if *he* failed to stop the madman who'd rigged bombs to blow up six of the planet's largest cities.

Jakab hadn't had to follow that order, as Damien had succeeded in stopping General Montoya from killing tens of millions of people himself, but the Hand would always have a soft spot for the ships that had stood ready anyway.

"You know you're going to have to shuffle that aside shortly, right?" Damien asked the Mage-Captain, gesturing to the Cross. "His Majesty has every intention of pinning the Solar Star on you as soon as we're back at Mars. After Antonius and the pirate rendezvous point..." He shook his head. "You earned it."

"I disagree, personally," Jakab replied. "I did my job."

The Solar Star was the Royal Martian Navy's *highest* award for valor, only awarded at the discretion of the Mage-King himself. Hands and Admirals could recommend it—and Damien had, in Jakab's case—but only Desmond the Third could decide to actually award it.

"We stopped a war, Kole," Damien told him. "His Majesty's already hung the only honor I'll take from him on me, so he's going to stick the Star on you."

"It is unwise to argue with one's King," Jakab admitted with a sigh.

"It is?" Damien asked with a smile. "I do it a lot. It's part of my job."

"And hence why you can get away with it," the Mage-Captain told him, shaking his head as he made his way to his desk and gestured for Damien to sit. "What can I do for you, my lord?"

"Our investigations here have mostly drawn a blank," the Hand admitted. "It's time for me to return to Mars and for our investigation into the attack on Andala IV to proceed in Sol. Given the events in Andala, I'd rather return aboard *Duke*. How long until she's ready to fly?"

"We made it here under our own power," Jakab pointed out. "I could kick all of the yard staff out and be underway in twelve hours."

"Which will leave you short, what? A quarter of your missile launchers still?" Damien asked.

"They're all *installed*," the Captain replied. "We could do the final hookups ourselves."

"Assuming I let you finish your repairs, how long until you can fly?"

"A week," Jakab told him. "We're already at the point where all of the work that requires the hull to be open is done. We're mostly on aligning and hookups now, but when you're talking about systems that handle gigaton-range warheads, this needs to be done carefully."

"We can spare a week," Damien said. "I'm waiting on Professor Christoffsen anyway; he wasn't planning on being back until your repairs were done, anyway."

"Our repairs will be complete on schedule," the Captain replied. "We can accelerate a few days if needed."

"A week is fine, Captain."

"Thank you, my lord." Jakab paused. "You and your staff are back aboard then?"

"We are," Damien confirmed. "We're...still short Secret Service people until we're back on Mars, so I'm probably going to keep Romanov for a bit."

"That's fine," the Captain told him. "You'll also want to meet with Lieutenant-Commander Anita Torres. She's the head of your new flag deck staff." The Captain smiled. "I took the liberty of arranging for us to take on a military team for you as we finished repairs; Torres is actually on the flag deck now, checking to see if she needs to make any changes or updates while we still have a shipyard at hand."

Damien had completely forgotten about the suggestion that he take on a Navy staff to support his security team and political staff and allow him to fully utilize *Duke of Magnificence*'s flag deck instead of interfering directly from Jakab's bridge.

"Well, that sounds like the best place for me to touch base with her," he said. "Do you need anything from me, Captain?"

"Not today," the cruiser commander replied. "I'd like to be briefed on whatever you have on the ship at Andala before we leave, though. Somehow, I suspect I'll be meeting her."

Despite having lived aboard *Duke of Magnificence* for almost a year, Damien had only set foot on the flag deck once, when he'd received his initial tour. He was very familiar with the regular bridge, though, and the flag deck was one short stairwell away.

The two major command centers for the warship were ninety seconds' brisk walk apart. At a run, abusing magic to control gravity, Damien figured he could make it under twenty if he had to. Since the bridge was also the simulacrum chamber that allowed access to the amplifier, that wasn't an irrelevant point.

Like the bridge, the flag deck was sealed away behind heavy security hatches. Seeing them open for once, Damien realized he'd walked *past* the flag deck at least a dozen times without realizing it was there—closed hatches, even security ones, were not uncommon enough aboard the ship to draw attention on their own.

Today, though, the hatch was open and a fire team of four Marines stood guard outside it. All four wore the shoulder flashes of Romanov's new company, which had been all but permanently assigned to Damien's security. Having an entire company of over a hundred of Mars's finest ground troops acting as glorified bodyguards bothered him, but he was no longer able to pretend he *didn't* need security.

"Lieutenant-Commander Torres is inside, my lord," the Corporal in charge informed him. "We're to keep everyone else out until she's finished her inspection."

"Does that include me?" Damien asked.

"She didn't exempt you, but we work for you, not her," the NCO pointed out with a laugh. "Go right on in."

With a smile, Damien strode past the Marines and into *Duke of Magnificence*'s flag deck. It was a smaller room than he'd perhaps expected, only about two thirds the size of the bridge below it and circular where the amplifier matrix required the bridge to be the same shape as the ship.

While the flag deck lacked the runes that linked the bridge into the amplifier, it had been otherwise designed in a similar fashion. The floor, walls and ceiling were covered in high-resolution screens that, when active, would show the world outside the ship as if you were suspended in deep space. Right now, they were turned off, faded to a dull gray that told no one anything.

A ring of consoles around the outside of the room showed where the Admiral's—or in this case, Damien's—support staff would work. A spherical hologram tank, easily three meters across, sat at the exact center of the flag deck, with a large chair festooned with controls next to it for the Admiral themselves to control the main display.

Unlike the all-surrounding displays, the holographic tank was online. The three-dimensional image was split into thirds. One third of it was showing an update on a self-diagnostic, another third showed space around *Duke of Magnificence*, and the last was focused on the construction slips for *Thunder* and her sisters.

Sitting in the Admiral's chair was a dumpy woman with dark frizzy hair in a Navy uniform. She wasn't *quite* overweight, but she was probably pushing even the Navy's physical fitness requirements. She was focused on the holographic tank, her gaze and attention flickering between

sections even as she used the controls in the command chair to manipulate the data in front of her.

"Lieutenant-Commander Torres, I take it?" Damien said loudly when
he realized she wasn't paying enough attention to see him standing there.

Torres jerked upright, flinging herself out of the chair into a credible
approximation of full attention and a sharp salute.

"My lord Hand! I didn't see you there."

"At ease, Torres," Damien said dryly. "I'm hardly offended you took
my chair. How's the flag deck looking?"

For a moment, it looked like the woman was trembling, and then she
managed to get herself mostly under control.

"We'll need to do some work," she finally told him. "*Duke*'s flag deck
hasn't been actively operated since she was commissioned, and it looks
like she missed an entire generation of hardware updates. The software
updates are straightforward and the main display is usable, but we need
to tear out *all* of the support consoles."

"How long and what's the difference?" Damien asked.

"Some of it's only incremental improvements, and most of the processing power pulls from *Duke* herself, but the updates can easily make a
twenty percent improvement in the efficiency of your staff," she told him
crisply. "Perhaps more important is that the staff I'm bringing over to
support you is used to working with the new equipment and will face a
noticeable learning curve catching up to the old gear."

"And how long to replace them?" he repeated.

"Five days," she replied. "They're canned modules; I can have the old
ones out and the new ones in before the rest of the repairs are done."

Impressed, Damien nodded.

"Go ahead, then," he ordered. If nothing else, it would give him the
ability to assess the ability of his new naval chief of staff. "Now we've covered the hardware, yourself."

"Myself?" she asked.

"I am sure that with the Navy's usual efficiency, I will at some point
receive your full record," he said. "I haven't yet. Summarize for me.
Where were you transferred from, and what are your qualifications?"

Torres swallowed and nodded.

"I was promoted to Lieutenant-Commander six weeks ago," she began. "Prior to that, I was the junior operations officer for Mage-Admiral Segal's staff for two years. Before that, I was junior tactical officer aboard the destroyer *Just Sword of Freedom.*

"Mage-Admiral Segal selected me personally to command your staff less than a week ago," she noted. "I...understand that I replaced someone else he didn't know directly. I am not sure of the reasons why, but I was told you would understand."

It seemed Mage-Admiral Segal was starting to share Damien's paranoia.

"I have two years' experience as direct deputy to Mage-Admiral Segal's Chief of Staff as we operated the Tau Ceti Station," she continued. "While I am certain there are more qualified officers available, the Mage-Admiral selected me as...a matter of trust."

"The Mage-Admiral understands my top concern at the moment," he told her. "What about the staff you're bringing with you?"

"I have four junior officers and sixteen technicians who will be joining us inside the next five days," she replied. "All sixteen ratings and petty officers are being transferred directly from Mage-Admiral Segal's staff. Two of the officers are from there as well; the other two are from *Righteous Guardian of Liberty* with Mage-Commodore Adamant's compliments.

"My understanding was that our priority was to find competent personnel we trusted completely," she finished. "My lord..." She paused. "I've always assumed that Navy personnel could be trusted, but the Mage-Admiral was acting like we couldn't trust anyone we didn't know ourselves. What's going on?"

"Send in your order for the flag deck repairs," Damien ordered. "Then meet me in my office. If you're going to work for me, Lieutenant-Commander, it appears we're going to have to fully brief you."

CHAPTER 26

DAMIEN SPENT the week waiting for something else to go wrong. To his surprise, it went without incident or interruption. Torres saw to the updating of the flag deck and the arrival of his new Navy staff with practiced efficiency. The repairs to the battlecruiser progressed around him, and finally, on the day before the repairs were supposed to be complete, Dr. Robert Christoffsen finally returned aboard.

When the pudgy, balding older man finally arrived in Damien's office, the Hand looked him over critically. Christoffsen held multiple PhDs in political and legal science and had been Governor of the Tara System—a Core World—earlier in life.

Now the Hand's political advisor, he was into his nineties, and even a few weeks seemed to have sapped his vitality.

"Are you all right, Professor?" he asked.

"My vacation in the sun and waves on Tara turned into a week-long emergency consultation with the latest Governor," Christoffsen told him. "My successor had a heart attack on us, and his Vice-Governor felt...unsure of herself. A week of backing her up seems to have everything back on an even keel, but it was hardly *relaxing*."

"No rest for the wicked, I see," Damien said. "You're not exactly coming back to work at the easiest time, either."

"I reviewed the briefing paper your Torres pulled together," the political advisor noted. "I assume there are aspects she wasn't cleared for?"

"I brushed over how we survived the bombardment and how I knew the runes were Martian Runic," Damien admitted. "She's not aware of the existence of Rune Wrights, and until *I'm* more comfortable with her, that isn't changing. Unfortunately, it appears our enemies *are* aware of Rune Wrights—and that I am one."

"That's a complicating factor," Christoffsen agreed. He grabbed a chair and took a seat, eyeing the construction yards through the observation window. "A lot of complicating factors this time around. A conspiracy at the heart of Mars?"

"I don't exactly want to believe it myself," Damien admitted.

His political aide laughed.

"Politics on Mars aren't pretty, my young friend," Christoffsen told him. "There's cabals and parties and factions galore. If you were going home to rest, they wouldn't be your problem. Desmond is perfectly capable of handling them himself.

"But if we're going *hunting* on Mars, you can't afford to be politically naïve," he finished flatly. "It sounds like our enemies hide in the Mountain, which makes this whole mess even more politically charged."

Damien stepped up to the transparent steel of his office window and looked out over the yards once again. From there, the core space station that guarded the yards and Tau Ceti *e* was clearly visible, a sign of the power and will of humanity overcoming *any* danger.

"Give me the highlights," he ordered.

"That could take a week."

"We don't have that kind of time," Damien said. "Skim the top for me."

The ex-Governor sighed.

"Remember that every conflict in the Protectorate seems to come to Mage versus Mundane," he said. "The Compact gives Mages certain rights and responsibilities, and whether they are too much or not enough is a constant source of tension.

"*Mirroring* that tension has always been the push-and-pull between the Council of the Protectorate and the Mage-King. One hundred and five Councilors, one for each world. They technically serve an advisory purpose and the Mage-King decides everything, as limited by the Charter and his ability to convince the system governments to buy in.

"In practice, Desmond and his father have both used the Council to make sure that the system governments will buy in, and the Council has effectively been writing our legislation for fifty years. *That*, however, is not part of their role under the *Charter*, so it's entirely at the Mage-King's discretion."

Christoffsen fiddled with his PC for a moment and threw a projection on the window of the one hundred and five worlds of the Protectorate, highlighting sections as he kept speaking.

"Forty-five of the Councilors are either directly loyal to the Mage-King or in agreement with his current agenda," he noted. "Those forty-five will usually vote as he wants. Fourteen are from the UnArcana worlds. They're fighting us on everything right now."

"They can't really admit that Legatus is behind our current spate of rebellions and piracy, can they?" Damien asked.

"No, they claim to just want us to spend less money," Christoffsen said dryly. "They have some support in that, but it's the system governments who have the right to deny the Navy funding—and they're all *terrified*."

"So, we have Loyalists and the UnArcana blocs." Damien tapped the lit up symbols on the window. "That's barely half the Council. Who else?"

"The Legislaturists," his aide replied. "They're going to be the problem. They're the ones who want to rewrite the Charter to explicitly give the Council the right to write legislation, not the Mage-King. The *smart* ones realize Desmond has to have a veto, but *some* appear to think that the *Council* should be the true government of the Protectorate, not the Mage-King.

"There are thirty-six Legislaturists," he concluded. "The remaining ten Councilors are more concerned with their planets' needs than the Council's infighting."

"So, that's the ground I'm on," Damien said quietly.

"It's more than that, Damien. Remember that many see you as not merely a Hand but as an adoptive member of the Alexander family," Christoffsen told him. "You are young for a Hand, photogenic, and keep

GLYNN STEWART

acting like a goddamn hero. You are the single most visible symbol of the monarchy after Desmond the Third himself.

"Everything you do in Sol will reflect not merely on the Mountain but directly on Alexander himself. You walk into dangerous waters, with shadowy enemies, and every eye on you." The older man shook his head. "I'm not sure I can guide you through this minefield, Damien."

"We'll do the best we can and deal with the consequences as they fall," the Hand said. "Do you know anything about this Royal Order of the Keepers of Secrets and Oaths?"

"No," the other man admitted. "If there are any records of them any-where, it's in the Archives at Olympus Mons. Unfortunately, I'm forced to agree with His Majesty—it is entirely possible that his grandfather *did* create this Order and *did* task them to keep everything we knew about these aliens secret."

"They suggested they might have to overthrow Desmond now he was hunting them," Damien pointed out. "I don't care *how* different Desmond the Third and the First are, I doubt the man who established a monarchy at the point of a Mage-led battle fleet would tolerate anyone turning on his grandson."

"No," Christoffsen agreed. "We'll deal with them, Damien."

"Of course we will," the Hand replied with a confidence he didn't feel. "That's the damned job, isn't it?"

CHAPTER 27

WHEN *DUKE OF MAGNIFICENCE* finally made her way out of the repair slip that had been her home for over a month, rebuilding the armor, systems and weapons lost under Damien's command, the Hand was aboard her flag deck, watching everything take place around him.

Despite the upgrades, the room didn't *look* particularly different to him. The big holo-tank in the center had been left unchanged, as had the command chair with its touch screens and displays, now linked into his personal computer.

One of the consoles that formed a ring around the holo-tank was Torres's—the one with the nicest chair, apparently—but for the moment, she was standing next to Damien, walking him through the menus for his chair's screens and the big tank itself.

"The menus and commands are kept as intuitive as possible," she told him. "They're designed for Admirals and such who..." She paused, clearly searching for a polite way to describe it. "Who don't have time to take retraining courses," she concluded.

Damien chuckled. That was a polite way of pointing out that Admirals were not the easiest beasts to direct and generally would want things shaped to *them* instead of the other way around.

"It's simpler than the controls to fly *Duke* herself, and I can do that," he pointed out. "I'll be fine, and if I'm not"—he gestured at the junior officers and enlisted who now held stations at the consoles—"there are a dozen of you here to help me through it."

She also chuckled, but hovered for a bit longer. A few moments of attempting to bring up a tactical plot of the system later, and he'd managed to bring up a schematic of *Duke of Magnificence*'s sensor systems.

"Fair," he conceded. "All right, Commander. Show me how to bring up the system plot."

Torres went through the iconography carefully but quickly, both bringing up the plot *and* leaving Damien comfortable he could do it himself if he needed to. And as a bonus, he also knew how to bring up a sensor schematic!

Clear of the fragile struts and repair pods of the immense shipyard complex at last, *Duke* rotated on his display as the big ship oriented itself on its final destination. The cruiser was an immense pyramid, four hundred meters tall and two hundred and ten meters square at the base, festooned with weapons of half a dozen kinds, and massing over twelve million tons unfueled.

A notice flashed up on Damien's chair screens, noting that the ship was going to full acceleration, a thirty-second notice proclaimed over the PA system everywhere aboard the ship *except* the bridge and flag deck.

The countdown flickered to zero and the image of *Duke* on the system plot began to move faster. At ten gravities flank acceleration, the yards drifted away behind them.

With his Gift, Damien could feel the magic pulsing through the floorboards, the gravity runes that fixed gravity in the ship at one gee shifting their power flow to reduce acceleration instead of creating gravity.

Duke was a well-built ship just out of a repair yard, with plenty of energy fed into the runes. Ten gravities was her designed flank acceleration, intended to carry her out to deep space, where gravity wouldn't interfere with the jump.

While Navy Mages with access to an amplifier could jump from and to a planet's orbit, it wasn't particularly *safe*. With a Hand's power behind it, such a jump could be done with relative simplicity, but it was still easier to take the just over two hours, in this case, to get twenty light-seconds clear.

It was, Damien had to concede, far more comfortable to watch the trip out aboard the flag deck than crammed into one of the—intentionally, he was sure—uncomfortable observer chairs on the bridge. And unlike his observation deck office, the flag deck actually had all of the video feeds, scanner data, and information available on the bridge. Including, though he didn't intend to *use* it outside of an actual battle, the ability to have the holographic tank show a miniature of the bridge in real time.

A full flag deck staff was probably excessive for his needs, though, he concluded as the ship made its trek outward. He really just needed enough people to keep the lights on and answer his questions.

The counterargument, he knew, was that his *last* mission had ended up with an entire fleet being commanded from *Duke of Magnificence*'s bridge. Hardly an efficient solution.

With a small sigh, he settled back into the chair to watch the trip out of Tau Ceti. The amount of loose rock drifting around the system required the defenses that protected the planets and made for messy navigation, but no one would deny it also made for a gorgeous view.

"I'm sorry for springing everything on you in one shot," the recorded image of Mikael Riordan, Governor-Elect of Ardennes, said. "It's easy to see how *tough* you are and assume, well, that you can take anything. And"—he sighed—"I didn't want to lose you. I figured putting all my cards on the table was the best plan."

Julia's boyfriend was a mousy man, of average height with brown hair loosely streaked with gray. Nothing about him would ever stand out in a crowd—not until you heard him *speak*.

She'd seen him captivate rooms when she'd been on Ardennes and met him during the rebellion there. Returning at the tail end of the election for Governor, she'd seen him enthrall *cities*. His vision of a better future, of an Ardennes that took the benefits of its years under a robber baron but built a happier, wiser world with them, could entrance *her*.

"I got your message, obviously," he continued with a small smile. "I know the thought is intimidating—you of all people know how much the governorship terrifies me! But...someone has to do it.

"People seem willing to listen to me, and I don't have it in me to walk away," he said. "I love you, but I know we haven't had that much time together, and I'm not just asking you to settle down in an estate and raise a swarm of kids—but then, you wouldn't be interested if I was, would you?

Julia attempted to imagine herself and Mikael with a big fancy house and a half-dozen children, and chuckled. While the image had a lot less revulsion than she would have expected, it certainly wasn't one either of them fit into.

"I'll be honest, Julia," he continued, "if you want to pass on the Minister for Defense, that's fine. I just want you here, with me. Unfortunately...if you marry me, you *are* the First Lady of Ardennes.

"And you know we need an outsider at Defense," he concluded. "If you don't want the job, I'm going to have to see if I can poach someone from the Navy." He shook his head. "And while the Navy *stopped* that madwoman, there's more than a few people here who don't trust anyone in the uniform right now.

"You don't need to decide straight away," he told her. "We have time—I won't be sworn in until the end of November. If there's some way you can come back before then, even if you haven't decided...I know your job doesn't run on a schedule."

He sighed and blew a soft kiss at the screen.

"Let me know, Julia. I can wait. I *will* wait. Just...let me know."

The message ended and Julia Amiri was left looking at a blank space where the hologram had been. The recording had arrived in a naval mail drop before they'd left Tau Ceti, and she'd taken a full day to getting around to watching it.

She was willing to marry Mikael Riordan. She hadn't been sure of that when she *left* Ardennes in such a hurry, but her impatient waiting for his message—and fear-driven procrastination after she *had* it—was enough for someone as self-aware as Julia to be sure of that.

Marriage hadn't exactly been in her life plans at any point, and certainly not since her brother and bounty-hunter crew had died and she'd somehow ended up in the Protectorate's Secret Service.

Minister for Defense, much as she didn't think she was *qualified* for the job, was in many ways more to her taste. First Lady she could take or leave, though she knew that Mikael would back her when *she* chose her duties.

She found herself missing Alaura Stealey. That Hand had dragged both her and Montgomery in from the cold, stood them up, brushed them off, and showed them how to make the galaxy a better place.

"What would Alaura do?" Julia murmured aloud, then smiled. Alaura Stealey would do whatever would help the most people.

Damien Montgomery had a *lot* of power to change the world and desperately needed a minder, an older and wiser mind to keep him on track and aware of the world around him. She knew, with harsh certainty, that Montgomery was *more* effective with her.

But was he enough more effective to offset the good she could do on Ardennes?

Julia sighed.

That wasn't a question she could answer on her own, and only one person could help her find the answer.

She found Montgomery in the observation deck he'd converted into his office. For a man who lived a surprisingly ascetic lifestyle, the fact that he'd claimed a massive space with transmuted steel windows seemed odd...until you realized that the cruiser had *three* such spaces and the loss of one had barely been noticed by the crew.

It was a luxury he could allow himself without hurting someone else, though it was certainly *possible* the young Hand hadn't thought it all the way through. She doubted, though, that Montgomery would have taken over the space if it had been *Duke's* only observation deck.

Montgomery stood with his back to the door, seemingly unaware of her presence. While the Marines and Secret Service Agents outside the door would never have let a threat into his space *quietly*, the woman responsible for his safety still hoped he was paying more attention than it looked.

Past him, she could see the glitter of stars in open space. Sixteen hours into their trip—two thirds of the twelve-light-year voyage—they were far enough from either star that they could truly be called lost in the void. More stars were visible there, with no close-by star to hide them, than could possibly be seen with the naked eye in any star system.

"No sun. No worlds. Yet we're almost as lit up as we would be at, say, Jupiter," Montgomery finally said after a moment's silence. Apparently, he *was* aware of her. "I never tire of looking at the stars. Grew up wondering what was out there.

"Now I'm wondering if we really want to know." He sighed. "You're not here to listen to me moan, Julia. What's up?"

Julia grabbed one of the several rolling chairs that had ended up in random corners of the office, and took a seat.

"You know I came back from Ardennes early," she reminded him. "It...wasn't because I'd heard you were injured. That news reached Ardennes about six hours after I left, from what I can tell."

"Ah," Montgomery said calmly. "Something went wrong?"

"Something went...awry," she replied. "Mikael proposed, the night he won the election. Wanted me to marry him...be First Lady...and he'd already asked me to be Minister for Defense."

"I can see the logic on the Minister for Defense," the Hand said slowly. "Normally, you most definitely *don't* want an outsider in that role, but with your candidates tarred by either serving Vaughn or being rebels..."

"Exactly his argument," she sighed.

"Since you're not handing me a resignation, I'm guessing there's more to it."

"I... I wasn't expecting it," Julia admitted. "I panicked. I ran. Give me a firefight or an assassin, I can handle that. A marriage proposal? Apparently, that was a flanking maneuver I wasn't ready for."

Her boss visibly winced and finally turned away from the window.

"Didn't say no, didn't say yes," he concluded. In the faded light from the stars behind him, the Hand looked even older than his thirty

194

standard years. Wiser, somehow, than his youthful features made him look.

Or maybe that was just what she *wanted* him to be.

"Do you need me to tell you I can't function without you?" he asked quietly. "To tell you you can do more good here than you could there?"

She laughed softly.

"It would make my choice easier," she admitted. "But I get the feeling I'd be asking you to lie."

"You can make a huge difference here, Julia," Montgomery told her. "With you at my back, I fear no threat, no enemy. I value your advice; I value your skills at arms..."

"But."

"But," he agreed with a nod. "I have other advisors. Political, military, even Romanov for small-team tactics now. I have other guardians— Romanov isn't Secret Service, but he does good work. There are Secret Service Senior Agents who'd do the job. I'm sure you could even find one *you* trusted to take over.

"Ardennes?" he shrugged. "The most qualified people served in Vaughn's military and government. Even those Riordan might trust, his *people* wouldn't. The rest were in the Freedom Wing, unacceptable to much of the government and, frankly, to the Protectorate.

"He could grab a Navy officer, but unless they were one of the captains from the Battle of Ardennes, Cor's shadow will hang over them.

"But all of Ardennes knows you," he concluded. "They remember you, in the heart of the battle, liberating the Bastille, standing at *my* side when we proclaimed Vaughn's defeat. You'd be welcomed, loved, even adored."

"There was a time it wouldn't have mattered," she said quietly. "I joined Stealey for revenge. I wouldn't have expected it to end here."

"She left a mark on the lives of all who met her," Montgomery agreed. "She showed us...that we could be better. That we could make *the galaxy* better. She'd say to go where you'd do the most good."

"And that's Ardennes," Julia admitted with a sigh. "My Lord Montgomery, will you accept my resignation?"

"Can you stay until this mess is over?" he asked. "I'm walking into a snake pit; I'd rather do it with my strong right arm at my side."

"I can stay," she promised. "But I'll need to let Riordan know. He can plan the damn wedding for when I get back—I just need to make *damned* sure he knows I'm not wearing a dress!"

CHAPTER 28

DAMIEN WOKE to a loud klaxon he'd never heard in his quarters before. He had finally managed to get to sleep, trying to get some rest before arriving in Sol, where he was going to get very busy very quickly, but now bolted upright in his small quarters near his office.

Since he mostly lived in the office, the room was barely large enough to hold a bed, a side table and a closet, and echoed *painfully* with the emergency klaxon.

"Battle stations," a voice announced as the klaxon cut off. "All hands report to battle stations. This is not a drill. All hands report to battle stations."

Damien grabbed his wrist PC from the side table and pinged the bridge.

"This is Montgomery. What's going on?" he asked.

"My lord, we're at Tau Ceti–Sol Jump Ten and we have an unidentified ship maneuvering aggressively," Jakab told him. "We don't have a clean enough scan to say if she's our mystery ship from Andala, but anyone *inside* missile range and maneuvering at me makes me twitchy."

"I agree," Damien replied. The Mage-Captain didn't need his approval to take the ship to battle stations—or even to defend himself if attacked. Opening fire *preemptively*, though, would be better done with the Hand's authorization.

"Our bogey's at ten million kilometers. That's *inside* our missile range, but if she's only got the half-dozen launchers she fired at TK-421, there's no way she can hurt us," Jakab pointed out.

"And how many missiles would *you* have launched to take out an armed courier?" Damien asked.

"*Maybe* ten," the Mage-Captain said with a snort. "I take your point, my lord."

"Do whatever you feel is necessary, Kole," the Hand ordered. "I'll be on the flag deck in three minutes."

It was the first time the Hand had ever had to make it to the flag deck in a rush, and he took over thirty seconds longer than he had told Jakab. It hadn't made *too* much difference—the strange ship was accelerating at roughly twelve gravities and had already been moving at a fair velocity toward *Duke*, but they'd still carved less than a light-second off the range.

"What's our status, Torres?" he asked as he settled into the command chair. The Lieutenant-Commander might have been on the flag deck when everything went down, but he wasn't certain. It was entirely possible she'd made it there well ahead of him.

"Range is just under nine point eight million kilometers," she replied. "Flight time for *our* missiles is six and a half minutes. No idea what they might have; CIC still hasn't confirmed an ID."

"Thank you." He brought up the tactical plot in the main holo-tank, an empty-looking display with only two icons on it. A few more taps zoomed in on the strange ship, allowing him to study what data they had.

As he did so, he *saw* the refresh of new data come through and the amorphous blob from the previous scans resolve itself into a familiar odd-looking bullet shape.

"Jakab, that's it," he snapped into the communicator.

"We see it, too," the Mage-Captain confirmed. "Sir...it's your call. She likely has comparable *weapons* to us, but she's only half our size. We've got her outgunned. Do we engage or wait to see what she does?"

There was, Damien reflected, a chance that the other ship was here by coincidence and it wasn't hostile. There was even a possibility that it *wasn't* the ship from Andala...except that no ship like it existed in the records of the Royal Martian Navy, and the vessel was very clearly maneuvering to engage *Duke of Magnificence*.

"No, Captain," he said quietly. "That ship is guilty of, if nothing else, the attempted murder of a Hand and a thousand innocents. If they choose to surrender, we'll talk, but I am *not* okay with that ship in weapons range of me. Engage at your discretion, Kole. Take the fucker down."

"My lord," the Mage-Captain acknowledged gruffly. He turned on the screen to focus on the rest of his bridge crew.

"All right folks, you heard the Hand," he snapped. "Carver—run the turrets, full defense; assume we're facing Phoenix VIIIs. These bastards seem to have the *rest* of our gear.

"Commander Rhine," he addressed his tactical officer. "Full salvo, all launchers. Fire when ready!"

Damien's current link to the bridge was a small screen on his chair, limiting his ability to see anyone's reaction to the orders from Jakab, but he saw the results of *Rhine's* actions on the main holographic tank with the tactical display.

A fountain of new icons emerged from *Duke*, dozens of missiles flashing across space at twelve and a half thousand gravities. Even at those tremendous accelerations, it would take them over six minutes to cross the void between the two ships.

Twenty seconds after *Duke* launched, a second flurry of icons emerged from the *other* ship.

"That's not right," he murmured.

"They launched before we did," Torres confirmed aloud. "They must have realized we'd have identified them from the active scans."

"Damn. What am I seeing, Torres?" Damien asked. Even as he spoke, though, he was fiddling with his controls, zooming in on the missiles and reviewing the data they had.

"Twelve point five kilo-gees," she said crisply. "Forty-five missiles. We're losing them to sensor jamming already—if they're not Phoenix Eights, they're close enough in capability to make no difference."

Damien did the mental equivalent of sitting on his hands. Mage-Captain Jakab knew better how to fight his ship than the Hand did.

GLYNN STEWART

"Steiner," Jakab snapped at his navigator. "Evasive maneuvers, if you please, and take us toward the bastard. Fifteen gravities."

Both ships were moving now, though everything they saw of the enemy was delayed more than thirty seconds. Fields of jamming swept out from the ships and the missiles, causing the tactical plot to surround every icon with a shaded probability zone where it *could* be.

Duke came under threat first, the missiles sweeping into the engagement zone of her Rapid-Fire Laser Anti-Missile turrets at over fifteen percent of lightspeed.

This was the environment an *Honorific*-class battlecruiser was *built* for, and a hundred RFLAM turrets flared to life. Their beams were invisible to the naked eye and the cameras that covered the flag decks walls with the view of the outside world.

The tactical plot drew them in automatically as tiny lines of white light. Every half-second, each RFLAM fired a tenth-second pulse at a missile. Lines flashed and appeared on the tactical plot with eye-searing speed, many of those flashes ending in explosions visible to the naked eye.

None of the missiles made it closer than a million kilometers, the gigaton explosions of their deaths three seconds or more old by the time the light reached *Duke of Magnificence.*

Their own missiles did better. The enemy ship had a full defensive suite, easily comparable to *Duke*'s in quantity though not quality. The weaker lasers, equivalent to those the Navy mounted on destroyers, couldn't engage nearly as far out as *Duke*'s defenses.

Watching the sensor data, Damien found himself holding his breath as the missiles carved their fiery path through the Keeper ship's defenses. Antimatter explosions marked the trail as missile after missile died—but over a quarter of the missiles closed to within a single light-second of the strange ship.

Then *something* flashed across the hologram, the computer unable to interpret the sensor data into anything useful, and a third of the missiles disappeared. A few seconds later, more energy flared, and this time Damien recognized it before the computer could.

"Amplifier," he said aloud. "Watch their closing rate, Captain Jakab. They have an amplifier."

"That's...a problem," *Duke*'s Captain said slowly as the last of his missiles vanished. He was silent for a moment.

"My lord Hand, we've never tested our counter-amplifier combat doctrine," he admitted. "Closest we came was Ardennes, and that was over before anyone was in amplifier range."

Damien nodded and leaned back in his chair.

"No one else knows any better either," he told his ship's commander. "Fight your ship, Mage-Captain."

The first missiles salvos had each been launched on their own, with no follow-up, to test the defenses of the other ship.

Duke of Magnificence was capable of emptying her magazines before her first missiles reached their maximum range. Testing the enemy's defenses before launching follow-on salvos wasn't always necessary, but in a situation with an unknown enemy, it could be valuable.

If the situation hadn't already suggested to Damien they'd be facing an enemy who'd read the same playbook, the matching test salvos would have been a strong indicator.

Now, with a solid idea of what they faced, *Duke*'s missile launchers spun to life again. Eighty missiles blasted into space, followed thirty seconds later by another eighty as the launchers reloaded at their fastest rate.

Icons began to speckle the display around the enemy ship as well as the light from their answering launches reached *Duke*. Two launches flared into space...and then Damien blinked in surprise as, suddenly, there were *two* Keeper vessels on the screen, the second emerging from a bright jump flare almost six million kilometers closer than the other.

"Picard Maneuver," he heard Jakab bark. "Steiner—*laser* evasive, now! Rhine, Carver—redirect what missiles you can; get our lasers on target!"

The Captain had barely finished giving his orders when the twelve-million-ton battlecruiser *lurched* like a drunken Marine, a laser beam slamming into the ship with brutal power, vaporizing a massive gash across the hull. Red lights started flashing all across one of the displays on Damien's chair as the ship took critical damage once more.

"My *gods*, that was a twenty-gigawatt beam," Torres exclaimed. "Those are *battleship* weapons—she only hit with one, but..."

Damien could read the damage display and understood Torres's unfinished sentence. That one hit had done more damage than the multiple near misses that had sent the cruiser into Tau Ceti's yards for a month. The schematic of the ship on his screens had a huge swathe of red and yellow marking sections the computer guessed destroyed or damaged.

"Kole?" he said quietly.

"They got us good, Montgomery," the Mage-Captain said in a strained voice. "We're evading, they won't land another hit like that until we're in basically amplifier range, but those lasers...I don't know if the old girl can *take* another solid hit. We're down a quarter of our launchers and the same of both our defensive and offensive lasers. They're stacking their earlier salvos with new salvos, doubling up the numbers."

Now that the light from the "original" ship had caught up, Damien could see what Jakab had meant by "Picard Maneuver." The enemy ship had made a twenty-light-second jump, dropping them eleven light-seconds away from *Duke*, allowing them to attack with lasers by surprise and stack new missile launches on top of old.

Damien was a trained Jump Mage, augmented with Runes of Power and more intimately familiar with the works of the amplifier and the jump spell than most Mages alive...and he wasn't sure he could have pulled off that jump.

The computer drew the invisible beams of the multi-gigawatt lasers in the tank for the humans, but both ships were now evading. While hits could be deadly at this range, the likelihood of hitting when your knowledge of the target's location was ten seconds out of date was low.

Watching the deadly dance of starship and laser beams, it took Damien a moment to realize there were no more incoming missiles.

Duke continued to belch out over fifty missiles every thirty seconds, but after the stranger had launched two final salvos, timed to coincide with her previous weapons, they'd stopped firing missiles.

"Rhine got her!" Torres snapped, drawing Damien's attention back to the laser fire. One of *Duke*'s twelve-gigawatt lasers had connected with the enemy ship. The battlecruiser's beams were lighter, but with five times as many in play, Jakab's people had a far better chance to hit.

Icons updated on the screen, notes attached to the enemy ship in the massive holographic tank, assessing the damage and pointing out the gas venting.

"Anything we took out doesn't matter at this point," the Hand said quietly. "Not enough damage to take out the amplifier, and all six lasers are still firing."

"Might help the missiles," Torres replied. "Gods know *we* could use help *against* theirs."

The double-stacked salvos had now entered the outer perimeter of *Duke*'s defense zone and the remaining RFLAM turrets were engaging. The gouge through the cruiser's armor and weapons told in the paucity of her defenses. Instead of the hundred laser turrets that had handily downed forty-five missiles, less than seventy now faced *ninety*.

On the screen showing the bridge, Damien watched Mage-Captain Jakab go from sitting in his command chair, primarily focused on the technical aspects of commanding his ship, to on his feet with his hands on the simulacrum.

It would be harder to pay attention to the bridge around him while linked into his ship like that, but it would allow him to use his magic directly in defense of the starship—a boost the battered cruiser desperately needed.

"Whoever's running their amplifier is good," Torres said quietly. "That's the first redirected salvo gone. We got some of the turrets, but the Mage is making up the gap."

Damien's focus was on *Duke* herself, his knuckles whitening as he gripped the arms of his chair. He'd used *Duke*'s simulacrum to turn the tide of a fight before, but Jakab was *far* more experienced at it than he was. He just had more raw power than the Mage-Captain did.

Missiles died by their dozens, but there were still dozens left—and a second salvo behind them. Damien found himself holding his breath as the trail of explosions reached toward *Duke of Magnificence.*

He could *feel* the magic flow through the runes around him as Jakab reached out to defend his ship. Tiny sparks were visible in the screens that suspended the flag deck in a simulation of the space around them. Each of those sparks, Damien knew, was a swathe of white-hot plasma hundreds of meters across.

Not all of those sparks lit the bright explosions of missile warheads— but many did, and the icons cascading toward *Duke* in the holo-tank suddenly dissipated, the survivors of the first salvo wiped away by the trained skill of *Duke*'s commander.

The second doubled-up salvo followed right on the first's heels. Slower now, launched from closer in or stepped down to arrive with the closer missiles, they were still traveling at over ten percent of lightspeed, giving the lasers under fifty seconds to intercept them all.

Duke's crew gave it their all, and explosions lit up the surrounding stars with flashes of antimatter fire. Power flared through the amplifier matrix, and more sparks flared into existence, taking missiles with them.

Damien had lived through enough space battles at this point that he could *feel* the moment it became clear it wasn't enough. The flag deck crew tensed, bracing for impact—and he rose from his chair, mentally transferring the tracks from the holographic tank in the middle of the room to the surrounding screens.

Without an amplifier, he could only do so much—but a long time before, he'd been taught a spell for just this circumstance, and now he had *much* more experience and power to throw behind it. He focused, studying the screens for a moment more—and then unleashed his power.

He couldn't wait to see if he'd had any effect. These screens weren't designed to enable what he was doing in the same way as the chamber that cocooned the simulacrum. He couldn't zoom, couldn't focus—all he could do was throw energy into the path of missiles and hope it was enough.

Again and again he lent his strength to the defenses. Seconds passed like hours...and then it was over, and his staff were staring at him in awe and shock.

"*How?*" Torres whispered from behind him. "Without an amplifier... you can't..."

"I am a Hand of the Mage-King of Mars," he told them. "I can."

Damien wavered slightly. He *could* do it, but without an amplifier, acting at those ranges would drain even him. He carefully grabbed the arm of his chair, turning back to study the tank. The Keeper ship was handling the missile salvos so far, but the salvos were creeping closer. They might finish this before they reached amplifier range.

Then his Sight *flared* as a massive charge of magic flashed into existence, an immense explosion of plasma and energy tearing a new hole in reality...*barely* clear of *Duke's* hull.

The big cruiser lurched from the shockwave but was undamaged as Damien checked the range. The Keeper ship was still ten light-seconds away—and no one except a Hand could use an amplifier past seven!

Damien was already moving by the time the ship stopped vibrating from the near miss, running past his shocked flag deck crew and out the door into the hallway. Two hallways and a ladder to the bridge, and he was already pushing past the fatigue to channel magic to speed his way.

A new gravity source, completely detached from the battlecruiser's artificial gravity magic, appeared next to the ladder. He leapt forward, letting the pull yank him through the air and into the alcove of the ladder with a bone-shivering catch of a landing.

Dropping down the ladder, he *felt* the gathering strength of the attack, recognizing it this time as he never had before, and reached out with his own magic. The power wavered through the air around him, time seeming to slow as he *saw* the other Mage's amplified strength start to take shape *inside Duke of Magnificence.*

Since doing nothing would inevitably result in death for him and everyone aboard, Damien grabbed every erg of power he could access, reached into the middle of the gathering power with it and *pushed*.

Somehow, it worked. The impending crush of energy was suddenly elsewhere, even a relatively tiny amount of force enough to fling it completely off target, though *Duke* lurched again as he reached the bridge, buffeted by more shockwaves.

Jakab looked up from the simulacrum, his face grim, as Damien charged in.

"That's where you are," he snapped. "Torres didn't know!"

"No one else can use the amplifier at this range," the Hand told him, but it was unnecessary. The Mage-Captain was already stepping back from the simulacrum, gesturing him toward it.

"They've missed us twice," he told Damien, his voice sharp with strain. "They likely won't miss us a third time."

"Steiner," Damien told the navigator, a pasty-faced man in his mid-twenties. "See if you can make them. Rhine—tell me you've got *something* up your sleeve."

"Give me sixty seconds and he'll have the shock of the day," the tactical officer promised.

"Let's see."

Parts of his suit were already smoking from the heat of the runes, but Damien's gloves were intact as he tore them off and laid his palms on the simulacrum. The small semi-solid silver model was covered in runes except for two points that were perfectly matched to the silver patterns inlaid in every Jump and Navy Mage's hands.

Linked into the ship at last, Damien let the magic flow through them, restoring and building up on his own reserves as he absorbed the information it fed him. In that moment, the bridge was ever so far away. He *was* the ship, seeing with her sensors and feeling her wounds.

A third blast of fire was taking shape as his power linked with the ship, but Steiner had pulled an appropriate twisting maneuver that had yanked them out of its way, and Damien took a moment to absorb everything.

Everything he saw of the enemy ship was still ten seconds out of date, but anything *he* did would take effect in real time. It was part of the advantage of an amplifier over the heavy battle lasers still filling the space between the two ships—the lasers had to travel the ten light-seconds back at lightspeed as well, and his magic did not.

He'd never been linked into an amplifier when someone *else* was using one before. The Royal Navy's doctrine basically treated them as super-fast lasers, to be defeated with the speed of light and maneuvering—and for anyone who *wasn't* a Rune Wright, Damien agreed that had to be the case.

He felt the fourth attack taking form. It wasn't going to be a direct hit, erupting partway into the wound opened by the battle laser earlier. Damien reached out and pushed again, sending the carefully constructed spell careening off into space, where it fired off a thousand kilometers from the cruiser's hull.

His opponent had to be confused. No ordinary Mage could do what Damien was doing...but on the other hand, his opponents had been disturbingly well informed so far...and he recognized the "taste" of the magic being thrown at him.

Even a Rune Wright couldn't identify an individual Mage by their magic, but Damien had learned long ago that magic that had gone through an amplifier felt different from regular magic—and magic that had gone through a *Rune of Power* felt different again.

The magic that had now tried to hammer *Duke of Magnificence* to dust had gone through *both*, which confirmed Damien's worst fears.

As the Hand on the other ship paused, probably trying to work out just what was happening, Damien lashed out with his own magic. Studying his enemy's maneuvers, he channeled power through his Runes and the amplifier and conjured *six* immense, kilometer-wide balls of arcing plasma from nothingness.

Everything he saw was still ten seconds old, so there was no way he could guarantee a hit with his first strike—but he came close. Two of his spheres appeared close enough to the Keeper ship to appear to flank it, and electricity *arced* from his plasma balls, transferring unimaginable levels of heat and energy to the enemy ship.

She *survived* but stopped accelerating for a precious few seconds. Damien was still gathering his strength from the strike and cursed mentally as he saw the other ship's engines and systems switch back on, reset from the massively powerful EMP the plasma arcs had triggered on their hull.

Then he saw Rhine's "shock of the day." Six salvos of missiles had already been too far out and going too fast when the Keeper ship jumped forward to be directed onto her—so instead Rhine had let them *pass* her, slow down, match speeds—and then come screaming back at the enemy ship in a single massive salvo of over *four hundred* missiles.

Their sensors took longer to recover than their engines, and it might not have mattered, anyway. The only way they could have lived was to have killed *Duke* before Rhine released the missiles to local control or jumped away.

Shaken by the plasma strikes, they did neither. Over a third of a *teraton* of antimatter explosives went off in a single heavens-shattering instant.

There was very little left of the enemy when the explosion faded.

CHAPTER 29

DENIS ROMANOV tried very hard *not* to look at the ship his shuttle was leaving behind.

"That's...awful," his pilot murmured, and he finally caved to the desire.

Duke of Magnificence looked like someone had taken a battle-ax built to the same scale as the four-hundred-meter-tall cruiser and bashed in one of the corners of the four-sided pyramid. The gouge started on one face and cut most of the way across the second, and that black splotch marked where over two hundred men and women had died.

"You should see the other guy," he finally told the pilot, and the young woman snorted softly.

"That's exactly what we're out here to do," she noted. "Did you bring your forensics evidence baggies?"

"We're hoping to find something a bit larger than that," Denis replied. "Do we have a sector yet?"

"Search pattern's downloading now," she replied. "CIC's best guess puts the simulacrum chamber or any bridge remnants here." She highlighted a section of the screen in front of them.

"Are we actually expecting trouble?" she asked, gesturing to Denis's exosuit armor and rifle.

"If I was expecting trouble, I'd be carrying a bigger gun," he replied. The rifle was almost too small to be used by an exosuited soldier. "We Marines are just the largest contingent of EVA-trained personnel aboard, *and* we're less useful than the EVA-trained techs for repairing *Duke*, so we got cleanup."

"Lucky you," she said. "And *I* get to haul you guys through a debris zone. It's like Academy worst-case exercises all over again."

"Let's just see if we find something *worth* landing on," Denis noted. "The Hand would *love* a living prisoner, however beat-up."

The pilot nodded, carefully guiding the spacecraft deeper into the cloud, mostly vapor but with a few chunks of physical debris, that had been an attacking ship.

"Sir," the pilot said after a moment. "Is it true..."

"What?" he asked carefully.

"That there was another Hand aboard *this* ship?"

Denis sighed.

"From what Montgomery said, it seems highly likely," he said quietly. "That's why we sent Marines."

Hopefully, the bastard was dead. Though Denis had made it quietly clear to *every* officer going in searching the debris that if they found a *living* Hand, no one would ask questions if they died before reaching *Duke*.

His people couldn't fight a Hand, but shooting a wounded one in the head?

Given his choices, Denis Romanov wouldn't even hesitate.

"I think that's the best you're going to get," the pilot finally told Denis, highlighting the chunk of metal in the screens. "It isn't much, but hell, even *Duke*'s sensors couldn't resolve just how many missiles we hit this bitch with."

That was a chunk of hull less than ten meters on a side, almost certainly from near the center of the ship, though clearly not the simulacrum chamber itself. It was melted and battered—but it was also the *only* significant piece left of the Keeper ship.

"Hold us at fifty meters; we'll jump the rest of the way," he told her. "Thanks."

"Part of the service," she replied with an airy wave.

Leaving the cockpit, Denis rejoined his old squad. He was getting comfortable with the rest of the company he'd been given, but the squad that was all that remained of his old platoon were still his strong right hand.

"All right, we have a fragment," he told them. "Not enough space for everybody. Chan—your fire team's with me."

He didn't hear any immediate response as he placed and sealed his exosuit helmet, locking himself in against the vacuum of space.

"We're good to go," Chan reported once everyone was linked in. "Please let us lead the way, sir."

"I'm not the Hand," Denis pointed out calmly. "It took me longer than it should to convince him he shouldn't make this sweep himself. I know my place in this kind of op."

The airlock door shut behind them and the five Marines were blasted out into space along with the air. Training and experience allowed Denis to readily control his course with the exosuit's jets, directing himself toward the designated chunk of debris.

In obedience to Corporal Chan's request, he hung back enough to allow the other Marines to land first, electromagnets in the boots locking them to plain metal floors. There were gravity runes on the floors of the ship section and they even appeared to still have power, but Denis wasn't taking any chances.

"Sweep for any survivors," he ordered. It was possibly someone who'd been in a proper ship-suit or had been close to an emergency locker had survived the destruction of the ship. Finding anyone like that was the main point of the trip, but he had little hope.

"Once we're sure we've found anyone on board, let's grab samples of anything you can find," he continued. "Hull metal. Furniture. Fabric. Bodies. Let's see what we can find."

The fire team obediently moved forward, spreading out through the dark and frozen remnants of a starship.

"Sir, you might take a look at this," Chan reported after a moment. Denis joined him in a few long strides to find him studying a door. "Look's like the Captain's briefing room, but check out the seal."

The commissioning seal on the door was in the same style as the ones the Royal Martian Navy had a bad habit of putting everywhere aboard their own ships, but where the RMN one had ROYAL MARTIAN NAVY across the top and the ship name across the bottom, this one simply had the name KEEPER OF OATHS.

The logo was a stylized mailed fist holding a scroll, etched in what was potentially real gold.

"Any atmosphere on the other side?"

"Not a drop," Chan told him.

No air meant no survivors—or at least, none that would complain when they kicked the door down. Stepping back to cover the door with his rifle, he gestured for Chan to open it.

One powered boot later, Denis followed the NCO into what *had* been a small briefing room. Now, the entire far wall was gone and it appeared the central table had been on fire until all of the oxygen left.

"Looks the same as ours," he concluded aloud, checking under the table. "Yep, computer setup is in the same place—slagged by the heat."

Chan had been checking the podium at the other end, looking for papers or data storage.

"Nothing here, either," he reported. "Damn, I was hoping, but it looks like this one's a bust."

"Let's check everywhere else," Denis ordered. "It's not *that* big a hunk of debris.

"The commissioning seal was the only thing of real interest we found," Romanov admitted later to a small meeting of Damien's advisors. The gold seal, cut with a hand laser from the door it had been mounted on, sat in the middle of the table.

The Marine looked disappointed to Damien, as if he'd hoped to bring back some kind of definitive evidence or gaudy loot to make the delay to study *Keeper of Oaths'* wreckage worth it. Just the name of the ship was telling, though, as it at least confirmed *who* the ship had belonged to.

"I'm surprised there was even *that* much left," Jakab told them. "We hit that ship with almost *four hundred* missiles."

"From what we saw, she was built to the same standard as Navy ships," the Marine replied. "Internal armoring, buffer sections, the works. Didn't leave anything useful, though."

"What about material samples?" Damien asked. Those had let them identify where the shuttles had come from, so he had hope for information from the wreckage of the enemy *ship*.

"My people and Jakab's MP forensics team have been going over what we got," Amiri told him. "It's...well, it's not much use. Even the one significant chunk had taken enough heat and radiation that we couldn't localize the hull metal.

"What *did* turn out to be of use was the commissioning seal itself." She gestured toward the golden symbol. "It was roughly central to the debris piece, so it got minimal radiation, and gold is significantly *easier* to trace than steel or titanium."

"Did you find the source?" Damien demanded.

"It's from Mars," she said flatly. "The John Carter mining complex, barely two hundred kilometers from Olympus Mons. While we can't be *certain* about the hull metal, our higher certainties—only about sixty or seventy percent likely, to be clear—place the source in either the asteroid belt or the Jovian Trojans."

"She was built in Sol," Damien concluded. "I'm not surprised." He sighed. "While I'm sure the rumor mill is having a field day and we *won't* feed it, I can confirm this for everyone here: there *was* a Hand on *Keeper of Oaths.*

"I can't say which one, and given how scattered and only semi-linked we all are, it may be weeks or more before we know who," he continued. "But we—*I*—killed a Hand today."

The room was silent.

"That's unprecedented," Christoffsen finally said. "Hands have died in the line of duty—Conrad Michaels most recently—but a Hand has *never* been killed by another Hand."

Conrad Michaels had taken the dubious privilege of being the most recent Hand to die in service to Mars from Alaura Stealey a month before, when his investigation into an arms smuggling ring had gone sour.

Two *other* Hands were now completing his investigation, with a Navy cruiser squadron backing them up. A Hand falls, another rises.

"I know," Damien told the Professor. "But...one way or another, a Hand was going to kill another Hand today. I suspect His Majesty will forgive me for not simply dying to avoid a political crisis."

He let that hang for another moment of silence, then turned to Jakab.

"Mage-Captain, can *Duke* get us home?" he asked.

"We're only two jumps out, and the matrix appears materially intact to our inspection," he reported. "We're down an engine, so we can't go over our ten gee flank if we *wanted* to, but we should be able to get back to Mars safely."

"It looks like I'm taking you from one repair yard to another," the Hand said softly. "I apologize. I'll... The dead—"

"—will be listed in the Navy rolls with honor," Jakab cut him off. "They died protecting a Hand. We'll get as many of them home as we can, and we'll hold a general memorial once we're back at Mars."

"I...will make certain I can attend," Damien told him. "I owe them that. And a thousand times more."

"Find the bastards who sent that ship after us, my lord," *Duke of Magnificence*'s commander replied. "When *they* have faced justice, our ghosts will rest easy."

"You have my word," the Hand promised. "Your dead *will* have justice."

CHAPTER 30

DUKE OF MAGNIFICENCE limped into Mars orbit in a vastly different state than anyone on the surface of humanity's capital world had expected. One of the battleships permanently placed in Mars orbit shepherded them in, *Reminder of Liberation* hovering over her smaller sister like any anxious sibling would.

Aboard her, with a heavy tread, Damien led his small party toward the shuttle bay. Once again, the ship had suffered carrying out his mission. It seemed he was doomed to lead the men and women of the Royal Martian Navy into battle.

Amiri and Christoffsen followed behind, a trio of Secret Service agents bringing up the rear to provide additional security even there. They'd all picked up something of his mood, staying silent as they made the trek from Damien's office—undamaged, despite everything—through the damaged battlecruiser to the shuttle waiting to return him to Mars.

He stepped into the bay, one of the largest open spaces aboard the massive battlecruiser, and stopped dead as he realized it was *full* of people. Front and center, a double file of Marines headed by Mage-Captain Denis Romanov, but behind them were...dozens, *hundreds* of the ship's crew.

"ATTEN-HUT!" Mage-Captain Kole Jakab's voice snapped out, and *every* off-duty member of *Duke of Magnificence*'s crew snapped to attention and saluted as one.

Blinking back tears and surprise, Damien returned the salute as carefully as he could, facing the spacers who'd fought for him *again*.

"My Lord Montgomery," Jakab said loudly, stepping forward in front of his crew and offering his hand. "It may have taken longer than we'd have liked, but we brought you home."

"I seem to have got your ship a little beaten up again, Captain," Damien admitted, taking the proffered hand. "We may have faced a few more trials than any of us expected along the way."

"We did," the Captain confirmed. "But we faced them together. And we've a few scratches to fix up, my lord, but once that's done, *Duke of Magnificence* and her crew will be ready to serve however you ask of us.

"We'd all be dead twice over without you," he said. "This crew will not forget, Lord Montgomery. Call, and we will answer. Command, and we will obey. For as long you'll have us, this is *your* ship and *your* crew."

Now he truly was blinking back tears.

"I could ask for no finer crew, no finer ship to have at my back," Damien told them, speaking to the crew more than Jakab. "I have asked more of you than I would have asked of anyone given a choice, and you have risen to that call again and again.

"Duty takes me home to Mars, but I know duty will carry me away from Mars as well. And when duty calls for me to leave this world behind, I would do so on no other ship, with no other crew."

"We made it this far together, my lord," Jakab told him. "Mage-Captain Romanov will join you on the surface once we've had a chance to sort out quarters for his company."

"Thank you," Damien said softly, quietly enough that none of the crew could hear him.

"Don't thank me," the Captain replied. "It was their idea. My crew knows *their* Hand, after all."

It was summer in the northern hemisphere of Mars around Olympus Mons, and bright green grass and trees crawled their way up the slopes of the immense mountain, winding through the wide thoroughfares and planned boulevards of Olympus City.

The City stopped below the snow line, not technically part of "the Mountain" people spoke of when they talked of the Martian government. The terraforming of Mars, a process accelerated by the first Mage-King and augmented to include, among other things, adjusting Mars's rotation to the same twenty-four-hour day as Earth, was now hundreds of years old. The complex Damien was headed to, however, predated that terraforming.

First carved into Olympus Mons to house the army the Eugenicists had later used to *conquer* Mars, the network of tunnels and caves now referred to with the same name as the mountain had then housed the monstrous forced breeding experiments of the Olympus Project, birthing humanity's Mages.

When DMA-651, the man who would later become Desmond Michael Alexander, had realized what the runes in the complex did, he had turned on his creators and destroyed them. Using the power of the Olympus Mons Amplifier, he had forced peace in the Solar System and made himself ruler of all humanity.

But the use of the Amplifier meant he had to live in the Olympus Mons tunnels—and the access to those tunnels turned out to be above the snow line on terraformed Mars.

Even as Damien looked down over the summer green of Olympus City, wind and snow buffeted the shuttle. His pilot was one of the veterans from Jakab's crew, however, and she handily guided the spacecraft through the turbulence until the air suddenly, literally magically, smoothed out as they approached the pad they'd been directed to.

The Hand breathed deeply, making sure his suit was perfectly aligned, his fist-like symbol of office was showing on his chest and his Mage medallion was secure on his throat. He'd left Mars a year before, officially an Envoy, informally an apprentice Hand.

He'd only been back once since: a single three-day visit for Alaura Stealey's funeral that had been more a blur than anything else.

The shuttle settled down onto the pad with a flash of superheated steam as a drift of snow evaporated under the thrusters. From repeated experience, Damien knew that the reinforced concrete of the pad would be skin-meltingly hot. That heat was one of the reasons Marine exosuits *existed*, though he hadn't known any of them to complain about the extra armor the rest of the time.

"Looks like you have a welcoming party, my lord," the pilot told him, and he looked at the external screens.

He'd half-expected a swarm of government officials, security, etcetera. Instead, there was a quiet cordon of Secret Service Agents around the pad, but only three people waited by the tunnel into the Mountain.

Damien recognized all three of them in an instant, though the youngest had shot up at least fifteen centimeters since he last saw her.

"I guess I'd better hurry," he told the pilot past the lump in his throat.

It wouldn't do, after all, to keep the entire Martian Royal Family waiting.

Shielding yourself from the heat of a landing pad was within the capacity of many normal Mages, though not all. There were tricks you could teach that would allow most Mages to do it, but even then, it was generally wiser to simply wait out the temperature. Most landing pads on major worlds had underground cooling tubes that would whisk away the heat in a few minutes.

For a Hand with even a single Rune of Power, it was a relatively small drain on power, often used to help awe whatever local powers they were going to have to work with.

Today, Damien simply used it to get across the pad to meet his King faster. He reached the cleared ground beyond the pad, releasing his power as it was finally cool enough to walk without it, and saluted Desmond Michael Alexander the Third crisply.

Any attempt at formality or ceremony promptly disintegrated two seconds later when the gawky form of the Mage-King's younger child slammed into him. Kiera Michelle Alexander, Princess of Mars, was fourteen years old and lankily carved from skin and bone at over a hundred and sixty centimeters—at this point, *taller* than Damien by a large margin.

She hugged with all of the grace and energy of an eager colt, and he returned the hug with a sheepish grin at the King.

Desmond Michael Alexander the Third, Mage-King of Mars and Protector of Man, simply laughed. He was a tall man with hair silvered with age, no longer the platinum blond of his two children. Like his children, he was carved from skin and bone, but what was gawky and endearing in the two teenagers was stern and foreboding to those who didn't know the man.

Though well into a vigorous second century, there were few lines on his face and he moved with grace and energy.

"I am the ruler of a hundred worlds, master of a Navy without peer in history, and wield magics unknowable by most of mankind," Desmond said calmly, "but I am not fool enough to believe I rule my children."

Kiera stepped back slightly, examining Damien's face.

"You look tired," she told him. Someday, she'd learn her father's social grace, but she remained as blunt as she had been when he left. "I saw some of the reports." She glanced back at her father. "You should have come home sooner."

"He's been busy, Kie," Desmond Alexander the *Fourth*, most commonly known as "Des" still, told his little sister as he shook Damien's hand. The eighteen-year-old Crown Prince of Mars had finally matched his father's towering height while Damien had been away, easily thirty-five centimeters above Damien's own diminutive size, though he managed to be even *skinnier* than his father with it. "Plus, I seem to recall you trying to scare him away."

The younger Alexander sibling flushed beet-red and looked away from Damien.

"I was *thirteen*," she pointed out from the lofty maturity of fourteen. "And...you look *awful*, Damien. Are you all right?"

"It's been a rough few weeks," he admitted, meeting the Mage-King's gaze. "I'm not sure I can talk about it yet, either. You'll have to ask your father."

"Fine," Kiera Alexander responded with an exaggerated sigh. "Or I can flutter my eyelashes at Chancellor Gregory and talk up 'wanting to be informed about the state of the nation'." Her pious tone was almost enough to convince *Damien*, and he knew the Princess's foibles.

So did Chancellor Malcolm Gregory, the man who helped run the day-to-day of the Protectorate Government. It would *work*, but only because the second-in-line to the Throne in the Mountain *did* need to be informed about the state of the nation, not because he'd been fooled.

"Come, Kiera, Des," the King said quietly. "I promised you could meet Damien at the pad, but he and I have work to discuss. He *will* be joining us for dinner, so you can bend his ear then. There will be a reception afterwards," he warned Damien, "but dinner will be quiet."

Damien recognized the order in the stressed word and nodded his obedience.

"So long as we get that talk," he murmured.

"Immediately," Alexander promised. "We cleared my afternoon when we saw that *Duke* had *battle damage*."

The Mage-King led Damien to a familiar old-fashioned, wood-paneled study with a roaring fireplace in one corner. A set of overstuffed chairs surrounded the fireplace, completing the illusion of a study pre-dating Earth's space age.

Of course, *this* study was buried deep inside Olympus Mons, had a gravity less than half of Earth's, had windows that showed a completely artificial scene, and processed the smoke from the fire with some of the most advanced carbon-capture technology in a hundred systems.

It was an illusion but one Damien knew Alexander found comforting—for all that the era was an illusion, the *age* of the room wasn't. It had been set up like this by Desmond Alexander the *Second*, and apparently, the current bearer of the name had fond memories of his father in this room.

The current ruler of all mankind got Damien into one of the chairs and grabbed two mugs of steaming tea.

"I have to agree with Kiera, though I'd normally be less forthright about it," he said finally. "You look awful, and your cruiser looks worse.

I'm sure there will be formal reports galore, which I will not have time to read all of, but summarize for me."

"We were attacked," Damien began slowly, considering. "Two jumps out from Mars, by the ship that hit Andala. They..." He sighed. "That ship was built like our best. Battleship-grade lasers. Phoenix VIIIs. An amplifier."

"Damn. How bad did it get?"

"Bad. Neither of us could hurt the other with missiles, so they surprised us with a micro-jump and the battleship lasers," the Hand said quietly. "Then they hit us with the amplifier—at ten light-seconds."

Alexander paused, his tea at his lips. He took a slow sip and swallow, then placed the drink on the tray next to his chair for it.

"One of ours," he said calmly. He wasn't referring to the ship. "How did you survive?"

"Has a Rune Wright ever been attacked by an amplified Mage before?" Damien asked.

"Not...that I am aware of," Alexander admitted. "My sister is the only Alexander to have gone into the Navy, and *you* seem to be the only person finding enemies with our own magical weapons."

"I could *feel* the attack spells forming," the younger man said. "And I managed to...shove it away somehow. I think it's the only reason we survived."

"And no one could have predicted that," the King said grimly. "Not even someone with *all* of the information. Ten light-seconds... They had a Rune of Power, didn't they?"

"Without question," Damien told him. "It had the right flavor of power. So, either I just killed a mystery Rune Wright we didn't know about or..."

"You just put down a rogue Hand we didn't know about," Alexander said. "You did what you had to do, Damien. I don't doubt that. Please tell me you found *something*. This is going to be an...ugly kettle of fish regardless."

"Our attacker ended up thoroughly vaporized, so not as much as I'd like. A commissioning seal calling the ship *Keeper of Oaths* and not much else." Damien sighed. "The seal was made with gold from Mars. The ship had our best tech. It had to have been built here, in Sol."

"Damn. I was hoping..."

"My lord, do you know *anything* about these Keepers? If they truly are a Royal Order, surely we must know something?"

"I know nothing," Alexander said. "I've had people look, but..."

"But what?"

"I asked my *fucking Hands* to look," the King snarled. "The people I trust *above all others*—but if *one* of you has betrayed me, *who the fuck do I trust?*"

"My liege..." Damien swallowed. "My liege, you *have* to trust us. We know there was one problem—but we also know they're *dead*. No one escaped that ship.

"I need resources and authority," he continued. "But if that ship was built in Sol, we can find her. If we can find where she was built, we can find who *had* her built. I will find you answers, my King. That is what you have Hands for."

Alexander held his breath for a long moment before exhaling in a massive sigh.

"And would you trust another Hand at your back with a gun right now, Damien?"

"None of my siblings-in-service would need a gun, my King," he said softly. "I wouldn't trust *anyone* behind me right now. Not until we're at the bottom of this."

"You are my Hand," the Mage-King of Mars finally answered him. "I charge you to follow this rabbit hole. Find who has betrayed us, find this Royal Order of the Keepers of Secrets and Oaths, find this Winton if you can.

"If you need ships, Marines, auditors, bureaucrats, ask. Any resource at my command is at yours. Even in Sol, I do not see all, but if there is a snake in the Mountain, I charge you to bring them to heel."

The relaxed setting robbed Alexander's word of not one gram of intensity, and Damien bowed his head.

"You speak for Mars," the Hand said quietly, "and I will obey."

CHAPTER 31

DESPITE HIS MANY responsibilities, Damien knew that the Mage-King made time to have dinner with his children at least three times a week. He hadn't been a *regular* attendee when he'd been on Mars—the dinners were probably the only quiet private time the King *got*—but he'd been one of the few people who *were* invited.

Tonight, both Damien and Chancellor Malcolm Gregory had joined the Alexanders for dinner. Gregory was an immensely fat man, his hair long lost to premature balding, with a perpetually befuddled smile. He was a mundane, with no magic whatsoever, and occasionally actually succeeded in convincing people he was an overweight, lovable idiot.

Gregory was certainly overweight, and was kind-hearted enough to qualify as lovable—but he was also possibly the smartest man Damien had ever met, a ruthless negotiator and businessman who had dedicated his life to the Protectorate.

"I don't see why I have to wait until I'm fifteen to get a Rune," Kiera asked. Her tone was more questioning than whiny, which Damien suspected meant she was on her best behavior.

"Because it *hurts*," Des told his sister dryly. "And however bad you think it hurts, you're underestimating it."

"Try period cramps sometime, dear brother," the girl said sweetly, causing her sibling to choke on his drink and glare at her. Damien managed to conceal his own choking *somewhat* more discreetly.

"You had those *twice*, my dear," their father reminded her in an indulgent voice. "And the only reason you had them *twice* is because you were too embarrassed to *tell* me or Dr. Sair the first time.

"That said," he continued, "both you and Des are right, but it's not *only* a question of pain tolerance. The first reason, though I will freely admit it's the weakest, is because I said so. The second is that, to date, no one *has* received a Rune of Power before fifteen, and I am not using my only daughter as a guinea pig.

"There are concerns around significant physical growth after the inlay," the King reminded her. "It is *also* a huge responsibility, Kiera. Those Runes make us *extremely* powerful, which comes with similarly sized responsibility. Every man and woman alive who bears one of those Runes, from myself and your brother to your Aunt Jane, to Damien and every other one of my Hands, has sworn their life to the service of the Protectorate.

"While getting the Rune doesn't require you to make that oath, it is a step along that path," he continued. "An utterly irreversible one. So, yes, my dear Kie, you are going to wait until you are fifteen, and I will repeat my explanation as often as you need me to. Because it's important."

Kiera sighed but nodded her acceptance of her father's explanation.

"Does it really hurt that bad?" she asked Damien. "Dad's were *years* ago, and well, who trusts their brother?"

"The four I did here on Mars were done under a local anesthetic," he said carefully. "Those were...uncomfortable. Painful, but...well, I did my first one without anesthetic. There's no comparison. That was *excruciating*."

She stared at him in horror. For various reasons, *that* part of the story had never come out before.

"Why?" she asked. "Wasn't that...well, stupid?"

"Rushed," Damien said dryly, with a glance at Desmond Alexander to be sure he was okay with the story being told. The Mage-King made a go-ahead gesture, and the Hand considered how best to tell the story.

"We were being chased by a crime lord with a stolen cruiser," he told the Alexander siblings. Des was leaning in with interest as well—and so was Gregory, for that matter. "*Azure Gauntlet*. Now, Alaura Stealey was on her way with an entire *squadron* of cruisers, but *I* didn't know that. We didn't have *any* guns on our ship, just the amplifier I'd built."

He shrugged.

"I had access to Shelly Monroe's Rune," he said quietly. More specifically, he'd had access to Hand Shelly Monroe's *forearm skin*, cut from her body after she'd been killed. "Being a Wright, I could see how it had to be changed for me, but I couldn't risk getting it even slightly wrong, so I didn't use any anesthetic.

"It worked. Mikhail Azure is dead and I'm still here. I'd do the same thing again in the same place, though I *now* know I could use a local anesthetic without problems," he finished with a grin.

It wasn't a pleasant memory, though not entirely due to the remembered sensation of cutting his own flesh with magic. He'd taken out the cruiser, but not before Azure had launched its missiles at the jump freighter. Without Stealey's arrival, he'd have died despite everything he and the rest of the ship's crew had done.

Kiera leaned toward him, her expression intent as she seemed to realize that she could ask *him* all of the questions about the Runes she might not be comfortable asking her father or trust her brother's answers.

"How does the silver work?" she asked. "I mean, it can't be just silver; that would...well, that wouldn't work."

"It's mixed with a polymer base," he explained. "That makes it flexible enough to move with your skin and tough enough to survive anything that doesn't completely *remove* your skin. Um. And some things that will."

Everyone around the table shivered, including Damien. He didn't know what *they* were envisaging, but he had memories of some of the burns he'd acquired on Ardennes.

Answering the Princess's questions was probably the easiest part of his job so far.

Several hours later, the quiet family dinner was a fond memory as Damien found himself the guest of honor at one of the Olympus Court's irregular formal receptions. While the Mage-King's court had avoided many of the pitfalls of royal courts of the past—the courtiers were all *employed*, if nothing else—and its ceremony was minimal, this still required him to chat and smile at people he barely knew by job description.

"We don't even need the slave saying 'you too are mortal'," he murmured to Gregory—his escort and political minder for the evening. "We can just make anyone who's too successful attend one of these receptions."

"Be nice, my lord Hand," the man second in charge of the entire Protectorate murmured back. "His Majesty doesn't like these affairs much more than you do, so they're rare—and they make a huge opportunity for new connections.

"By the time the evening is done, at least three new long-term romantic relationships, one political marriage and two multi-billion business deals will have been set in motion. *And* they get to honor a bona fide hero, who stopped a near–civil war. It's a win all around."

"Do I get a cut of the business deals?" Damien muttered, to a chuckle from the Chancellor.

"The couples might name babies after you," he replied. "But after the whole Antonius affair, there'll probably be enough babies named Damien on Sherwood and Mínglìàng for the whole Protectorate."

Damien concealed a wince as the next individual came up. Spotting the same golden hand hanging on the newcomer's chest, he straightened to attention and gave the tall, heavily built man a crisp salute.

"Montgomery," the stranger rumbled, offering his hand. "Hans Lomond. It's good to meet you at last."

It took the younger Hand a moment to get past being almost starstruck. The graying, still powerfully built man he was shaking hands with was the longest-serving Hand alive. It had been *Hans Lomond* who'd hunted down the men who'd murdered and flayed Shelly Monroe, beginning the sad story that had ended with her forearm skin and its inlaid rune in a store in Darkport. Lomond was a living legend.

"My Lord Lomond," he replied, "it's good to meet *you*. I am honored."

"I was here on business, but it never hurts to pass up a chance to remind the rest of the Protectorate that we're the ones who deal with the dirty messes they create when they mess up policy," Lomond said grimly. "Good work at Antonius. Bit of a softer touch than I tend to find necessary, but it seems to have worked out this time."

"A harsher touch would have started a civil war," Damien said quietly. "It's always better to find the right nail, even when you *are* a hammer."

The older Hand chuckled.

"Alaura was always a soft touch," he pointed out. "It worked for her, most of the time, but, well, there's a reason she had cybernetics and I don't."

Alaura Stealey had taken a grenade to the stomach when a negotiation had gone sideways. Lomond wouldn't have had that problem, as he generally didn't *bother* to negotiate. The old Hand was a legend—but so was Stealey, and Damien opened his mouth to defend his mentor.

"And yet her record speaks for itself," Gregory interrupted, cutting off Damien's reaction. "I believe Stealey is currently credited with stopping no less than *eight* rebellions with no further loss of life."

"She was good," Lomond admitted. "Most of us don't have tongues quite so silver, and it's naïve to think we aren't sent on missions that match our talents!"

"Indeed," Gregory allowed. "His Majesty's Hands include both hammers and...more complex tools."

Lomond chuckled again.

"And we know which one I am and which Stealey was," he allowed. "I'll leave you to the rest of the crowd," he told Damien with a jerk of his head at the line behind him, "but if you need to run your current problem past older, if not necessarily *wiser*, heads, look me up. I'm on planet for at least another week or two."

"Thank you, my lord," Damien said, inclining his head. As Lomond walked away, heading for the snack table, the younger Hand glanced over at the Chancellor. "And thank *you*, my lord," he murmured as the next guest approached. "I might have said something rash without your intervention."

"Lomond wouldn't have taken it as badly as you might fear, but we must show unity in public," Gregory murmured back. "Appearances are power, after all."

This wasn't the first formal reception Damien had attended at Olympus Mons, though it was the first that had been for *him*, and he'd known roughly what to expect. He was still flagging by the time the line of several hundred officials, officers, and bureaucrats had made its way past.

At the very end of the reception line was a small black woman, only a few centimeters taller than Damien himself, wearing a tight-fitting dress with the golden hand of her office dangling, somewhat distractingly, into her cleavage.

He took her hand and bowed over it.

"My lady, I didn't realize we had quite so many Hands on Mars," he admitted. He searched his memories, trying to establish *which* Hand this was. She wasn't significantly older than he and likely wasn't Martian-born—her ethnicity wasn't *nearly* mixed enough for her to be one of the products of even the less-vicious programs the Eugenicists had implemented on the general population—which meant she had to be...

"Charlotte, my Lord Montgomery," she introduced herself. "Charlotte Ndosi."

That made her the *second* most recent Hand and the woman who'd apprenticed with Alaura Stealey while he'd been studying on Mars.

"A pleasure to meet you," he murmured.

"Likewise. Alaura spoke of your...adventures, on occasion," Ndosi told him with a smile. "And to answer your question: three Hands on Mars is a little unusual, but there's usually two of us floating around. We..." She shrugged. "We burn out, frankly. And His Majesty appears *damned* good at picking it up and ordering us home for a while."

"What *I* burnt out on is apparently on everyone's lips," Damien replied. "But you seem to have been...quieter in your affairs than I."

She smiled and chuckled softly.

"Most of us, with a few exceptions"—she nodded toward where Lomond was holding court with a pair of Navy officers—"*try* to avoid our situations exploding into outright shooting. Negotiate, compromise, find the middle ground." She shrugged. "Of course, there are *always* assholes, but when an interstellar corp tries to strongarm a planetary government and gets cut off at the knees by a Hand, no one wants it to make news.

"Too much compromise gets a little toxic, though, and you've got to sit back and grab some fresh air, or your compromises start getting *too* pragmatic," she observed. "I've been here a month, and I'm here until His Majesty sends me out again, which he has thankfully started making noises toward."

"It's good to be home," Damien admitted. The degree to which he wasn't sure if anyone he met was a Keeper was dragging on him, but it was still good to be around friends.

"That's everyone," Gregory told him. "I need to go disperse and mingle, but if you and Hand Ndosi want to catch up, you can find the drinks table. If anyone needs you, we'll find you," he finished with a wink.

Damien glanced at Ndosi, who was looking at him with an unreadable expression.

"Thank you, my lord Chancellor," he told Gregory.

"The drinks table is over there, Damien," the attractive woman told him with a smile. "Shall we?"

CHAPTER 32

WAKING UP the next morning and processing that he wasn't alone in the bed in his unreasonably large but still underground suite in Olympus Mons, Damien had to admit to himself he wasn't entirely sure who had seduced whom.

He was reasonably sure Ndosi, currently curled up into his spare pillow in a distractingly naked fashion, was the one who'd suggested going back to his suite. Beyond that was a haze of fine liqueurs and conversation that had progressed to kissing and then, well, to waking up naked with *two* golden Hand chains of office sitting on his dresser.

Both before and after the reception had turned out to be *very* pleasant, and he smiled softly as he ran his hand gently up Charlotte's side. She shifted, unfolding from the pillow like a cat as her eyes snapped open. There was a moment of stiffness as she awoke, but then she relaxed, leaning into his caress with a soft sound.

"Good morning, my lady Hand," he said quietly.

"Good morning yourself, my lord Hand," she replied, her eyes barely half-open. "I think your quarters are nicer than mine."

"I lived here for three years before taking up the Hand," he pointed out. "What's the longest you've stayed here?"

"Three months, just after Alaura died," Ndosi said quietly, shifting herself to lean against him. "I missed the funeral and needed some time. Then a month this time." She chuckled. "I've been on Mars more than not the last year, it seems sometimes. It's...a good place to recover."

"It is," Damien agreed. "This helps," he told her with a wink.

"It does," she said with a smile, guiding his caressing hands across her body. "Do you know how long you're here?"

"Until I'm done with my current case, and then until Desmond has more work for me," he told her. "You?"

Implicit to both of their questions, he was sure, was that this tryst would be just that...a tryst. The Hands of the Mage-King might return to Mars, but they spent their time all over the Protectorate. Trying to make this more than that was unwise, and distracting as Charlotte's nakedness was, he didn't think this could be more.

"It shouldn't be more than a couple of weeks," she admitted. "I'm not on a case here. You are?" she asked. "Not much work here for Hands."

"Someone tried to kill me," he told her grimly. "We think the ship came from Sol, so we're trying to trace it."

"Damn," Charlotte replied. "Let me know if I can help!"

"We're keeping it quiet," Damien said, distracted as she guided his hands to her breasts. "We're worried about leaks."

"At least we know we can trust each other," she told him, gently pushing him back down to the bed. "Brothers and sisters in service to Mars, that's the Hands.

"Now," she continued with a wicked smile as she straddled him, "I've a *definite* idea of how I can help right now!"

The suite of rooms Damien had in Olympus Mons was the size of a largish house and included his office, a space *almost* as large as his commandeered observation deck aboard *Duke of Magnificence*. Since, even on Mars, his personal security was run by professional paranoids like Julia Amiri, there was a "waiting area" between the access to the rest of the tunnel complex and his house, a quiet space with a pair of comfortable couches, usually occupied by the two Secret Service Agents of his working detail.

With Charlotte Ndosi having gone back to sleep, it was time for him to get to work, but he stopped in his tracks as he stepped into the normally quiet waiting area.

The two Agents of his normal Martian working detail were in their normal spots, flanking the security door leading into his suite like statues in expensive suits. The *rest* of the room, however, was *also* crowded with that particular class of polite and deadly young men and women who guarded the Protectorate's VIPs.

Any visitor would have been unable to find a seat, as both couches were full of Secret Service Agents, four he recognized as his and six he didn't recognize at all. A second group were Marines, clad in light body armor and carrying only carbines, but he recognized their shoulder flashes at least as being Romanov's new company.

A fire team of four under a Corporal he recognized after a moment as Chan was guarding the *outer* door. A pair of "extra" Marines, he realized, were both Mage-Lieutenants, Combat Mages whose brand-new shoulder flashes also marked them as Romanov's people.

The last members of the crowd were *another* four young men in plain black suits, presumably *more* Secret Service Agents, who were lounging against one of the walls in position to support Chan's people if anything somehow happened to attack the suite buried in the heart of the Protectorate's capital.

Damien's people had Ndosi's outnumbered by two, and while everyone seemed to have come to a comfortable agreement, the other Hand's security team were eyeing the two Marine Mages uncomfortably.

"Good morning, everyone," he said softly after a moment. "I *presume* your discretion. Do any of you need to speak with me before I grab Corei and Wang here and go about my day?"

That got him a mix of chuckles and uncomfortable looks. The two Mage-Lieutenants waited a moment to see if anyone else said anything, then stepped forward in an eerie synchronicity.

The pair looked alike enough to be brother and sister, both with short-cropped blond hair, golden medallions proclaiming them as fully trained Combat Mages and pristine uniforms over athletic bodies.

"My lord Hand," the woman greeted him. "We've just been assigned to Mage-Captain Romanov's company, and he asked us to introduce ourselves to you. I am Mage-Lieutenant Andrea Forbes and this is Mage-Lieutenant Mykyta Kozel."

"A pleasure to meet you," Damien murmured. While having more Mages relatively easily accessible wasn't a bad thing, he hoped that Romanov had selected them carefully. He suspected, though, that Lieutenant White's betrayal had made even more of an impact on the Marine than on him.

"May we walk with you, sir?" Forbes asked after a moment, not so subtly glancing around the room. "Corporal Chan seems to have the security of your quarters in hand."

The noncom threw them a confirming salute, and Damien glanced back at where Corei and Wang were guarding the door, and gestured for them to follow him into the corridor.

He was still leaving enough people behind that he was sure that Charlotte's guards weren't going to steal his cutlery or anything else dangerous.

"Care to explain the crowd, Agent Corei?" Damien said dryly.

"Well...her working detail showed up with your working detail, right after you two got back from the party," the agent replied. "They weren't going to leave until she left, obviously, so we all settled in. Your quarters *normally* have a four-person detail watching the main area who are less obvious in presence, but we messed up on our interfacing with Romanov's people, so we had four of ours *and* four of his.

"Since we realize that, like us, they had to have a backup team hanging just out of sight of the principal, we invited them in once we, um, realized Hand Ndosi was staying the night." Corei managed to get that out with a straight face, to Damien's amusement.

"Turned out her support detail was larger than we expected, but we had the Marines to even the numbers, so we, well, shared the watch and made sure you two had your privacy."

"Which was appreciated," the Hand admitted, turning his attention to the Marines as he led the way deeper into the Mountain.

"While I'm glad to have you," he told them, "you'll understand that my team is under a pretty heightened state of awareness right now. How can I be sure you came from Romanov?"

The two Marines exchanged concerned glances.

"I suppose you could call him, my lord?" Kozel finally suggested. The Mage, who had so far let Forbes do the talking, had a very quiet voice with an odd pitch to it.

With a sigh, Damien did just that, linking into the Mountain's internal datanet, as his communicator's transceiver wouldn't reach very far through solid rock.

"Romanov, it's Montgomery," he greeted the Marine. "Did you send two new Mages to meet with me?"

There was a pause on the other end.

"Yes," the Marine replied slowly. "And I guess that simply showing you their orders would be less of a reassurance than I assumed. My apologies, sir. I keep thinking of Mars as safe ground."

Considering *his* activities of the prior night, Damien shook his head.

"We all do," he admitted. "And it *should* be. Can these two be trusted?" he asked, meeting the two Marines' gaze calmly.

"Kozel and Forbes? Yeah. I went through Basic and RMMC OCS with them. They're solid, they had no idea what I was asking about when I asked about the Keepers, and neither of them is bright enough to lie to me successfully."

"They *can* hear you," Damien pointed out gently as both of the Mages winced.

"Then remind them that I *remain* their superior officer," Romanov said in a serious tone. "I trust them to have my back and yours, my lord. That's what's important."

"Thank you, Captain," the Hand told him.

"I don't think I need you two at this moment," he continued to the two Mages as he ended the channel. "Check in with Romanov and

Special Agent Amiri for your duties. We have reason to believe we have enemies on Mars, so, well, don't trust *anyone.*"

Both of the Marines looked painfully young as they nodded their understanding.

Damien ended up being over half an hour late to meet with Christoffsen in the Archives. While he was the one who'd *set* the time, he couldn't bring himself to regret the delay, though he did feel bad for making the Professor wait.

"Professor?" he called as he stepped into the onyx cavern of the Olympus Mons Archives. Carved early in the human occupation of the Mountain by the Eugenicists, the Archives were an immense cavern with multiple floors, each partially open to the floor beneath, all carved from black stone.

The lighting reflected back from the polished stone, allowing a tiny number of lights to reasonably illuminate the huge chamber full of stacks of server hard drives, three hundred years of different physical data storage mediums, and even climate-controlled cases of paper documents.

The active records and accounts of the Protectorate were backed up in one set of these servers, much like the data center he'd raided on Tau Ceti, but most of this was cold storage that couldn't be accessed remotely. About a third could be accessed from inside the Mountain, but even ignoring the data that was on paper or detached storage media, over fifty percent of the data in the Archive could only be accessed there.

It meant that the data in cold storage was rarely accessed, but it was *in* cold storage because it was rarely accessed. Inconvenient or not, the Archives contained *everything* the Protectorate government had ever done or written, not merely that which had been regarded as important enough to preserve.

Enough was classified, regardless of age, that researchers were only allowed in under supervision. That restriction stopped few of the researchers who were aware of the Archives' existence from regularly scheduling appointments, though the security systems had informed him that his political aide was the only person in the Archives right now.

"Professor?" he called again, wandering deeper through the stacks of servers and data.

"Ah, there you are, Montgomery," the older man replied, appearing suddenly from behind a set of shelves full of late twenty-first-century data storage disks, all labeled with the official logo of the Martian Republic—the short-lived government of Mars before the Eugenicists took over.

"Come," the ex-Governor and ex-academic turned political advisor ordered. "We have a lot of work to do."

He led the way to a group of consoles set around a sturdy metal table holding a meter-tall stack of data readers for the over two dozen different forms of media stored in the Archives.

"The program Jakab's people put together cleared TCNI's database in under five minutes," Damien pointed out as he eyed the consoles and readers. "How much work do we actually have to do?"

"That was *one* database," Christoffsen pointed out. "One database, already organized in a specific way that the people writing the spider were familiar with, and you were sweeping for something you had *all* of the possible references for.

"The Archives contain just over *ten thousand* databases," he continued, gesturing expansively around them. "That's *excluding* anything on hard storage, though that's mostly pre-Protectorate or extra-Solar, so we *shouldn't* find anything in those."

He removed his stiff gray blazer and slung it over his chair, eyeing the stacks around him balefully.

"If this needle-hunt you've got me on, my lord, takes us into the hard storage stacks, we *are* going to have to find minions you can trust," the Professor concluded. "*I* am certainly not trying to go through the Archive Index on my own!"

CHAPTER 33

EIGHT HOURS later, Damien was starting to go cross-eyed. He'd also acquired a new respect for Christoffsen's capabilities as a researcher. Damien
had used a canned program to search the databases at TCNI and was using
something similar to sweep through the databases here in the Archives.

Christoffsen was using something he'd presumably written himself,
dropping various modules of code into and out of the program as he
turned from one database to the next, sweeping the immense sea of data
he and Damien had access to for any sign of the Royal Order of Keepers
or *Keeper of Oaths* herself.

They'd cleared maybe a tenth of the databases. These were *old* records, from the founding of the Protectorate, and they were not organized
or consolidated particularly well at all. Damien didn't expect to find the
ship in these files, though he'd looked, but he was hoping to find some
information on the founding of the Keepers.

He stood up and stretched, trying to loosen muscles tightened by
hours of fruitless research.

"Is this going to get us anywhere?" he asked quietly. "It feels like
there should be a better way."

"We are looking for something that was *buried*, my lord," Christoffsen
replied. "The Keepers were clearly meant to be secret, so we're not going
to find the standard charter and founding documents for a Royal Order."
He stretched himself. "I've got spiders running on some of the larger
databases, but we could be at this for days."

Before Damien could put together a constructive response to that, his wrist computer chirped an incoming communication.

"This is Montgomery," he answered it.

"Hi, Damien, it's Charlotte," the other Hand greeted him. "How's your evening looking?"

Damien glanced around the immense stacks of data storage around him.

"Long and potentially excruciating," he admitted. "What do you need?"

He wasn't going to admit *aloud*, where his aide could hear him, that he was hoping for a rescue from the data search.

The woman chuckled.

"Well, I hate to interrupt, but *I'm* headed into Olympus City for dinner and was wondering if I could steal you? I know an adorable little French restaurant, very quiet, very private."

Damien sighed and began to make his apologies when Christoffsen interrupted him.

"We'll be at this for *days*, Damien," the ex-Governor told him. "Go. Don't choose a night in a library with an old man over a night out with a beautiful woman!"

Damien wondered if his entire staff had been told Charlotte Ndosi had spent the night in his room at their morning briefing or something similar.

"My attempt to admit I'm working has been overruled by my staff," he told her with a chuckle. "Where do you want me to meet you?

The Mountain had an entire *fleet* of air and ground vehicles available for use by government staff and its semi-irregular residents like the Hands and other traveling representatives of the Mage-King. Ndosi's people had a pair of black sedans waiting for them—one for the Hands themselves plus one bodyguard each, and one for the *rest* of the security details who would accompany them into the city.

It was quite the cavalcade for a quiet date, and from the way the vehicles moved as they traveled out of the tunnel complex, Damien quickly concluded that both vehicles were armored and almost certainly possessed hidden weapons.

Despite the excessive nature of the convoy in his mind, they made it to Ndosi's "adorable little French restaurant" in the city. It turned out to be a terraced patio on the higher end of the city, where the diners could look out over both Olympus City with its glittering skyscrapers and the vast green expanse of the foot of the mountain.

It was easy to call Olympus Mons a mountain and forget just how *huge* it was. Not only was the entire complex that ran the Protectorate buried inside it, but Olympus City itself was built along the lower slope of the mountain. Even the green fields of crops in full summer growth that stretched for dozens of kilometers past the City were still, technically, on Olympus Mons.

The tuxedoed maître d' at the door was clearly expecting them, bowing and ushering them to a set of tables on the top terrace. Damien and Charlotte were seated at a quiet table at the far end of a terrace, and their guards took over the two tables between them and the rest of the restaurant.

"Quite a view, isn't it?" Ndosi asked as they opened the menus. "Stealey brought me here the first time I was on Mars. It's one of the best places to see the city from *and* the food is good."

Damien opened the menu and perused it carefully. Somehow, he wasn't entirely surprised to see the entire menu in French without translation. He could, with difficulty, read and speak Mandarin as well as his native English. Otherwise, his language ability was limited to using the translator in his wrist computer.

"She and I only spent a few days together on Mars," Damien said quietly, struggling through the handful of words he knew to identify a dish before giving up and picking one at random. "Most of my time here before was...busy."

"So I've heard. His Majesty ran you pretty ragged, as I understand?"

"If I was getting college credits, my best guess is that I'd have picked up three master's degrees along the way," he replied. "Law, criminal justice, and thaumaturgy, plus another equivalent range of studies in being a Rune Wright that I don't think anyone would recognize."

They shared a small chuckle.

"Is it true you're as strong as the King now?" she asked softly.

"No," Damien told her. "The Runes build on your own natural strength, and I was a middling Mage at best before the Runes. The Alexanders..." He shrugged.

Even in an open-air restaurant, with guards at the entrance and the white noise generator one of the Secret Service Agents had subtly slipped next to their table, he wasn't prepared to say aloud what he and Ndosi knew to be true: that the Alexander family was *heavily* genetically modified prior to birth to make sure they kept both the Rune Wright Gift and the immense magical Gift of the first Mage-King.

They weren't *quite* clones. While the Mountain's geneticists couldn't *create* the Rune Wright Gift, they had a pretty good idea of what portions of the code needed to remain unchanged to *keep* it, and they allowed as much genetic randomness from the children's mother in as they could.

Even with an equal number of Runes of Power, all three adult Alexanders could tie Damien in knots.

"I'm not as strong as the Mage-King," he concluded, "though it's an academic difference, really."

He glanced over the menu again.

"I don't suppose they have a *translation* of this anywhere, do they?"

With a little bit of help from their computers, the pair of Hands muddled their way into an astonishingly delicious meal as the sun slowly set over Olympus City. The waiter, speaking in accented English, was prompt and efficient, and the view was incredible.

"It's amazing how little these people know about what's going on in the Protectorate," Ndosi noted as they sipped wine and watched the last of the sunset over the city. "The news is *there* if you look for it—the courier networks are reasonably efficient—but, well, the Antonius Incident almost kicked off a civil war, and I doubt half the people in that city down there could even tell you where Antonius is."

"They don't need to," Damien pointed out. "Our job is to make sure that *nobody* needs to worry about something like that, that any danger will be cut short before it happens." He sighed. "I'd love to be more successful at it. A *lot* of people died in Antonius before I worked out enough of what was going on to stop it."

"And if we'd sent, say, Lomond, would any fewer have died?" she asked. "He's not *quite* the bull in the china shop he pretends to be, but he favors straightforward solutions. Would, say, restricting both militias to their home systems have saved the Antonius colonies?"

He sighed.

"No. It's hard to be sure, though—the instigators might have simply written it off as a bad deal."

Two mining facilities, with over a hundred thousand people between them, had been destroyed by agents of powers unknown—but suspected to be Legatus—to try and trigger that civil war. There certainly would have been ways to still make it look like the other system militia was involved, though being able to locate all of the ships of each militia would have reduced the chances.

"And what about Legatus?" she asked softly. "Do you think *that* conflict is something we'll be able to head off before anyone gets in danger?"

"No," he admitted. "But I also suspect more than half of the people out there"—he gestured over the terrace—"know about that tension and have their worries. We know they have plans. We have plans of our own."

She arched an eyebrow at him.

"I haven't heard any such thing," she noted.

"If you don't know, it's not my place to tell you," Damien replied, realizing he may have made a mistake. He'd assumed that the other Hand was cleared for Project Weyland by virtue of *being* a Hand, but since his *own* involvement was peripheral, he had no authority to brief her.

Charlotte made a throwaway gesture and smiled at him.

"I know how that works," she admitted. "Gorgeous as the view is, shall we be getting back to the Mountain? I do have further plans for the evening," she told him with a wink.

CHAPTER 34

SIX DAYS.

Damien and Christoffsen, guarded by Amiri, Romanov and their Secret Service and Marine minions but basically working alone, had been grinding through the databases for six *days*. Only the evenings stolen by Charlotte Ndosi stopped the Hand from going out of his mind.

He was *competent* to do this kind of research, but he didn't enjoy it. His political aide, nicknamed the Professor for a reason, seemed to find the challenge of it all fascinating. The older man cut through the databases with practiced skill, easily clearing twice the number that Damien did and with a higher degree of certainty.

After six days of nothing, though, it took Damien a solid ten seconds to realize what the notification alert from his console meant. He'd become used to the soft *click-click* of a search complete with no results, so when the console instead went *ding!*, announcing a hard match, it was a shock.

"What have you found?" the Professor asked, coming around to look over his screen.

Damien was pulling the data as the other man asked, bringing up the records and watching in surprise as he found a near-complete match to his data on *Keeper of Oaths*.

"The ship," he told his aide absently, running through data. "No wonder it was an odd size—it was designed by Desmond the *Second*."

"Wait, I'm missing something," Christoffsen said slowly.

"The ship. It's clearly a Martian design, bigger than a destroyer but smaller than a modern cruiser—which is because it was designed on top of a cruiser hull *ninety years ago*," Damien explained, pulling the data.

It was *everything*. Full designs and specifications. The engines weren't right and the weapons suite had been upgraded, but the basic design and its oddities had been preserved from the original specifications for the Mage-King's father's work on the "Special Purpose Vessel."

"So, it's a cruiser with battleship guns," his aide said, reading over his shoulder. "Why would they have duplicated the old design that closely for that?"

"They didn't," Damien said quietly. "They duplicated it for this." He tapped the rune matrix layout and studied the notes, confirming what his first glance had suggested.

"The amplifier matrix was written to be tunable," he continued. "From the notes, it wouldn't work for anyone without a Rune of Power, but for someone *with* the Rune..." He shook his head. "An experienced Rune Scribe with enough information on what the Rune of Power did and what the matrix was designed to do could tune the matrix to a Hand, increasing their power while using the amplifier even *more*."

If the runes had worked as designed, Damien hadn't had the range advantage he'd thought he'd had. The other Hand had struck from farther away than any regular Mage could, and apparently farther than even another *Hand* could have.

"Without a Rune Wright to recode the matrix around the tuning, they had to use *exactly* the matrix Desmond's father wrote," Damien concluded aloud. "So, they built an obsolete ship, a hundred-year-old cruiser, upgraded with modern engines and weapons, entirely so they could use that matrix and tune it to whichever Hand was using the ship."

"Are you sure she's new?" Christoffsen asked. "They could have just upgraded one of the original ships."

"I'm sure," Damien said grimly. "We only built two of them, and I recognize both Hands they were built for. Both died in space and their ships went with them."

"Damn," his aide said, tapping a command to transfer the same file to his own system.

Damien tuned out the other man, delving deeper into the data. While it wasn't the ship that had attacked him, it was the only information he could find. The original pair of ships had been built in secret in the Jovian Yards almost a hundred years before, and both had been destroyed, with the Hands they'd been tuned for, before the current Mage-King had taken the throne.

"I wish this was more immediately useful," he finally admitted. "Knowing where they got the idea is handy but doesn't help us."

"Having the exact specifications should help track down who built it, shouldn't it?"

"Not much more than the data we already had would have," Damien replied. "I have schematics now, as opposed to just sensor data, but still..."

"How about knowing when the data was pulled and by who?" Christoffsen asked with a laugh.

"What? You can..."

His aide flipped the file *he'd* been looking at onto Damien's screen. An access log. It showed his access today, when the files had been transferred into cold storage—roughly seventy years ago—and a flurry of accesses five years before by Hand Lawrence Octavian.

"Damn," Damien murmured. "Bets that Octavian hasn't reported in in the last week?"

"I am *not* taking that bet."

"Octavian hasn't been near Sol in about six months," Amiri reported to the gathering of Damien's staff in his office. "He was, however, recently involved in mediating a trade dispute in the Alpha Centauri System. His last report home, according to what's on file, anyway—he may have made a verbal report via RTA to His Majesty without it being recorded—was three days before we left Tau Ceti."

"That's plenty of time for his ship to have met us outside Sol," Damien noted, studying the group for a moment. Romanov was the newest addition, the Marine calm and serious despite having been dragged into the heart of his nation's government.

Christoffsen and Amiri were just as calm, though with more reason. Both of them had been with Damien in Antonius, defusing a near-war *after* its first massacre. Dealing with a conspiracy at the heart of Mars was, in many ways, a quieter task.

"I don't suppose he's officially assigned *Keeper of Oaths?*" the Hand asked his chief bodyguard.

"Octavian is—was—from one of the Martian First Families, descended from one of the Mages adopted into the Eugenicists themselves," she said quietly. "His family is unimaginably wealthy, so he travels on a personal yacht."

"Potentially, only as far as *Keeper*," Damien noted. "Unfortunately, I never met Hand Octavian, and I'm forced to the conclusion that I may have killed him—but given that there were four hundred and eighty-six *other* people on that ship, he's not the one I'm going to cry over."

The room was silent for a long moment. Damien was perched on his desk, gaining a tiny bit of the height his frame denied him, looking down at where his staff had occupied the set of comfortable chairs that normally filled the reading nook in the corner with its fake fireplace and serving table.

"Where do we go from here, my lord?" Romanov finally asked. "If Octavian had *Keeper of Oaths* built, how does that help us?"

"If nothing else, she was crewed by the Keepers," Amiri pointed out. "Wherever she was built, they saw almost three hundred people come aboard her. Where did they come from? The schematics were modified to upgrade her weaponry—Octavian wasn't qualified to do that, *or* to tune the Runes to himself. He was His Majesty's *trade* czar."

"Finding the ship would allow us to learn how it was funded, who provided the designs, even, for that matter, if Octavian involved *himself* in the process at all," Damien noted. "From Mars, I can readily access the Deimos Yards facilities' computers. The ship wasn't built there.

"So, she was either built at Earth or Jupiter," he concluded. "Given the...nature of the work we do at the Jovian Naval Yards, I'd really, *really* like to find that she'd been built at Earth." He sighed. If nothing else, the entirety of Project Weyland and the top-secret rearmament project being run in fear of Legatus was at the Jovian Naval Yards.

"Of course, *Duke of Magnificence* is in for more repairs, so we'll need a ship to get to Jupiter," he noted. "I think that's our next stop."

"I think I can do more good remaining here and continuing to search the Archives," Christoffsen told him. "There may be answers here we have not yet found."

"I agree," Damien said. "Romanov—can we have one of your platoons and Mages stay with Christoffsen? No matter what happens, we need him safe."

"Certainly," the Marine replied. "Depending on how we're traveling to Jupiter, I likely will not be able to bring the entire company with us regardless."

"There are jump ships at the disposal of the Protectorate Government," Amiri pointed out. "Same as the cars and planes, and since it's only one jump, we don't even need to have a Jump Mage assigned."

"Of course there are," Damien sighed. He kept forgetting that he was at *Mars*, the center of the Protectorate's power. He was by no means limited to his own resources.

Damien sent Ndosi a message, and the other Hand met him at the exit out onto the landing pad. Even with the doors out onto the mountainside closed, some of the chill of the snow outside made its way into the tunnel.

Clad in a long black dress that matched her skin, Charlotte shivered and wrapped her arms around Damien, he guessed as much to warm herself as to say goodbye.

"I won't be gone particularly long," he told her. "I just wanted to make sure you knew I was off-planet for the next day or two."

"We never know where we get sent," she reminded him. "I could be gone by the time you get back. Duty is a harsh mistress."

"We both knew that when we took the Hand. I'm not yet on true leave here, though, and my investigation leads me to Jupiter."

"Why Jupiter?" she asked, shaking her head at him. "There really isn't much out there."

Jupiter had been too far out for there to be much of a human presence before the Eugenicists had seized control of Mars and rendered most of the long-term plans moot. Earth had kept the colony there supplied, but it hadn't grown much before the Mage-King took over.

It had always been the perfect place for the Royal Navy to build and work in secret. While the Yards were known to take very high-end clients as well, *those* clients never visited the Yards themselves, usually going through everything except final inspections on Mars.

"Only the Yards," he said quietly. Since he was there, he'd probably inspect the Project Weyland slips as well. It wouldn't hurt to remind everyone that the highest levels were concerned around *that* secret. "Sadly, I don't believe they have a souvenir shop; I can't bring you back a postcard."

She smiled at him and shook her head.

"I think their souvenirs start at 'destroyer' size and go up," she noted. "Looking for a ship, then?"

"I can't say too much," Damien told her. "I trust you, but...we've had too many leaks from far too high on this one," he finished grimly.

"Well, travel safe," she told him, leaning down to kiss him thoroughly. "And hopefully, I'll still be here when you get back!"

CHAPTER 35

THE JUMP-YACHT *Doctor Akintola* was only a little larger than the armed courier Damien had visited Andala VI aboard. Unlike TK-421, however, *Akintola*—named for one of the Eugenicists anyone chose to remember, one who had betrayed her fellows to help the Mage-King overthrow their control of Mars—was completely unarmed.

And had literally gold-plated faucets.

Doctor Akintola was a luxury ship, with every interior fitting completed to the highest standard. Intended to be flown by a small crew or by a Mage VIP like Damien themselves, even the crew sections were finished in plush carpet with woven silver gravity runes, leather seats, and hardwood paneling from Earth itself.

Even the simulacrum chamber at the heart of the spherical ship was a step above almost any vessel Damien had been on before. Instead of expecting the Ship's Mage to stand next to the simulacrum, a reclining leather chair had been mounted on rails, allowing the Mage to sit and adjust their seat to allow them to hold the magical icon comfortably.

Screens on flexible mounts surrounded the chair, easily responding to gesture commands to align themselves around the Hand as he relaxed into the seat.

"We may need to get Jakab one of these," he observed. "This is disturbingly nice."

"They tested the concept on Navy ships," Amiri told him. Since Damien was fully qualified to pilot the ship himself and there was no permanently assigned crew—there were six of the yachts in Mars orbit but only four rotating crews and three Jump Mages—he'd forgone crew to allow Romanov to pack two entire platoons of Marines alongside Amiri's Secret Service agents into the richly-appointed ship.

"And?" he asked.

"It's too distracting and too comfortable if you're trying to command the ship as well," she said. "A Navy Captain has access to a lot of the same displays, but *not* when they're using the simulacrum. The amplifier demands too much attention; layering on the data access led to overload and dramatically increased decision-making time and reduced quality."

"That's a shame," Damien replied, luxuriating in the cushioned leather. A few gestures across the panels linked him into Mars Orbital Control.

"MOC, this is *Doctor Akintola*," he informed them. "We are executing our previously-assigned flight plan and leaving orbit at five gravities in sixty seconds."

That flight plan took them in the rough direction of Jupiter, though it wouldn't have mattered if he was going in the opposite direction. All he needed was to be far enough away from Mars to jump without risk.

"Understood, *Akintola*," an older female voice replied. "Be advised that one of our charted debris fields is closing on your flight path. Not close enough to require diversion per our scanners, but watch your proximity alerts. There is a chance of small debris having separated from the cloud."

"Understood, MOC," he replied as he swung his fingers across the haptic interface. He could have brought up the data faster working through the command pad on his wrist computer, but he couldn't resist the shiny toy.

One of the screens lit up with the debris cloud they mentioned, wreckage from one of the battles of the Eugenicist War. Many such clouds, lacking in anything worth scooping up and only minimally hazardous to navigation, had simply been tagged and left. Cleaning up the *dangerous* wreckage of the Eugenicist War had taken fifty years. Cleaning up the harmless debris was an ongoing "as we have time" project for the Navy and several salvage companies.

Given that estimates ranged from twelve to twenty *thousand* ships destroyed over the hundred-year course of the war—smaller than today's vessels but still interplanetary warships—they'd be at it for at least another hundred years.

Damien adjusted his course a fraction of a degree, still inside his flight plan but giving himself a few dozen more kilometers from the cloud that had probably been a UN Martian Expeditionary Force squadron or something similar once, and triggered *Doctor Akintola*'s engines.

At five gravities, the distance to Mars rapidly increased, the world shrinking behind them. First slowly, then more rapidly as their velocity built.

The debris cloud grew closer, and an itch started on the back of Damien's neck that had him checking the ship's systems and shaking his head.

"Our VIP transports seriously have no defenses whatsoever?" he asked aloud.

"They're intended to either hang out inside defensive perimeters, like we're doing," Amiri pointed out, "or have escorts. If you're feeling paranoid, I'm sure we can borrow a battleship or two. The Martian Squadron wouldn't even *miss* them."

Damien chuckled. The Martian Squadron was the only full squadron of battleships in the Protectorate, with *six* of the immense fifty-million-ton warships permanently positioned in orbit. With two more orbiting Earth, fully two-thirds of the massive ships were in Sol.

"I don't think the itch between my shoulder blades justifies borrowing battleships," he said dryly. "I wouldn't mind a defense turret or three, though."

"You're an all-powerful Hand," she replied. "Who needs lasers when we have you?"

He laughed again, relaxing slightly. They were in orbit of *Mars*. Who could possibly threaten them here?

Ten seconds later, he remembered why it was unwise to *even* think things like that as the threat detectors—which the defenseless VIP transport *did* apparently have—started screaming.

"What the hell is that?" Amiri demanded.

"Targeting sensors," Damien said grimly as a gesture summoned a manual control joystick into his hand. Settling his grip, he focused and then took direct control of the spherical little ship, spinning it into a spiraling evasive course as he pushed up the acceleration with his other hand.

"They have active lock," he announced, trying to discern anything *else* from the screens around him. "I can't tell you what they *are*, but they've got our number. Trying to evade."

Without the gravity runes, his careening, twisting antics would probably have crippled everyone aboard, but they only bought him a tiny reduction in the signal strength of the radar hitting his hull.

Finally, however, the pathetic sensors on the runabout picked up the threat. Still over ten thousand kilometers distant, a dozen antimatter drive missiles flared out of the debris cloud they'd been hidden in. Their sensors had locked onto him, and there was *no* way he could evade the military-grade computers driving their maneuvers.

"I don't suppose anyone believes those are left over from the War?" he asked.

"Phoenix VIIIs," Amiri said quietly. "Following you around, I've become *far* too familiar with them."

"Great," he muttered. All he had was seconds, and not many of them. He could *try* to stop them. Even without an amplifier, he could probably handle twelve missiles still only twenty seconds or so into their burn.

On the other hand, he wasn't planning on staying here *anyway*, and while the jump matrix was harder to make a high-interference jump with than an amplifier, he *was* a Rune Wright.

"Flash a warning to the Martian Squadron," he ordered. "Then stand by to jump."

Updating his calculations to jump over an hour early took time. Not much time, but every second was precious and he was mustering power to try to defend the ship anyway when the numbers popped up on his screen.

Inhaling sharply, he committed the numbers to his mind, grabbed the simulacrum, and *stepped*.

The numbers were wrong. He knew it the moment he committed to the jump—he'd run his calculations assuming he had an *amplifier*, not a jump matrix. The jump matrix was basically the same, but it was prevented from doing anything except amplifying the jump spell by limiter matrices.

They also slightly but measurably changed the results for the jump spell. Across a light-year, the impact became irrelevant as the interference smoothed out. Across less than a light-hour, the impact was several light-seconds.

He'd jumped from close enough in that it was a strain, which the jump matrix made worse. With the calculation error, he also *arrived* too close in.

His entire body *rippled*, the magic tearing through him in waves as both his power and reality itself objected to the change. For an eternal moment, the ship *hung* in a way he'd never felt before, trapped in a reality that insisted they were in two completely different places.

Damien pushed past the pain, channeling more power through the matrix as he bent the universe to his will and *felt* the missiles enter the space where his ship was, their sensors confused by a ghost they could *see* but not *touch*.

Then, in a sudden rush, it was over.

Doctor Akintola erupted into reality once more a million kilometers from Jupiter, alarms screaming throughout the ship as its computers tried to deal with the fact that, for a few seconds that the computer would have been able to process, the ship had had *no* physical presence.

Damien all but fell out of his chair, pain wracking his body as he began to vomit, again and again across the leather seat until his stomach was empty and he was curled into a fetal position on the floor.

It took a few minutes for him to recover enough to sit up and realize that nobody *else* on the yacht's bridge was doing much better. At least one of the Secret Service agents at the door was completely unconscious, and the other was barely working up the energy to crawl over to check on him. Amiri managed to lever herself back to her feet at much the same time as he uncurled.

"What was that?" she asked slowly, massaging her temples and eyeing the several pools of vomit scattered around the room.

"Jumping from too close and arriving too close," he told her. "Nobody on the ship is going to be in good shape." He touched his own temples and groaned as pain spasmed through his skull. "On the other hand, no one appears to be shooting at us here."

"Great." His bodyguard winced. "What do we do?"

"There are cleaning robots, but I don't think they can handle this," Damien admitted. "Help me up," he ordered. "We need to find some cleaning supplies."

"You can't just magic it away?" she asked hopefully.

"If you're willing to let all that sit for an hour or so while I rest, sure."

"Right. Cleaning supplies."

CHAPTER 36

SEVERAL HOURS LATER, with everything cleaned up and following a careful arcing course through Jupiter's moons and rings, *Doctor Akintola* finally approached the massive collection of smelters, girders, and half-constructed ships that made up the Royal Martian Jovian Naval Yards facility.

Two destroyers were already headed toward them as Damien hit a command on the screens surrounding him, opening a channel.

"Jovian Yards, this is Hand Montgomery," he told them. "Transmitting authentication codes." Another command triggered that sequence. "I'm here to inspect the Weyland hulls."

And to interrogate the Yardmaster and her associated computers, but there was no point explaining that. His involvement in Project Weyland gave him a reason to be out there that no one in the know about the quiet armaments program would question—and he was quite sure that the Keepers were entwined deeply enough into the Martian government that *they* knew.

"Authentication confirmed, my lord Hand," a transmission responded after a moment. "I am Mage-Commander Honshu of *Sterling Voice of Judgment*. We will escort you in... You look like you've had better days."

"You have no idea, Mage-Commander Honshu," Damien replied. "I make our ETA to the main station eleven minutes."

"We have the same. Enjoy the view, my lord. Not many people will see it before the girls are done."

Cutting the channel, Damien quickly double-checked his course and then focused his cameras on the only set of hulls present in the yards. He heard Amiri suck in a breath of shock and smiled to himself.

The Jovian Yards had the facilities to build or repair roughly a hundred million tons of warships—two battleships or a hundred destroyers—simultaneously. Or it *had* had, at least.

The yard slips had been completely dismantled, the girders and mobile repair pods spread across an even-larger volume of space anchored on four huge chunks of rock pulled from the Trojans. Material was being cut from those rocks as Damien watched, a stream of autonomous miners and piloted control craft shaping and moving thousands of tons of raw material toward the smelters—and then from the smelters to the seven immense hulls starting to take shape in orbit above Jupiter, shielded from view by the gas giant and its moons.

One was nearly complete, an immense half-kilometer spike in space that flared out to a quarter-kilometer-wide hammerhead at its tip. The base hull was only the beginning, Damien knew, with weapons and armor still remaining to be installed on the hull itself, not even considering the crew quarters, power supplies, engines, and rune matrices necessary to make her a warship.

"What *are* those?" Amiri asked as he kept the camera focused on the furthest along ship.

"*Mjolnir*," he tapped the nearly complete ship. "*Masamune. Excalibur. Fragarach, Durendal. Zulfiqar. Kladenets.* Project Weyland, Amiri. Our answer to the carriers we fear Legatus is building.

"Mars's first dreadnoughts."

Yardmaster Misaki Tsukuda was a tiny woman from Japan on Earth. She was one of the few adults Damien had met who shared his own lack of height, though her reputation suggested she'd adapted to her height in a more...stereotypical manner.

"Lord Montgomery, we were not warned to expect you," she greeted him as he entered the boarding gallery of the Yard facility's Station Alpha. "I was told I would have full control and be advised in advance of all inspections!"

"No," he replied calmly, "you weren't. I *know* you weren't, Yardmaster, because I helped write your quarantine protocols. His Majesty has full control of all visitors to this facility now, and you were told there would be unannounced inspections by either Alexander or his designated representatives.

"Do I need to explain what this means?" he asked, tapping the fist-shaped golden icon hanging on his chest. "I am here on His Majesty's behalf for an update on Project Weyland. We have other questions as well," he noted quietly, glancing around the mostly empty boarding gallery, "but everything we have to discuss requires more private surroundings."

"Everyone in the Jovian Yards has been fully cleared, my lord," she said stiffly. Her willingness to defend her people did her credit in Damien's mind. "We did a lot of transferring and rearranging when we took the Yards over for Project Weyland, I trust everyone out here now."

"Good," Damien allowed. "Nonetheless, Yardmaster, we need to speak in private. Can you arrange a tour of the Weyland hulls?"

She sighed.

"We have a lot going on, my lord. I know the timeline is long enough that one day may not *seem* like much, but if we can avoid interrupting the work?"

Damien smiled.

"Miss Tsukuda, I understand you perfectly," he told her. "I want to *see* them, but I certainly don't need to be close enough to get in the way."

She relaxed—slightly—and nodded.

"We should be able to use my private shuttle," she told him. "It is secure, I promise you. But," she continued as Amiri stepped forward, "your staff is of course welcome to sweep it."

The Yardmaster's private shuttle had artificial gravity runes in its main observation compartment and an outer hull that had been partially transmuted to be transparent. Other than those two relatively functional luxuries, it was a surprisingly spartan spacecraft with no more amenities than any other commuter shuttle.

The transparent wall, however, allowed them to study *Mjolnir* from a distance as the pilot carefully skirted the actual work zones. An overlay allowed Tsukuda to control the zoom, and she focused in on the shape of the dreadnought.

"The *Mjolnir*-class ships are still a work in progress as the design continues," she noted to Damien. "*Mjolnir* herself was commissioned as a test-bed two years back, where the other six were initiated after the Sherwood-Míngliàng incident. While we've been working on *Mjolnir* for longer, we've learned enough that the other six are only about twelve months behind her.

"*Mjolnir* is about another two years from completion," Tsukuda warned him. "The squadron will be done about a year after that, having taken three years to build. The *second*-wave ships, once we've worked through the whole process and run up seven vessels, we expect to only take two years to build from scratch."

"How big is she?" he asked.

"Eighty million tons, seven hundred meters from the base of the pyramid to the front of the hammerhead," she reeled off. "She's got higher-density beams than our current generation of warships, faster launch cycles, and more efficient power generators. She may only be sixty percent bigger than our battleships, but she has almost three times their firepower and survivability.

"They chose the name *dreadnought* for the class with intent, my lord. Once they're complete, nothing in space will be able to fight them. Their only real vulnerability is an amplifier at close range."

Damien winced.

"That brings me neatly to my other point in visiting," he said. He'd been briefed in on Weyland after the Sherwood-Míngliàng incident, asked for his input on how the ships could best stand up against the kind of mass gunship attack he'd faced there.

Bringing up his wrist computer, he opened the files he'd prepared and brought up a three-dimensional image of *Keeper of Oaths*, based on the schematics they'd pulled from the Olympus Archive.

"We're looking for the origin of this ship," he told her. "I have reason to believe it may have been built here, potentially commissioned by a Hand. They would have been *very* exact on a lot of specifications and brought in their own people to do the amplifier matrix."

Tsukuda was very still, staring at the hologram as it gently spun in the air.

"My lord," she said carefully, "you know I am bound by my office, my oaths, and my contracts not to reveal His Majesty's secrets. For Weyland, for example, only two Hands are cleared to know anything about the project. Even with a Hand asking, there are questions I cannot answer."

Her loyalty and discretion did her credit, though her refusal was *frustrating*.

"I can assure you," he said quietly, "that this is not one of *His Majesty's* secrets. No Hand has the authority to bar another Hand from a project. Only Alexander can do that."

"So *you* say," she told him. "But I was bound not to unveil anything about that ship without the permission of His Majesty or..."

"Or Hand Octavian?" Damien asked quietly.

Her lips whitened as she pursed them for a long moment, then nodded.

"I've already said more than I should have, my lord," she confessed. "I can say no more without permission."

Fortunately, Desmond the Third, at least, had foreseen this possibility and had provided Damien with one more arrow, one not normally provided to *anyone*, not even the Hands.

He tapped a command on his wrist computer, rapidly bringing up a different file. *Keeper of Oaths* flickered and disappeared, replaced by the image of the Mage-King of Mars.

"This recording represents a Royal Order, a High Warrant for Grand Treason," Alexander's voice intoned solemnly. "Damien Montgomery, my Hand and Voice, has been charged with investigating treason among my

Hands and Court. He speaks with my Voice...even to the Hands of Mars.

"By my Order, deny him nothing."

Tsukuda stared at the space where the hologram had hovered for a long moment.

"*Chikushō*," she swore. "I've...never seen anything like that."

"Only seven High Warrants have ever been issued," Damien said quietly. Four had been for Hands. Two for Core World Governors. One for a member of the Council of the Protectorate. Only two men *ever* had been given that authority permanently, as First Hand of the Mage-King, charged to pass judgment on his Hands and Voices as well as the rest of the realm. "The situation is dire, Yardmaster. We fear Hand Lawrence Octavian has delved into treason and shadows, and the very fate of the Protectorate may rest on finding out just what he was doing."

"I'll need access to files I don't have here," the small woman finally told him. "We need to return to the station."

Back on Station Alpha, Tsukuda led Damien to her office. Reaching the door, she glanced back at where Julia Amiri and another Agent trailed them.

"We need to speak in private, ladies," she said calmly but firmly. "I'm no threat to a Hand."

Amiri looked ready to object, but Damien cut her off with a swift gesture.

"I'll be fine, Julia," he told her. While he could think of half a dozen ways that the Yardmaster *could* threaten him—poison topped the list, for example—she didn't *seem* to be plotting his demise. "You'll be just outside, and I *do* have both a panic button and healthy lungs."

His bodyguard looked rebellious but nodded her agreement. Until this mess was resolved and she went to join Riordan on Ardennes, she had to keep him alive.

After that, Damien already had a plan, though he'd run it past Amiri before he did anything permanent.

"Thank you, Julia," he said quietly as he followed Tsukuda into the office, allowing the door to slide closed behind them.

The office was gorgeous. At some point in Tsukuda's twelve-year tenure out there, she'd had enough Japanese red pine shipped from Earth to completely panel over the steel walls of the station. One wall was covered in a screen, currently pretending to be a window out onto *Mjolnir*'s construction, and the other three each held two calligraphied scrolls.

The desk also looked to have been imported from Japan, though Damien recognized the telltale black markings of built-in electronics that would link to the Yardmaster's wrist computer. The desk *looked* old-fashioned but was clearly very modern.

Tsukuda went straight to one of several standing cabinets, all in the same wood as the paneling and the desk, and pulled out an unmarked white ceramic bottle and a single matching cup. Wordlessly, she filled the cup with a clear liquid and slugged the entire drink.

Damien took a seat in a comfortable chair facing her desk and waited. The woman was upset by more than just the fact that he'd demanded access to her files, and he wouldn't begrudge it if she needed liquid courage.

She poured another cup, swallowed half of it, and studied one of the calligraphied scrolls carefully.

"It might help to know that Lawrence Octavian is my sister-in-law's cousin," Tsukuda finally said, studying the scroll. "This one is his work." She tapped the artwork. "Done before he was a Hand. I imagine you can guess the quote, given the kind of men and women who become Hands."

"'Death is lighter than a feather, duty heavier than a mountain'," Damien said softly.

"Exactly. I've known Lawrence for twenty years. He's...rude and arrogant at the best of times, but he had the record and skills to back his attitude. He was a trade negotiator for first the Guild and then the Protectorate before he became a Hand. His sense of duty was impressive.

"You'll understand that I find the thought of Lawrence Octavian committing *treason* almost impossible, but you have the authority to compel my cooperation. Give me a minute to check my files."

"I don't know if Hand Octavian is guilty, Yardmaster," Damien told her. "But *Keeper of Oaths* attacked the Navy ship carrying me. I need to know everything you know about the ship."

She nodded slowly and stepped over to her desk. Waving her PC over the scanners linked it into the desk's systems, bringing up both a projected screen and a keyboard.

"Lawrence came to me about five years ago, a year or so after he was elevated to Hand," she explained. "He had a unique design, utterly archaic, that he wanted us to work on. He had all the papers necessary to install Navy systems, but he wanted to make sure that *nothing* where the rune matrix was involved changed. We had to work around the matrix— he had his own people come in for that instead of using ours.

"Gravity runes, amplifier, everything was done by the Scribes he brought in."

Tsukuda finally found what she was looking for, replacing the exterior view with a rotating schematic very similar to the one Damien had provided. Studying it, he could pick out the differences. This one had the modernized weapons and battleship-grade lasers the original design had lacked. The engines and reactors were bigger, the nozzles smaller, more modern.

"Do you have any data on the matrix at all?" he asked.

"None," she said simply. "Lawrence told us it was super-classified, even more secret than the regular amplifier matrix. Something to do with the new rune he was sporting as a Hand."

Studying the schematics, Damien saw where the rune matrix details would normally be included. All it contained was swathes of black, basically marking those parts of the ship as "do not change."

"So, you upgraded the design for him?"

"We did," Tsukuda confirmed. "Upgraded it, refined it, and then ran it past him for approval. He came up with the money for the construction costs—I assumed it was Protectorate funds, but I'll admit I never checked. He certainly *could* have paid for it himself, though I don't think even the Octavians would have found that kind of expense easy."

Most likely, it had been funded by the Keepers, so Damien nodded.

"The ship was finished about three and a half years ago, about eighteen months before we started seriously locking down the Yard for Weyland," she concluded. "I never heard the name until you mentioned it. She left us as Hull Twenty-Six Seventy-Seven. Lawrence took possession of her personally with a small passage crew of people who definitely *weren't* Navy. A little suspicious, but he was a friend and a *Hand.*"

All of that was *useful,* but it didn't give him any more leads. The ship design had been upgraded there, so the people involved in *that* weren't going to lead him to anything. The passage crew could have been anyone. The only real link he could have would be the runes themselves.

"The Scribes Octavian brought," he said. "Were you given any information on them?"

"Not even their names," she admitted. "They came aboard a government jump-yacht much like yours and moved directly aboard the ship. They stayed aboard her while they worked. Except for when they arrived and when they left, I don't think they spent more than five minutes on the station."

"But they were aboard Station Alpha?" he asked. "This is a Class One military facility, so everything in the boarding gallery is recorded, correct?"

So was just about everything else aboard the station, though that was something no one liked to think about too much.

"Yes," she said slowly. "That's...cold archive data. It'll take some time to access—and even aboard a military station requires a warrant."

"Would you like your warrant written or verbal?" Damien asked. "You have my order to pull all records of those Rune Scribes, and I'll have a written warrant in your hands within the hour. Is that acceptable, Yardmaster Tsukuda?"

With a deep sigh, she nodded.

"It will take us a day or so to pull the correct data," she admitted. "You are welcome to stay in our visitors' quarters, but my understanding is that *Doctor Akintola* probably has better quarters."

Damien chuckled softly. He'd taken a glance inside the main VIP room aboard the yacht.

"Suffice to say I'm not sure if there's a bath in my quarters or a *swimming pool*," he noted dryly.

CHAPTER 37

"STORM OF UNRELENTING FURY was thankfully close enough to your position to intercept the missiles before they became a threat to anyone else," Mage-Captain Jakab reported in the hours-old recording Damien was watching. "SolCom is now backtracking the debris cloud and trying to see who may have planted the missiles—it had to have been done after your flight plan was filed, which reduces our time frame, but... it's Mars local space. If they can narrow it down to less than fifty ships, I'll be stunned."

Duke of Magnificence's Captain shrugged.

"They'll dig, and my people will help. We don't have much else to do while we fix the latest set of holes. Give us a few days and we may have some new leads for you," he concluded. "I hope you're not relying on it, though. There's a *lot* of traffic around this planet.

"Let me know if there's anything you need us to handle before you're back."

The recording froze. Transmitted hours before, it had taken most of an hour to cross the distance between Mars and Jupiter at the speed of light. Damien had seen it before, but he was playing it for his people now.

"SolCom is good," he concluded to Amiri and Romanov. "But let's be honest, it's quite possible Kole is underestimating the number of ships that may have passed close enough to drop a pod of missiles into the debris cloud. We can't rely on that."

"What do we have?" the Marine Mage-Captain asked slowly. "We know the ship was built here, but nobody here seems to know much beyond that."

"We've got this." Damien tapped his PC, replacing the frozen recording of his cruiser's captain with an equally frozen image of the boarding gallery on Station Alpha. Seven men and women were in the image. One was the tall, obviously mixed-race form of Lawrence Octavian, clearly a member of Mars's first families.

Only three of the other six had visible faces, and all were somewhat blurry.

"This, sadly, is the best shot we have of the Rune Scribes Octavian brought to the Yards to install the rune matrix on *Keeper of Oaths*," he said grimly. "Very clearly, none of the *Scribes* have a clue they're being recorded—but Hand Octavian *did* and was guiding them on a path that kept them clear of the cameras.

"Fortunately for us, we did manage to get three clean faces out of the mess of video that Yardmaster Tsukuda was able to provide me," Damien continued. "Normally, I would simply send the images to Mars and ask the MIS to identify them for me. Since I'm not sure there is *anyone* in this system who didn't come with us that I can trust, we're going to need to return to Mars and access their databases directly."

"Surely, we can trust the Investigation Service?" Amiri asked. "Or, perhaps more accurately, we have friends in the MIS we can trust?"

"Most of my friends in this system are in the top of the government," Damien admitted. "The MIS people I know are scattered across three systems, and none of them are Sol. If *you* know anyone, of course?"

"Every MIS person I know is either in the same systems as you or the type of Fringe officer who issues bounties," she admitted. "Denis?"

Romanov blinked.

"Why are you looking at *me?*" he asked.

"You grew up here," Damien pointed out. "Neither of us did."

"I think I have a friend's cousin who went into MIS," he said slowly. "But no one I'd trust this far. But..."

The Marine paused, and Damien gestured for him to carry on.

"If you have a thought, Denis, please share it," he ordered. "I'm hardly perfect; there's a reason we're having this conversation."

"Most likely, the Keepers are based on Mars," Romanov said slowly. "You were talking about checking out both Jupiter *and* Earth. If we proceed to Earth, they may think we didn't find anything out here, and it would *also* allow us to access the MIS databases there. The planetary databases are mirrored to each other for ease of operation."

"How do you know that?" Amiri asked. "*I* didn't know that, and I've been briefed on MIS procedures here."

"I don't know anyone in MIS," Romanov replied, "but I do know some cops back on Earth. If we want to do this completely under the radar, they *do* have access to the system databases with the right warrant."

This time, Damien took *Doctor Akintola* out the full two million kilometers, making sure they were well away from the interference of Jupiter's titanic gravity well. The view as they made their trip outward was mind-boggling, half of the gas giant's moons currently visible as the yacht burned away from the planet in all of its glorious colors.

Once they were past Ganymede, the massive half-built hulls of the dreadnought squadron rapidly became invisible, shielded from prying eyes by Jupiter and its children. Damien wished he could regard the construction of the new ships, an immense leap in firepower over the ships the Martian Navy currently had, as pure paranoia. An unnecessary precaution.

But someone had blown two small colonies apart from orbit, killing over a hundred thousand people, to try and start a civil war already. That a conspiracy appeared to have nestled itself into the heart of the Protectorate's government didn't make him any more comfortable that war could be averted.

It wasn't like they could challenge Legatus and slap them down. They didn't have enough evidence—and the sad truth was that even if they did, Damien wasn't sure that politics would allow them to, anyway.

It wasn't like the UnArcana worlds didn't have a *point* about the flaws of the Protectorate, after all.

The Keepers themselves were a sign of that. Born of the first Mage-King's paranoia, ordered to conceal secrets likely inherited from the Eugenicists... He shivered.

The Eugenicists' sought-after "master race" had turned on them in the end, but that didn't mean the Mages hadn't ended up in charge anyway. Damien had never really questioned that, though he had grown to question the Compact that called for Mages to try their own and similar rights.

Now, though...if *one* conspiracy had survived amidst the Mage rulers of the Protectorate, who was to say there was *only* one? The Eugenicists had been a cult and a conspiracy before they'd overtaken Mars and become a government. Enough of the Mages who'd worn a Eugenicist uniform had been allowed to defect that Damien had to wonder.

"Scanners look clear, Damien," Amiri told him, her voice cutting through his thoughts.

He checked the numbers himself and nodded. They were far enough out from Jupiter that he could jump now, but he stared at the simulacrum for a long moment.

"Damien?" Amiri asked. "Are you all right?"

"This whole sneaking around because we can't trust our own people is starting to wear *really* fucking thin," he said sharply. "This is *Sol*. We should have infinite resources: money, ships, trustworthy people." He shivered. "This conspiracy bullshit is getting to me."

"It's getting to all of us," she told him. "Though, frankly, your job has enough of that everywhere else, too. I don't see His Majesty sending you anywhere quiet and calm to, I don't know, judge a cat show, do you?"

The image of a room full of cats being carried around, groomed and presented for Damien—who was only vaguely familiar with the critters at best—to judge made him chuckle.

"Fair," he admitted. "It's the job, but...damn, Mars is supposed to be where we come to relax."

"Then fix it," Amiri said. "That's *also* your job. Can't say any of the rest of us could do it."

He smiled sheepishly and slowly nodded.

"Earth, then," he said aloud, laying his hands on the simulacrum. "I'm going to miss you, you know."

"I know. But you'll do fine."

It was strange. Despite having spent three years in Sol, Damien had never actually been to Earth. Yet the blue-green orb beneath him looked heart-achingly familiar to his eyes. It wasn't the faint purple of his home-world's oceans or, indeed, exactly the hue of any of the oceans he'd visited since leaving his home, but the blue looked perfect and normal to his eyes. The green, the fluffy white clouds, everything looked strangely *right*, even to eyes that had never seen it before.

"All right," he said slowly as Romanov settled in behind him in the tiny shuttle, which was barely big enough for his two senior bodyguards and the minion apiece they'd brought. "Now, this will sound stupid, but which one's Ireland?"

"Well, firstly, we're currently orbiting above Mexico, so you can't see it," the Marine officer pointed out. "But." He leaned forward and tapped a sequence into the computer, which happily provided a waypoint.

"Those are the coordinates for the Dublin Metroplex Spaceport, near where I grew up," he explained. "One of the girls I grew up with now runs the Sector Six Office of the Dublin PD. It's twenty minutes by taxi or transit line from the DMS."

"We'll probably want to keep my presence on Earth quiet," Damien noted. "While the Keepers know I'm on the planet, if they realize I'm talking to cops, they may draw, well, the right conclusions."

"I can talk to Wanda on my own," Romanov offered. "I'll need a warrant, something to cover *her* ass as she accesses the databases for us."

"I can give you a digital one," the Hand agreed. "Amiri and I will hang out at the spaceport, if you end up needing us we can catch up."

"Backup is handy," the Marine agreed, sounding even more serious and subdued than usual. "I'm not the target, but that doesn't mean the Keepers won't take a shot if I'm in the open."

"If you go down, it makes Montgomery more vulnerable," Amiri agreed. "Watch your back. We can commandeer a spaceport security chopper and be on your six faster than you might think, but we still won't be right there."

"I'll be careful," Romanov promised.

CHAPTER 38

DENIS ROMANOV always felt a little bit more comfortable, a little bit more able to stand straight, when he stood on his home planet and humanity's mother world. The air in Ireland was clear and fresh, the pollution of previous years cleaned away—first reduced by dint of great effort and then erased later by vast amounts of magic.

The city hadn't changed much in the last ten years. A few more suburbs sprawling out in the distance, another couple of older blocks demolished and replaced with arcology-esque apartment towers. Sector Six was next door to Sector Seven, where he'd grown up. The Sectors *had* older names, and he was sure most people might even use them—but he'd grown up in an arcology tower and his interest in his homeland's history was minimal at best.

A fleet of automated electric taxis, combined with an interlinked system of monorail streetcars, tied Dublin—and most major Earth cities these days, for that matter—together. Leaving his charges behind, Denis hailed an autocab and gave it the address of the Sector Six Police Office.

Twenty-two minutes later, the vehicle delivered him to the office, what had once been a manor house surrounded by landscaped ground. The manor house, now the sector police dispatch, remained but the grounds had given way to a slightly classier style of apartment buildings than the one he'd grown up in.

The office looked utterly out of place, which he suspected was the point. Anyone looking for help would see the older building and then realize it was the police station. It served as a beacon.

The cab unlocked its doors and released him after he tapped the payment scanner with his Marine Corps payment chip. Anything he did in Montgomery's service was charged to the Hand's accounts. So far as Denis knew, Hands' budgets didn't *have* limits—at least, not in the context of anything smaller than starships and armies, anyway.

He'd traded his uniform for plain civilian clothes, slacks and a dress shirt of a simple style that seemed to stay relatively constant across centuries. None of the uniformed police officers or civilians paid any attention to him as he strode up the steps of the station and into the front lobby.

The lobby had been a grand entrance hall once but was now a somewhat comfortable waiting area. Two uniformed officers held down desks, clearly doing triage of who was and wasn't important enough to be hurried in.

It didn't *look* like there was anything in place to stop anyone going past those two into the offices deeper in the building, though Denis suspected no one would make it through any of the doors without being intercepted.

He approached the woman on the left, who looked *slightly* less harried, and cleared his throat loudly as she continued with whatever electronic paperwork she was doing.

"Wait until you're called, please," she said sharply. "We'll get to you."

"I need to speak to Captain Wanda Skellard immediately," Denis told her calmly.

"Unless you have an appointment, please wait until you're called," the officer repeated, still ignoring him.

"What part of 'immediately' is difficult to understand?" he asked. "Your job, Corporal, is to assess who actually needs to get in to see the officers in this station. If you ignore them, you're not *doing* that, are you?"

Finally, the woman looked up at him, and he saw her angry retort die unspoken as she saw the golden medallion at his throat. Not only was he a Mage, but he'd be *very* surprised if a fully trained police officer didn't recognize the sword etched into the medallion that marked him as a fully trained Combat Mage.

"And you are?" she finally asked carefully.

"Mage-Captain Denis Romanov, RMMC," he introduced himself. "I'm here on the Mountain's business and I need to speak to Captain Skellard immediately."

"She is in a meeting," the officer told him after spending a moment checking a schedule. "I could page her?"

"I can wait until she's done. I'll be outside her office," he told her with a small smile, and swept past the guardian desks. "Please let her know I'm waiting, if you could."

Now that the officer was doing her job, he had no reason to *continue* making her life difficult.

Wanda Skellard showed up five minutes after the hour, clearly *not* having left her meeting for him. She looked exactly like Denis remembered, allowing for ten years' difference. She'd left the arcology at eighteen when he'd been fourteen, determined to make a life for herself.

The example of the tall woman striding down the hallway toward him with her own personal thundercloud was directly responsible for his being where he was now.

"Denis Romanov," she greeted him, her tone flat. "I'll confess this isn't how I expected to find you in my station. Come in," she ordered, the easy authority of having kicked her way from a slum to a prestigious command in ten years showing in her words and motions.

"Captain Skellard," he returned the greeting, bowing his head and following her into her office. He'd expected some kind of plain utilitarian space and was instead confronted with what had probably been the den when the manor was originally built. Paneled in *very* old oak with an equally old oak desk, every inch of her office dripped power and prestige.

Sector Six contained some of the wealthiest neighborhoods in Dublin. It was a plum appointment, and one he knew the girl from his block had *earned*.

"Call me Wanda, Denis," she told him as she dropped into the much-more-modern ergonomic chair behind her desk. "From what my poor abused front desk tells me, you're a Captain yourself these days. The Marines have been good to you, huh?"

"As good for me as Dublin Police has been for you," he agreed. "No one's ever been surprised to see Wanda Skellard succeed, though."

"Where I half-expected you to end up in here for gang trouble, even *after* I heard you'd gone to the Marines," she replied genially. "Mage or not, you were a *pain* as a kid."

"I learned better," he told her seriously. "Even before I went to the Marines, to be honest."

"Fair," she allowed. "It's not like I ever went back. You?"

"Mom married the Sarge; I visit them once a year or so," he replied. "It's... Well, nothing ever changes in the welfare towers. Nothing's permitted to break, but no one ever cares to make it work *better*.

"I'm here for work, though," he continued. "I need a favor."

"No offense, Denis, but if I let old times' sake drag me into trouble, I wouldn't have this office," she pointed out.

"I was relying on 'old times' sake' to get me in here, not to convince you to help me," Denis replied. "I need access to the MIS identity databases."

The joking friendliness vanished instantly. Suddenly, Skellard's feet were flat on the floor behind her desk, her face was level, and her eyes had gone gray and cold as she focused on him.

"Talk fast, Denis," she ordered in a clipped tone, one he recognized from his superiors in the Corps. "Accessing those databases without a warrant would cost *me* my career and put *you* in jail."

"In front of a court-martial, at least," he confirmed, and tapped a command on his wrist PC. "You should have the warrant on your system by close transfer now."

She held that cold gaze on him for a long moment and then checked her computer. The Sector Captain studied the warrant for a long, long moment.

"Denis, this is a Hand's Warrant," she said slowly. "Hands don't ask Sector Captains to look up identity databases. They have MIS falling over themselves to look up this shit."

He sighed.

"How deep down the rabbit hole do you want to go, Wanda?" he asked quietly. "It's legit; you can tell that without me saying it. Do you need the explanation?"

"What the hell have you wandered into, Denis?" she asked in turn, her voice concerned instead of harsh now.

"My company has been seconded to Hand Montgomery for his personal security," he explained. "I report to his Secret Service lead, but otherwise I share responsibility for the life and safety of one of the Hands of the Mage-King of Mars.

"This appears to come with a lot of *other* tasks," he noted, "including trying to get a database search done without anyone knowing about it. There are reasons."

"Down the rabbit hole, huh?" she said slowly. "All right, Denis, how badly would knowing the answers hurt me?"

"Possibly fatally," he admitted. "We *should* have that chance removed, but...people have died over this already."

"I have my Sector," Skellard noted. "One hundred thousand citizens, two hundred and fourteen cops. Our job is to keep them safe, no matter what. *That* gives me problems sleeping at night. I wouldn't take a Hand's burden for anything. This'll help?"

"It will," Denis promised. "And the warrant covers you. He has the authority to make the request; we're just...well, finding someone we can trust."

"Ten years later, you still trust me that far?" she asked.

"Yes."

She sighed.

"Fuck you, Denis Romanov," she said with a smile that took the bite from her words. "I presume you've got faces for me and not much else?"

"Only two of the faces were clear enough for Captain Skellard to pull details from the databases," Romanov informed Damien and Amiri as the Hand piloted the shuttle back up to *Doctor Akintola*. "The other was *just* shaded enough that we couldn't get a clear ID."

"That's two more than I was afraid of," Damien admitted to the Marine. When he'd first seen how carefully Octavian had guided his people through the boarding gallery, he'd worried that even having found *Keeper of Oaths'* construction slip wouldn't help them.

"Who have we got?" he asked.

"Rune Scribe number one is this young lady," Romanov flipped an image to both Damien and Amiri. Still paying *some* attention to the shuttle and its automated course, Damien laid it onto the cockpit window as a translucent overlay.

"Jessica Philips, Rune Scribe, Mage, graduate of Curiosity City University with a Masters in Thaumaturgy and Runic Studies four years ago," the Marine concluded. "She was a grad student at the time, and one from a poor family at that. Her involvement was almost certainly motivated by money."

"Can we find her?" Damien asked.

"Eventually, almost certainly," Romanov answered, "But not quickly. She left Sol eighteen months after graduating; records say she went to the Kaber System. MidWorld; relatively advanced, but no RTA. We'd need to physically go there to find her."

"I'd really rather *not* do that," the Hand said dryly. Kaber was fifty-two light-years from Sol, hardly a quick day trip out to ask some questions.

"We don't have to, because Rune Scribe number *two* was Miss Philips's *professor*," the Marine said, flipping a second ID photo over. "Dr. Periklis Raptis, PhD in Runic Studies, Masters in Third Millennium Solar History and Thaumaturgy."

Dr. Raptis was a swarthy older man, a fringe of shockingly white hair that surrounded a liver-spotted bald patch drawing all attention in the picture.

"He was and remains the Head of Martian Runic Studies at CCU," Romanov explained. "He's a tenured professor teaching several classes, including first-year History of the Eugenicist War and fourth-year Rise of the Protectorate History classes, plus between four and eight Runic Studies courses a semester."

"Busy man," Amiri observed. "Surprised he teaches the history classes."

"Always has, according to the CCU website. I guess they're his hobby."

"And an interest in that period would tie neatly into working with the Keepers," Damien said quietly. "The bastards probably know more about the war than anyone else. Part of the damned secrets they keep."

"We can probably use MIS resources to trace his movements over the last while," Amiri pointed out. "But the truth is, he's probably most easily found at his school."

"So, that's exactly where we'll go," the Hand concluded as *Doctor Akintola* came into view. "The Keepers probably expected us to spend longer on Earth, going through the shipyard records if nothing else. If we move fast enough, we may be able to interrogate Raptis before anyone knows we've identified him."

"Does it ever go that smoothly?" Romanov asked, sounding honestly curious.

"No."

CHAPTER 39

RETURNING TO MARS at last, Damien found himself tensing as they emerged from the jump, focusing on the sensor displays around him as he watched for some kind of threat. Here of all places he should be safe, but...he could no longer take that for granted.

By the time they made into orbit, he had finally started to relax. No new missiles had appeared out of the shadows, and the jump-yacht was now, not particularly *subtly*, under the protective guns of two of the Martian Squadron's battleships.

"*Doctor Akintola*, this is Olympus Control," a voice came over his channel. "Our holding patterns are currently full; I've been requested to redirect you to the transfer station."

Damien sat bolt upright.

"OC, I'm going to need to request authentication on that," he said calmly. "This is Hand Montgomery."

"I understand that, my lord," the controller replied, her voice strained. "Believe me, my lord, this is *not* normal. I have *four* Councilor delegations on approach for a private meeting with His Majesty. Authentication is Lima Victor Tally Ho Six Five Niner."

The code was solid: no one at Olympus Control was under duress that the controller was aware of. He sighed. He could fly from the transfer station to Curiosity City just as easily as he could do so from Olympus Mons, but he'd been hoping to meet up with the Mage-King first.

If there were *four* members of the Council of the Protectorate in the Mountain, though, that wasn't happening either way.

"My apologies, Hand Montgomery," the controller told him. "Be advised any shuttle flights for the next hour are going to run into the same problem. If you want to hold in orbit, it'll be ninety to a hundred and twenty minutes before we'll have a clear entryway."

"Understood, Olympus Control," he finally allowed. "We will proceed to dock *Akintola* at the royal transfer station."

Damien, Amiri, and the rest of his security detail had made it onto the transfer station and were heading for a waiting shuttle when they were intercepted by a trio of suited young men in matching black suits.

"My Lord Montgomery, Agent Ishmael," the leader said quietly. "Authentication Kilo Tally Mike Seven Delta Seven. We're with the Service. If you could come with us, please?"

Damien glanced at Amiri, who nodded calmly. The code was legit, then—he'd trust her judgment on that.

"What's going on, Agent Ishmael?"

"I can't say anything in public," the Secret Service Agent said calmly. "But if you, Agent Amiri, and Mage-Captain Romanov will come with me, I can take you to the individual waiting for you."

"Denis is getting his people off of the ship and coordinating with the ground," Damien replied. "It's just me and Amiri."

"That's fine, my lord. I was asked to bring you; the inclusion of your bodyguards is for your comfort."

"He's legit," Amiri said quietly.

"All right, Agent Ishmael," Damien said. "Lead the way."

The young man nodded, almost a small bow. He led them through a side door and down a somewhat dingy corridor leading away from the main sections of the station.

After several minutes of similar back corridors, Damien was starting to get nervous.

"Agent, what is going on?"

"My principal is...not on the station, if you understand me," Ishmael said after a moment's hesitation. "He wished to meet with you in complete secrecy. The situation, I am led to understand, deserves such."

Further questioning was cut off as they emerged into a *very* different part of the station. Here, gravity runes were inlaid into thick, traffic-resistant carpet, and the walls had been painted in murals of soft green and blue.

Damien had seen the VIP section of the station before, and wondered just *who* he was meeting. The presence of another grim-faced trio of Secret Service Agents reduced the likely possibility dramatically, and he wasn't entirely surprised to be ushered through a pair of double doors into the reception area of one of the nicer hotel suites containing Hand Hans Lomond.

"Hand Lomond," he greeted the other man. "Why all the cloak-and-dagger?"

"Because you're not meeting *me*, Hand Montgomery," the older man said cheerfully. "I haven't been briefed on your current mess, and I don't really expect to be. I'm His Majesty's hammer, and this doesn't sound like a problem for a hammer.

"Today, though, I'm just the taxi driver," Lomond continued. "Got him up here without anyone the wiser."

With the Mage-King tied up meeting with the Council, the only "him" who could convince Hands to help him sneak around out of sight would be...

"Well, shit," Damien said aloud.

"Like I said, I don't know what's going on," the older Hand told him. "In fact, I'm heading out-system in about ten minutes—we think we may have found Julian Falcone's latest hiding place, and I'm taking a trio of cruisers out to pay a visit."

"Good luck," Damien assured him. Once, long before, he'd passed through Darkport, a slave-trading port run by Julian Falcone. The man had ended up in jail but had broken free after less than a year—and many of the criminals broken free *with* him had ended up involved in the pirates attacking Sherwood and Mínglìàng.

"I've had my ear to the ground for a long time, though, Montgomery. Something stinks on Mars, and it feels like you've stirred it all up. The kid wants to help, and he *could*, but I don't think he realizes just how bad the snakes' nest you're walking into is."

"I wasn't planning on encouraging him," Damien noted.

"If you need backup, I can postpone my trip," Lomond offered. "The Navy can handle Falcone without me. We can call Ndosi, muster up everyone. I don't know *who* is fucking with you, Montgomery, but they can't fight three Hands."

"My problem isn't firepower," the younger man demurred. "The problem is finding a shadow."

Lomond sighed and nodded.

"And that's why I go squish pirates," he said brightly. "And leave the shadows—and the *family*—to you."

"Thanks *so* much."

Desmond Michael Alexander the Fourth, eldest child of the Mage-King of Mars, Rune Wright, and Crown Prince of the Protectorate, looked more than a little guilty as Damien entered the room he was hiding in.

Des towered over Damien, but that didn't seem to be making him any more comfortable as the Hand stalked across the room.

"Does your father even know you're here?" Damien asked.

"Yes," Des replied. "Of course, he thinks I'm seeing Lomond off," he admitted.

"As opposed to *what*, exactly?" the Hand demanded. "Please tell me you at least have your *bodyguards* here?"

The youth flushed.

"Of course. Agent Ishmael brought over a dozen Secret Service Agents with him, *and* we had Lomond's detail with us aboard the shuttle up. Was rather crowded, all things considered."

The boy was irrepressible, and Damien sighed. He hadn't been a lot better in his own not-too-distant youth.

"What do you *want*, Des?" he asked. "This is a giant mess, and not one you need to be anywhere near!"

"I want to *help*," the Crown Prince exclaimed. "I have a full set of Runes of Power, I'm trained as a Jump Mage, I'm as powerful as you or Father. I'm no good to anyone sitting around the Mountain learning how to make nice with politicians!"

"When you inherit from your father, making nice with politicians will be your job," Damien pointed out. "Politics is sadly a more useful skill for running the Protectorate than being a fully trained Combat Mage—something you're not, Des.

"Even if you were, this isn't a mission I can *use* backup for," he continued. "It's a question of shadows and answers, conspiracies and lies, and the *last* thing I need is to be watching an eighteen-year-old with phenomenal cosmic power but not the sense to *duck*."

The tall youth winced.

"Honestly, you'd have been better off asking your father to send you with Lomond," the Hand pointed out. "That's a straightforward assignment, one that would give an idea of just what the people your father commands are sent to do."

Des sighed.

"I...I thought you'd be easier to work with than Lomond," he admitted. "He's...intimidating."

"Des?" Damien said dryly. "I wouldn't have let you tag along up to the transfer station. I think you find him easier to *manipulate*, if nothing else."

The youth flushed and sighed.

"Is there *anything* I can do to help?" he asked plaintively.

"You're better off asking your father that than me," the Hand pointed out. "He's the one with all the problems of mankind loaded onto his shoulders. I only carry some of the burdens for him."

"These Keepers," Des said quietly. "They scare him. A lot. He thinks Great-Granddad may have betrayed his own Charter and Compact, and the consequences could be bad. The Council is already chipping at the Mountain's power. If they know the first Mage-King set this into motion..."

"That's going to be a headache." Damien shook his head. He did *not* want the Mage-King's job—and Winton had thought that was a prize to tempt him with! He knew enough *other* headaches of his boss's to be sure of that. "But this is a situation that needs discretion and speed. I need to be on my way down to Mars to follow up a lead."

"Can I help?" Des repeated, and the Hand sighed, realizing that there *was* something the boy could do.

"Here." He loaded a datachip into his wrist PC and transferred all of his files and research, including the IDs they'd managed to make, onto it. "If you want to help? Make sure you deliver this to your father—into his hands, no one else's. I'm not betting that my enemies don't know where I'm going and what I'm doing, so let's make sure my *friends* do as well."

"I will make sure of it!" the Crown Prince promised, as if he'd been asked to do something far more important than act as a secure courier.

"Tell no one, Des," Damien told him. "I'm starting to hate secrets, but this has to stay in the shadows a little while longer."

CHAPTER 40

FINALLY IN A SHUTTLE and descending toward Curiosity City, built on the edge of what had been the Gale Crater and was now the Gale Crater Sea, Damien began to plot his next moves. He was missing the assault shuttle he normally flew in, though, as the runabout had space for only four passengers.

Flying the shuttle himself allowed him to cram Amiri and three Secret Service Agents into the spacecraft, but that left Romanov and his company sorting out their own ride down to the surface. He would miss the extra firepower, though he was relatively sure he didn't need it to interview a university professor.

With a few commands, he opened up a call to the Curiosity City University's primary reception.

"Good afternoon," he greeted the young man who appeared on the other end cheerfully. "This is Hand Damien Montgomery. I'd like to make an appointment to speak with Professor Periklis Raptis."

The receptionist paused and took a moment to collect himself before replying.

"CCU is always ready to help His Majesty's Hands," he said brightly. "I can pull up Professor Raptis's schedule and slot you in whenever he's free. What time will you be arriving?"

"Roughly three PM local time," Damien told him. "If possible, I'd like to meet with the Doctor immediately at that point; I have some questions with regards to his work, but my time, as you can imagine, is very limited."

"Of course! Professor Raptis is free at three o'clock," the receptionist told him eagerly. "I'll add you to his calendar and let him know you're on your way!"

"Thank you."

That gave the Rune Scribe and potentially Keeper an hour to try and run away. Damien had a plan for *that*, too.

A second set of commands raised the Curiosity City branch of the Martian Investigation Service.

"This is MIS Curiosity City; how may I help you?" another cheerful young man, almost a clone of the one at CCU except actually in a uniform this time.

"Connect me to Director Agnes Wong, please," Damien asked. "This is Hand Montgomery."

The junior cop swallowed hard and obeyed with impressive alacrity, not even checking to see if the woman who ran the city's branch was free or not.

"This is Wong," an older woman with the dark brown skin and slanted eyes of a Martian native answered as the call connected. "This better be good."

"This is Hand Montgomery, Director Wong," Damien greeted her. "I'm going to need to commandeer your resources for a matter of Protectorate security."

She nodded slowly with a grumbling cough.

"We are at the service of His Majesty's Hands," she told him.

"I have reason to believe that Professor Periklis Raptis of the Curiosity City University may shortly attempt to flee the University and, most likely, the city," Damien replied. "If he does so, I need him intercepted and brought in. Alive."

"*If* he flees?" she asked with an arched eyebrow.

"'The wicked flee where no man pursueth'," Damien quoted at her. "If the good doctor is innocent, he will happily meet with me and we will have a nice chat. If he is *not*, the last thing he'll want is to be in the same room as a Hand."

Wong chuckled.

"Sir, *I'm* pretty innocent, and I'd rather not be in the same room as a Hand," she pointed out. "I have an aerial unit in the area I'm diverting. They'll be in position in two minutes, sweeping for his car. I don't have ground units anywhere nearby; if you want a ground sweep, I'll need to secure local police."

"Do it," Damien ordered. "No details, only that there's a warrant for Raptis's arrest." He dashed off said warrant as he spoke. If the Professor wasn't a Keeper, if he'd only worked with Octavian for money or for some other acceptable reason, he could always void the warrant later.

"My lord, you haven't given *me* more details than that," Wong pointed out. "If he runs, we'll catch him."

"Thank you, Director. It's nice to be able to rely on the MIS."

He leaned back in the cockpit seat as he cut the channel, glancing at Amiri in the copilot's chair.

"Do you trust them?" she asked.

"For this? Yeah," he allowed. "We'll have to see what Raptis does."

The old rune scribe was the only lead he had. One way or another, Periklis Raptis would lead him to the Keepers.

The main entrance to Curiosity City University was marked by a statue of the rover the city was named for—an eleven-meter-tall heroic bronze of the robot that had confirmed water on Mars and allowed for the initial, very non-magical colonization of the red planet.

Even under the current time constraint, Damien couldn't help but stop in the oval of soft grass and stare in awe at the sheer incongruity of it. One wheel surmounted a stylized mountain and the arm-like camera eye looked benevolently over the city named for it.

Smiling at both the absurdity and the absolute seriousness of the monument, Damien strode across the front courtyard to the glittering glass structure of the main administration building. Blinking against the reflected light, he stepped into the lobby and looked around for the young man from earlier.

He found him, along with several other young men and women who were probably students working on their summer break, behind an immense desk that ran across one wall.

The youth spotted him as he headed toward the desk and stepped out to meet him, eyeing the trailing quartet of suited Secret Service Agents uncomfortably.

"Hand Montgomery," he greeted them. "Professor Raptis said he'd meet you in his office. Do you need a guide?"

"Please," Damien told him. "Lead the way."

He followed the student deeper into the building. Thankfully, once they were out of the main lobby, the glass was tinted on the inside, eliminating the reflection entirely. Raptis's office was on the end of the administration building closest to the Akintola Building, where the Runic Studies department held most of its classes.

Reaching the door, Damien stepped up and rapped sharply on it.

"Professor Raptis?" he asked through the door. "This is Hand Damien Montgomery."

Only silence answered and the Hand mentally sighed. Gesturing for Amiri and the other Agents to move up, he rapped harder on the door.

"Professor Raptis, please open the door," he said gently. Mentally counting down from ten, he waited for someone to answer.

At zero, he made a chopping gesture with his hand and sliced the deadbolt in two. Shoving the door open, he pushed his way into the empty office before their guide even registered what he'd done.

The office was large but cluttered, with bookshelves covering every inch of the walls and several holo-displays set up in the middle of the room around the desk.

There were clear signs of a rapid exit, with entire bookshelves emptied onto the floor, presumably to extract a handful of papers or books. There *had* been a console built into the desk, but the entire electronic portion of the desk had been slagged with magical fire, as had a stack of papers and datachips pushed up against one of the holo-projectors.

"Well, it seems the Professor wasn't interested in that interview," Amiri said quietly.

"Indeed," Damien said absently as he tapped the code for Director Wong's office.

"Wong, this is Montgomery," he greeted her. "Raptis has fled his office. Did any of your units pick him up?"

"Negative," the MIS Director replied. "We have a hard lock on his car; it hasn't gone anywhere. He *might* have slipped past the constables CCPD had in place, but they had a pretty good subtle net up a full half-hour ago. He didn't leave on the ground or by air, my lord."

"Damn," the Hand murmured. "Search the room," he ordered the Agents. "If he had a getaway plan, let's hope there's some clue left here."

"Is there anything MIS can do?" Wong asked.

"See if you can trace his movements," he ordered. "There has to be *some* clue where he's gone."

"We'll do that," she promised. "I also have a team of *my* people, not CCPD, on their way to his house. I'll let you know what we find."

Julia stood back, watching the Hand with one eye as her team began to tear apart the cluttered office. He was getting better at hiding his emotions, but after a year, she could tell when he was frustrated. All of their leads right now ended there.

"Maybe we shouldn't have given him any warning," she told him.

"No. If he was a Keeper, he would never have consciously betrayed them," the Hand replied distractedly. "We needed to know where he ran. We still do."

Julia nodded, studying the room and looking for clues. She'd hunted men for money once, in darker corners of the galaxy than her mostly Sol-born Secret Service Agents had ever seen. They were stripping bookshelves and moving them away from the wall, but...

The pattern for a secret exit wasn't there. There wasn't enough missing space in the walls.

"However he left, it wasn't from here," she said aloud, turning to their nervous-looking guide. "Kid, what's your name?" she asked gently.

"Aaron," he half-whispered. "Aaron Chun."

He didn't *look* like a Chun, but as she studied the youth, she picked out the key features of Mars's classic mixed racial features despite the blond hair.

"This building has a service basement," she told him. "Where's the nearest access?"

"I...think it's this way, ma'am," he said quickly. "Follow me."

"Keep searching," she ordered her staff. "Damien?"

"Go," he said softly. "I need to touch base with Romanov."

She nodded to him and followed Chun out into the corridor.

"The maintenance accesses are locked," he told her as he led the way. "I'm not sure if Raptis had a key." He paused. "Um, I don't have a key."

Reaching the door, Amiri studied it. It was a perfectly normal-looking door, with a small MAINTENANCE PERSONNEL ONLY, KEEP OUT sign above the lock.

"I don't need one," she told him, pulling out an auto-picking device and slapping it onto the lock. It wouldn't work on anything particularly secure, but against the locks a maintenance door was secured with, it took less than a second.

The youth stared at her in surprise as she stepped through into the stairwell and descended into the depths of the building. She replaced the auto-picker with another tool she'd learned to use as a bounty hunter, and acquired an even better version of as a Secret Service team leader: a thermal scanner calibrated for footprints.

In the busy corridors above, it would have been useless. Here, where only a handful of maintenance staff came through in any given day, it showed the thirty-minute-old trail leading down clearly.

"You stay here," she ordered the kid. The last thing she needed was a teenage anchor as she chased down their only lead to the Keepers.

Once the boy was out of sight, she drew her sidearm. Raptis *probably* wasn't a threat—but he was a Mage and she wasn't.

The single trail of footprints led her through the surprisingly clean mechanical rooms of the CCU administration building, crossing several other, older tracks as they went, until they finally ended at what looked like a plain concrete wall.

It was *possible* that the Rune Scribe had teleported through, but the footprints went *right* up to it. Running the thermal scanner over the wall suggested the presence of a door but gave no clue how to open it.

She sighed. Most likely, it was a radioed command code from the professor's PC, which meant *they* were going to need explosives. By the time they got the tunnel open, their prey would be a long, long way away.

CHAPTER 41

"WHAT'S YOUR STATUS, Romanov?"

The Hand's voice echoed in Denis's helmet, sealed away from the noise of his people loading into the shuttle.

"I have half a platoon on a shuttle ready to go and another three squads loading," he replied. "I can have eighty men on your position in twenty minutes. Ten if we have the clearance for a combat drop."

Montgomery chuckled.

"I'm on a college campus, Mage-Captain," he replied. "I don't expect to need an assault landing. Do you have word from your people guarding Christoffsen?"

"I've checked in with Mage-Lieutenant Forbes," Denis told his boss. "They've been allowing the academics back in, but it's been quiet. No issues, though the Professor doesn't seem to have found anything either."

He'd also, from what Andrea Forbes had said, started trying to use the Marines as research assistants. Since RMMC Marines tended to be capable and *smart*, most of them seemed to be taking it in good humor as an educational opportunity. Since Mage-Lieutenant Forbes was even more capable and smarter than her Marines, she'd assigned the ones who *weren't* taking it well as outer security.

"Julia is following her instincts from her bounty hunter days," Montgomery told him. "I expect her to find something useful—at least, more useful than *I'm* finding in the man's office—but I don't expect to catch Professor Raptis at this point. We won't need backup here beyond MIS data-crunching.

"I want *you* to reinforce Professor Christoffsen's protection," the Hand ordered. "I'm hoping he's found something useful in the last few days, but I'm afraid that if he *has*, he's a target. Drop that first squad ASAP. You're not cleared for combat, but you *are* cleared to emergency-override Olympus Control. Understand?"

"Yes, my lord," Denis replied, already thinking through the risks. The academics *probably* weren't a threat, but if someone had the ability to change the bookings, they could have sneaked their own people in.

"We'll keep the Professor safe," he promised.

"Good. Let me know once you're in place," the Hand ordered.

Letting the channel close, Denis smiled and opened an intercom to the pilot. She'd be unlikely to complain about the change in plans—how often, after all, did a pilot get to override ground control?

Four shuttles dropped from the transfer station like homesick rocks, targeting the landing pad closest to the Archive chambers where Christoffsen was working. It wasn't *quite* a combat landing—but it was enough that the civilian shuttles carrying the visiting Councilors' staff were being cut off before they complained.

"This is *Olympus Mons*," the controller snapped. "You can't just charge down from orbit and tell us to 'make it happen'!"

"Control, I'm operating on the direct authority of Hand Montgomery, who has identified a potential threat to the security of the Protectorate," Romanov told the woman. After half a dozen go-arounds, the pilot had dumped Control on him and focused on flying. "I know we're not exactly *used* to emergencies here, but the Hand *has* that authority and *I* will fulfill my orders.

"We're not going to hit anyone on the way down, but I suggest you give my pilots as much of a safety zone as you can," he continued gently. "My Marines *will* be on the ground in fifteen."

"You can't just land Marines at Olympus Mons."

Denis smiled.

"I suggest you check with His Majesty whether or not he included that in his Hand's authority," he pointed out, "but either way, we're landing."

Denis led the way off of the shuttle onto the cooling tarmac and found a single soldier in red exosuit armor waiting for him. There was no insignia on the armor, but the Marine Mage-Captain came to attention and saluted the wearer anyway.

The Royal Guardsman might have a rank technically junior to his, but there were thousands of Marine Captains across the Protectorate. There were only two hundred Royal Guards—all of them fully trained Combat Mages, all of them Marines of at least ten years' service, as many of them as possible combat veterans.

The Royal Guard was the mailed fist behind the silk glove of the Secret Service, and they never left Olympus Mons unless the Mage-King did.

"Guardsman Han," the exosuit introduced herself. "Mage-Captain, what is the situation?"

"We have reason to believe that the conspiracy Montgomery is tracking has infiltrated the Mountain and may be moving on Professor Christoffsen to prevent him communicating his discoveries to the Hand."

Han nodded once.

"We are not maintaining any particular surveillance on the Professor," she noted. "I believe you have a platoon already guarding him?" A small hand gesture took in the *four* shuttles, each carrying an entire squad of Marines, behind Denis.

"And given the intelligence these people seem to have had all along, they'll be ready for that," he pointed out.

"I see your point," Han allowed. "You don't need my permission," she continued, "but the Captain wanted to make sure *we* knew what was going on. Care for some company?"

A full company of Marines, three Combat Mages...versus an unknown level of threat from an organization that had commanded at least one Hand and a capital ship built to custom specifications.

"I would *love* some company, Guardsman."

The Archives were much busier now than they had been when Denis had visited the Hand and Professor during their first phase of research. His platoon was scattered throughout the room, some on guard duty, some on more academic pursuits.

The Marines were in the majority in the room, but there were still at least thirty researchers of one stripe or another, digging through papers, hard storage, and the information databases. The arrival of a *new* group of Marines started to draw attention as his people made their way in.

The Archive was *huge*, and even filing over another eighty Marines in body armor and carrying carbines into the space didn't noticeably crowd it. His people knew their brief and immediately moved to secure entrances and exits, unboxed cased heavy weapons and set up barricades even as the academics started to recoil away from them.

Ignoring the researchers—identifying if any of them were a threat was Kozel's job—Denis crossed the old library cavern to where he spotted Forbes and Christoffsen still at the same set of consoles the Professor had started on weeks before.

"Good to see you, boss," Forbes greeted him. "Did you have an overdue book?"

"Not this week," he replied seriously. "Professor Christoffsen, please tell me you have something?"

"About a hundred and twenty Marines tramping around the library," the old ex-Governor turned political aide said dryly. "And while I have learned quite a good deal about the origins of our enemy, I have learned nothing of immediate use."

"Damn," Denis muttered. "Montgomery was hoping," he admitted.

"Our biggest lead on Mars evaporated; he was hoping for context that could help us *find* something."

"Context I can give you," Christoffsen replied. "But I'm not sure knowing that the Keepers were created by direct order of the first Mage-King in Twenty-Two Sixty helps us *find* them. I can tell you they were a creation of the early days of the Protectorate, and that they took a *lot* of the Eugenicists' files from this place," he waved a hand around the Archives. "None of that is *useful*, however."

"How were they funded?" Han asked. Denis glanced at the red-armored Guardsman.

"Sorry?" he asked.

"The Guard were quietly briefed on the Keepers after Montgomery returned," she said softly. "They have a lot of resources, and they're not being funded by the Protectorate—not without having co-opted an entire *army* of auditors, anyway.

"If the Mage-King wanted them kept secret, he would have provided them with some kind of funding arrangement. What was it?"

"Follow the money," Christoffsen said aloud. "I didn't think of it—I looked to see if anyone was benefiting *today* but not how they were being *funded*. The ship was paid for out of Octavian's personal funds, and I have ten of said auditors trying to see if anyone paid him *back* for it, but..."

He shook his head, turning to one of the Marines with him.

"Shelly, fetch me the second datachip from yesterday," he told her. "It was a blue one, archival of land grants under the Terraforming Agency."

"You already searched that, though," she replied, though she went digging for it obediently regardless.

"I was looking for the wrong thing," Christoffsen said sharply, his voice distressed. "I didn't *think*—dammit, I *know the date the King created them*."

The young Marine found the blue chip and the older man slotted it into the reader, warming up his data searches.

There was nothing Denis could do to help with that, so he glanced around the Archive, checking the status of his people. The defenses weren't perfect—the room wasn't particularly defensible—but unless he was facing Mages and exosuits, they would hold.

"There! *There!*" the Professor exclaimed. He threw a map up on the display and stabbed at a point on it.

"January fifteenth, two thousand two hundred and sixty," he announced aloud. "*All* of the land grants that day were made in the Hellas Montes."

"The Hellas Montes are a planetary park," Forbes objected. "There's nothing *there* except a few tourist traps."

"And in the heart of the park, five hundred square kilometers that were granted to Caleb Octavian and then transferred into a holding company that has never done *anything* with them," Christoffsen replied. "No roads enter the area. None of the tourist traps are near it. It's in the middle of nowhere, where no one would ever go. Where else would you hide a secret library?"

"That's a huge area," Denis said quietly. "I'm not sure that's enough."

"It's a starting point," Christoffsen said. "I'm relaying to Montgomery now."

A few keystrokes later and the old man leaned back, the excitement fading as he exhaled.

"Not as much of an answer as I hoped, but more than we had," he said aloud. "It's been transmitted. Down to the Hand now. If they wanted to stop me, Mage-Captain, they are too late now."

And *then* the entire mountain trembled beneath their feet and the lights went out.

CHAPTER 42

"FIRE IN THE HOLE!"

Damien felt the ground tremble and waited for the MIS demo team to check the area before going around the corner himself. The overly neat basement of the CCU building was now covered in concrete dust, and the secret door Amiri had found had been blasted off its hinges.

The other side looked like a...garage. It was dustier and clearly less well maintained than the basement behind them, but it had clearly held a vehicle of some kind for a long time. A dimly lit tunnel stretched away from them, marked with a clear set of tire tracks in the dirt.

"Find where this comes out," he ordered.

"Yes, sir," the Martian Investigation Service team lead replied, gesturing one of his people forward with a small airborne drone. "It's probably not too far," he concluded. "Maybe two klicks at most; more than that would be unsafe."

And two kilometers would have put Raptis well outside the perimeter established by the Curiosity City cops.

He called Director Wong and quickly filled her in.

"We'll try and backtrack the time once we have the exit point," she told him after she'd processed it. "But...that line goes through downtown. If it emerges into a parking garage, without knowing what the vehicle *looks* like, we won't have much of a trail.

"Find what you can, Director," he replied. "I don't demand the impossible, merely the extremely difficult."

"We'll do what we must. I have a team breaking down the door of Raptis's house as we speak. We'll rip the place apart; hopefully, we'll find some kind of clue."

"Hopefully," Damien echoed. "I don't suppose we have full records of aerial travel?"

"We can scan them, but there's enough private short-range flight that we can't guarantee an unscheduled flight was a risk."

"Check," he ordered. "We'll want to investigate them anyway."

"We'll find Raptis, my lord," she promised. "This is *Mars*. No one can evade us here."

Damien wasn't sure he believed that anymore, but he nodded anyway.

Damien had returned to his shuttle, studying what information he had and trying to decide his next move, when the datapulse arrived. Anything from Christoffsen was flagged for his immediate attention, and he threw it onto the shuttle's cockpit screen to study what the old man had sent.

The cover note was short and abrupt, noting that the land parcel shown had been transferred to the ex-Eugenicist Caleb Octavian— Lawrence Octavian's great-great-great-grandfather—on the same date that the Royal Order of the Keepers of Secrets and Oaths had been created by order of the first Mage-King.

"Director Wong," he raised the MIS woman again. "I need you to run a satellite scan for me."

"We're still digging through the data for flights leaving here," she replied. "What do you need?"

"I'm sending you an area of the Hellas Montes Park," he told her. "Did any of those unscheduled aircraft go there?"

She was silent for a long moment.

"Yes," she said finally. "This makes no sense, my lord. A helicopter left a downtown rooftop helipad roughly as you were arriving at the

University. They went directly into the park and appear to have landed... but there's nothing *there*. Just...wilderness."

"Give me the coordinates," Damien ordered. "Then...continue your investigation of the house and the tunnel, but I think you can mostly stand down. If you've got where Raptis landed, your part in this is done."

"We'll remain on standby regardless," Wong told him. "We'll see what we find."

It was time to call in the Marines. Romanov was busy, but it wasn't like *Duke of Magnificence* didn't have two *other* Marine companies he could call on. He was reaching out to raise Mage-Captain Jakab when a planetwide alert slammed onto his wrist PC.

"This is Admiral Amanda Caliver aboard *Defender of Mars*," the voice of the woman in charge of the orbiting battleships announced, and he realized that *every* military and police com on the planet was receiving the transmission. "The Mountain is under attack. Unknown forces have disabled both the geothermal and fusion power plants in Olympus Mons, crippling the interior and exterior defenses.

"A secondary series of attacks appear to have disabled Olympus City's power plants as well.

"I am declaring a humanitarian and security crisis. All military personnel are to report to base immediately. All police forces are to move to secure their local areas and stand by to provide support to OCPD and the Royal Marines.

"We will be launching Marine landings into Olympus City and to reinforce the Mountain's defenders immediately. Stand by for individual instructions via your local chain of command.

"Until further notice, Mars is now under martial law."

And Damien Montgomery was *not* getting his Marines *or* police backup.

He'd been worried about an attack on Christoffsen. He'd forgotten that Winton had threatened the *Mage-King*.

Julia listened to the message and, without a word aloud, gestured for her Secret Service Agents to follow her into the shuttle. They settled in behind her as she dropped in beside Montgomery.

"What's the plan?" she asked.

"We should head to Olympus Mons, make sure Desmond and the rest are safe," he replied slowly.

"And would you, powerful as you are, make a difference when the Mage-King is surrounded by hundreds of Marines and Secret Service Agents and the Royal Guard? Hell, Desmond himself is a walking weapon of mass destruction."

"If the King is under attack, we have a duty."

"And what if that's what the Keepers are counting on?" she told him. From what she could tell, the Hand was closing in on the bastards who'd bombed Andala and killed Kurosawa. They had to be running scared. "If they're keeping secrets, they probably have records of some kind? The kind they'd need a huge distraction to move without people noticing?"

"A distraction like martial law and having every man and woman in uniform on the goddamn planet watching the Mountain," he said quietly.

"Exactly. Damien, our King is *probably* safe and *certainly* doesn't need you," she pointed out. Her charge had a bad habit of swinging between thinking he was completely unimportant and thinking he had to solve *everything*.

"But no one else has all the pieces we've put together," she continued. "What if they're running scared? How close are we?"

"We have them," he admitted quietly. "Christoffsen tracked a land grant that was buried in the middle of a park, made to the first Mage Octavian—a defected Eugenicist. It was made the same day that the Keepers were established.

"A chopper left here without a flight plan and headed right to that land grant. I have coordinates that I think are their base. Their home. Most likely their records, as you say."

"Then what are we waiting for?" she demanded. "This shuttle has enough fuel to make it to orbit and back twice; we can do a nice short suborbital, can't we?"

"We can."

"Then let's go end this fucking case so I can go get married, shall we?"

He chuckled.

"Strap in, people," he ordered. "Apparently, our bride-to-be is getting impatient."

Hand lights flickered to life across the Archives, accompanied by panicked questions and shouting from the researchers, none of whom had expected to see the perfectly safe underground cavern have *any* problems.

"What's going on?" was the primary refrain.

"Everyone, *shut up!*" Denis bellowed. "Lights to the center, check on the civilians. Perimeter teams, go thermal. Watch the doors, watch your backs," he ordered.

With some order beginning to form around him, he turned his attention back to Christoffsen and Guardsman Han.

"What happened?" he asked the exosuited soldier.

"Something cut the primary, secondary, and tertiary power systems," she reported. "The trembling was explosives collapsing the boreholes for the geothermal plant. I'm not sure what shut down the fusion and fission plants, but given that the thorium reactors' *existence* is classified, that's concerning on its own."

"Should you be going to protect His Majesty?" Denis asked.

"I'm in contact with Guard Control," she reported. "They have battery power, but the thorium fission plants are supposed to provide our final emergency power source. The Mage-King is secure, the Throne Room is secure, the kids are with him. If the King is in the Throne Room, any attack on him won't work.

"Frankly, Mage-Captain, you and the Professor are more vulnerable, and since the Professor just cracked open the damn Keepers like a crab dinner, I think everyone would prefer we kept *him* alive."

"Wait," Denis said slowly, "you think someone knocked out power to the entire complex as a preamble to attacking *us*?"

"It's sufficiently likely that I've been ordered to secure the Archives and protect Dr. Christoffsen," she said calmly. "Just in case."

CHAPTER 43

THERE WAS NO subtlety to arriving in a shuttle, even a small un-armed runabout like the one Damien had taken to Curiosity City. The spacecraft came screaming in on the coordinates Wong had identified, still traveling at the speed of sound as they entered the parcel of land be-longing to the Octavian family in the middle of a planetary park.

"I'm not seeing anything here," Amiri told him from the copilot's seat. "Just...trees."

"Slowing down over the last spot the satellites had the chopper," he replied, looking out through the cockpit as the shuttle came to some-thing resembling a more reasonable speed as he looped around. "Wait—what's that?"

"That" was a glint of metal through the trees. His bodyguard had clearly seen it as well and started tapping commands on the screen as he directed the shuttle in the direction of the glint.

"Son of a bitch," she murmured as he brought the shuttle through a break in the trees and into a hover above a three-quarters-full vehicle park.

A helicopter—presumably the one whose trail they'd followed—still sat in the middle of a concrete landing pad. Half a dozen robotic tow trucks sat silently off to one side, and a cleared zone tucked against the side of the mountain held another five choppers and half a dozen shut-tles identical to the one Damien was piloting.

"Those are all government spacecraft," Damien said quietly. "We found our target."

"This thing has no guns," she told him. "That's a *lot* of vehicles to leave behind you."

"It's an orbital shuttle," he reminded her. "It doesn't *need* guns for this."

With a carefully calculated course, he swept the spacecraft down through the vehicle park, suspending the shuttle barely five meters above the ground and directed the thrusters at each vehicle as he swept over.

On full power at that range, engines that could lift the craft from the ground to orbit *melted* steel and overheated ceramics to the point of shattering. The shuttles had apparently been at least partially fueled, as explosions buffeted Damien's craft as he swept back around, making certain none of the vehicles were intact.

No one was going to escape today. After Andala, after *Keeper of Oaths* and the dead aboard *Duke of Magnificence*...the Keepers would surrender or be destroyed.

"Got a bead on the entrance?" he asked.

"There's a path leading up the mountain," Amiri replied. "It's the only manmade feature I can see, so I'm guessing that's the way to our door."

Damien adjusted the shuttle, landing the slightly scorched but intact spacecraft in a clear space away from the wrecked vehicles around him.

"We've already knocked. Let's go find the door."

Once they were outside and on the ground, the path leading up the mountain was clear and obvious. Someone had put a *lot* of effort into cultivating and trimming the trees around the landing pad and vehicle park to conceal the facility as much as possible. If they hadn't known exactly where the helicopter had disappeared, Damien wasn't sure they could have found the place.

The path was similarly concealed but was a smoothly paved straight line under the trees. It ascended smoothly up the mountainside, though the tree canopy arching over it blocked his view of the destination.

There were no signs, no people. The only noise was the crackling fires of the wrecked vehicles. He'd have to call the site into the Park Rangers once they were done to make sure the fire didn't spread, but for now...

Silence.

He looked up the path, absently recognizing the natural beauty of the place the Keepers had made their own. Damien suspected what waited for him inside their base. He didn't want to be right, but he steeled himself for it anyway.

"Julia," he said quietly, gesturing Amiri to him. "I want you to take your people and fly the shuttle back to Olympus Mons. The autopilot can handle that."

"Not a chance," she replied sharply. "You need us to watch your back."

"Not today." He shook his head. "Julia, you're one of the few who know what it means for a Rune Wright to go to war. I can't be responsible for your safety."

"You'll still die if someone shoots you in the back of the head."

"And if I and whoever I end up fighting start throwing antimatter around?" he asked softly. "I can protect myself, but if I'm protecting you and your people as well, I might just get us all killed."

"Until this case is done, my job is to keep you alive," she snapped. "I will *not* abandon you."

"Your part in this case is done," he stated flatly. "Julia, I don't need you for this. Having you here will put both you and me at risk. Go. You can help more at Olympus Mons than here—and you can make sure that whatever happens, His Majesty knows where this place is."

"And if you die?"

"Then I died doing my job and I didn't take you with me," Damien told her. "You've watched my back for a long time, Julia. I don't even know how many lives I owe you, but you can't watch my back today. I *need* you to go back to the Mountain and tell Desmond what we've found.

"I need you to go back to Ardennes, no matter what happens, and help Riordan put his planet back together," he admitted. "This... This is up to me."

"*Why?*" she demanded. She wasn't arguing anymore—both of them knew it was an order he would not permit her to refuse.

"Because unless I'm severely mistaken, I'm going to find a Hand in there," he told her quietly. "And that's something we need to deal with in the family."

As Damien stepped under the trees, the shuttle engines roared to life behind him. The little runabout was designed to function entirely without a pilot. Its computer was entirely capable of taking Amiri and her people back to Olympus Mons on its own, which meant *they* would be safe.

His own fate was an entirely different question.

The path was wide and clear, obviously carefully maintained—probably by robots, from the ruler-straight edges of the shrubs and lower branches that touched it. The evening sunlight was streaming through the canopy, tinging the concrete path with a calming shade of green as he made his way up the side of the mountain.

It was incongruous at best. Damien was here to fight a war, to end a conspiracy that had killed people under his command, tried to kill thousands of innocents—*had* killed God alone knew how many people protecting their secrets.

But the path leading up to their secret library was a soothing, relaxing place that managed to do *nothing* for his peace of mind. Knowing what was coming made it creepy.

Finally, after about a quarter-kilometer, he reached the end of the path. An opening had been cut into the side of the mountain with magic, angled to be invisible from above, containing a large set of double doors surmounted by a sigil of a mailed fist holding a scroll.

The symbol was the only sign he was in the right place. There was no text, no explanation, just a set of armored doors in the middle of nowhere with that symbol carved into the stone above them.

His arrival had not been subtle. He was a little surprised nothing had tried to shoot at him on approach, but he had certainly made his presence known. The Keepers knew he was there. They knew who he was, more than any enemy he'd ever faced, he suspected.

With a deep inhalation and a surge of magic, Damien Montgomery, Hand of the Mage-King of Mars, blew the doors apart and strode into the lair of his enemy.

CHAPTER 44

DAMIEN HAD no idea if the doors had been locked, but they had been armored to withstand almost any conventional weapon. Converting half a gram or so of the metal at the exact center of the door to antimatter, however, was far more than any mundane material could withstand.

He strode through the shattered wreckage of the doors, summoning shields of force around himself to stop any bullets from unexpected corners. The shields couldn't be sustained forever, but while he held them, it would take more than a bullet to the head to stop him.

The double doors led into a small antechamber with another set of doors at the other end. The space was carved out of the raw rock, with gentle lighting showing delicate woodland murals painted across the smoothed stone. The inner doors were armored to the same level as the outer doors and he glanced around for defenses.

There weren't any. Just the doors. With a gesture, he blew *those* apart inwards, clearing his immediate path, and stepped over the debris into an immense open lobby.

If the space had started as a natural cavern, there was no sign of it anymore. Easily two hundred meters long and fifteen high, supported by immense pillars and marked with second- and third-floor galleries, the space looked like it should be the heart of a museum, not the entrance to a secret underground base. It was massive enough that the debris from the wrecked doors hadn't actually *touched* anything in the room.

Mirrored airshafts in the roof delivered sunshine, diffusing a mix of natural and artificial light to fully illuminate the massive space with a consistent level of light that glittered off glass cases and covered bookshelves.

The place *was* a museum. Artifacts and books that no one outside this deathly secret order had ever seen or even known existed. Knowledge hidden away—Damien couldn't even *guess* how important it was, how much knowledge of the origins of magic had been concealed from humanity.

There were hundreds of hiding places in the room and he held his shields as he walked forward into the center of the room. He could *feel* the eyes on him, and he stopped in the middle of the room and waited.

His Sight told him he wasn't alone. Even amidst the runic artifacts hidden in the cases, he could See the runes of the Mages around him... and the Rune of Power ahead of him.

"I know you're here," he said aloud. "I know you know what I am, so that can't be a surprise.

"Your 'Royal Order' is guilty of treason and mass murder," he continued. "If you lay down your arms and submit to the Mage-King's justice, he may be merciful. Yield or be destroyed."

For a long moment, silence was his only answer and he began to reach for his power. If they would not answer, then he would *make them.*

Then the Rune of Power ahead of him shifted. A black-clad figure emerged from behind a column on the second floor gallery and jumped the railing. With the tiniest of bursts of magic, Charlotte Ndosi landed gently on the floor in front of him.

He'd guessed.

No. He'd *known.* Lomond had clearly known nothing, and yet everything suggested there was a Hand on Mars funneling the Keepers information. If it wasn't Lomond and it wasn't Damien, then Ndosi was the only option.

"I'd hoped it wasn't you," he said quietly.

"This still doesn't have to end in violence," she replied.

"Only if you lay down your arms and surrender," Damien told her. "Your Order has gone too far. Bombarding a planet? Ambushing a Hand? Launching missiles in *Mars local space?!*"

"I doubt it matters, but no one here knew what Octavian was doing," Ndosi replied. "And I don't have a goddamn *clue* who put those missiles there, Damien. But you've chased us since you came back, and I swore an oath to defend the secrets of this Order."

"Even from your King?" he demanded. "Even to the point of attacking Olympus Mons?"

"A distraction," she told him. "We wanted to take Christoffsen into custody, try and convince him to see our side, but you'd wrapped too much security around him. We needed to keep the *rest* of the Mountain away from our capture team."

She sighed.

"If it makes you feel any better, those capture teams were called off when you started slagging our escape vehicles. The whole point in neutralizing Dr. Christoffsen, after all, was to stop him leading you to here, and the distraction will help us evacuate the place anyway."

"What is this place?" he asked.

"The Secret Library, the place where we stored everything Desmond Michael Alexander felt he had to keep hidden. He was right," she concluded. "You don't know what you've scratched the surface of, Damien. You could destroy the Protectorate if you unveiled what we protect.

"Please...join us," she asked. "We could explain everything. You will understand then."

Her eyes said, unspoken, that they could be together then.

"Lawrence Octavian dropped kinetic weapons on an archaeological dig site," Damien said quietly. "Your 'Winton', whatever his real name is, kidnapped and threatened an eighteen-year-old girl to force me to talk to him. Hell, he offered me the Throne in the Mountain. Threatened the Mage-King of Mars to whom we both owe our allegiance.

"Your Order, whatever its reason, whatever its purpose, has gone too far. It's over, Hand Ndosi. Stand down or be destroyed."

"I swore an oath, Damien," she said quietly. "And like you said, we know what you are."

She gestured for him to look behind him.

The Mages emerged from behind columns on each level. At least twenty, all marked with the projector rune of a Combat Mage. Against any conventional threat, even against a *Hand*, it was overkill—especially backed *by* a Hand. Against Damien... He wasn't sure even he could win that fight.

"Please, Damien," she said softly. "We serve the same cause; we just have more information than you do. There's a *reason* this stuff is secret."

"A Hand threatening another Hand," Damien replied. "An attack on the Mountain by our own people. What would Alaura have said?"

Ndosi winced. Alaura Stealey had recruited and trained them both. She'd been one of the best Hands of their generation in Damien's opinion, and she would have been heartbroken to learn one of her pupils had fallen this deeply into treason.

The other Hand looked conflicted for a long moment. As she opened her mouth to say something, however, several of the Mages took advantage of Damien's distraction.

Out of nowhere, fire and lightning hammered his shields, the force sending him flying even as his shield absorbed enough heat and kinetic energy to protect him from harm.

Steadying himself behind his shield, he summoned the full array of his power. The time for talking was over.

More fire lashed across the room with deadly focus, the deadly beams ripping into the column Damien had landed behind as he took cover. His shields were strong, but against twenty Mages, even a Rune Wright could sustain a defense for only so long.

His attackers reacted to his attempt to hide by opening fire with grenade launchers. They were *very* willing to wreck their own library to kill him, it seemed.

At least half a dozen of the weapons bounced around the corner toward him, but he deflected them away with a blast of force and charged after them. The explosions covered his emergence from behind the stone column, allowing him to quickly assess the threats.

The Mages were working in teams of five, focusing both magical and weapons fire on particular locations as they tried to sweep him. Ndosi was on her own, but her Rune made her the largest threat. She hadn't, so far as he could tell, attacked him yet...and even in the middle of a battle, he couldn't bring himself to strike first against a woman he'd slept with.

Instead, he targeted the team of Mages on the third-floor gallery. Power surged through him and he *ripped* the balcony from the walls, flinging a hundred tons of stone—and five Mages—across the room at another of the teams, crushing eight of his attackers with a single strike.

"He's moving!" a voice screamed. "*Take him!*"

Twelve beams of force and fire slammed into his shields simultaneously, a skilled unison that drove him back once more. He gave way a few steps, preparing another attack—and then a brutally powerful force strike slammed through Mages' attacks, flinging him off his feet and against the wall.

He'd never fought a Hand before, and he struggled against the sheer power of Ndosi's will for a moment. Even under the pressure of her attack, however, he was able to stop her Mages' attacks from reaching him—and theirs, unlike the Hand's, were *lethal* strikes.

Ndosi was still trying to take him alive. She should have known better.

Damien focused power and turned his shield into a mirror, reflecting *every* attack back in a flash of magic that overrode the other Mages' control of their Gifts. The reflection lasted bare moments and took more energy than jumping a starship, but faced with this many Mages, it *worked*.

Energy hammered into walls and pillars, *most* of his attackers dodging or defending themselves. Despite a growing sense of fatigue, he followed up the deflection with strikes of his own, tight beams of superheated plasma that cut through magical shields, flesh, and the stone of the columns they tried to hide behind.

One of the columns collapsed under the strain as his attacks sliced through it, its unimaginable weight ripping it free from the roof as it was severed from the base. Hundreds of tons of stone crashed to the floor of the massive chamber, the ground itself shaking, glass cases and book-shelf fronts shattering in a crescendo of noise.

Over half of his opponents were down now, but the survivors opened up with grenade launchers again. With the ground itself trembling under Damien's feet as part of the library roof came down, he missed the weapons until it was too late.

Six high-explosive grenades bracketed him and detonated at close range within a second of each other. His shields compressed under the impact, energy backlashing into him with overwhelming heat and force.

Somehow, *somehow*, he held it together—even as the backlash drove him to his knees. He began to rise, only to be hit by a follow-up salvo of magic. His shields stopped *most* of it before collapsing, but one beam of fire slammed into his shoulder.

Force and heat flung him across the room again, and he used his own magic to carry himself farther, crashing down mostly safely into one of the piles of debris, buying himself a moment of time.

Before he could *do* anything with it, however, a force field settled onto him, pressing him onto the ground. Looking up, he wasn't surprised to see Ndosi approaching him, her hands outstretched and her Rune of Power flaring with light and energy as she pinned him in place.

"Yield, Damien," she ordered. The surviving Mages were behind her, adding their own strength to the spell holding him in place. "Even you have limits. Even you can die. I don't want to kill you."

He relaxed under the magic, feeling into the weave of it, identifying where the Hand's magic began and where the other Mages were sup-porting her. If they'd still had all twenty Mages, they might have been able to hold him. If he was uninjured, a mere eight supporting the Hand would never have been enough.

Looking up, he met Ndosi's gaze and smiled sadly.

"I'm sorry, Charlotte," he told her quietly—then struck.

It was a tiny piece of magic, really. Something he'd taught himself long before to carve the first Rune of Power on his own flesh.

Charlotte Ndosi was a powerful Mage in her own right. Augmented with a Rune of Power, she ranked highly even among the Hands...but without the Rune, she would be no match for a Rune Wright with *five*.

His power tore through her Rune and *broke* it, ripping the silver polymer from her skin in an attack that sneaked through her defenses because it was almost gentle in its action...and vicious in its results.

Her power *collapsed* and the spell went with it. Damien was on his feet, fire flashing from his hands as the Mages began to realize what had happened.

All but one went down in moments, but the last deflected his strike and ran to Ndosi's side. Damien thought the man was going to try and help the Hand, and hesitated for a precious moment.

Instead, the Mage shot her. Four shots echoed around the cavernous chamber and the woman's small body lurched with each blow.

"Stop!" Damien bellowed, raising power to strike the man down—but the shooter simply threw him a salute and vanished in the crashing noise of vacuum filling.

He'd teleported away, leaving Charlotte Ndosi bleeding out on the chamber floor.

She was, amazingly, still alive when Damien reached her, kneeling in the blood and dust. None of the bullets had been instantly fatal, but it was obvious even to him that her lungs had been pierced in multiple places and the woman had at most minutes to live.

"We've got to get you help," he told her.

"No time," she gasped out. "You have...to run. Now."

"I'm not running, Charlotte," Damien replied. "This place...it isn't worth a Hand."

"Have to...disagree," she said, her voice growing weaker and more interspersed with bloody coughs. "Swore... an oath. Dead man's switch. Nuke."

His heart ran cold. If she died, the entire place would blow up. *That* was why the last Mage had shot her. To make sure the whole place was incinerated.

"Octavian...was supposed to recruit...to co-opt...not destroy," she whispered. "Someone...betrayed us...as well. So...much blood."

He wasn't sure if she was talking about herself, the room, or how many people were now dead because of Lawrence Octavian.

"I can teleport us both, get you to a doctor," he assured her.

He reached out to grab her, but she grabbed his hand instead. Blood was still dripping from where he'd destroyed her Rune of Power.

"Sorry, Damien," she got out clearly. "I am a Keeper and my oaths will be kept."

He felt her magic trigger before he could stop her, the last ounces of energy Charlotte Ndosi had sweeping through the air around him—and carrying him away in the familiar warping sensation of a teleport.

Blinking against the setting sun, he managed to orient himself and turned back toward where the mountains should be. She hadn't moved him far, maybe twenty kilometers.

He was still close enough to see the mountain explode when the nuke went off—taking the Royal Order of the Keepers of Secrets and Oaths into history—along with their secrets, their library, and Hand Charlotte Ndosi.

CHAPTER 45

MAGE-CAPTAIN Denis Romanov, Royal Martian Marines, wasn't expecting to find anyone in his borrowed office when he came in the morning after everything went to hell. The room had been temporarily handed over to him to help him coordinate security around the Archives and Montgomery's quarters, interfacing his Marines with the Secret Service for both the Hand and the rest of the Mountain.

Despite that, he found Julia Amiri perched on the edge of his desk, waiting for him.

"Special Agent Amiri," he greeted her. "How can I help you?"

"It's just Julia now," she told him with a smile. "As of this morning, I've officially resigned from the Secret Service. I'm catching a Navy courier this evening, heading to Ardennes."

"Getting married, I hear?"

"To my shock and surprise, yes," she admitted. "Still wrapping my brain around it, but... First Lady and Minister for Defense. My now-fiancé knows how to throw a party, it seems. But, nonetheless, I have one last task to discharge for both Montgomery and the Secret Service."

Denis eyed her askance as he took a seat behind the desk.

"Which is?"

"Montgomery's security detail needs a new chief," she told him. "Like most Hands, he's picked up extras beyond the Service: you and your company. Honestly, your people have always outnumbered the Secret Service detachment assigned to him, though you've been thankfully cooperative in regards to working with us."

"The Secret Service is responsible for the Hand's security," Denis pointed out. "I was mostly just...assigned to help out."

"Which you did with skill and aplomb," Amiri agreed. "And let's not pretend I'd be comfortable leaving Damien's safety in the hands of a stranger."

"Ma'am, like you said, the Secret Service is in charge of his security," he said slowly.

"Indeed," she agreed. "You've been seconded to the Secret Service for the last couple of weeks, and we're impressed. We'd like to offer a more permanent position. You'll be the Special Agent in charge of Montgomery's detail, much as I was. You'll remain technically seconded from the RMMC and continue to accrue seniority as a Marine Captain.

"Before you ask, yes, you will actually receive both salaries," she continued with a grin. "We're well aware that this kind of poaching, regardless of technical seniority, does set you back in the Corps. But...Damien needs someone watching his back, and you've been doing better than I would have expected."

Denis exhaled slowly.

"That's...quite the leap to consider," he admitted.

"I'm just the presenter," she told him. "You have a few days to make up your mind; no one's looking for an immediate answer. You'll probably stay attached to Damien for a while regardless, though, and this way, you're in charge of the whole mess."

"It's tempting," he said. "I'll have to think about it but...I'll admit you've probably got your man."

Normally, the Royal Guards' presence around the Mountain was subtle. They were a backstop to the Secret Service, not intended to act as formal or ceremonial guards. In the aftermath of the Keepers' abortive attack on the Mountain, however, they were *far* more obviously present.

Two red-exosuited Guardsmen led Damien to the Mage-King's office, where another pair of red-armored Guards let him in. The Secret Service agents were still around; they just seemed to fade away next to their armored and magic-wielding big brothers.

Which was probably just fine with the Service, and a deadly mistake for anyone trying to attack the Mage-King.

"Damien," the Mage-King greeted him as he entered the room. Desmond Michael Alexander the Third stood next to a window that made Damien want to pull the man away. Armored with transmuted titanium or not, near the peak of Olympus Mons and therefore opening onto unbreathably thin air or not, the window still made him a target.

"Your...interesting case files were less disturbing before they managed to reach not merely to Mars but into my home," Alexander continued. "We have confirmed, by the way, that Lawrence Octavian left his mission at a time that would be consistent with *Keeper of Oaths'* interception of *Duke of Magnificence*.

"He has not been seen since. Congratulations, you are now the only person to have *ever* killed two of the Mage-King's Hands."

Damien winced. There was no avoiding that. *Two* of the twelve Hands of the Mage-King had been up to their necks in the Keepers, and both were now dead.

"I wish there had been another choice," he admitted.

"In neither case did you have another choice," his King replied. "Octavian picked his fight, knowing the consequences if he was discovered. Ndosi..." Alexander sighed. "Ndosi linked a *nuclear bomb* to her vital signs to make sure the Keeper's secrets were never uncovered. I only wish I knew what my grandfather charged them with that made them *so* fanatical."

"Beyond that aliens were the source of the runes in Olympus Mons, I don't know," Damien said quietly. "But that on its own gives me some ideas."

"Everything we thought we knew," Alexander said. "*Everything* we knew about the origin of magic and the Protectorate is now called into question. The consequences could be severe."

Damien nodded wordlessly.

"The Keepers launched their attack at a bad time for us," the Mage-King continued. "Three Councilors, including the Legatus Councilor, were here when the Mountain came under attack. All of them now have access to sensor footage showing a nuke was detonated on Mars.

"They're already asking questions. Shortly, they will learn that two Hands are dead, and then they will ask *more* questions. We have never let the death of a Hand go unavenged before, but they were guilty of *treason*."

"So, we tell them the truth," Damien suggested. "They *are* part of the government of the Protectorate. Don't we owe them honesty?"

"You of all people know there are secrets we keep from them," Alexander replied pointedly. "They question the power of the Mage-King. If they know Hands betrayed us, it will be a weapon they will use against the Mountain.

"Telling them the truth will trigger a constitutional crisis we don't need—and will put *you* on trial for the deaths of two Hands, Damien. They have always had the right to question the actions of my Hands. There is no way they will let a Hand killing two others go unquestioned, unchallenged."

"So, we lie," Damien said flatly. "Perhaps we set up a brand-new Royal Order to keep the secret. And then in, what, a hundred years they start killing to protect that lie?"

It was Alexander's turn to wince.

"I wasn't planning on going that far," he said. "Just...holding out for an opportune moment."

"I suspect that the Keepers did have conditions under which they would release their secrets, an 'opportune moment' to tell everyone," Damien noted bitterly. "Why else keep the data and not just destroy it?"

"We've just seen the consequences of lies and deception, my King. We...*must* tell at least the Council the truth. We've broken the Keepers' power, but some of them escaped."

"What you suggest threatens *my* power and *your* safety," Alexander snapped. "You serve *me*, Montgomery. If I order you to keep the secret, would you betray me?"

"No," Damien sighed. "But I *would* resign. This is a threat to the heart of the Protectorate. We do not have the right to keep it secret...but if you order it, I will. I will also give you back your Hand and go home. I'm sure Commodore McLaughlin would love another Jump Mage."

"You'd be Governor inside a year," Alexander pointed out with a sigh. "I doubt Miles McLaughlin would wait a *month* to announce his resignation in your favor—probably along with pointed hints about his granddaughter's marital status.

"My daughter would kill me," he concluded. "And..." He sighed. "You're right. All we could do is spin out time, and our political position versus the Council is desperately in need of...clarification.

"I'm not joking about a trial, though, Damien," Alexander warned. "Are you prepared to face that?"

"My liege, after all I have done in your service, *defending* my actions seems...necessary," he replied. "And, frankly, somewhat less likely to get me killed. I'll face the Council's judgment."

"I'll back you. You did what had to be done." The Mage-King of Mars sighed. "You just may have set into motion the shock that will finally fracture our nation."

ABOUT THE AUTHOR

GLYNN STEWART is the author of Starship's Mage, a bestselling science fiction and fantasy series where faster-than-light travel is possible–but only because of magic. His other works include science fiction series Duchy of Terra, Castle Federation and Vigilante, as well as the urban fantasy series ONSET and Changeling Blood.

Writing managed to liberate Glynn from a bleak future as an accountant. With his personality and hope for a high-tech future intact, he lives in Kitchener, Ontario with his partner, their cats, and an unstoppable writing habit.

OTHER BOOKS
BY GLYNN STEWART

For release announcements join the
mailing list or visit **GlynnStewart.com**

STARSHIP'S MAGE
Starship's Mage
Hand of Mars
Voice of Mars
Alien Arcana
Judgment of Mars
UnArcana Stars
Sword of Mars
Mountain of Mars
The Service of Mars
A Darker Magic
Mage-Commander (upcoming)

Starship's Mage: Red Falcon
Interstellar Mage
Mage-Provocateur
Agents of Mars

Pulsar Race: A Starship's Mage Universe Novella

DUCHY OF TERRA
The Terran Privateer
Duchess of Terra
Terra and Imperium
Darkness Beyond
Shield of Terra
Imperium Defiant
Relics of Eternity
Shadows of the Fall
Eyes of Tomorrow

SCATTERED STARS
Scattered Stars: Conviction
Conviction
Deception
Equilibrium
Fortitude (upcoming)

PEACEKEEPERS OF SOL
Raven's Peace
The Peacekeeper Initiative
Raven's Course
Drifter's Folly (upcoming)

EXILE
Exile
Refuge
Crusade
Ashen Stars: An Exile Novella

CASTLE FEDERATION
Space Carrier Avalon
Stellar Fox
Battle Group Avalon
Q-Ship Chameleon
Rimward Stars
Operation Medusa
A Question of Faith: A Castle Federation Novella

SCIENCE FICTION STAND ALONE NOVELLA
Excalibur Lost

VIGILANTE
(WITH TERRY MIXON)
Heart of Vengeance
Oath of Vengeance

**Bound By Stars: A Vigilante Series
(With Terry Mixon)**
Bound By Law
Bound by Honor
Bound by Blood

TEER AND KARD
Wardtown
Blood Ward

CHANGELING BLOOD
Changeling's Fealty
Hunter's Oath
Noble's Honor
Fae, Flames & Fedoras: A Changeling Blood Novella

ONSET
ONSET: To Serve and Protect
ONSET: My Enemy's Enemy
ONSET: Blood of the Innocent
ONSET: Stay of Execution
Murder by Magic: An ONSET Novella

FANTASY STAND ALONE NOVELS
Children of Prophecy
City in the Sky

Made in the USA
Coppell, TX
26 September 2022

83649245R00194